"What has occu[...] a mistake. I beg that you'll speak of it to no one. If my aunt was to hear..." Kathryn could not finish what she had started.

Ravensmede's voice rumbled low, little more than a whisper. "Why did you not speak earlier? Inform me of my...error?"

A hot blush flooded her cheeks. "I tried—"

"Miss Marchant, someone should teach you—" deliberately he leaned down and allowed his breath to caress her ear "—the perils—" his lips hovered by the side of her face, so close yet not touching "—of allowing yourself—" he closed the last small space that divided them, until he felt his thighs brush against her skirts "—to be kissed by a rake."

* * *

Mistaken Mistress
Harlequin® Historical #815—September 2006

**Praise for Margaret McPhee's debut novel
THE CAPTAIN'S LADY**

MARGARET McPHEE
Mistaken Mistress

TORONTO • NEW YORK • LONDON
AMSTERDAM • PARIS • SYDNEY • HAMBURG
STOCKHOLM • ATHENS • TOKYO • MILAN • MADRID
PRAGUE • WARSAW • BUDAPEST • AUCKLAND

ISBN-13: 978-0-373-29415-2
ISBN-10:   0-373-29415-8

MISTAKEN MISTRESS

www.eHarlequin.com

Printed in U.S.A.

Please address questions and book requests to:
Harlequin Reader Service
U.S.: 3010 Walden Ave., P.O. Box 1325, Buffalo, NY 14269
Canadian: P.O. Box 609, Fort Erie, Ont. L2A 5X3

Chapter One

May 1815

'*Kathryn, my sweet dove, you're the only woman for me. Say that you'll be my wife, I beg of you!*' *Lord Ravensmede plucked her svelte figure into his arms and placed an ardent kiss of love upon her perfect pouting lips. His glossy dark hair mixed with the rich red-brown ringlets dancing temptingly at the sides of her beautiful face. He moved back to stare into her eyes, eyes that were of a serene silver coloration and not at all a bland grey. '*I love you, Kathryn Marchant!*' he declared with passion and kissed her again, mindful not to spoil the arrangement of her new and highly fashionable lemon silk dress.*

'Kathryn, Kathryn! Stop wool-gathering and attend to me at once! Are you deaf that you cannot hear me calling you?' Lottie stared at her cousin with narrowed eyes. 'For heaven's sake,' she whispered loudly, 'you're here to assist me, not gawk around like an imbecile.' Her voice resumed its normal tone and with one white and perfectly manicured hand she gestured vaguely in the direction of the floor. 'The hem of my dress has caught on the buckle of Miss Dawson's slipper. Disengage it before any damage is done.'

As Kathryn stooped to free the offending article, which

proved to be more difficult than anticipated, she listened to Lottie's conversation. *Dear Lord*, she thought. *The pair of them are as vainly empty-headed as ever!* Then had the grace to blush when she remembered the content of her own sweet daydream.

'Jane, I declare they're both prodigiously handsome. I couldn't pick which man is the better of the two.'

'Well, they're rakes, both of them. My mama has warned me to stay clear of their sort.'

'Tush, Jane, you're such a ninnyhammer at times. They may be rakes, but they're titled and wealthy to boot…and so devilishly good looking. Would your mama say no to you landing a lord?'

'They're looking over here, Lottie.'

'No!'

'Yes, indeed, it's true.'

'Look away, quickly! Don't let them see that we've noticed them.'

Not only did Miss Dawson avert her head but, in a moment of preoccupation, which can only be supposed to have resulted from her excitement over the gentlemen in question, she also stepped back.

Kathryn gasped as Miss Dawson's large foot inadvertently trod on her fingers. The good that resulted from this was that Lottie's dress was freed in an instant. The bad, aside from Kathryn's bruised digits, was that a small tear appeared in the hem.

'Dear Lord, I don't believe it! My dress is ruined. This is the first time I've worn it and, thanks to Kathryn, it's ruined. I may as well go home this instant.' Tears pricked at Lottie's blue eyes, rendering them brighter and bluer, if that were at all possible. The tiniest flush of pink crept into her cheeks, completing, in Kathryn's mind at least, the perfection of her beauty.

'No, dear Lottie. It's scarcely noticeable. A small stitch will soon have that remedied,' Miss Dawson soothed her friend.

Lottie's pale eyebrows arched in irritation as she peered down at Kathryn, who was trying her best to conceal the damage. 'You did that on purpose, just to ruin my evening!'

Then she turned to Miss Dawson once more. 'Kathryn's such a spiteful cat. You'd think she'd be grateful, wouldn't you? Saved from destitution by the kindness of *my* family.'

Miss Dawson's eyes opened wider. She tried to speak. 'Lottie—'

But Lottie was in full rant as she warmed to one of her favourite subjects. 'And what does she give in return? Humble gratitude? Most certainly not.'

Miss Dawson tried again. 'Lott—'

'If you would be so kind as to let me finish, Jane. As I was saying, all she gives is jealousy and stupidity!'

'Indeed, life can be so tedious sometimes, Miss Marchant, don't you think?'

The deep masculine drawl caused Lottie to jump. She turned startled eyes in the direction from which it had sounded. Her expression of spiteful fury transformed instantly to one of demure innocence. 'Lord Ravensmede,' she uttered faintly. And looking beyond the breadth of his shoulder, 'Lord Cadmount.' Belatedly, and with a countenance that had stained ruddy, she made her devoirs.

Kathryn looked up from her knees and saw Lord Ravensmede so very far above her. *Not like this. Please, don't let him see me like this!* She swallowed her embarrassment and rose swiftly to her feet, allowing the two quizzical glances to wash over her. The thumping of her heart was so loud that she feared the whole ballroom would hear it. On either side of her were the taller forms of Miss Dawson and Cousin Lottie in all their finery. And not three feet in front stood the subject of her daydreams—the Viscount of Ravensmede. This time there was no lemon silk dress for Kathryn, no pretty dancing ringlets. The reality of their meeting stood in stark contrast to her dream. Still, she mustered a stiff little smile.

Ravensmede's gaze did not linger, returning instead to Lottie, who was frantically fanning herself to remove the scalded heat from her cheeks. She batted her eyelashes, looked coy, and did not offer to introduce her cousin. Neither did his lordship request an introduction. Indeed, he had looked at her, in Kathryn's own view, as if she were no more than a crumb upon the floor.

Attraction retreated. Indignation rallied. Anger advanced. Quite clearly Lord Ravensmede's handsome looks were not matched by a handsome temperament. Why, he was possibly one of the rudest men Kathryn had ever met. And then it dawned on her exactly why Lottie had made no introduction. Lord Ravensmede thought her a servant, and Lottie, dear Cousin Lottie, wanted it to appear so to excuse the chastisement he had interrupted. Two fiery patches erupted on Kathryn's cheeks. She might be an orphan, and poor. She might live under the name of companion and work as a servant. But through all her shabby misery she still had her good name, and that knowledge lent her courage. Might well they talk of a breach of manners! She set a stubborn tilt to her jaw and in a frosty tone uttered their given names. 'Lottie, Jane, gentlemen—' she eyed Lord Ravensmede with special dislike '—please do excuse me.' She saw the arrogant arch of his eyebrow. With a degree of satisfaction and her head held high, she turned on her heel and walked away.

Ravensmede noticed her then, the small sparrow of a girl with her ancient grey gown and her ruffled dignity. The look that she shot him from those stunning silver eyes was not one the Viscount was used to seeing in women: disapproval, dislike and disappointment all wrapped up into one. A spark of interest ignited. Ravensmede followed the retreat of the girl's straight back until she disappeared into the crowd. Even then, he continued to trace her steady progress weaving through the crush of guests until he heard Cadmount say with the glimmer of a laugh, 'One just can't get the staff these days.'

He watched while Miss Dawson creased with embarrassment and glanced nervously at Miss Marchant, whose bland prettiness seemed only mildly perturbed. Neither replied. Ravensmede tucked the matter away for later consideration and idled away a little more of his time before announcing, 'Ladies, please excuse me. I have a rather pressing engagement.' Then he headed off on the real purpose behind his attendance at so dull an affair as Lady Finlay's ball.

Kathryn had almost made it out of the ballroom when she was halted by a woman's haughty voice.

'Just where do you think you're going?' Aunt Anna loomed behind her, reticule in hand, resplendent in a cream-and-rose creation.

'The ladies' retiring room.' Kathryn forced a politeness to the words that she did not feel. It was the only way of dealing with Aunt Anna. Every other means only worsened the situation. That she was reliant on her aunt and uncle's charity for the roof over her head and the food in her belly was something that she never forgot. Neither, for that matter, did they.

'You've left Lottie alone?' The question was in her aunt's usual imperious tone. Kathryn could have sworn that it was edged with accusation.

'No. She's with Miss Dawson.' Kathryn looked at her tall well-dressed relative and waited. She omitted to mention the conditions under which she had abandoned the younger women. No doubt Aunt Anna would find out soon enough.

Mrs Marchant frowned, as was her habit when addressing her niece, and averted her gaze. 'Then you had best be quick about your business. You're here as Lottie's companion, try to remember that. My patience wears thin with reminding you.'

Still Kathryn stood, betraying nothing, her face a mask of polite indifference.

'Well, what are you waiting for? Get on with it.' Mrs Marchant waved her hand in a dismissive gesture.

Kathryn turned and walked away.

She sighed and rubbed at her brow to ease the knot of tension. In truth Kathryn had no need to visit the retiring room; it was merely an excuse to avoid the loathsome Lottie. No matter the cost, Kathryn knew that she needed some little time away from the spoiled spite of her cousin and the arrogant disregard of Lord Ravensmede. She'd already done quite enough damage on the Lottie front, the repercussions of which would no doubt be reaped in the very near future. And as for Lord Ravensmede...

Walking as briskly as she could, she passed unnoticed through the throng of hot, perfumed bodies and escaped into the hall. Quite where she was going she did not know—anywhere would do as long as it gave her the respite she sought. Just five minutes to cool the splurge of temper that had risen too readily. Over the past three years she had learned to school such reactions, to bear all with a stoic countenance. It was better, after all, to show nothing. And now, despite all of that practice, she had almost lost her temper.

Five minutes. It surely wasn't too much to ask. Five paltry minutes, and then she'd turn her feet around and return to face it all once more, as if she had never been away. No one need notice. Indeed, no one ever did notice plain Kathryn Marchant, which is why Aunt Anna and Uncle Henry had agreed to have her to live with them after her papa's death. She was the perfect backdrop against which to exhibit their own sweet Lottie, and, of course, it saved on the expense of employing another servant. It was something that Kathryn had firmly resolved not to dwell upon, as such thoughts could do nothing except produce a bitterness that was unworthy of all that her dear departed mama and papa had instilled in her.

The hallway had become a corridor, which continued through a set of doors towards the rear of Lady Finlay's large mansion house. Not another soul was to be seen. Evidently Lady Finlay had the servants engaged elsewhere and no other guest would be so rude or so bold as to wander so freely. The corridor became a gallery and Kathryn paused to examine the paintings that lined the walls. Faces, some faintly reminiscent of the elderly Lord Finlay, peered down at her. Just as she was examining a lofty-looking young man's features, footsteps sounded in the distance.

Lord above, she could not be found here! Why, just imagine Aunt Anna's reaction to the news that her niece had taken it upon herself to inspect her ladyship's family portraits. Glancing around in panic, she spied a single door at the end of the gallery, just at the point where the corridor turned and led away to the right. The footsteps grew louder.

Kathryn did not wait to hear any more. Within the blink of an eye she ran towards the door, and, finding it to be unlocked, whipped into the room beyond. Just in time, for the footsteps, large and plodding, passed her hiding place and continued off into the distance. She heaved a sigh of relief and turned to look at the place in which she now stood.

It appeared to be a large room with a few items of dustsheet-covered furniture clustered around its periphery. There were no candles burning and no fire within the blackened grate. Yet the centre of the room was bathed in a silver light that flooded in through a pair of glass doors. The magical illumination drew Kathryn like a moth. Lottie and Aunt Anna were no more. All else was forgotten as the moonlight lulled her under its spell. Through the panes of glass she could see the deep darkness of the night sky studded with the glitter of distant stars. But the moon itself was what held her attention—huge and white, a glowing orb amidst the darkness. Kathryn stared with increasing fascination. Such a feeling of peace. Within the silent silver room anger ebbed, indignation crumbled.

There had been nothing unusual in Lottie's behaviour; Kathryn had long since grown used to her cousin's high-handed ways. What was it, then, that had instigated her outburst? The question perhaps should have been *who* rather than *what*. And the answer, to Kathryn's chagrin, was patently obvious: Lord Ravensmede.

It was one thing to escape the reality of her life by daydreaming, but quite another when those dreams involved a particular nobleman. Unfortunately, she had been thus affected since first seeing the arrogant man across the floor at Almack's Assembly

Rooms a month ago. It was just an imagining, a game that she played inside her head, nothing more. Harmless, or at least it had been until now. But she had reckoned without this evening. She knew that no man of quality would look twice at such a plain penniless creature as herself. Witnessing the obvious disdain in which Lord Ravensmede held her was humiliating, as if the cloth had been torn from the mirror and she had been forced to stand exposed before it. Kathryn's life did not make for a pretty picture.

She thought of the past eight years, of the deaths of her parents and her sister. Nothing of Aunt Anna's dislike or Lottie's tantrums could compare with the pain that those losses had wrought. At first she had thought it intolerable, but as the weeks became months, and the months, years, Kathryn had learned to live with the ache buried deep in her heart. She could take whatever Aunt Anna wished to throw at her. Wasn't that what daydreams were for? To make life bearable? To make one impervious to hurt? Lord Ravensmede could not be allowed to change that. His behaviour was an abomination of all that was gentlemanly. He was as arrogant a scoundrel as his reputation told. For certain his place in her dreams was now forfeit. She would not think of him again. Most definitely not. And all the while the cool silver light stroked her with its comforting caress.

Kathryn could never be sure of what it was that made her suddenly draw back into the darkness of the shadows, but barely had she done so when the door creaked open and a large figure slipped inside. The door closed with a quiet click.

'Amanda?' The whisper was clearly that of a man.

She stood quiet and motionless, hoping to hide her presence from the stranger.

The soft tread of his footsteps sounded against the floor.

Her back hugged the floral-print wallpaper. *Please stay where you are and come no further.*

'Amanda?' the voice whispered again and a figure advanced into the moonlight.

The breath caught in Kathryn's throat as the light illuminated his face. *Dear Lord, no! It cannot be*. As if summoned by her thoughts, there stood the stark figure of the Viscount of Ravensmede.

His head lifted, as a hound that scents the hare, and it seemed that he could see through the darkness to look right at her.

Do not see me. Pray, do not know that I'm here. Kathryn tried to quieten her ragged breathing.

'Amanda, what game are you playing? Have you forgotten our little arrangement?' He walked slowly, determinedly towards her.

A meeting with his inamorata, except that it isn't Amanda, whomever she may be, who is here. She swallowed hard, and heard the smile in his voice.

'Very well, we'll proceed as you prefer. I must agree that it is a rather entertaining novelty...for now.'

There is nothing else for it; I will have to own my identity. Kathryn was just about to step forward when his fingers touched to her wrist. A short sharp intake of breath. She made to warn him of his mistake, only to find herself in the Viscount's arms and her would-be protestations silenced by the warm touch of his lips. She stiffened and tried to pull away.

But Lord Ravensmede clearly had other ideas. His hands stroked sensuously against her back, imprisoning her with their caress. His heat burned through the fabric of her bodice.

She pushed hard against his chest, her fingers all too aware of the unyielding muscle beneath. Panic gripped her. She struggled. Opened her mouth to scream.

Slowly, deliberately, he intensified the kiss, his tongue tracing a spell against her lips before it probed within.

Something fluttered deep within her, and all her good intentions disappeared in a warm fuzzy haze. Kathryn moaned and gave up all semblance of resistance as reality and daydream merged within the passion of the moment.

She didn't understand what was happening to her. Knew that

her behaviour was reprehensible. But her blood surged wild and strong, and the sensations assailing her would not be denied. Taste of nectar on her tongue. Touch of lips that slid against hers—demanding, enticing. Smell of clean masculinity mixed with the subtle undertones of bergamot. Even when every rational thought screamed out that she should stop she could not. Common sense fled. Kathryn answered the call of Lord Ravensmede's body. She relaxed into his arms, her rigidity shed like a cloak upon the floor. So warm, so comfortable. She sighed and nestled closer. For that one brief moment in time Kathryn was the woman of her dreams, neither poor nor dowdy, but desirable and loved. Dewy breath caressed her cheek. A soft whisper tickled her ear.

'Amanda.' The name rolled lazily off his tongue.

Kathryn descended back down to earth with a crash, all her dreams shattered in an instant. *What am I doing letting him kiss me? It's not Kathryn Marchant that he holds so tenderly, but another woman altogether. If he knew the truth...* 'No!' Her whisper was loud and urgent. She thrust herself back from him.

'What the...?' His puzzlement was palpable.

'No!' she said again, louder this time and with quiet determination. She tried to move away. But she had reckoned without Lord Ravensmede.

He stepped closer, backing her up against the wall. 'What's wrong? Was the diamond bracelet not to your liking?' One large thumb drizzled slowly down her cheek to brush against the soft cushion of her mouth. 'Come, Amanda, we're both hardened players of this game.'

Kathryn's heart thundered in her chest, her pulse leaping at her throat. Her whisper was loud against the hiss of silence. 'You're mistaken, my lord. I am not...'

Ravensmede halted her words with an ardent kiss. 'Am I then mistaken in that? Or in the fact that your kisses are the sweetest I've ever tasted?' His hands slid over her shoulders as he pulled her to him. 'Trembling like a virgin, Mrs White? Did

I not know just how determinedly you had courted my attention, your timidity might be believable.' He made to kiss her again, but was thwarted by Kathryn's wriggles and succeeded only in planting a chaste kiss upon the tip of her nose.

The time for speaking was past. Kathryn knew she had but one opportunity for escape and she created it with a sudden exclamation. 'My lord, there's someone at the window!' When Ravensmede turned to look over his shoulder, she bolted and ran for the door. Blood pounded in her temples and her breath shortened. Movement sounded behind her, but she did not look back, just kept running. Her fingers reached forward, the tips touching to the cool brass of the doorknob before their contact was severed. A strong arm wound around her waist and yanked her back against a wall of solid muscle.

'What the hell is this about, Amanda? You've been flirting with me for months, practically begging me to visit your bed, and when finally I agree you flee as if the very devil is on your heels. Let's resolve this matter once and for all, madam.' He waited with patience, but did not loosen his grip.

A thousand thoughts whirled through Kathryn's brain. Plans to escape, words of excuse, fear and panic, but through them all she knew her time had come. There was no alternative other than to let him see the truth and await his reaction. Dear Lord, if there was any other way! She steeled herself to the task, to the revulsion and anger she knew that she would see in his face. There could be no further prevarication. She ceased her struggle.

'An explanation, please, if you would be so good, Mrs White.'

'I did not mean for this to happen, my lord.'

She allowed Lord Ravensmede to turn her in his arms, knowing full well it would be the last time ever she would feel his touch. The shadow had lightened a little, but as she looked up she could see nothing more than the dark outline of his face, and was thankful that it was so. 'I am not Mrs White,' she said simply.

Silence stretched between them.

Abruptly he pulled her across the room to stand before the glass doors. Moonlight captured his stunned features, proclaiming the perfection of each contour, every plane. Dark eyes glittered incredulously, raking every fibre of her being until she thought she could stand his silent scrutiny no more. She stood stiff and erect, her pride holding all else in check.

'I am Miss Kathryn Marchant, the cousin of Miss Lottie Marchant.'

No reply, just the soft sound of his breathing, and the continued pressure of his hands around her upper arms.

A tremble set up in her legs. 'I only sought some…somewhere where I could be alone.' The words were stilted, awkward. 'I did not know that…that the room was to be used by another…others,' she corrected.

Still he did not speak.

'What has occurred here has been a mistake. I beg that you'll speak of it to no one. If my aunt was to hear…' She could not finish what she had started.

His voice rumbled low, little more than a whisper. 'Why did you not speak earlier? Inform me of my…error?'

A hot blush flooded her cheeks. 'I tried—'

He raised an eyebrow. 'Not very convincingly.'

'I could not, my lord.'

'Could not, or would not, Miss Marchant?'

She quailed beneath the intensity of his stare.

'You play a very foolish game…a downright dangerous game.'

The touch of his fingers burned where they contacted the bare skin of her arms.

'Don't tell me you have not heard of my reputation?' he mocked, then glanced away as if there was something he could not quite fathom. When his gaze slid back to hers there was something in it that caused her heart to race even faster.

She did not answer. Aridity threatened to close her throat. When finally her words came they were nothing but a hoarse whisper. 'Please excuse me, my lord, I must return to my cousin.'

'Really?' There was a lazy drawl in Ravensmede's voice that did not match the glint in his eye.

'Indeed, my lord.'

His lordship showed not the slightest inclination to withdraw his hands.

Beneath the magical glow of the moonlight her skin was pale and smooth as alabaster. Her hair was still pinned back, but some of the curls had escaped to dangle enticingly against her cheek and throat. One finger lifted a curl from her cheek, then slid down to trace the delicate line of her jaw. His gaze followed where his finger led, then meandered back to her eyes that appeared opalescent in the moonlight. Fringed with long dark lashes, glittering with unshed moisture, her eyes were quite simply beautiful. And contained in the stare that she returned him Ravensmede could see shock and guilt…and passion. She was playing with fire. Already the heat within him kindled.

'Miss Marchant, someone should teach you…' deliberately he leaned down and allowed his breath to caress her ear '…the perils…' his lips hovered by the side of her face, so close yet not touching '…of allowing yourself…' he closed the last small space that divided them until he felt his thighs brush against her skirts '…to be kissed by a rake.' Her clean feminine fragrance filled his nose. Where their legs touched he could feel the slight tremor running through her. He watched her eyes widen, but she did not try to pull away. 'Shall I, Kathryn?' he exhaled the question in a soft breath. He looked at her a moment longer, then gently, insistently, covered her mouth with his, massaging her lips in a slow, sensual motion.

She tasted sweet and innocent…and completely alluring. Desire leapt. Their first kisses had not lied. He wanted nothing more than to deepen the kiss, to drink in every last drop of her. Attraction scorched as hot as if he were the greenest of lads. He wanted to reach in and touch her as she had touched him. Temptation loomed large. And Nicholas Maybury, Viscount of Ravensmede, had never been a man to deny himself.

'By the heavens, Ravensmede! You arrange an assignation with me then fill my place with another before I arrive!' A woman's shrill voice shrieked at full volume from the doorway. 'You, sir, are a damnable scoundrel!'

He felt the girl jump within his arms, heard her sudden shocked gasp. It was with a great degree of reticence that he removed his embrace. 'Mrs White, how very good of you to join us,' he said.

The voluptuous young widow's eyes slid towards Miss Marchant and narrowed further.

He sensed rather than saw the girl's withdrawal. 'Miss Marchant and I were just admiring the night sky.'

A derisive snort sounded from the beauty. She stepped fully into the room, leaving the door gaping wide behind her. 'I know full well exactly what you and...Miss Marchant...were doing and it had nothing to do with the stars! Don't take me for a fool, Ravensmede!'

'I must insist that you're mistaken, my dear Mrs White.' He moved to stand between the two women, shielding Kathryn from the other's view. Mrs White's abundant bosom expanded before his very eyes, rising and falling with alarming speed. There was about her face a slyness that he had not observed before. He wondered that he ever could have mistaken one woman for the other, for in the clear moonlight there was certainly nothing of a similarity between them. Amanda White was tall with a curvaceous figure. Kathryn Marchant was not. And yet it was the smaller, slimmer woman in the unfashionable plain gown that he wanted; the woman whose eyes were cool silver, and whose lips were hot with untapped passion.

'I know what I saw, sir,' Mrs White said harshly. 'Miss Marchant, indeed.' Her head bobbed to look down upon Kathryn's pale face. 'My, how your standards have dropped if you have taken up with such a plain little specimen. You know, of course, that she's nothing but a poor companion.' Her pretty face hardened into malice as she stared. 'But then gentlemen will be gentlemen and have *whatever* they can from *whoever* will give it. It signifies nothing other than the perfidy of men in general. You, my lord, are no exception to the rule.'

Kathryn skirted Lord Ravensmede's large frame and made for the door, but not before Mrs White had moved to block her exit.

'You're a trifle late in leaving, Miss Marchant. In fact, you never should have arrived. Scuttle back to your aunt, I'm sure she'll be very interested in this evening's activities.' The widow laughed, a cruel and petty sound.

Through the dimness Ravensmede could see Kathryn's face, white as a ghost, her eyes huge and round, staring with a horror that even her controlled façade could not disguise. Such vulnerability, such innocence. In one fleeting moment her life had been ruined…and he was not without blame in the matter. It was one thing to have a little fun, quite another to allow the woman to suffer. He knew what would happen if Mrs White's gossip was allowed to spread. Guilt flickered. It was not a familiar feeling for Lord Ravensmede, and it led to contrariness.

'Miss Marchant,' he said with more asperity in his tone than was necessary, 'return to your family.' It sounded cold and imperious even to his own ear. She walked towards the door as if heading to her own execution. 'We shall continue our study in astronomy another time.' And he meant it. Kathryn Marchant's kisses had shattered the monotony of his boredom and awakened a long-forgotten part of him. Ravensmede had no intention of just letting her walk out of his life. But first, and more importantly, he had to deal with Amanda White. He waited until he heard the soft click of the closing door.

'Mrs White, I apologise for the misunderstanding this evening. The situation, as I said, was one of complete innocence, even if it may have appeared otherwise.'

The widow said nothing, just looked at him with her heavy-lidded eyes and an expression of smug irritation.

Rose-scented perfume wafted to greet his nostrils. Overstated, cloying, like its wearer. Strangely he had not noticed it before. 'You're a woman of some standing—' that was certainly one way of putting it '—with a compassionate nature.' There was nothing of those traits in the look she returned him, but Amanda White was above all a vain woman, and it was to this weakness that Ravensmede played. 'I know that when I ask that you make no mention of this affair, you will indulge my request.'

'Of course, Lord Ravensmede. Your request is my pleasure.' Her pale eyes glittered coldly; a veil of insincerity covered her. She stepped closer, arranging her posture to exemplify the voluptuous curves of her figure. Rosebud lips parted as if in invitation. 'But, first, have we not unfinished business to attend to?'

Lord Ravensmede looked at the woman before him, at the artfully arranged hair, and the costly silver-and-blue dress. Her generous bosom swelled, tempting, teasing in design. And then her cruel derisive words to Kathryn Marchant rang clearly in his mind, dampening any interest he may have had. Revulsion rippled down his spine.

'I'm afraid that that can no longer be the case.'

The pale eyes narrowed.

'This evening's…incident…has no bearing on the matter. Circumstances have changed.'

The pouting lips narrowed to a thin line.

'You're welcome to retain the gift that I sent.'

'Of course.'

Ravensmede said nothing, just allowed the silence to stretch to discomfort, and watched the widow's anger and irritation grow.

Mrs White's gaze broke first. 'If that is all, Lord Ravensmede, I shall bid you good evening. There is suddenly a matter that I simply must discuss with the ladies.' She turned to leave.

'Not quite all, Mrs White.'

Her movement checked. Hope leapt. 'My lord?'

Ravensmede could hear the deliberate reversion in her tone: from shrill annoyance to husky enticement. The ghost of a curve touched at his lips. 'Gossip is such a vulgar pastime, don't you think?'

She hesitated. 'I cannot agree, sir.' There was a furtiveness to her expression.

'Allow me to persuade you otherwise—a banker's draft for two thousand guineas to be delivered to your address tomorrow morning in exchange for your silence.'

Two thousand guineas! Mrs White's eyes bulged. And then she recovered herself. 'I might consider it…' she sniffed '…if the sum were perhaps three thousand.'

Ravensmede's smiled a chilling smile. It was enough to make the hairs on the back of Amanda White's pretty white neck stand on end. 'Two thousand guineas,' he said, 'take it or leave it. Make your choice before the offer is withdrawn.' He stepped towards her. 'And should you choose wrongly, Mrs White, let's just say you may find your own reputation a little the worse for wear.'

'Are you threatening me?'

'Would I do such a thing?' He raised an arrogant eyebrow as if the very suggestion amused him. 'I'm merely illustrating the rule of cause and effect. Gossip about Kathryn Marchant and you'll not find a welcome at any decent house in London.'

Anger flashed in her eyes. 'Don't be ridiculous! You know nothing, Ravensmede, nothing that you could use against me.'

He shrugged his shoulders in a nonchalant manner. 'Perhaps, but everyone has something to hide, a secret. Consider yours very carefully. For should I have reason, I would discover it.'

'You could not!' she exclaimed, but there was a definite echo of fear in her voice.

'My wealth and power are considerable. And everybody has a price. You of all people should know that, Amanda.'

She paled and took a few steps back.

He slipped his watch from his pocket and glanced down at the face. 'Time's up, Mrs White. What is it to be?'

She cleared her throat. 'I'll accept the money.'

'Bravo.' He looked at her a little longer with that same lazy expression. 'Might I be so bold as to suggest that you would benefit from a sojourn in the country. A few weeks away from the heat of the town…'

'I'll think about it,' she ground out from between gritted teeth.

'Please do,' he said as if they were having the politest of conversations.

They stared at one another with barely concealed dislike across the small distance.

'Good evening, my lord.'

She turned and was gone, leaving Ravensmede to ponder on what he had just done to one of London's most coveted women…and all for the sake of Miss Kathryn Marchant.

Chapter Two

Kathryn sat composedly watching her cousin being whirled around the dance floor by a young gentleman whose features bore a startling resemblance to a horse. On the other side of Lottie's empty chair Mrs Marchant was chatting to Mrs Brown, the tinkle of her laughter ringing out into the ballroom.

Kathryn concentrated on the music and tried to disguise her mounting worry. As the minutes ticked slowly by without a sign of either Lord Ravensmede or Mrs White, she began to hope that they had left the ball. But that would mean only one thing, and, despite everything, it was not a pleasing thought. She heard again the echo of his parting words: *We shall continue our study in astronomy another time.* Surely he did not think… But hadn't she given him every reason to believe so? So caught up in her remembrances was she that she did not at first notice the arrival of the beautiful woman accompanying Lady Spey. Only the overpowering scent of roses alerted her.

'Mrs Marchant, may I present Mrs White, who is a friend of mine.'

Kathryn senses reeled. *No!*

'Mrs Marchant!' the husky voice gushed. 'How very pleased I am to meet you. I've heard only good things about you.'

'Mrs White, the pleasure is mine.' Mrs Marchant puffed out her chest in a self-important manner.

The widow turned to view Kathryn. 'And this must be your—'

'Niece,' supplied Mrs Marchant in a rush.

'Ah,' Mrs White uttered softly, 'this must then be Miss Kathryn Marchant.' She sauntered closer and inclined a regal head. And never once did her pale ice eyes leave Kathryn's face. 'Such a delight.'

'Mrs White.' Kathryn bobbed a curtsy and forced her face to a mask of politeness. For the briefest of moments her eyes met the scrutiny, and held. Amanda White's sly smile widened.

'Please say that you won't object to my being seated with you, my dear Mrs Marchant.' It was not so much a question as an assumption. Amanda sat down with a show of elegance and proceeded to monopolise Mrs Marchant.

Kathryn sat rigid. Perspiration prickled beneath her arms. The length of her back had adhered to the grey silk of her dress. Even her palms were cold and clammy. And still she waited, while Mrs White played her cat-and-mouse game. Each time those pale eyes slanted her way, each time that husky voice lowered conspiratorially to utter, *My dear Mrs Marchant*, Kathryn's heart lurched. Every nerve in her body was stretched taut, vibrating with expectation.

'But Kathryn—' the widow broke off to pat Kathryn's cold white hand '—you don't mind if I call you that, do you?' and without waiting for an answer rushed on, 'You look so pale. Are you ill?'

Kathryn licked the dryness from her lips. 'I'm quite well, thank you.' And all the while she wanted to scream, *Tell her, if that's what you mean to do, and be done with it.*

But Mrs White had no intention of ending her game, not when her humiliation still burned so painfully. Ravensmede might have bought her silence, but Kathryn was ignorant of the fact. The widow fully intended to exact a measure of revenge upon the girl for the remainder of the evening. A slow, delicious torture, and one that would not leave Ravensmede unaffected. Amanda White relished the prospect. She drew Kathryn a malevolent smile and turned her attention back to Anna Marchant.

Kathryn's overstretched nerves began to fray.

'That woman has the cheek of the devil.'

Cadmount followed Ravensmede's focus and smiled lazily. 'The Winsome Widow White, I perceive. I thought you and the lady had reached an arrangement?'

Lord Ravensmede bestowed a withering look upon his friend. 'Not the kind of arrangement that you think. Matters have altered.'

'What are you not telling of the Winsome Widow?' Cadmount studied his friend for a moment. When no answer was forthcoming, he added, 'Or rather, should I ask which new face has captured your interest?'

Ravensmede lifted one haughty eyebrow.

'I know you too well, my friend.' Cadmount chuckled. 'You don't fool me for an instant.'

'Perhaps.'

'Come on, let's head to Brooks's. I've a mind to enjoy a turn at the tables and a drink or two. This place is so full of blasted chits and tabbies as to wear a man's soul.'

Ravensmede smiled at that, but his eyes soon drifted back to where Kathryn Marchant sat drained and rigid. Her chestnut hair was scraped back in a chignon from which the escaped curls still hung defiantly. Despite the pallor of her cheeks her back was straight and her head held up. She was afraid, but she was fighting it with courage. And courage was something that Lord Ravensmede had ever respected.

He thought of the harangue he had interrupted between pampered Miss Lottie Marchant and her cousin; thought too of how hard Lottie had tried to portray Kathryn as her servant. He remembered the feel of Kathryn's lips beneath his, and how slender her body was within his arms. Just the memory brought a stirring in his nether regions. Finally he allowed his thoughts to turn to Amanda White. The widow was no fool; she was unlikely to jeopardise the little agreement they had just reached. But a warning shot wouldn't go amiss. As he stood there, beneath the bright glow of the chandeliers, surrounded by the crowd and the melodic strains of the band, he knew just what to do.

Cadmount's perceptive gaze lit upon Kathryn. He decided to test his theory. 'Drab little chit.'

Ravensmede glanced up.

'Miss Marchant's cousin. The one she would have us believe is her servant.'

Ravensmede donned a slightly amused expression. 'Only to those with a less discerning eye. The only drab thing about Miss Kathryn Marchant is her dress. Clothing is easily replaced.'

'It's like that, then? I'm impressed. One would hardly have guessed it from the look she gave you earlier this evening. Were you a military man, you would surely have made Commander-in-Chief for your ability to claim victory from the most hopeless of situations.' Cadmount widened his eyes in feigned surprise and tried not to appear smug.

Ravensmede resumed his watch. 'You're making assumptions, dear boy.'

'Afraid it's what I must do if you won't spill the beans, old man.' Cadmount looked at the awkward little group. Their tension was palpable even across the room. 'It's rather interesting that the Winsome Widow is so friendly with Mrs Marchant. Didn't think they'd get on. Wonder what she's up to?'

'Baiting Miss Marchant, I should guess.' As if to confirm Ravensmede's words, Mrs White's gaze flitted to meet his. The widow looked pointedly at Miss Marchant, then back to the Viscount before delivering a nasty smile.

None of it was missed by Cadmount. 'Now what could the very respectable Miss Marchant have done to so upset the widow?' he mused, and looked speculatively at his friend.

The flicker of a smile crossed the Viscount's face. He said nothing.

'Care to enlighten me?'

'No.' Ravensmede didn't even look round. 'What do you know of her?'

'The Winsome Widow?' Cadmount's forehead wrinkled in mock puzzlement.

One dark brow raised in sarcastic denial. 'I was referring to Miss Marchant, as well you know.'

Cadmount scratched at the dark blond of his curls, sniffed knowingly and reeled off the information. 'Family lost their money in some confounded investment venture that went awry. Poor as church mice. Father shot himself little over three years past, the mother and sister died about eight or nine years ago; Miss Marchant must have been little more than a child at the time. Henry Marchant is the father's brother. The girl's lived with his family ever since. Have it from the best sources that she's little more than a domestic in that household. Anna Marchant doesn't take to her too well. That's as much as I know.'

'Caddie, I'm the one who's impressed. Should you wish to purchase another commission, consider military intelligence. Undoubtedly you'd go far.'

They laughed.

Then Cadmount said knowingly, 'So Brooks's will have to wait?'

'For now.'

Cadmount picked distractedly at his nails and deliberately yawned. 'Shouldn't take too long, damned chit looks as if she's about to keel over any minute now.'

The corner of Ravensmede's mouth twitched. 'Not if I have anything to do with it. How are your dance steps these days?'

They shared a look of mutual understanding. No need for further explanation between old friends.

'It'll cost you a bottle of your finest brandy.'

'Done!'

'You do know that you'll be delivering a monumental snub to the widow, don't you? I mean, the whole town is aware that she's been chasing you for months and what do you do? Head straight in the direction of the good lady and ask the plainest chit in the room, who just happens to be sitting by her side, to waltz. No denying that it don't look too good for Mrs White.'

'How very perceptive of you, Caddie,' drawled Ravensmede. 'Mrs White will soon learn the wisdom of good advice, and her departure from London might suddenly seem rather more urgent.'

The pair set off at a sedentary saunter in their deep-blue fitted tail-coats.

'Now to really set the cat amidst the pigeons!' Cadmount said under his breath. 'I hope the chit's worth it, my friend, I sincerely do.'

'It's so unusual to meet a young lady with an interest in astronomy, don't you agree?' Mrs White's voice grated against Kathryn's ear. 'I was just telling your aunt, it's such a curious trait to observe in a female.'

Kathryn gritted her teeth and looked round. The widow was enjoying herself immensely. Beyond the gleam of Amanda White's dark curls Aunt Anna's face was scowling in perplexity. It was time that things came to a head. Temptation beckoned. 'Perhaps, but I understand it to be a most enjoyable pastime.' She was relieved to hear that her voice held no trace of fear. Indeed it was positively calm. The words acted, as Kathryn knew they would, as a burr to Mrs White.

The lady's face contorted to a sour grimace before she recollected herself. 'For those of a certain set. Hardly a fitting activity for a young lady. Wouldn't you say, Mrs Marchant?'

Aunt Anna might not have understood to what Mrs White was alluding, but she definitely detected an underlying current of dislike aimed at her niece. She smiled and shifted a little closer to the widow. 'Completely, Mrs White. Please do call me Anna.'

'Thank you, Anna. And you must call me Amanda.'

The two women smiled in unity.

'There is a rather delicate matter which I'm not fully at liberty to discuss.' Mrs White held her fan over her mouth. 'You must think me foolish not to know how to proceed, but, with your valuable experience of raising such a beautiful daughter, and then your great kindness in inviting your niece into your home as a member of your family, there's no one better I can think to ask.'

Anna Marchant patted her hair and tried not to look superior. 'I've always tried to set an example. Lottie has just to make a match and my job will be complete.'

'Miss Marchant...that is, Miss *Lottie* Marchant, will have no lack of interest from *suitable* gentlemen.' Mrs White shot a glance at Kathryn. 'She's a credit to her mother,' she said. 'Which is why I must ask for your help on behalf of a friend whose charge has just been discovered to have behaved in a most improper manner with a gentleman. I declare the guardian to be quite distraught.'

'Is the girl known to me?' Mrs Marchant's curiosity got the better of her.

Mrs White nodded her beautiful ebony head. 'Most definitely. But do not press me to tell you. I'm sworn to secrecy.' She batted her fan, then added, 'It does so prey upon my mind. I'm in such a quandary as to what to do for the best. Will you trust me as I trust you, dearest Anna?'

'Of course, Amanda.'

'In that case I feel I may speak of it to you.'

Ruined. Cast out, penniless and in shame. There would be little hope for the future. Kathryn waited for the life-changing words. Stared at the floor, wishing it would open up and swallow her whole, and waited. Waited, and waited some more. And then she heard them.

'Miss Marchant, may I enquire whether your card is marked for this dance?' The deep timbre of the voice sent a shiver down Kathryn's spine. She looked up into the moss green eyes of Lord Ravensmede.

'I'm afraid I don't have a dance card. I'm here as a companion to my cousin.'

'Then I'll take it that you're free to accompany me on to the floor.' And with that he took one of her hands in his and pulled. Glancing over at the two older women, he inclined his head. 'Always a pleasure, ladies.'

Kathryn had only the briefest moment to revel in the slack-jawed gawking expressions of her aunt and Mrs White before she found herself clamped firmly in Lord Ravensmede's arms and waltzing across to the other side of the room. It all happened with such speed that she did not know whether to laugh or cry. The former won.

Lord Ravensmede raised a wry eyebrow. 'My dancing is a source of amusement?'

'Not at all.' The vestige of a smile remained upon her face. 'I was merely thinking that your timing is impeccable, my lord. Mrs White is on the brink of revealing all to my aunt. The question is whether she'll await my return before she delivers her denouement.'

'I fancy that Mrs White may have suffered a change of heart,' he said softly and glanced directly down into her eyes.

Kathryn suddenly felt acutely conscious of the touch of one of his hands upon her waist and the other encompassing the fingers of her right hand. 'I can only hope that you're right, my lord.'

His head gestured subtly in the direction of a couple some distance away.

'Mrs White and Lord Cadmount! How very clever. But you only defer the inevitable, my lord. That lady won't be quieted for long.' For someone so perilously close to doom she felt rather light-hearted.

He was still looking at her in that strange way. 'Are you quite recovered?'

A warmth swept into her cheeks and her voice became a

little gruff. 'Yes, thank you. I'm concerned only that…' She paused, and glanced towards Amanda White.

'That Mrs White will seek to destroy your reputation?'

'Yes.'

His hand gently squeezed her fingers. 'You have nothing to worry about.'

'I think, my lord, that you underestimate just how much I've heated Mrs White's ire; it will be a long time in the cooling.'

'I underestimate nothing,' he said softly. 'As I said, you need not worry. I shall see that Mrs White holds her tongue.'

Kathryn's heart kicked to a gallop. 'And how do you propose to do that, my lord?'

He smiled a devastatingly wicked smile.

Kathryn did not remain unaffected; the pulse leapt to a fury in her neck, she missed a step, and almost trod on Lord Ravensmede's toes.

His smile deepened.

Kathryn grew even more flustered. 'I'm sorry, but it's a long time since I've danced.' Her cheeks grew warm and pink. 'I didn't mean to embarrass you by my mistake.' And then she realised just how her words could equally well apply to her earlier misdemeanour in the moonlit room, and her blush intensified.

There was a twinkle in his eye. 'I assure you that I'm not in the least embarrassed.'

She looked away. The music filled the small silence between them.

'Do you enjoy waltzing, Miss Marchant?'

Her eyes flitted back to find his gaze upon her. At least the conversation had turned to safer ground, or so she thought. 'Yes, very much so, my lord.'

'Good. Then we'll waltz the next time we meet.'

Their eyes met, and held. 'I did not mean…' Kathryn's words trailed off unfinished. 'There's really no need. My aunt would not approve.' Her teeth nipped at her bottom lip.

Lord Ravensmede gave a short dry laugh. 'And you, of course, would never do anything of which your relative would not approve?'

The colour staining her cheeks deepened. She knew exactly to what he was referring.

'Then it's settled.'

The regulatory inches between them seemed to shrink. 'I don't think that…' She swallowed hard.

Lord Ravensmede's focus did not waver for a moment.

Kathryn's words of refusal remained unspoken. The final bars of 'Ach! Du lieber Augustine' sounded and she noticed the stares and whispers behind fans. Hardly surprising given that the heir to the Earl of Maybury had just danced with a woman little better than a servant, and it was the waltz of all dances. Despite the attention, and her shabby clothes, and worst of all the prospect of what awaited her back at the seats, Kathryn felt neither shame nor embarrassment, nor even apprehension. She smiled at his lordship, thanked him and allowed him to lead her back to her grim-faced relatives.

Mrs White seemed to have disappeared. So too had Lord Cadmount. And it wasn't long before Ravensmede followed suit. Only Aunt Anna and Lottie remained to scowl their disbelief at Kathryn.

'Whatever have you done to make Lord Ravensmede dance with you?' Lottie was incredulous. 'It's quite unheard of, a man of his calibre dancing with someone like you.' Her lower lip pouted to a petted curl. 'It should have been me that he asked.' She ground her slipper against the floor. 'Say it's so, Mama, say it.'

'Of course, my dearest.' Aunt Anna shot a foul look at her niece. 'It was probably the result of some wager or joke at Kathryn's expense.'

Kathryn said nothing. At least their preoccupation with Lottie told her one thing: that Mrs White had not made her revelation…yet. She supposed she ought to smooth things over or life in the Marchant household would be miserable for the rest of the week…as if it were ever anything other. A smile tickled the edges of her mouth. 'Lottie, I'm sure that his lordship approached us with the intention of asking you to dance. As you were already on the floor with Mr Richardson, he asked me, but only out of courtesy.'

Lottie's eyes flashed a hard, bright blue. 'I wasn't dancing when he returned you to us. Why did he not ask me then?'

'He had an urgent appointment, or so he told me upon the dance floor.' Beneath Kathryn's demurely folded hands her fingers were firmly crossed. 'Otherwise I'm sure he would have sought you as partner for this quadrille.'

Lottie appeared temporarily placated, but had seemingly developed the most frightful headache.

For this reason, or so it was said, the Marchant ladies bid a hasty departure from Lady Finlay's ball.

From where she stood, Kathryn could see almost the whole of the drawing room in the house in Green Street, as well as herself, reflected in the large gilt overmantel mirror. She was a drab grey figure against the yellow painted walls. The room seemed loud and gaudy, even beneath the subdued lighting of the candles flickering in the drop-crystal chandelier and ormolu cherubim wall sconces. A large group portrait of Mr and Mrs Marchant with Lottie seated demurely between them hung proudly between the two large Palladian windows opposite the fireplace. It had been painted two months previously by Mr Jackson. Kathryn's gaze alighted briefly on the cosy Marchant family captured on canvas before moving on to the lavish sets of curtains. Fringed and tasselled gold-and-yellow damask curtains festooned either side of each window. Not one of them was closed. A thin blind of cream material had been pulled down to create the illusion of privacy. Kathryn could feel the press of the sofa at the back of her knees. Its cream covering decorated with mulberry-coloured roses seemed too cheerful for a house that was so lacking in that sentiment. She shifted her feet uneasily, and was thankful for the cushion of the gold-and-burgundy patterned Oriental rug through her thin worn slippers.

'It has been one of the worst evenings of my entire life,' sobbed Lottie and flung herself into the nearest chair. 'And the blame rests entirely with Kathryn!'

'Now, now, Lottie,' cajoled her mother. 'I have told you already. Lord Ravensmede cannot possibly be interested in your cousin. I dare say it's all part of some jest the gentlemen were playing.'

'It d-didn't look like a jest.' Lottie's eyes were red and swollen from the sobbing and the feigned headache was fast becoming a reality. 'No one would have realised that it w-was.'

'Of course they did, my angel.' Mrs Marchant touched a gentle hand to Lottie's wet cheek. 'If you don't cease this weeping, your looks will be quite spoiled for tomorrow and then what will Mr Dalton say when he calls to collect you for your carriage ride?'

A suitably mollified Lottie turned to Kathryn and sniffed. 'Mama is right. You're such a spiteful cat that it serves you right that you are long on the shelf. When did a gentleman ever call for you to take you driving in the park? Never! And they never will because you look positively ghastly, and everyone hates you!'

Kathryn should have let the comments go; they were not worthy of a reply. But she did not. Although she had long since reconciled herself to a life with neither husband nor children, it still hurt to have the fact rubbed in her face. So for the third time that night Kathryn succumbed to impulse. 'And you, Lottie, are behaving little better than a spoiled and pampered brat,' she said wearily.

Lottie set up a wail. 'Mama, but hear what she's saying to me! Will you let her get away with such insolence?'

'Kathryn Marchant!' exclaimed Mrs Marchant. 'Close your mouth this instant! Do not dare to presume that you can insult Lottie before my very eyes! Haven't you caused enough damage for one night?'

'Aunt Anna—'

'Be quiet!' said Mrs Marchant. 'It's my job to instruct you in the ways of polite society as your papa would have wanted, Kathryn. It would be remiss of me not to do so.' The pink feathers in her bandeau quivered as she shook her head with mock sorrow. 'It's for your own good.' The feathers positively swayed in delight. 'As a punishment, all social outings shall be forbidden.' She looked for a response on Kathryn's face.

Kathryn gave none.

'In addition you'll have no dinner for a fortnight.'

Still no hint of emotion registered on Kathryn's face.

'And…you shall assist cook in the kitchen for the same duration. Mrs Moultrie will, of course, be under strict instructions that dinner is prohibited to you.' She smiled at the ingenuity of her little plan.

'As you wish, Aunt.' Still her gaze held steady.

'When not required by Mrs Moultrie you shall help with the laundry. That, at least, might teach you to know your place. You are here to help Lottie, not attempt to spoil her evening in a fit of jealous spite. Such malice cannot be allowed to go unchecked.'

Kathryn's eyes flickered to some point in the distance, knowing full well the game that her aunt played. What matter if Aunt Anna punished her a thousand times, as long as Lord Ravensmede and Mrs White held their tongues? It was not a hope in which she trusted.

'And you will apologise to Lottie for the foulness of your tongue.'

'She was unkind in her words to me,' said Kathryn.

'She is upset. And little wonder! This season is about making a match for Charlotte, not about you making an exhibition of yourself by dancing with the most libidinous nobleman you can find!'

Lottie looked smugly on.

'I did not—'

'And the waltz of all dances! For heaven's sake, girl, if you have not a care for your own reputation then at least have some consideration for your cousin. Through the goodness of his heart Mr Marchant has taken you into his home, fed and clothed you. And what thanks do you give him? None save to plague his own daughter with spite.'

'No, that isn't true. I merely—'

'You merely tried to steal a better match for yourself. Did you think to catch yourself a viscount, miss?'

Kathryn frowned her indignation. 'Of course not!'

'I have tried my best to see that you dress demurely and behave in a modest and sober manner, but bad blood will out.'

'What do you mean?'

'I mean, my dear, that your mother was the exactly the same: wanton.'

The word seemed to echo between them. The blood drained from Kathryn's face. 'You go too far, Aunt. My mother was not wanton. How can you cast such an unfair slur upon her name?'

'Why else did she run off with Robert Marchant? She was little better than a bitch in heat. It was hardly surprising that her family disowned her!'

'Take that back! You know nothing of my mother. She was a good and kind woman. She eloped with my father because they were in love.'

'Of course that's what she would have told you,' Anna Marchant sneered.

'My mother spoke the truth, unlike you. I won't believe your lies!'

The older woman's eyes narrowed with malevolent intent. 'You are a foul little trollop just as she was.' She advanced quickly and captured Kathryn's upper arms in a cruel grip. 'But if you think that I will allow you to ruin things for Lottie, then you're sadly mistaken.' Her fingers tightened, biting into Kathryn's flesh. 'I tolerate you here as Lottie's companion, nothing more.' The vice-like grip began to shake Kathryn. 'Start behaving with a modicum of decorum and modesty if you don't want to find yourself out on the street. How long do you think you'd last out there?' screeched her aunt. 'You'd be in a bordello or have your throat slit before a single day was out.' The rough shaking intensified.

'Take your hands off me!'

With no warning whatsoever Kathryn found herself thrust down against the sofa. 'Oh, I haven't even started with you, miss,' said Anna Marchant in a voice that chilled Kathryn to the bone.

A week later the Viscount of Ravensmede still had not forgotten Kathryn Marchant. Indeed, she was the topic of his conversation with Cadmount, and not for the first time.

'The girl's avoiding me. Why else have we seen Mrs Marchant and Miss Lottie Marchant, but no sign of Kathryn? I have endured three balls, an evening at Almack's and two routs! Imagine what this is doing to my reputation.' Ravensmede's long legs stretched out before him as he lounged back in the wing chair.

'And mine.' Cadmount loosened his neckcloth and, in a flippant gesture, dropped it over the side of his chair. 'Sir,' he slurred, 'you obviously haven't looked in the betting book in Brooks's of late.'

One dark eyebrow quirked. 'Enlighten me, Cadmount.' Despite the languor of his manner, there was a darkening of his eye and a quickening of his heart. Surely Amanda White had not reneged on their agreement so soon? Two thousand guineas should have silenced her for good. Money well spent...if she stayed silent. And she shouldn't even still be in London. He carefully refilled each glass and sat back, waiting.

'A fine drop of brandy, I do declare.' Cadmount's lips smacked with pleasure. 'I'd dance all night with the Winsome Widow for a case of this. Are you sure it was just the one bottle you promised me?'

A green gimlet eye stared back at him. 'The betting book?'

Cadmount took another gulp of brandy. 'Yes, the betting

book.' He stopped and rubbed his fingers over the golden stubble upon his chin. 'Should shave more often. Wingham says the ladies prefer a smoother approach.' He guffawed at his own joke.

'Hell's teeth, man, spit it out! What does the damnable book say about Kathryn Marchant?' For once, Ravensmede's usual aplomb had deserted him.

Cadmount blinked in confusion. ''Bout the chit…why, nothing.' He took another a drink and then looked knowledgeable all at once. Tapping the side of his nose, he leaned forward to his friend and said, 'Say no more, old man, understand it perfectly. Li'l Kathryn is your ladybird.' One wavering forefinger pressed to his lips. 'Sshh! Won't say a word.'

The amber liquid swirled around Ravensmede's balloon glass. 'Sorry to disappoint you, but there's no such understanding between Miss Marchant and myself.'

'Absolutely not.' An enormous grin erupted on Cadmount's face.

Ravensmede smiled in return. 'You are the most infuriating man when you're in your cups.

Cadmount's grin deepened, and he hiccuped.

'Brooks's betting book—what does it say with regard to me?' There was no hint in Lord Ravensmede's voice that he had drunk the same quantity of brandy as his friend.

A smile. 'That you'll be wed before the summer is out.'

Ravensmede laughed as a wave of relief swept through him. 'They think I'm on the hunt for a bride because of my attendance at Almack's? Seeking some precious chit just out of the schoolroom? I think not. You know me better than that, Caddie.'

'Indeed I do, sir,' avowed Lord Cadmount. 'Thirty-two years old, heir to an earldom, no wife, no nursery, old man breathing down your neck. Thank God I'm only a younger son. No such pressure.'

'Are you always this philosophical when you're foxed?' Ravensmede demanded somewhat sourly.

'Always.' Another gulp of brandy. 'If Kathryn Marchant's

not your girl, then why have we been trailing round one blasted place after the other in search of the little lady, and all the while missing out on the finer things in life? Beats me why you're behaving like a green lad over her. She's not your type at all!' Even the worse for several glasses of brandy, Archibald Cadmount knew exactly how to nettle Ravensmede.

In return, Ravensmede slowly and deliberately set his glass aside. 'You're quite right in thinking that I would like to make Miss Marchant my mistress.' He recollected vividly those soft supple lips beneath his, the gentle swell of her hips, and the sound of her wicked chuckle of laughter when he plucked her from beneath Amanda White's nose. 'However, she's an innocent and,' he added drolly, 'I haven't stooped quite so low as to start deflowering virgins.'

'You could always make an exception in her case.'

Silence followed the scandalous suggestion.

Cadmount waited to see if things were bad enough for Ravensmede to take the bait.

'Perhaps…' Ravensmede's eyes flicked shut. A vision of Kathryn Marchant's pale face arose. His mind meandered to imaginings of just how soft and white her skin would be beneath that hideous grey dress. Temptation loomed large. He quelled it with impatience. 'But then again, maybe not. She's made her feelings quite clear: a no-show at any of her cousin's outings this week. I've never forced a woman, and I don't intend to start now.'

'Glad to hear it, old man. Had you made an arrangement with her?'

Ravensmede thought of his promise to dance with Miss Marchant, and of her conspicuous absence from her cousin's side. 'Of sorts.'

Cadmount looked impressed. 'By Jove, this must be a first. A lady that turns you down. She won't have you. Hah! Well, it's about bloody time!' A snort of merriment resounded throughout the library. His eyes closed, but not before they had alighted on Lord Ravensmede's wry smile.

The clock ticked upon the mantel. Logs crackled within the grate.

A flicker of Cadmount's heavy-lidded eyes. 'Are you for Lady Campbell's gathering tonight?'

'I think not. I've other fish to fry.'

This time Cadmount's eyes remained shut and within a few minutes the soft sound of a snore was upon his lips. Ravensmede rose without a noise and left the library.

A sleepy whisper murmured behind him, 'Chit might as well as thrown down the gauntlet. Twenty guineas he'll have her in his bed before the month is out, whatever the right or wrong of it.'

But had Archibald Cadmount known Miss Kathryn Marchant, he would have wagered very differently.

Chapter Three

The street was thronging with bodies as Kathryn wove a path through the crowds. Although the afternoon was well advanced, the street vendors were still plying their trade, which was fortuitous, as it was on an errand of procurement that she was employed. Despite the dusty heat and the overpowering smells arising from the pigs and piles of rotting rubbish nearby, she was glad to be free of the house in Green Street, no matter how short the duration. The week had passed slowly, with Aunt Anna and Lottie taking delight in meting out Kathryn's punishment. No doubt it somehow acted to salve the snub that Lottie felt Ravensmede had dealt her at the ball. Kathryn had endured without complaint, and indeed had striven to appear positively cheerful. There was nothing like it for irritating Lottie, or Aunt Anna for that matter. Little did they know how she enjoyed her brief excursions from the house. It was only twenty minutes since Lottie, on overhearing that there were no potatoes left, had demanded a dish of potato pudding for dinner. Upon Lottie's insistence, Kathryn had been dispatched to fetch some more. It was supposed to be a degrading experience, and one that would teach her a lesson.

A while later, and overhead the dazzling sun still shone down from a cloudless blue sky. A soft humming sounded from Kathryn's lips as the notes of the music danced through her head. Her feet neatly avoided a pile of fresh horse manure and, as the tempo increased, she skipped over the stream of bloodied water running down from a nearby butcher's shop. *The noisy street had vanished. A cooling breeze fanned her face as she breathed in the fresh country air. She was beautifully composed as the gentleman swept her into his arms and they began to glide with effortless grace across the neat lawns of the country mansion. One two three, one two three, she counted the beats as her delicately embroidered slippers scarcely touched the ground. Lord Ravensmede was smiling, his green eyes twinkling in the sunlight... Ravensmede!* Kathryn banished the thought and the noisy bustle of London reappeared. She adjusted the sack of potatoes balanced on her hip and continued her steady pace.

Ahead she could see the golden glint of the railings surrounding St James's Park. The green grass and the cool sparkle of the canal beckoned enticingly. It wouldn't take long, just to shelter beneath the cool dapple shade of the trees, to feel some little sense of space. Without a moment's hesitation her dusty feet padded up the street and into the park. Carriages containing fine ladies rolled by. Smartly dressed gentlemen astride their horses trotted past. The grass was fresh and springy beneath Kathryn's shoes. Ahead the air rippled with a heat haze.

She had just paused to watch two swans upon the water when a small family group passed close by. A familiar voice caught her attention. Glancing round, she saw, with some consternation, Miss Dawson walking arm in arm with her younger sister. Kathryn became suddenly all too aware of her situation. There could be no hiding the large and conspicuous sack of potatoes, and Miss Dawson was sure to mention any such meeting to Lottie. And then Lottie would know exactly what Kathryn had been up to during her errand. Quite deliberately Kathryn averted her face and walked in the opposite direction. She needn't have worried. With half her hair escaping from her bonnet, a smear of dust on her chin, a soil-stained dress, and the presence of the exceedingly dirty sack on her hip, she appeared more like one of the inhabitants of St Giles's Rookery, and not anyone connected to the respectable household of Mr Henry Marchant.

A close shave. Without further ado she disappeared behind the breadth of a large oak tree. It was only here that she laid down her burden. Hidden quite well as she was from view, she not only sat herself comfortably on the grass and leaned her back against the gnarled bark, but also dispensed with her bonnet and set about repairing the worst of her hair.

Lord Ravensmede reined his horse to a standstill, unable to quite believe his eyes. Surely that could not have been Miss Marchant he had just witnessed vanishing behind that oak? The slight figure certainly bore a striking resemblance to her graceful form, even bowed as it was with some large and weighty object. Perdition, he was becoming obsessed with the chit. First, she had been in his thoughts for the past week. Now, he was imagining that he saw her at every turn. It did not sit well with his lordship. His hand moved to twitch Rollo's rein, then stilled. What if it really was Miss Marchant? He had a thing or two to say to that young lady. No matter how much Ravensmede might deny it, he felt aggrieved by her snub, especially in view of the effort he had made to silence Amanda White. His leg slid over the saddle and he jumped down to the ground.

Having securely tethered the gelding to a nearby tree, Ravensmede proceeded on foot with some caution. Thus, he walked directly to the opposite side of the massive oak without the slightest noise. He heard the hushed melody from her lips before he saw her: 'Ach! Du lieber Augustine.' It had been playing when he danced with her at Lady Finlay's ball. The memory tugged a smile at his mouth. He moved leisurely around the trunk.

She was sitting on the grass, her legs drawn up beneath her, intent on scraping her mass of red-brown hair up into a chignon. The hairpins were held at the ready between her lips. And all the while her soft humming filled the air. At her side lay a lumpy and rather grubby sack. Ravensmede stared, intrigued with the sight. What an earth was the girl up to?

He stepped forward. 'Miss Marchant, a pleasure to make your acquaintance once again.'

Kathryn jumped, dropped the hank of hair she was attempting to secure, and almost inhaled one of the hairpins. The remainder of the pins scattered on the ground as she exclaimed with undisguised horror, 'Lord Ravensmede!'

Ravensmede watched while she scrambled unceremoniously to her feet, brushing any remnants of grass from her skirt. In one glance he took in the worn shoes caked in dust, the soiled dress, and the fatigue in her eyes. The bridge of her nose and cheeks were smattered with freckles that had not been there a week ago, and dirt streaked her chin. He held out his hand to take hers. Kathryn stared at it as if it held a dagger. 'Miss Marchant,' he said with the utmost politeness, and with slow deliberation touched her bare fingers to his lips. Not only was she gloveless, but her hands were reddened and rough, almost as if she had been scrubbing floors or laundering. A frown flitted across his brow at the thought.

Kathryn saw the look and, snatching her fingers away, clasped her hands behind her back. 'What are you doing here?' she blurted, then, remembering her manners, 'I mean…I didn't expect to meet you here.'

'Apparently not.' Ravensmede's gaze dropped to the sack and wandered back to her face. Crimson washed her cheeks and he thought he saw a flash of anger in her eyes before it was masked.

She held his gaze boldly. 'Please don't allow me to interrupt your walk, my lord.' Her cheeks burned hotter.

Ravensmede smiled lazily. He was not to be dismissed so easily. 'I assure you it's no interruption. Perhaps I could join you.'

The girl seemed speechless for a moment at the audacity of his suggestion. He was fully aware that it was rather inappropriate. 'I'm afraid that's not possible, my lord.' As he knew it would not be. Her voice was firm, her body poised for flight.

'Indeed, I must be getting back to Green Street. I've been away too long as it is.' Her eyes scanned for the pins, and, having located them in the soil by an exposed tree root, she bent to retrieve them.

Ravensmede saw her purpose and, with surprising agility for a gentleman wearing such tight-fitting buckskins, stooped to reach them first. Their fingers brushed; an intense awareness tingled in the air between them. He stared into the widening clear grey eyes. Realised that he wanted her, even dressed as she was in the guise of a servant. A determined interest stirred. Jaded boredom faded. His gaze dropped to her lips.

Kathryn withdrew her hand as if she had been burned. 'I do b-beg your pardon,' she stuttered, and rose swiftly to her feet.

Ravensmede followed, his eyes still trained on her face. The pins lay forgotten in the dirt. He closed the distance between them and reached out for her.

A woman's laugh sounded from the other side of the oak. 'Come along, Mary, we mustn't be late.'

It was enough to burst the growing bubble of tension.

Lord Ravensmede recovered first, dropping his hand to his side, and did not move. He was so close he could see the dark sweep of her eyelashes and the glitter of perspiration on her cheekbones.

One step back and then she halted, an expression of confusion on her face. 'I should leave.'

Ravensmede was not fooled by the small gruff voice.

She stepped aside and bent to retrieve the sack.

'Wait.' His hand stilled her outstretched arm. Neither the material of her dress nor his fine leather gloves dampened the arc of excitement that sparked between them.

She looked pointedly at his fingers; only when he removed the offending articles did she raise her gaze to meet his. 'My lord?'

'May I be so bold as to enquire the nature of your burden?' His horsewhip flicked towards the sack.

Her eyes lowered only momentarily before her chin raised a notch, as if in challenge. 'Potatoes.'

'Potatoes!' That would explain the preponderance of sandy soil about her person. 'You've been sent to buy them?' His lordship asked the question with a nonchalant air, as if lugging a huge sack of the damn things was an everyday occurrence for a gently bred companion.

She nodded once, that fierce little gaze never faltering for a minute.

'I see,' murmured Ravensmede with a sudden clarity of perception. The sinister hand of Mrs Marchant loomed large. 'And this is one of your usual chores?'

'No.' Her fingers plucked nervously at the material of her skirt.

Ravensmede waited in silence, a look of expectation upon his face.

'I'm assisting Mrs Moultrie in the kitchen this week.'

'And last week too?' he asked in a gentle tone. He suddenly understood why Kathryn had not accompanied her cousin and aunt on any of their recent outings.

More plucking at the material. 'Yes.'

'Surely Henry Marchant is not so strapped for cash that he cannot employ a kitchen maid?'

She said nothing, just looked at him.

'It seems that you are out of favour with your aunt of late.'

Her eyes held his for a moment longer before glancing away.

'Kathryn?'

She shivered.

The tips of his fingers brushed against hers. 'Why might that be?'

She shook her head in denial.

'Kathryn,' he said again, more gently this time. 'Will you not tell me the reason?'

A soft sigh sounded in the air. 'Please, Lord Ravensmede, I must—'

'You have not told her of our study in astronomy at Lady Finlay's ball?'

Her cheeks reddened. 'Of course not!' Indignation flashed

in her eyes. 'I don't wish to sound rude, my lord, but the reason that I'm assisting in the kitchen is none of your consideration.'

Ravensmede looked at her with growing intensity. 'On the contrary, Miss Marchant,' he said quietly, 'it is everything of my consideration.'

Miss Marchant ignored his remark and continued, 'Now, if you will please excuse me, my lord.'

'No,' he said with a wicked glint in his eye.

The poor girl paled.

'How long is this…punishment to endure?'

A guarded look closed over Miss Marchant's face. 'I didn't say anything about a punishment.'

His eyes held hers. 'How long?'

Her gaze flickered away. She made to step back.

Ravensmede touched his fingers to her chin, guiding her focus to his. 'Let me help you, Kathryn.'

For an instant, just one fleeting moment, he saw the softening of her expression, the hope that shone in her eyes. 'Help me?'

'If you were to be under my protection…'

A pause, followed by a dawning realisation. And then it was gone, replaced instead with hurt disbelief, and finally furious humiliation. 'Certainly not!'

He had never had such an offer so adamantly refused.

She jerked away, leaving his fingers suspended in mid-air. 'I don't need your *help,* Lord Ravensmede.' Her voice was cool, her words clipped. 'I bid you good day, my lord.' She bent to retrieve the sack of potatoes.

But Ravensmede was there first. He watched her cheeks blanch and her eyes widen.

'My offer stands, Miss Marchant. If you should change your mind, you need only send me a message. Perhaps in time you will view matters differently.'

Her nostrils flared with fury. Her small breasts rose and fell with the quickening of her breathing. 'I will never accept such an offer!' Her hand tugged at the sack.

But Lord Ravensmede held firm. In one easy motion he tucked the sack neatly beneath his arm. 'My horse is tethered close by. We'd best fasten this to Rollo's saddle and make our way smartly to Green Street if these potatoes are on this evening's menu.' There was a teasing note in his voice, and the suggestion of a smile. Then off he sauntered towards the gelding, leaving Kathryn staring after him.

The sack was securely attached to the horse when he heard the rustle of her skirt behind him.

'Lord Ravensmede, surely you cannot seriously mean to accompany me home?' The glorious spread of hair had disappeared beneath a bonnet that matched the unfashionable brown coloration of her dress. The glare of sunlight exposed the fragility of her face, highlighting the smudges below her eyes.

A muscle twitched in Ravensmede's jaw. 'But of course, Miss Marchant. It would not be gentlemanly to do otherwise.' He'd be damned if he let her struggle beneath the weight of that load.

Panic rose in her voice. 'No, it won't do. You mustn't! Please pass me the potatoes at once.'

Ravensmede turned to face her, a twinkling in his clear green eyes. 'Have no fear, they're fixed firmly in place and shall not dislodge.'

'My lord,' she said in a stage whisper, 'I must insist that you return my potatoes and cease this…this…' she plucked the word from the air '…madness, at once!'

The corners of Ravensmede's mouth twisted upwards. 'I believe that I've already explained my position, Miss Marchant.' He tried not to laugh. 'The potatoes are quite safe.' One dark eyebrow arched. 'Now, if you wish to avoid a scene I suggest that you take my arm and let us be on our way.'

Several murmurs alerted Miss Marchant to the interest growing around their conversation. At least two ladies were staring. She sighed and tentatively touched her fingers to his sleeve, only to find them firmly tucked within the crook of his arm.

With Miss Marchant secured on one side, and Rollo and

the precious cargo on the other, Lord Ravensmede made his way towards Green Street.

Blast the confounded man! How dare he take such a liberty! She'd have rather balanced the potatoes on her hip to Stepney and back than endure this. What could he be thinking of? His offer of help? Help, indeed! Like a fool she had thought it an honest offer until the truth of his meaning had dawned. What kind of woman did he take her for? Well, he would soon learn that Kathryn Marchant had no need of his sort of help, not now, not ever!

She sneaked a look up at his face. His strong handsome features showed not the slightest hint of discomfort. In fact, if she hadn't known better, she could almost have sworn that he was actually enjoying himself. Such behaviour was only to be expected from a man with Ravensmede's reputation. Not that she knew exactly what it was that he was actually guilty of, only that there were many pursed lips and raised eyebrows at his arrival, and that he had a penchant for women, gaming and drink…in that order.

Her eyes dropped to the burgundy coat, the matching waistcoat and immaculately arranged neckcloth. And lower still to the buff-coloured pantaloons that hugged the muscles of his thighs in a quite indecent fashion. The pristine condition and expensive cut of his clothing only served to emphasise the tawdry state of her own. Realising that she was staring at his lordship's thighs brought her gaze rapidly up, only to meet with an amused pair of green eyes.

'Do I meet with your approval, Miss Marchant?' His voice was a slow delicious drawl.

'Most certainly not,' she snapped, feeling her cheeks begin to burn. Then, realising just how rude she sounded, added, 'I appreciate that your intention to relieve me of my burden is one of kindness. It is, however, quite unnecessary.'

That slightly mocking gaze found hers once more. 'On the contrary, Miss Marchant, I assure you that I'm never kind.'

Emerald lights danced in his eyes, rendering them such an unusual colour that it took the immense application of Kathryn's will-power not to stare.

Not trusting herself not to deliver him a sharp retort, she bit her tongue. They strolled along in silence and all the while she took care to keep her face turned from him.

It was some minutes before he spoke again. 'It appears that I've unwittingly offended you, Miss Marchant. Or have you just a natural aversion to my company?'

Her head swung round with surprise at the directness of his question. It was a big mistake. Those alluring eyes were on her again. A tingling sensation crept across her skin. Her tongue tied itself into knots and she quickly glanced away. 'I…I'm…'

His voice lowered, so that the words would reach her ears alone. 'It did not seem so at Lady Finlay's ball.'

She stared at him aghast. 'You appear to be labouring under some false impression of my character, my lord.' Her hand tried to wriggle free of Ravensmede's arm.

He did not release her. 'Where precisely have I erred?'

As an elderly lady peered down at her from a passing carriage, Kathryn ceased her struggle.

Keeping her expression carefully bland as if they were discussing the weather, or other such matters, she whispered, 'How can you ask such a thing?' She glanced around and recognised that they were close to Green Street. 'Please hurry, my lord. I have kept Mrs Moultrie waiting some considerable time.'

If anything, Ravensmede's feet dragged.

'My lord, I'm very late.' Agitation raised her voice, and she tugged at his arm to propel him faster.

His lordship stopped stock-still. 'What are you so afraid of?'

'Nothing.'

A cynical brow raised. 'I'll speak to your uncle. The situation may change if he realises that your shoddy treatment has not gone unnoticed.'

Kathryn paled at the very thought. Heaven forbid that he

should do such a thing! 'No!' She licked her suddenly dry lips. 'Thank you, but no. It would serve only to make matters worse.'

Ravensmede looked at her, then slowly resumed walking towards Green Street. Once they reached the Marchant residence he loosened Rollo's load and made to mount the steps up to the front door.

'Lord Ravensmede.' Kathryn gently pulled at his arm.

'I won't see you struggle beneath this weight.'

Her fingers tightened around the broad band of muscle. She looked up into his face and bit at her bottom lip. 'Very well. Then please come this way.' She made to walk around the side of the house.

The Viscount of Ravensmede showed no sign of moving. 'I find I have a preference for the front door. I've never used a servants' entrance in my life, and I don't intend to do so now.

Kathryn's heart missed a beat. The blood drained from her face. She composed a breath. 'Please, my lord.'

The green eyes held hers, and in his gaze was understanding and determination. 'It's better this way,' he said softly, and, tucking her hand into his arm, walked up the steps.

The bell rang. And in that moment of waiting, Kathryn was never more aware of the absurdity of her situation. The tall handsome aristocrat by her side, a sack of potatoes under one arm, her own hand tucked in the other, standing at the front door of the house in Green Street for all the world to see. Footsteps sounded from within. The trickle of fear surged and she felt suddenly that she might be sick. She tried to remove her hand from Lord Ravensmede's arm.

His lordship's hold tightened.

The door opened.

Kathryn swallowed hard.

'I'm here to call upon Mr Marchant,' said Lord Ravensmede and thrust the sack into the unsuspecting manservant's hands. The sack was followed by Ravensmede's card.

The manservant stared first at the potatoes, then at Lord

Ravensmede, and finally at Kathryn. He blinked once or twice, seemingly unable to find words.

Ravensmede gestured Kathryn in ahead of him. 'After you, Miss Marchant.' Once within the hallway he raised Kathryn's hand to his lips. 'So fortuitous to have met you again,' he said gallantly, and finally released her.

'Lord Ravensmede,' she said, and gave a small curtsy. Even her breath was shaky.

'Ever your servant,' he said and bowed.

With a very straight back, and very precise steps, Kathryn walked away…while she still could.

Only then did the manservant remember himself enough to stop gaping and fetch the master of the house.

Lord Ravensmede was wiping his hands on a pristine white handkerchief when Henry Marchant entered the drawing room.

'Lord Ravensmede! What an unexpected pleasure.' Mr Marchant bustled forward, unable to believe just who had called upon him. His lordship might be considered one of the worst rake-hells in London, but, as the current Viscount of Ravensmede, heir to an exceptionally wealthy earldom, and in receipt of a considerable allowance, he was not a man that Henry Marchant felt any inclination to snub. Ravensmede made the Marchant monies look like a pile of pennies, and he was what Henry for all his hard work could never hope to become—an aristocrat. As the initial surprise waned Henry began to calculate just how advantageous Lord Ravensmede's visit might prove. Mr Marchant was, after all, in possession of a young and attractive daughter, and his lordship had ever been known to have an eye for a beautiful woman. The possibilities danced before him. 'Please take a seat. Would you care for a drink?'

'Brandy, if you have any.'

'Most certainly,' said Mr Marchant. He poured the brandy into two crystal glasses and passed one to Lord Ravensmede. Ravensmede made himself comfortable in the chair and lei-

surely perused the surrounding room before turning his attention to Henry Marchant. 'Perhaps you may be able to assist me,
Mr Marchant.'

Mr Marchant's chins wobbled in delight. 'Of course, my
lord, in any way that I can.'

'It is the most peculiar of situations.'

'Indeed?' The older man leaned forward.

'I chanced upon your niece while I was out. She was
carrying a sack of potatoes.'

There was the smallest silence before Mr Marchant spoke.
'*Potatoes*, you say?'

'Most definitely potatoes,' said Ravensmede, and waited.

A subtle pink coloration crept into Henry Marchant's complexion. 'I don't understand. What on earth would Kathryn be
doing with potatoes?'

'My question precisely, sir. Naturally no gentleman would
allow a lady to carry such a burden.'

'No, no, of course not,' Mr Marchant added in bluff agreement.

'I therefore carried the potatoes in her stead.'

'You?' said Mr Marchant weakly.

'Me,' said the Viscount of Ravensmede, and smiled grimly.

'Good God!' came the whispered reply.

'Financial straits are always embarrassing, sir, but it is a gentleman's duty to spare his womenfolk.'

The colour of Mr Marchant's cheeks deepened to puce. He
stuttered so much as to almost choke on the words. 'M-m-my
finances are all in order. You are mistaken, sir, in your thoughts.
I employ a house full of servants.'

'Indeed?' Ravensmede paused. 'Then why was Miss
Marchant sent to do a servant's job?'

'I've no idea, but rest assured, my lord, I shall discover what
this business is about.'

'I'm glad to hear it.'

'Kathryn is very grateful for my family's charity and tries
to make herself useful in return. Perhaps that was her intention

in this instance—well meant, but poorly judged. There is, after all, no fathoming the workings of the female mind!' Mr Marchant laughed. It sounded false and uneasy in the room.

Ravensmede raised a single eyebrow.

Mr Marchant hurriedly cleared his throat. 'As I was saying, I mean to get to the bottom of the matter. Kathryn came to us when my brother tragically died some number of years ago. She has been welcomed into the bosom of my family. I've never been one to flout my duty, my lord, and I trust that no one would suggest otherwise.'

'Heaven forbid, sir.' Ravensmede took a swig of brandy and stood to leave. 'You stock a fine brandy, Mr Marchant.'

Soothed by Lord Ravensmede's response, Mr Marchant sought to redeem something of the situation. The thought of a match between the Viscount and Lottie was still rather tantalising. 'If you would like to call again, my lord, under more auspicious circumstances, I have some rather splendid cigars.'

'How very kind,' said Ravensmede with an irony that was lost on Henry Marchant, and departed.

Lord Cadmount attacked the game pie with obvious exuberance. 'Nothing like an afternoon practising the pugilistic arts to fire up a man's appetite. Didn't mean to land you such a planter.'

'You got lucky. It was a very respectable left hook, and my mind was elsewhere.' Three hours' boxing had not taken the edge off Ravensmede's disgruntlement. It was a sentiment that had failed to shift since his earlier encounter with Miss Kathryn Marchant.

'So I noticed.' Cadmount forked a great mound of meat into his mouth. There was nothing but the sound of cutlery scraping against plates and noisy mastication coming from Cadmount. He licked a smear of gravy from his lip. 'Ain't been happy for a while. Can see it in your face. Been winning at the card tables; cellar is stocked with the best of bottles; plenty of luck with the ladies too. But something ain't right.

Known you too long for you to pull the wool over my eyes.'
Cadmount resumed his attack on the enormous piece of pie
before him. 'Pressure from the old man getting too much?
Is he still trying to force that heiress upon you—what's her
name—Pitten?'

'Francesca Paton.' Had it been anyone else sitting across the
table, Ravensmede would have quelled them with an arrogant
stare. Archie Cadmount was different. He was one of the few
people that Ravensmede trusted. The two men were as dissimilar in temperament as they were in looks. But since their
youthful days at Eton they had remained true friends. And
because it was Cadmount, Ravensmede spoke the truth. 'And,
no, things are no worse than usual. My father can say what he
will, but I'll be damned if I'll let him dictate my life.'

'Still sore about him forbidding your commission?'

'While you were risking your life in the Peninsula to put a
halt to Boney's forces, I was here doing what I've been doing
for the last twelve years, what I'm still doing. Men are dying
for England and I'm here drinking, gambling, whoring…
What's the bloody point?'

'Ain't your fault that you're heir to the earldom. Ain't your
father's fault either. Maybury just wants to ensure things are safe
for the future. Only son and all that. Can't have you going off
and getting yourself killed. Can't blame the old man for that.'

'Maybe not,' said Ravensmede. 'But tell me this, Caddie—
if you hadn't been obliged to come home because of your
brother, would you choose to still be out there fighting, or
sitting here in London leading a comfortable existence?'

'Point taken. But if you ain't happy with things as they are,
perhaps it's time for a change. Perhaps Maybury is right,
perhaps it *is* time for a wife and a nursery.'

'Hell's teeth, Caddie, not you too! I'll marry when I'm good
and ready and not before.'

'Stubborn to the bone,' murmured his friend. 'Always were,
always will be. Stubborn and wilful.'

Ravensmede gave him a crooked smile. 'You know me so well.'

A little pie remained on Cadmount's plate. He set about remedying that with one final flourish of his fork and pondered on his friend's unhappiness. Clearly a change of subject was required. Something to cheer Ravensmede. Something with which the Viscount was enamoured. He paused to savour the richly flavoured gravy. 'By God, but that was good. If you ever tire of Lamont's cooking, send him to me.' The claret was drained in one gulp and he eyed Ravensmede. Inspiration came to him. 'Made any progress with the Marchant chit?'

Ravensmede sipped his wine with a nonchalance that he did not feel. 'I happened to chance upon Miss Marchant while I was out this afternoon. She's not treated well within the Marchant household, but refuses to consider possible ways out.' He looked away to conceal the depth of his emotion. 'Blasted girl's pride will be her downfall.'

A snort of laughter sounded in the dining room. 'Turned you down again, did she?'

The blue-shadowed jaw-line tightened. 'Something like that.'

Cadmount snorted again. 'Good for her.'

Ravensmede did not want to reveal the full extent of his encounter with Kathryn Marchant. He knew full well what he had offered the girl. Could still taste the sourness that the ignoble offer left upon his tongue. And yet he wanted her, even here, even now, knowing all that he did. Any mention of what she had been doing or her tired appearance would be an act of betrayal. Instinctively he knew that Kathryn would not want others to know of her circumstance. Living as she did could not be pleasant. He thought of her lugging the sack of potatoes across St James's Park, of her seeking refuge behind the old oak tree, ashamed to be seen. Despite her dusty worn clothes and her red chapped hands she had been happy, humming that tune, with a faraway look in her eyes. Happy, at least until he had arrived. He set his fork down upon his plate.

Cadmount eyed him with interest.

Ravensmede's finger tapped thoughtfully against the stem of the glass. 'There must be something I can do, Archie. I'll be damned if I'll just leave her to that family's devices.'

Lord Cadmount knew things must be serious. Ravensmede never, but never, used his given name. It looked as if Kathryn Marchant might be just the tonic that Ravensmede needed. 'She turned you down, old man, and if she ain't under your protection then there's nothing you can do. Unmarried lady and all that. And she *is* a lady,' he said. 'Wouldn't look too good for li'l Miss Marchant if you start charging in there, pistols blazing. Not to put too fine a point on it, Ravensmede, any association with you is likely to leave a lady's reputation a little the worse for wear. No offence intended.'

Ravensmede thought grimly of his meeting with Mr Marchant. Hardly charging in with pistols blazing, rather a case of letting the man know that his treatment of the girl hadn't gone unnoticed.

'Best thing you could do is to stay away.' A large dollop of puréed potato was scooped into Cadmount's mouth. It did not prevent his continued conversation. 'Unless, of course, you're prepared to contemplate a more respectable alternative.' The adroit blue gaze slid to Ravensmede.

Lord Ravensmede picked at the fillet of sole, before pushing his plate away.

'Stands to reason,' Cadmount released a loud and resonant burp, 'why did you turn down the splendid Mrs White if your interest in Miss Marchant isn't in earnest? I mean, the Winsome Widow's practically offering herself on a platter. Don't think that I'd send *her* packing. And from where I was standing, it looked like you were about to devour the Marchant chit on the dance floor. If it ain't serious, why else did you waltz with her?'

Ravensmede's eyes glowered in the candlelight. 'Why indeed?'

Cadmount affected not to notice. 'I know you'll go your own way, you always do. But for what my humble opinion is worth, if you've any regard for the girl you'll stop sniffing round her skirts and leave well alone. There's no family to hush a scandal, and no man waiting in the wings to salvage her reputation. Don't ruin her life, Nick…unless you mean to offer her marriage.'

One haughty eyebrow cocked. 'Still on that old theme? I'm beginning to think that you're in league with m'father.' He savoured the taste of the claret against his palate. 'I've no intention of marrying Miss Kathryn Marchant or anyone else.'

'Good thing you'll be leaving her alone then. Besides…' he looked pointedly at Ravensmede '…I don't suppose the chit is quite what Maybury has in mind for your bride.'

'Don't push it, Caddie,' Ravensmede said quietly.

Cadmount laughed, and shrugged off his serious garb. 'Then it's to Brooks's this evening and the faro tables.' He slapped the table and belched again, grinning all the while. 'It's not as though Henry Marchant will starve or beat the girl.' And with that parting comment Lord Cadmount went to relieve himself.

Ravensmede remained alone at the dining table. Starvation. Beatings. For some reason the thoughts weighed uneasy on his mind. He rubbed at his chin and tried to banish the image of a small heart-shaped face. His dark brows puckered. Damn Kathryn Marchant's pride, and damn Archibald Cadmount's warnings. He could no sooner leave the girl to her fate than he could pluck out his own eyes. Whether she wanted it or not, Miss Marchant was about to become the recipient of his help…whatever guise that it might come in.

Chapter Four

It was ten o'clock and Kathryn was busy helping Nancy wash the linen. The coarse soap stung at their hands as they scrubbed within the cold water, but neither woman complained. They chatted about Nancy's young man and her sister's new baby boy.

"'E's as bright as a button, miss, truly 'e is. All downy black 'air and big blue eyes, and such a big smile for a little fella.' The front door bell sounded. 'Wonder who that could be?'

Kathryn tucked a stray curl back up into her cap with a soapy finger. 'It's rather early for visitors. Unless, of course, there was some scandalous affair last night at Lady Campbell's after Aunt Anna and Lottie left. Just think what they might have missed!'

The scullery filled with their chuckles.

'You ain't 'alf a laugh, miss.'

A delicious aroma of eggs and chops and toast wafted through from the kitchen. Kathryn's stomach growled so loudly that Nancy pulled a face.

'Lawk! Sounds like someone ain't had no breakfast!'

Kathryn just shrugged and carried on with the scrubbing. Her stomach protested at being ignored.

Nancy peered suspiciously at the other girl's pale face. ''Ave you ate somethin' this mornin', miss?'

'There was a to-do over the potatoes yesterday that dis-pleased my aunt. Breakfast is forbidden for the next week.'

Nancy knew exactly what the 'to-do' was about. Indeed, the servants had talked of little else since that fancy lord had brought Kathryn and the potatoes home. But Nancy was wise enough to make no mention of it.

'Don't worry. I'm not really hungry. It's just that smell causing all the rumbling down there.' Kathryn's eyes dropped down to indicate her stomach.

'But you didn't 'ave no dinner last night neither. Let me get you somethin'.'

Kathryn's soapy hand reached out towards the maidser-vant's, and squeezed it affectionately. 'Thank you, but no. I don't want you getting into trouble on my behalf, and it would be just like Mrs Moultrie to spot what you were about. She seems to inform my aunt of every detail. No, Nancy, kind as your offer is, I shall last very well until lunch.'

'She's a bloody bitch, that one,' came the sharp reply. 'Sorry, miss. I know I shouldn't be swearin' in front of you, but I couldn't help myself. She's a mean-hearted woman.'

Kathryn smiled at what a shock it would cause if she were to ask Nancy to which woman precisely the maid was referring. Swallowing down her bad grace, which she feared was getting out of hand, she changed the subject. 'When will you visit your sister again?'

The maid was just about to reply when the clatter of foot-steps sounded from the kitchen. Mrs Moultrie's scowling jowls appeared in the doorway.

'The master and mistress are up early this morning so you best get upstairs and strip the beds. It's a fine day, so don't be dallying.' A jaundiced eye stared smugly at Kathryn. 'No outdoor chores today, miss. Mrs Marchant says as there's plenty to keep you busy in here.'

'I'm sure that my aunt is quite correct.'

Mrs Moultrie sniffed and waddled back to her kitchen.

* * *

Upstairs the visitor was being shown into the dining room by a somewhat awed footman.

Even the master of the house had lost his normal staid countenance and was eyeing the doorway of the dining room in a rather apprehensive manner. The *Morning Post* lay discarded upon the table.

Anna Marchant recovered from the shock first and greeted their guest with a feigned smile and a nod of her golden head. 'Lord Ravensmede, what a pleasant surprise and so early in the morning. Please do join us for breakfast.'

'Indeed,' agreed her husband a tad too heartily. 'Make yourself comfortable, my lord.'

Ravensmede passed his beaver and gloves to the footman and sat himself down at the table. The dark ruffle of his hair and colour in his cheeks bespoke a man who had been up since the crack of dawn. He wore an aura of strength and vitality, quite unlike his host and hostess, who had not long crawled from their beds and were still feeling not quite up to scratch.

'Sorry to trouble you at such an unearthly hour,' he drawled with absolutely no hint of sincerity. An invisible speck of dust on the sleeve of his impeccable dark green coat required his attention, leaving Mr and Mrs Marchant perched on the edge of their seats.

'Will you take something to eat, my lord?' Mr Marchant's chins stretched into a smile.

Ravensmede's waved his hand in a dismissive gesture. 'No, thank you, sir. I've already broken my fast.' He watched the shadow of anxiety cloud Henry Marchant's face.

Mr Marchant cleared his throat. 'Regarding the matter you brought to my attention yesterday, my lord, it was a silly misunderstanding and shall not happen again.' His gaze flickered to Mrs Marchant, then back to the Viscount.

His wife looked on coldly, dislike bristling beneath her pleasant veneer.

'Good,' said Ravensmede, 'But I'm here for quite a different purpose, sir. I wondered if I might call upon Miss Marchant this afternoon to accompany me for a drive in Hyde Park.'

'Yes, indeed you may, sir.' The words were out before Ravensmede had even finished his sentence. 'Lottie's the apple of my eye. A darling girl. And a diamond of the first water, even if I do say so myself.'

His lordship did not immediately correct the man's mistake. He thought of Lottie Marchant and her bland prettiness, so like a hundred other young women. He checked the twitch at his lips.

'My daughter will be more than happy to accompany you, won't she, my dear?'

Anna Marchant inclined her head in agreement.

Lord Ravensmede's haughty brow raised just a little. 'But, sir, you misunderstand me. I was speaking of Miss Kathryn Marchant.' He paused to watch the shot go home.

Henry Marchant's countenance coloured and his wife was staring as if the very devil had just appeared.

'My niece?' The words ground slowly from Mr Marchant's mouth.

'I take it you have no problem with my request.'

Unless he had gauged the Marchants wrongly, then they would do nothing other than comply.

Mr Marchant nodded once. 'Fine by me, sir.'

Anna Marchant's top lip curled with disdain before she forced it once more to the semblance of a smile. 'Unfortunately, my niece is indisposed with a chill. It will take some days before she's fully recovered, and I doubt that the outdoor air would be advisable for her state of health.'

Ravensmede's expression did not alter from unassailable boredom. It was the one he used when engaged in card play and it had never failed him yet. 'Indeed, madam, I send my condolences. In that case, I won't waste any more of your time.' He executed the tiniest of bows and made to leave.

Mr Marchant made haste to repair any damage. 'I'm sure she will be recovered by next week, if you would care to call then.'

If looks could kill, Henry Marchant would have been a bloodied corpse upon the rug, a victim of his wife's malice.

'Perhaps,' said his lordship ambiguously and strolled out into the hallway just in time to see Kathryn Marchant running down the stairs with a basket full of crumpled sheets between her hands.

'Miss Marchant,' said Lord Ravensmede, in a tone of absolute correctness. 'I trust you're feeling well enough to be out of bed?'

Kathryn stared at the tall athletic figure that had just emerged from the dining room. 'Lord Ravensmede?' Was she dreaming? Her fingers loosed their grip on the wicker strands, leaving Anna Marchant's dirty sheets to tumble out in full display down the staircase before her.

The lady screeched in the background. 'Kathryn, what are you doing up there? No doubt she has developed a fever to make her behave in such an obscure manner. I cannot begin to think what on earth she is doing with that linen. Leave it at once and return to your room.' As Nancy appeared over Kathryn's shoulder she added, 'You, girl, why are you using the main stairs? Get this mess sorted out at once! I'll speak to you later.'

Aunt Anna's harsh words pulled Kathryn's attention from the Viscount. 'Aunt, please do not be cross with Nancy. I insisted that we come this way. These baskets are so wide it makes the servants' stairwell difficult to squeeze down. I did not think...' The words trailed off and she glanced apologetically in the direction of Lord Ravensmede.

'You never do,' came her aunt's withering reply.

Ravensmede looked directly from the sheets to Mr Marchant. A flush appeared on the older man's cheeks.

Ravensmede allowed a small awkward silence before turning his attention back to Kathryn. 'You appear to have recovered from your chill, Miss Marchant,' he said in a voice that was silky smooth.

Kathryn's brow wrinkled in bewilderment. 'I'm quite well, thank you, my lord. Whatever made you think that I was not?'

Ravensmede cocked an eyebrow in Mrs Marchant's direction.

'Kathryn, you silly girl, you don't know what you're saying! It must be the fever.' Anna attempted to shoo her niece back up the stairs. 'And have a care not to waken Lottie.'

'Shall I send my own physician to attend Miss Marchant?' The deep voice arrested the ladies' progress. He stepped forward, extending his hand to touch his fingers against Kathryn's forehead. 'How strange, no heat at all. A miraculous recovery wouldn't you say, Mrs Marchant?'

Anna Marchant's mouth compressed with fury.

Her husband tugged helplessly at his neckcloth. 'Just as you say, sir, a speedy and fortuitous recovery.'

Ravensmede stepped back, fixed his beaver hat on his head and carefully donned his gloves. 'Then I shall call at four.' The piercing gaze rested on Mr Marchant, 'Good morning, sir', flitted to his wife, 'madam', and finally alighted on Kathryn, 'Miss Marchant.'

The three stood slack-jawed and silent as Lord Ravensmede sauntered from the house in Green Street.

Kathryn had changed into her best walking dress: a slightly faded blue muslin purchased five years ago. It was dated in appearance, but clean, and she knew that the colour suited her well. Her hair was caught back in a knot at the nape of her neck and was well hidden beneath the mud-brown bonnet, which had been a gift from Aunt Anna when her own had fallen apart. A fichu, a rather tight spencer, sturdy walking shoes, darned gloves, and a small home-made reticule, all in a matching shade of greyish brown, completed the ensemble. Standing in front of the mirror, Kathryn surveyed her reflection with a critical eye. Her face was so pale that even her lips had lost their rosy hue. She looked exactly like she felt: tired and washed out. And she had yet to face an afternoon in Lord Ravensmede's company. The prospect was really rather daunting. Why would a man like him be interested in a woman like her? The answer was plainly evident. He had made his intent very clear. Raising her chin a notch, she determined to set his lordship firmly in his place with regard to that. A noise sounded behind her.

'Ah, Kathryn, getting ready for Lord Ravensmede?' Lottie swept an appraising gaze over her cousin. 'You look…like someone far past her last prayers.'

Kathryn said nothing, just watched while Lottie flounced into the bedchamber and sat herself down upon the single battered chair.

'There's only one reason that Ravensmede would be taking the likes of you for a drive, and we all know what that is.' One pretty slippered foot swung repetitively. 'Let's just say that it's certainly not marriage he has on his mind.' A snigger escaped her. 'What have you been up to with his lordship, Kathryn?' Lottie leaned forward, a smug gloating look upon her face.

'Stop it, Lottie. I didn't ask Lord Ravensmede to take me driving. Indeed, I would much prefer not to spend any time in his company. I was as surprised as you to hear that he had made such an offer.'

'And is that the only offer he has made you?'

On seeing the barb hit home and two patches of colour flow into her cousin's cheeks, Lottie continued, 'That night at Lady Finlay's, when he waltzed with you, where were you when you stormed off out of the ball room? In the retiring room? I don't think so. More like reaching an agreement with the Viscount of Ravensmede!'

Kathryn turned, eyes flashing, fists clenched to control her fury. 'Lottie, how can you make such wicked allegations? You know very well that it's nonsense.'

Lottie did not reply, just smiled knowingly.

'Please excuse me, Cousin.' Kathryn could not bear to stay in the room a minute longer.

A snide laugh followed her. 'You may run, Kathryn, but you won't get very far. Mama has a little surprise planned for you.'

She sat alone and tense in the drawing room awaiting the sound of the bell. If Lottie thought such a thing, then the rest of the world was likely to view it in much the same vein. She would have to deter Lord Ravensmede in no uncertain terms. Her gaze fixed on the blackened fireplace. She forced herself to relax, to breathe deeply. In, and out. Tension ebbed. *The fireplace disappeared. Her mother's face smiled kindly. A soft hand reached out to softly stroke her hair. The wind whipped at her face, sea air inhaled deep into her lungs. Mama was laughing and pointing to the shimmering water and the rolling white waves. Lottie's cruel words receded into oblivion. Meaningless. Gentle fingers stroked her cheek. 'Kathryn,' Mama whispered. Kathryn smiled beneath the caress. 'Kathryn.' The voice was deeper, slightly more insistent, not like Mama's at all. She touched her hand to Mama's.* Her eyelids fluttered open, and she looked up into the clear green eyes of Lord Ravensmede. A gasp sounded, her own, and she was up and out of the chair, breathless with confusion. 'Lord Ravensmede, you startled me!'

'My apologies, Miss Marchant. I did not mean to.' He was regarding her with such scrutiny as to set Kathryn's cheeks aflame.

'Good afternoon, Lord Ravensmede.' Mrs Marchant breezed into the room. 'We seem to have found Kathryn at last. I shall tell Lottie she can call off the search.' The bright blue eyes narrowed as they flicked over Kathryn's reddened face.

Ravensmede extended his arm in Kathryn's direction. 'I shall return your niece safely before six. Try not to concern yourself, ma'am. I shall see to it personally that there's no deterioration in her health.'

'Indeed, Lord Ravensmede, I don't doubt it. But I will, of course, be present myself to witness your attentions. Lottie and I will accompany Kathryn this afternoon.' Mrs Marchant almost cackled at the deliverance of her cunning plan. 'It would be unseemly to allow my niece out without a chaperon.' She did not add the words 'and in your company'. She did not need to.

Lord Ravensmede delivered the woman a glare of such glacial proportions that she actually stumbled back. 'Such a thought is anathema to my sensibilities. Which is why I've brought my grandmother in just such a capacity. She preferred to wait in the barouche while I came in to collect Miss Marchant.' The inferred insult was obvious. 'Perhaps you would care to step outside to meet her?'

Anna Marchant moved swiftly to the window and looked out at Lord Ravensmede's barouche complete with an elderly lady dressed entirely in gaudy purple.

Kathryn looked from her aunt to Ravensmede and back again.

'But of course, Lord Ravensmede,' Mrs Marchant uttered between gritted teeth. 'How very thoughtful of you.' Every step those daintily clad feet took on their way out to the barouche warned of a mounting violence. 'I shall await Kathryn's return with impatience.' She slid a meaningful look at her niece.

Kathryn did not miss the promise held so clearly in those cold blue eyes.

The day was warm, but that had not prevented the frail little lady being almost hidden beneath the thickest pile of blankets.

'Grandmama, may I introduce Mrs Marchant, Miss Kathryn Marchant, and...' he indicated the sullen-faced young woman who refused to leave the doorway '...Miss Charlotte Marchant.'

Anna Marchant dropped a graceful curtsy, hid the malice from her face and smiled charmingly. 'Such a pleasure to meet you, Lady Maybury.'

The old lady subjected each of the offered females to a piercing stare from eyes that were a faded version of Ravensmede's own, and let out a cackle. 'The little chit looks nothing like the other two. I fancy Mr Marchant may have been cuckolded there.' Then, as if she hadn't just dropped a monumental insult, she dabbed a lilac lace handkerchief to her nose and declared in an imperious tone, 'Nicholas, how much longer do you intend to keep me waiting? Even the greys are getting bored.'

For the first time since meeting her Ravensmede bestowed a smile upon Mrs Marchant, then he took his leave of her, lifting Kathryn neatly into the barouche and bowling off down the road at what could only be described as a reckless pace.

The entirety of London's *ton* had decided to partake of the afternoon air within the green surround of Hyde Park, or so it seemed to Kathryn when they entered. So many pairs of curious eyes turned upon her, so many hushed whispers and veiled finger pointings. She hid her discomfort well and smiled at Ravensmede's eagle-eyed grandmother. The old lady fussed around with her blankets, oblivious to the heat of the day, raised a withered hand in the direction of a distant carriage and then turned her attentions to Kathryn.

'Well, let me have a good look at you, gel.' A quizzing glass appeared from beneath the blankets. One greatly enlarged faded eye gave a close scrutiny, missing nothing of the worn attire or the way Miss Kathryn Marchant kept her head averted from her grandson's person. 'Not got the fair locks or the silly prettiness of the other two,' came the succinct observation.

Kathryn heard the sharpness in Lady Maybury's voice. Those unused to her ladyship's company had been known to quail under her blunt comments, but Kathryn sensed no malice beneath the harsh veneer. 'No, my lady. Mrs Marchant is my aunt, and Charlotte, my cousin. I've lived with them since my father died.'

'And your father was...Robert Marchant?'

Kathryn's eyes opened wide. Forgetting her reserve, she twisted round to face Lady Maybury. 'You knew him?'

'No. When you've been alive for as long as I have, there's not much you don't eventually get to hear of. Refresh my memory.'

'Grandmama!' said Ravensmede, remembering Archie Cadmount's brief account of Kathryn's history, 'Miss Marchant may not wish to speak of her family.'

'Tush and nonsense, Nick!' exclaimed the old lady heatedly. She then bestowed a look of obvious affection upon her favourite grandson.

For the first time since leaving Green Street Kathryn looked directly at his lordship. 'Really, I don't mind, my lord.'

Ravensmede kept his eyes upon her. And in his breast rose that same inexplicable feeling that had enveloped him on seeing Kathryn Marchant seated all alone in the drawing room with her mind a thousand miles away. Who was it that she saw behind those closed eyes? Someone who had the power to make her smile, someone she was happy to have caress her cheek. A suitor from the past, or some secret lover? The thought did not please him. That velvet-smooth skin washed with the merest hint of colour as she turned once more to his grandmother.

'As you said, my father was Robert Marchant, the elder brother of Uncle Henry. My mother was Elizabeth Thornley, from Overton. She died of consumption almost eight years ago. Soon after, my sister died too, of the same illness. My father…' Her voice wavered. 'My father suffered an accident.' She couldn't bring herself to tell them the exact nature of the 'accident', or how she had spent the time since his death trying to forget the horrendous image that seemed branded on her memory. 'He's been dead for just over three years. Uncle Henry and Aunt Anna were kind enough to offer me a home.' Her fingers tightened against the seat.

'What of your mother's relatives? Have you no contact with them?' the Dowager Countess demanded, but there was a distinct mellowing in the sharpness of her tone.

Kathryn's fingers plucked at the muslin of her skirt, and her lashes swept low before she answered, 'They didn't approve of my parents' marriage. I've never met them.'

'I see.' Lady Maybury raised her quizzing glass once more. 'And why are you not yet married?'

Kathryn blushed. 'There was never time for that.' She did not speak of the pain of nursing her mother and sister, nor of

the years of caring for her grief-stricken father. Neither did she
mention the torment of her father's death. 'And now I'm my
cousin's companion.'

A tutting sound escaped the crinkled lips. 'Stuff and
nonsense! No time indeed!'

On seeing the deepening hue of Kathryn's cheeks, Ravensmede came to her rescue. 'You mustn't tease Miss Marchant
so, Grandmama. It really is quite cruel of you.' Besides he
didn't want his relative getting ideas about arranging a marriage
for the girl with the first convenient man; not when he had other
plans for Kathryn Marchant.

Of all his family Ravensmede was closest to his paternal
grandmother. Even so, that did not mean he was blind to her
tendency for bossy dominance and interfering in matters that
did not concern her. Not that it was a family trait by any means,
or so he told himself. He made a mental note to have a word
with her at a more opportune moment.

The dowager snorted, but changed the subject all the same.

They stopped on several occasions to allow Lady Maybury
to converse with other ladies, to all of whom she insisted on
introducing Miss Marchant. The afternoon was progressing
splendidly and even Kathryn had begun to relax and enjoy the
bright sunshine and wonderful cooling breeze when the unfortunate incident occurred.

The tiny ragged figure appeared as if from thin air to mate-
rialise directly in front of Lord Ravensmede's barouche. Even
with the wealth of his driving experience and his renowned skill
with the ribbons, there was little that Ravensmede could do to
stop the team in time. As it was, his expertise allowed him to
pull the team hard to the right-hand side of the path and, in all
probability, it was this reflex that prevented the collision and
saved the child's life. As the horses ground to a halt, he glanced
round to check that his passengers had not been dislodged by
the abruptness of his stopping. Kathryn was tucking the blanket

around his grandmother, who was complaining in a most quer-
ulous tone of voice. Her gaze met his as he heard the soft
murmur of her voice reassure the old lady.

He moved quickly, reaching the child in a matter of seconds.
With firm but gentle hands he examined the body lying so still
upon the ground before him. She was a small girl, three or four
years of age at the most. Her hair was dark and matted; her
clothes dirty and ragged. There was no blood, and no lacera-
tions of the skin. Neither were her limbs twisted. She looked
unhurt, as if she were just sleeping. He heard the commotion
as his grandmother struggled to climb down from the carriage.
'Stay where you are, Grandmama. The child does not appear
badly injured, but I don't yet know the extent of the damage
caused. You may find it distressing.'

Lady Maybury spluttered her indignation. 'Fiddlesticks! If
you're bent on shaking me around this carriage as if I'm a
bowl of dried peas, then at least have the decency to allow my
curiosity!'

Ravensmede recognised the stubborn tone of her voice. Resistance would be futile, and more to the point, a waste of time.
With a barely stifled sigh of frustration he ignored her
comments and turned his attention once more to the child, only
to find Miss Marchant crouched on the opposite side of the poor
motionless body. And the concern clear in the gaze that met his
caused a peculiar sensation within his chest.

Her darned gloves were unceremoniously cast aside and
two little work-worn hands were engaged in feeling the length
of the child's body to measure the extent of the hurts, just as
he had done. Upon her face was a look of such focused intensity of which Ravensmede had never seen the like. He heard
the movement of his grandmother behind him; felt her hand
touch briefly to his arm.

'Is the child…?'

Kathryn glanced up for the briefest of moments. 'Thank the
Lord, she's not dead. But I fear that she may have broken her

leg.' She raised the little girl's skirts to expose her ankles and shins. 'See how swollen and red it is below her knee. Mercifully she's fainted and so cannot feel the pain.'

'It's fortunate indeed that she was thrown clear. She ran straight in front of me. There wasn't much I could do.' A frown wrinkled Ravensmede's brow. 'She should be seen by a doctor. Let's hope that the leg is not broken.'

A moan escaped the little girl's lips.

'Hush, child. You're safe now.' Kathryn rubbed the child's dirty, scrawny arms. 'You've had an accident and hurt your leg, but everything is going to be fine. Can you tell me your name?'

'Maggie,' the child whispered, scarcely loud enough to be heard.

'Well, Maggie, just you lie still until we can get your leg mended. Be a brave girl.'

Ravensmede watched in amazement while Kathryn gently stroked the child's filthy hair, her voice crooning softly to calm the little girl's panic. That a grubby, unknown street child could engender such a tender, caring response! Most young ladies of the *ton* would have run a mile rather than touch such an offensive specimen of the lower classes. But then, again, why should he expect Miss Kathryn Marchant to be like most young ladies, when she had so far proven herself quite dissimilar in every aspect? It seemed she was determined to provide him with further evidence of her rather unique qualities as she began to strip off first her spencer, then her fichu.

He felt the flicker of the familiar hunger that he'd come to associate with her. Without thinking, he licked his lips. Anticipation hardened the angles of his face. And then he remembered where he was, and that his grandmother was at his shoulder. 'Miss Marchant, what do you think you're…?' The question trailed off unfinished as he watched her wrap the garments around the child's body.

'No doubt it's the shock that has chased the warmth from

her. We mustn't allow her to become chilled.' Kathryn appeared to be so completely focused upon the little girl that she betrayed not the slightest inhibition at her partially disrobed state and spoke as if tending an injured child was an everyday occurrence in her life.

Lord Ravensmede stared at what had been exposed by the missing fichu. He stared at the tender skin above the shabby dress's neckline. He stared as he had never stared at any woman before. And the expression on his face was not one of lust or desire; rather, shock more aptly described the sensation. Shock that was rapidly progressing to anger. For Kathryn Marchant's skin bore marks that should adorn no woman.

'Nicholas.' A firm hand touched to his shoulder. Elderly green eyes gazed down into his, and he saw in them the reflection of what he felt. Lady Maybury gave a barely perceptible nod of her head before subtly drawing her grandson's attention to the rapidly massing crowd.

An indefinable curse growled from the Viscount of Ravensmede before he hastily shrugged off his coat and swept it around Kathryn's shoulders.

Wide grey eyes met his with blatant surprise. 'My lord? There is no—'

Ravensmede smoothly cut her off. 'It would not do for *you* to catch a chill, Miss Marchant.'

'But it's a warm day and...'

The full force of his powerful gaze turned upon her. Anger spurred his actions and hardened his voice. Those marks, in faded hues of blue and purple, green and yellow, were still vivid enough against the white of her skin. Bruising. Made perhaps a week or so ago. Made by cruel fingers, if the patterning was anything to go by. What the hell had happened to her? Who was the scoundrel that had hit her? He slammed the brakes on the route his thoughts were taking. Hyde Park was neither the time nor the place.

He was brought back to reality by his grandmother's voice.

'Wrap the child in one of my travelling blankets. There's plenty warmth in those.'

His eyes fleetingly met Kathryn Marchant's once more, before he gathered up the urchin in his arms, complete with Miss Marchant's draping clothing, and walked to the carriage. 'I'll have Dr Porter treat the child at the house.' And, so saying, he deposited the small bundle into one of his grandmother's travelling blankets, ensured that both ladies were safely aboard, and set off for Berkeley Square.

Kathryn's eyes opened wide at the magnificent mansion before her. Ravensmede House was quite the grandest abode she had ever seen. And this was only one of his lordship's properties. She did not dare to think of all of his other houses. The image of one of London's most infamous rake-hells carrying the swaddled bundle with such care up the grand stone stairs would stay with her for ever. In that moment it seemed that the summer breeze had stilled, and her breathing too. The liquid warmth of tenderness erupted in her heart. It was obvious that there was very much more to Lord Ravensmede than his reputation suggested.

Ravensmede withdrew the toe of his boot from the fender and his elbow from the mantelpiece, and turned to face the drawing room chairs in which both Kathryn Marchant and his grandmother were seated. 'Dr Porter has been up there for some considerable time. I hope that the child's injuries are not worse than we thought.'

The dowager arched a quizzical eyebrow at her grandson.

Ravensmede seemed not to notice. 'Little Maggie seemed most reassured by Miss Marchant. Perhaps if Miss Marchant were to go to her... But no, I'm being too presumptuous...'

Kathryn carefully replaced the fine china cup upon the ornate saucer. 'No, not at all, Lord Ravensmede. I should have thought of such a thing myself. It was very kind of your housekeeper to sit with Maggie, but the poor child will be feeling frightened and alone.' She brushed down her skirts and rose, all the while remembering similar feelings from the years following her mother and sister's deaths. It was not something that she was content to let any child suffer. She pushed the memories away and concentrated on the child lying up in one of Lord Ravensmede's guest bedchambers. 'If you do not mind, I will stay with her until the doctor is finished.'

'Of course, Miss Marchant,' Ravensmede said politely. 'It's for the best.'

He reached over and rang the bell.

He did not speak again until the maid had arrived and escorted Kathryn from the drawing room.

'Well?' the dowager enquired of her grandson.

Ravensmede moved to sit on the sofa close by his grandmother's chair. 'Well,' he threw back at her. 'Judging from the bruises covering her neck and chest, I think that someone has tried to throttle Miss Marchant.'

'I'm not blind, boy!' she snorted. 'I saw them all right. I'm quite sure half of London did too when she whipped off her spencer and fichu in the middle of Hyde Park!'

'She was trying to help the child.'

'And exposing herself in the process.'

'She was unaware of what she was doing.' Ravensmede's eyes darkened. 'It would seem that I'm required once more to call upon Henry Marchant. The man is in need of guidance when it comes to his treatment of Miss Marchant.' He cracked his knuckles and balled one hand to a fist.'

'And have the whole of London gossip as to why the bachelor Viscount of Ravensmede is intervening in that man's treatment of his niece. Damn it, Nick, you don't even know if Henry Marchant's your man. She might have got the bruises elsewhere.' Lady Maybury drained the tea from her cup and swiftly refilled it.

'Indeed she might have. But as her uncle, it's his responsibility to ensure her safety. Whether he lifted his hands to her or not, the blame still lies with him.'

The dowager watched her grandson closely.

'I'll be damned if I just deliver her back into his hands. I suspect that his wife lies behind the problem. Mrs Marchant had her niece in the kitchen and laundering the bed-linen, as if she were a blasted maid of all.' Belatedly he remembered to whom he was talking. 'Please excuse my language,' he muttered.

Nothing had stirred Nicholas to such a passion in a very long time. Lady Maybury's focus sharpened. 'You seem to have developed rather a concern with Miss Marchant.'

Ravensmede lay back languidly and stretched his legs out before him. 'What I'm concerned with is righting an injustice,' he said in a lazy tone. 'Hitting a woman goes far beyond the pale for any man, least of all the most charitable Mr Henry Marchant.'

'I agree entirely, but you had no notion of Kathryn's bruises when you asked me to act as chaperon.'

'I enjoy her company. She's an interesting woman.'

'And an attractive one.'

'A very attractive one.' Ravensmede met his grandmother's gaze.

'Her mother was a Thornley of Overton,' she said. 'Kathryn Marchant is a lady. And a young, unmarried lady at that.'

Ravensmede knew the turn the dowager's thoughts were taking. 'She is indeed. I do not mean to ruin her, if that's what you're thinking.'

'Then what exactly is your interest in the gel? Marriage?'

A dark eyebrow quirked in disbelief. 'Certainly not. I like Miss Marchant, and suspected her situation was unhappy, although I had no notion of the extent of her mistreatment. My interest in the girl, as you so aptly put it, is purely philanthropic. Would you have me turn a blind eye to her suffering?'

They looked at one another for a moment longer, before

Lady Maybury finally said, 'So what exactly is it that you are proposing?'

Ravensmede's mouth formed a charming smile, and then he proceeded to explain his plan in full.

Chapter Five

A soft knock at the door heralded Kathryn's return.

Lord Ravensmede slipped from the room to speak with the physician.

Lady Maybury patted the empty chair by her side. 'Come and sit here, Miss Marchant. Tell me how the child fares.'

'Thank you,' said Kathryn, and sat down where the dowager indicated. 'The doctor says that Maggie's leg is not broken, only bruised. As Lord Ravensmede said, she's had a very lucky escape.'

'Lucky, indeed,' said her ladyship.

'She doesn't seem too distressed, but the poor little thing is exhausted. The doctor says that she needs rest. She was dozing off as I came away.'

'Excellent.' The dowager beamed. 'The child could not be in better hands. Dr Porter attends all our family and is one of the best physicians in London. Treated Nicholas when he was a boy. I remember twenty years ago when…' She went on to reminisce over her grandchildren's childhood ailments and the antics that caused them, much to Kathryn's amusement. In light of Lady Maybury's stories her aristocratic family did not seem quite so daunting. They were still laughing when Lord Ravensmede returned.

The clock on the mantel chimed six. 'I hadn't thought it so

late,' said Kathryn. 'I must return home. My aunt was expecting me before now.'

'Oh, but we have not even begun to discuss the other matter.' The Dowager Countess's small eyes brightened.

Kathryn did not miss the conspiratorial look exchanged between Lady Maybury and her grandson. She felt herself stiffen involuntarily and eyed the elderly lady with suspicion. 'What other matter?'

Lady Maybury crowed a small sharp chuckle. 'Well, my dear, you're nothing if not blunt!'

'Please do forgive me, my lady.' Kathryn looked away awkwardly at her sudden lapse in manners.

'It's a trait I admire,' declared Ravensmede's grandmother. 'Can't stand these milk-and-water misses who are scared to say what they think. Would agree with anything I say. Faugh!' The sunburst of wrinkles deepened as the top lip curled with contempt. 'Much prefer a gel who'll tell me the truth!' A smile replaced the frown. 'So, Miss Marchant, how do you find me?'

The grey eyes widened and she stared at the dowager. 'How do I find you?' she repeated with rising incredulity.

'That, indeed, is the question,' affirmed Lady Maybury with a twinkle in her eye, and the same mischievous look that Kathryn had seen cross her grandson's face on occasion.

A short pause sufficed to frame Kathryn's reply. 'Why, I find you to be very nice, and I've enjoyed your company greatly this afternoon.' It was the truth no less.

'Splendid!' her ladyship returned in increasingly exuberant tones. 'Then you'll have no objection to accepting my offer.'

'Your offer?' Kathryn said slowly, aware that she sounded rather like a simpleton who could do nothing other than repeat the questions asked of her.

The faded green gaze locked on to hers. 'To become my companion for the next two months of my visit.'

'Oh, no, my lady. I'm afraid that would be quite impossible. My aunt and uncle—'

'Nonsense!' chirped the grandam. 'I've already made my mind up and I don't mean to take no for an answer.'

'But—' She tried again, to no avail.

'I've a need for a companion. Can't stay in London with only Nick for company. He'll drive me mad before the week is out.' She snorted in the direction of her grandson.

Kathryn glanced over to see a smile curve Lord Ravensmede's lips.

'I'm afraid that my grandmother is quite right. All those wild card parties, the brandy, the gambling… She needs someone to keep her on the straight and narrow. I confess it's a job beyond my capabilities. Why, just look at the shocking influence she's already had on me.' The straight white teeth flashed and one dark eyebrow raised in a crooked gesture.

For all that she tried to resist, Kathryn felt the smile tug at her lips and looked abruptly away from temptation. Was it possible? Could she really just leave the torment of her life within the Marchant household? A brief flame of hope flickered…and then expired. Uncle Henry and Aunt Anna were her relatives, had offered her a home, albeit a miserable one, for the last three years. Wasn't it her duty to act as Lottie's companion until her cousin was successfully married? And if Aunt Anna had her way, a husband for Lottie would be netted before the Season was over. Perhaps then she could… Such thoughts were futile. Lady Maybury desired her as a temporary companion only during her visit to London. And afterwards? It was quite beyond question. She raised her eyes once more to Lady Maybury. 'I thank you for your generous offer, my lady. Indeed, it's most kind of you to even consider asking me, but I'm afraid that I'm forced to decline. It's my duty to act as Lottie's companion until she's—'

'Surely Mrs Marchant attends all of the society events along with her daughter?' The elderly voice was severe in the extreme.

'Yes, but—'

'Then, what does the chit need a companion for? As an unmarried and young lady you can hardly be expected to act as her chaperon can you?'

Kathryn felt the net closing around her. 'No, but—'

'I suppose I should not be surprised that you prefer to accompany a pretty, young chit to dances than spend your time assisting an old woman who is not much longer for this earth.'

The dowager seemed to shrink before Kathryn's very eyes, her narrow shoulders closing in, her velvet cheeks growing gaunt. A hollow cough rent the air.

Guilt stabbed at Kathryn's breast. 'No, it isn't—'

'Do not worry yourself, Miss Marchant.' A blue-veined hand dabbed a delicate lace handkerchief to each faded eye. A sad little sniff…and then the dowager played her trump card. 'I shall contrive my best to attend the injured child upstairs, but at my age…' The words trailed off. 'Such a strain on my health, the worry of it all…' Lady Maybury sniffed again and a tremor quivered upon her lips.

Dear Lord, but the old woman was clearly distraught and in danger of working herself into a fit of the vapours! Kathryn leapt forward and took one frail old hand within her own.

'That poor urchin…' There was what sounded to be a definite sob in her ladyship's voice.

Kathryn gently rubbed the paper-thin skin covering the back of Lady Maybury's hand. How could she make her understand that it really was not her choice at all? That she would much rather leave behind the house in Green Street and live her life as the dowager's companion? But it was not a matter of want. 'Dear Lady Maybury, please do not think that I don't want to accept your kind offer, or help little Maggie. There's nothing I would rather do, but—'

The old lady clung to her, her eyes brightening of a sudden. 'Oh my dearest gel! I knew that you would see sense; that you wouldn't be so heartless as to sentence an old lady to a season of loneliness and ill health. I cannot tell you the relief!' Ravensmede's grandmother's smile was wonderful to see.

'But—' started Kathryn uselessly, and stopped. The old lady was looking at her with such expectation that she could not correct the mistake. It would be a cruel and heartless woman that could shatter such joy. Who knew the effect such a shock would have on the lady's health? Kathryn swallowed down that sinking feeling and forced a smile to her face. And not once did she allow herself to look in the direction of the lady's grandson standing so tall and silent by the fireplace.

The small girl lay still within the great bed, her brown pansy eyes trained upon Kathryn's face.

'How old are you, Maggie?'

'Four,' the little voice whispered back.

'And do you remember where it is that you live?'

'Whitecross Road, the top room in Number Sixteen.'

'Good girl! You're really very clever. I'll send a message to your mama and papa so that they know where you are and aren't worried about you.'

Two fat tears rolled down the cheeks that Kathryn had just cleaned. 'Want to go home. Want me ma.' A hiccup sounded.

Kathryn wiped the tears away. 'Of course you do, moppet. And when you're better, so you shall. The doctor's looked at your leg and do you know what he said?'

The question distracted Maggie away from the sobbing she was poised to commence. 'What?'

'He said that it isn't broken at all, only bruised, and that it will get better very soon. But until then you're to rest in bed and eat lots of food.'

Maggie's eyes opened wide at the prospect. 'Lots an' lots of food?'

'Lots and lots and *lots*!' confirmed Kathryn with a grin. 'And I'll be here to tell you stories and talk to you, so you won't be lonely at all.'

Maggie smiled up into the kind face that hovered above hers. A creaking of the door and Lord Ravensmede materialised by the bed. Kathryn struggled to get to her feet, but was stayed by a warm hand touched to her elbow.

'No need to get up on my account.' His voice was both deep and melodic, without a hint of the practised drawl he used when he was out.

She raised her eyes to his and felt a shimmer of excitement ripple down her spine. Just his proximity caused her heart to race. Her fingers fluttered to rearrange the fichu that she had recently replaced. Averting her face, she sought to turn her mind from inappropriate thoughts of the Viscount of Ravensmede. 'Maggie is a very clever girl and has told me where she lives.' With great gentleness she stroked the child's forehead.

Ravensmede smiled. 'Very good.'

Whether this remark was addressed to herself or Maggie, Kathryn remained unsure.

Maggie was regarding the tall dark-haired man solemnly. 'Are you the pa?' she asked quite suddenly.

'The pa?' Ravensmede looked rather bemused.

'Are you?' The round dark eyes had not wavered from his face.

Ravensmede glanced with amusement at Miss Marchant.

'You *must* be.' The strands of black hair so carefully combed out by Kathryn bobbed up and down as the child nodded. 'And you must be the ma,' added Maggie with certainty to Kathryn. 'Where are your little girls an' boys?'

Crimson flooded Kathryn's cheeks. 'Hush now, Maggie, you're tired and need to sleep. I'll come back and see you later.' A small kiss was dropped to the little girl's forehead.

'Promise?' the baby voice queried.

'I promise,' vowed Kathryn and rose to her feet, casting the child's previous innocently uttered questions from her mind.

Ravensmede opened the door and waited for her to pass through, before following her out into the passageway.

A throaty laugh sounded. 'Ma and pa!' And the look that

smouldered from those green eyes caused a dancing sensation deep in Kathryn's belly.

She kept her gaze straight ahead, concentrating on each step, the pink-and-gold patterned carpet, the pale gold-coloured walls with their wall sconces and elaborate gilt-framed paintings, anything other than the man walking by her side. He was so close she could almost feel his heat scorching the full length of her left-hand side. Living in the same house as Lord Ravensmede was going to prove difficult in more ways than one.

Firstly, there was the simple fact that he was a bachelor, coupled with the not-so-small problem of his reputation. Secondly, Aunt Anna and Uncle Henry were not likely to receive the news of her move well. Finally, and perhaps most importantly, was the strength of her own inappropriate reaction to the Viscount. From their first encounter over Miss Dawson's shoe, to that unwitting kiss and the subsequent calamity with the potatoes in St James's Park, Kathryn was well aware of the trouble resulting from that very reaction. The more she thought on it, the more she came to realise that, even as Lady Maybury's companion, living under the same roof as Lord Ravensmede was likely to prove a dangerous pastime—and one that she could not afford to risk, even if it did mean an escape from Aunt Anna's cruel treatment. All she had left was her reputation, and that wasn't something that she was prepared to jeopardise. She did not want to hurt Lady Maybury, or leave Maggie for that matter, but the alternative was far too threatening to contemplate. The decision made, she pressed her lips firmly together and stopped abruptly.

Ravensmede had stepped past her before reacting to her halt. 'Miss Marchant?' He sauntered back to stand beside her.

'My lord, I…' The words were rushed before her fragile resolve could fail. 'I know that I agreed to your grandmother's most kind offer, but upon further reflection I'm afraid that it is—'

Ravensmede took her hand within his and raised it lightly to his lips. 'For your kindness to my grandmother you have my gratitude. She's very dear to me and I would not like to see her ill or distressed. Her heart is weak and the family have been advised that she must be spared all that we can. Any shocking news, any great disappointment is to be avoided. That's why I'm so relieved that you have the generosity of spirit, Miss Marchant, to indulge an old lady's whim.' Warm lips pressed against the roughened red skin of her hand.

Kathryn felt the breath catch in her throat. She blinked several times to clear her head. And stifled the groan.

'Grandmama is rather set in her ways. As you may already have noticed, she's very much determined to do things in her own style, even if it does rather fly in the face of what is deemed convention.' He smiled. 'She often takes irrational sets against people, but rarely have I seen her warm to someone as she has to you. My grandmother likes you, Miss Marchant, and that really is quite an achievement.'

It seemed that there was no way to extricate herself from the agreement. *But surely the Viscount himself can see the position in which I would be placed?* Kathryn's thoughts flitted back and forth. 'My lord—'

'Please, call me Nicholas.'

Kathryn recoiled as if he'd slapped her. Call him by his given name? Indeed she would not!

The smile deepened. 'Or Ravensmede, if that is your preference.'

She gritted her teeth and started again. 'Lord Ravensmede…' Confound the man, but he was laughing at her. Anger flushed her cheeks and she raised steely eyes to his. 'This is a serious matter, not some tomfoolery for your amusement.'

His mouth straightened but those mesmerising green eyes were still brimful of laughter. 'Indeed, Miss Marchant, I assure you that I had no such thought.'

With a tug she rescued her hand from within his. 'You cannot be unaware that living here as your grandmother's companion would place me in a somewhat awkward position.'

The green eyes opened wide and innocent. 'Whatever can you mean, Miss Marchant?'

Her anger deserted her of a sudden and she sighed. 'Just that you are a bachelor and that, as an unmarried lady, perhaps I'm not best placed to accept the position offered.' There, she had said it. She found sudden fascination in the patterned carpet.

'How old are you, Miss Marchant?'

She looked up in surprise. Of all the answers she had expected this had not been one. 'Four and twenty, my lord.'

'Ravensmede,' he corrected.

Two spots of colour burned high in her cheeks. 'Ravensmede,' she repeated softly.

The corner of his mouth squinted up in a boyish gesture. 'Then you're hardly a schoolroom miss, and quite old enough to be considered suitable as a lady's companion. That, coupled with my grandmother's lineage, will ensure that no disadvantage attaches itself to your reputation.'

Her cheeks were glowing with all the subtlety of two blazing beacons. 'I'm well aware that I'm considered to be left on the shelf, but that has no bearing on the concern that I've raised.' The thump of her heart echoed throughout her body and she wished that she were anywhere but here, standing beside Lord Ravensmede, listening to him confirm his notion of her as an old maid.

He watched her closely. 'That was not my meaning, Miss Marchant. I'm sure that there's many a gentleman who would be only too happy to make you his wife.'

Kathryn swallowed her embarrassment well and attempted to force the conversation towards safer ground. 'You mentioned your grandmother's lineage?' she said demurely, as if her face were not aflame.

That not-quite-serious expression was back on his face. 'She's the daughter of a duke, and the widow of one of the wealthiest earls in the country. If Grandmama is for you, Miss Marchant, no one will dare be against you.'

She digested this information in silence for some minutes.

It seemed that Lord Ravensmede had just removed the last of her reasons to refuse Lady Maybury's request. 'Then I hope I may prove useful in my new position.' Quite deliberately she turned and walked slowly towards the staircase, throwing the words over her shoulder as she went. 'When does Lady Maybury wish me to start?'

'Immediately.'

She nodded once. 'Then, I shall return first thing tomorrow morning.'

'I fear you misunderstand me, Miss Marchant. My grandmother needs your assistance *now*.' His gaze held hers.

'Very well. I'll return to my uncle's house to inform him of what has happened and pack up my clothes.'

'There's no need. I will dispatch a letter to Mr Marchant. Your clothes may be sent over later.' There was a determination in his voice that she did not understand.

'I cannot just leave for a drive in the park one afternoon and not return! It's a preposterous suggestion!'

A hand on her shoulder spun her round, and she found herself imprisoned by his grip on her upper arms. 'And what of your aunt and uncle, what of your cousin—is their treatment of you not equally preposterous?' His eyes stared down into hers.

Her skin scorched beneath the touch of his hands. 'I...I've never said so.'

'You don't need to.'

Surely he could not know? She had spoken to no one. Her heart was beating wildly within her chest. 'I won't renege on my agreement with Lady Maybury, if that's what you're afraid of.'

'I know you would not hurt an old lady's feelings, Kathryn.'

Her eyes widened at his use of her name.

'Nevertheless, I cannot permit you to return alone to Green Street. As I said, I will write to Mr Marchant with a full explanation.'

His confident assertion pricked at her pride. '*Cannot

permit?' Her tone was incredulous. 'I don't think that it's your place to say such a thing, Lord Ravensmede.'

The green eyes did not betray their surprise by as much as a flicker. 'If you're bent on such a journey, then I must insist on accompanying you. My grandmother is quite fatigued by the drive and subsequent incident with the child. Trailing her back across town is quite out of the question. Therefore, we should ready ourselves immediately, Miss Marchant, unless you would prefer to wait until it is dark…'

Kathryn knew very well what his lordship was saying. Arriving alone with Lord Ravensmede to take her leave of them, no matter Ravensmede's assertions as to Lady May-bury's influence, there could be no doubt what it would look like. Aunt Anna and Uncle Henry would have an apoplectic fit. She ground her teeth. 'I have no need of your escort. I'm perfectly happy to go alone.'

'No.' The single word was decidedly emphatic.

'Lord Ravensmede, you're behaving most unreasonably.'

A dark eyebrow raised. 'Are you so very eager to return there? Do they treat you so well that you're loath to leave them?' There was an undercurrent to his words that made her shiver.

'It's not so strange a request.'

'You haven't answered the question, Miss Marchant.'

There was silence.

'It seems that you leave me little option, my lord. Write the letter if you must.'

And this time he did not chide her for the use of his title.

It had been several hours since a letter had been dispatched from the Viscount of Ravensmede to Mr Henry Marchant and still there had been no reply. Kathryn eyed the soft white cotton of the borrowed nightdress with some reticence. She was still uneasy about her sudden new-found position and the means by which it had been effected. Ravensmede's refusal to allow her to return alone to Green Street worried her. Undoubtedly he was stubborn and arrogant and used to getting his own way, but she had never thought him to be so downright unreasonable. It flew in the face of all she knew of him. But then she had to concede that her knowledge of Lord Ravensmede was remarkably scant. And he *had* made her a most indecent proposal in St James's Park.

Her fingers reached out and lifted the garment to her lap. Lady Maybury had seemed to think nothing remarkable in her grandson's overbearing attitude; indeed, the old lady appeared to positively encourage Ravensmede. She was still half-expecting Uncle Henry to come charging over, demanding to know what precisely was going on. But hadn't her uncle always been too keen to court the favour of the aristocracy? If she knew Uncle Henry, he'd be carefully weighing up the best response to further advance his own schemes. She sighed just as a light knock sounded at the door and a young maid entered.

'I'm Jean, miss. Come to help you undress for bed.' She bobbed a little curtsy.

'Thank you, Jean, but I'm used to dressing and undressing myself.' Kathryn watched the crestfallen face and suddenly realised why. 'Are you an abigail?'

The thin face flushed. 'No, miss, I'm a chambermaid, but I'm a quick learner and...' The maid waited to be dismissed.

'Perhaps it would be nice not to have to struggle round to reach the buttons on this dress,' Kathryn said with a smile. 'Do you mind if I change my answer?'

'Oh, no, miss, not at all.' And Jean bounded across the bed-chamber to begin work in the lofty realms of a lady's maid. She started with the careful removal of Miss Marchant's fichu, folding the worn length of material into a neat pile before turning to tackle the buttons of the faded blue afternoon dress. It was only then that the smile dropped from her face, replaced instead with a look of shock. The narrow brow wrinkled in con-sternation and the brown eyes rounded as two new pennies.

'Is something wrong?' Kathryn eyed the maid with some concern.

The gaze dropped to the floor and two small spots of colour mounted in the thin cheeks. 'No, miss.' She skirted round to release the back buttons that secured Miss Marchant's dress, taking care not to meet the lady's eyes. The dress, petticoats and stays were removed in a matter of minutes. 'Shall I help you into your nightdress, miss, before brushing your hair?' The slender hands strayed towards the folded nightdress.

'No thank you, I can manage from here myself. Thank you, Jean, I shall see you in the morning.'

The maid bobbed a curtsy and almost ran from the room, leaving a rather puzzled Miss Marchant looking after her.

Still clad in her threadbare shift, Kathryn unpinned the heavy coil of her curls, sat down at the dressing table, and began to brush her hair using the silver-backed hairbrush from the set laid out on the mahogany surface. The golden glow from the fireplace illuminated the room, and the candle still sat where she had left it on the small table beside the bed. Her eyes glanced up to the oval looking-glass and froze. The brush ceased its action, hovered in mid-air and quickly resumed its position upon the dressing table. And all the while Kathryn's gaze did not waver.

From the mirrored glass a pale thin figure stared back, a ghost of the woman she had once been. Her stomach tightened and sank at the sight. For there, in front of her very eyes, was the obvious reason for the maid's strange behaviour. How could she have so easily forgotten? Reddened fingers reached up and cautiously traced the large purple black smudges adorning the skin around her collarbone, then shifted down to touch each and every one of the bruises peppering her thin arms. Beneath each eye was the faintest trace of shadow and her cheeks had about them a slight gauntness, lending her whole face a look of worn fatigue. Indeed, she looked little better than the poor child recovering in the bedchamber further along the passageway. Little Maggie, who had lain so still and cold on the ground in Hyde Park as to chase every thought from Kathryn's head save for those concerned with the child's welfare. Little Maggie, over whom Kathryn had so readily draped her fichu and spencer. And, by removing her fichu, she had unwittingly exposed her shame for all to see. Dear Lord! The bruises could not be missed. Not by Lady Maybury. And certainly not by Lord Ravensmede. So absorbed had she been in the accident and all that ensued that not once had she remembered the presence of those ugly telling bruises. A groan escaped her at her own ineptitude. She knew now why the Viscount had been so downright stubborn in his refusal to allow her to return to Green Street. He had seen the bruises and drawn his own conclusions.

Humiliation scalded her cheeks and caused an aching in her heart. Her fingers kneaded at the worn linen of her shift. But Kathryn did not cry, even though Ravensmede had viewed the shameful marks upon her body, even though she now knew herself to be an object of pity and curiosity. Jean's eyes had been telling enough and she did not doubt that by tomorrow morning the story of her darned underclothing and smattering of bruises would be the main topic of conversation below stairs. Her chin jutted out as she held her head high. Let them talk. She had survived worse than a little tittle-tattle, much worse. Gossip would not touch her, as nothing had ever touched her since her father had placed the muzzle of a Manton in his mouth and pulled the trigger.

She had cried then, for days—or was it weeks? When the tears had finally stopped she had vowed they would never come again. That was when she had discovered the power of daydreams. Dreams that took her away from the pain of reality. Dreams that made life bearable. And the worse things got, the more Kathryn dreamed. Resolutely she raised the brush to the thick hank of chestnut hair curling over her shoulder and began slowly, steadily, to brush.

'I like this toast. Is there more?' Maggie demanded as she sat plumped up in the big bed. Sunshine shimmered on her black locks, coating them with a blue sheen and bleaching her small elfin face white.

Kathryn laughed. 'Of course, moppet, but first you have your ham and eggs to eat. Let's see what room you have left when they're gone.'

The brown pansy eyes widened in awe. 'Ham *and* eggs *and* toast?'

'Most definitely.' Kathryn positioned the full plate on the child's tray.

A large grin spread across Maggie's face and soon she was too busy eating to manage more than the odd unintelligible word uttered through a mouthful of half-chewed food.

Kathryn sat in the chair beside the bed. Sipping the hot coffee chased away the thick-headed feeling that had troubled her since waking. The bed had been both warm and comfortable, a far cry from the hard, lumpy truckle bed in her room at Green Street. But she had slept poorly, tormented by worries, and nightmares from the past. Her escape from the bosom of Henry Marchant's family was not likely to be that simple. She nibbled at the toast, finding that the previous week's starvation rations had rendered her unable to eat much before her stomach protested its fullness. A crumb was displaced from the bodice of her blue muslin dress with the flick of a finger before she caught sight of Maggie's little face looking at her with a rather guilty expression. 'Is something wrong? You seem to have stopped eating?'

The black head shook in denial. The dark eyes peeped up through long lashes. 'You ain't got no eggs or ham. You can have some of mine if you want.'

Kathryn knew what it had cost the child to make such a generous offer. A child who was no doubt used to going hungry. 'It's very kind of you to offer, Maggie, but I've already eaten some eggs before I came to see you,' she lied. 'I'm afraid you'll have to eat them all yourself!'

Maggie wasted no time in complying. 'Where's the pa?' she questioned between mouthfuls of egg.

The thought of Ravensmede in the role of a father brought a wry smile to Kathryn's face. 'Lord Ravensmede is probably still sleeping.' She had no idea when he had returned, or, indeed, if he had returned at all. 'He was out late last night and is bound to be very tired this morning.'

The gentleman in question chose this precise minute to make his entry. 'Good morning, Miss Marchant, Miss Maggie.'

Maggie giggled, spluttering a piece of half-chewed ham down her chin.

Kathryn remedied the accident with a starched white napkin while returning the greeting. For someone who'd been up half the night, he was looking bright-eyed and refreshed.

'The ma said you was in bed 'cos you was out last night. But she was wrong, 'cos you're here.' Maggie smiled up at the tall dark-haired man, not intimidated by his lordship in the slightest. 'Where was you?' she asked sweetly.

'Maggie!' Kathryn admonished. 'You mustn't ask Lord Ravensmede such questions.' But her cheeks glowed and not just because the child had unwittingly revealed that the 'ma' had noticed his absence the previous evening.

Ravensmede sat himself down on the bed and tousled Maggie's hair. 'I was very busy, but now I'm back to check whether you're eating up all of your breakfast.'

If the Viscount's reputation was true, Kathryn had a very good idea exactly what Lord Ravensmede had been 'very busy' doing throughout the night. She sought to change the subject. 'Maggie's leg is much better this morning. Dr Porter will be pleased when he calls again this afternoon to decide whether she may go home.'

'Home to *my* ma and pa,' declared Maggie in a cheerful tone.

'Indeed so. They were very worried when I told them about your sore leg. If you're to stay here much longer, they'll come and visit you.' The Viscount's eyes twinkled.

Kathryn could not prevent herself exclaiming, 'You've spoken to them yourself?'

His gaze met with her incredulous stare. 'But of course. What else did you expect?'

She smiled. 'From what I've heard, certainly not that.'

'Then you should not believe everything that you hear, Kathryn.' He said her name like a caress.

'And you should not seek to encourage an unwarranted reputation, sir!' The smile deepened to a most unladylike grin.

His lordship arched a dark eyebrow and said, 'I assure you that my reputation is most deserved, Miss Marchant.'

If it had not been for the glimmer of the smile that lurked too readily behind his lips, she would have withdrawn. As it was, Miss Kathryn Marchant, who had for the past three years striven to be as quiet and unnoticeable as could be, was engaging in what could only be described as a rather flirtatious conversation with a notorious rake. But he was so damnably arrogant that he deserved to be taken down a peg or two. 'Indeed, sir? Perhaps it is rather overrated.' Had she just said such a comment? It barely seemed possible. Surely she must be in the grip of some madness. She most certainly knew she was when she saw his lips slide into a sensual curve.

'Would you care to put it to the test?' The suggestion in his gaze caused the heat to rise in her cheeks.

Standing up abruptly, she smoothed her skirts down with the palms of her hands. 'Certainly not. Now, if you'll excuse me, I had better get on.' And, so saying, she gathered up Maggie's tray containing the emptied plates and cups.

A pair of strong arms reached across the bed and deftly lifted the tray away. The teasing sensuality had vanished. Instead, the stark contours of his face contained what looked to be anger. 'You are a guest in this house, Miss Marchant, along with my grandmother. I pay my servants well to do such things.' The tray was deposited unceremoniously on an occasional table and the bell pulled. 'If you would be kind enough to attend the library in ten minutes, there is something which we must discuss.'

A shiver stole down Kathryn's spine. Clear grey eyes raised to meet green. 'My lord?'

'My name is Nicholas, Kathryn, I would that you used it,' he said soberly and softly closed the door.

Chapter Six

Ravensmede was about to ignore his grandmother's advice. The source of the foul markings on Kathryn Marchant's skin was like a needle that pricked at him constantly. Even during last night's journey to Whitecross Road to call upon little Maggie's parents he could scarcely concentrate on what he had to say because of the blasted matter. Hitting a woman, any woman, was something that sickened Ravensmede to the pit of his stomach. The fact that it had been Kathryn on the receiving end of someone's vicious temper exacerbated that response a hundredfold. He controlled his mounting fury admirably.

Someone had been liberal with their fists, that much was evident, and there was no point in meeting Henry Marchant until he knew the truth of it. No matter what Lady Maybury said, Ravensmede had every intention of getting to the bottom of the sickening assault...and today. Waiting for Kathryn to tell them in her own time was simply not soon enough. The brandy hit the back of his throat like a brand. He swallowed it down. Too damn early in the day, but he needed something to dampen his temper.

A quiet tap at the door sounded and the subject of his concern presented herself. She was still dressed in the shabby muslin gown that she had worn yesterday. He noticed that the periwinkle blue coloration brought out the creamy white hue of her skin, and the red lights in her hair. The fichu had been arranged to cover every trace of the bruising. She was so slender as to appear fragile, something he had no memory of either on that first night at Lady Finlay's ball, or later in St James's Park. No doubt the bastard had been starving her as well. The thought of Henry Marchant curled his fingers into fists. With calm deliberation he forced his hands to relax. A deep breath, and he was ready to face her.

'Kathryn.' He smiled and gestured towards one of the two large wing chairs around the fireplace. 'Sit down.' As the day was fine and warm, and showed every promise to continue as such, the hearth was empty. Sunshine flooded in through the large bow window, highlighting a halo of red around the rich brown of her hair. He positioned himself in the opposite chair, stretching out his long, pantaloon-clad legs before him.

She sat demurely, hands folded motionless in her lap, as if she were a model of relaxed serenity…as if she had not been beaten and starved by her so-called family. Her eyes glanced up, but the question in them remained unasked. He would have to tread very carefully. 'Would you like some tea?'

'No, thank you, my lor…Ravensmede.' Her fingers gripped tighter and then relaxed.

'Then I will come straight to the point. Mr Marchant has arranged to call here at three o'clock to discuss your new position. My grandmother will explain the urgency of her need for a companion. In view of her age and the injured child upstairs, I'm sure that your uncle will understand why it was imperative that you commence as Lady Maybury's companion with immediate effect.' And if Henry Marchant dared to raise the slightest objection he'd see to it that the man was put firmly in his place.

Her gaze was trained on the blackened grate. The rigid tension across her narrow shoulders tightened at his words. 'Will he be accompanied by my aunt?'

Now why should that matter so much to her? For suddenly he knew that to be very much the case. 'In truth, I do not know. Do you wish to take your leave of her?'

There was a pause, just long enough to be obvious. 'Naturally. They are my family. It's only polite, after all that they've done, that I take my leave of them all.' And still her focus did not waver from the grate.

'And what have they done, Kathryn?' The question slipped softly from his lips.

Startled eyes raised to his and quickly looked away again. A whisper of pink touched to her cheeks, before the small chin was thrust defiantly up. 'Why, they took me in and offered me a home when my father died. I...I'm very grateful for their charity.'

The time had come to say what must be said, to discover the truth. He leaned forward by the smallest fraction. 'But it wasn't charity they had in mind when they dealt you your bruises, was it? And I would hazard a guess that it wasn't gratitude you felt in receipt of those markings.' His voice rumbled low and quiet, each word enunciated clearly, no hint of the practised rakish drawl.

The chestnut-coloured head whipped round to face him, her breast rising and falling dramatically beneath the outmoded gown. Within her eyes flashed anger and something else that had gone in an instant. She faced him with her fear concealed. It seemed for a moment that his words had rendered her speechless, but she recovered herself well, forcing her emotions back under control. When her voice finally sounded it was quiet and careful, as if she were attending to his grandmother or the child that lay upstairs. 'Lord Ravensmede,' she began, 'you are mistaken. The...bruises...that you happened to see upon my person are the result of a small accident, nothing more. Through my own clumsiness I tripped and fell. The blame rests entirely on my own head and no one else.' The slender fingers began to twist themselves together.

His eyes flitted to her hands, saw more than he was meant to see, and returned once more to her face and the darkened gaze that had been rapidly averted while she told her story. 'You make a very poor liar, Kathryn.'

The colour heightened in her cheeks and she shot him one brief infuriated glance. 'I'm telling you the truth, sir. You've drawn the wrong conclusion.'

'I don't think so.' He watched the small white teeth nibble delicately on the fullness of her lower lip and did not speak again until those stormy grey eyes slowly dragged round, as if not quite of their own accord, to meet his.

'We have nothing further to discuss, sir. I shall be ready to meet my uncle at three o'clock.' With that she rose and made to step away.

But Ravensmede had no intention of letting Miss Marchant evade him quite so easily. Within an instant he was towering over her. 'On the contrary, we've only just begun. Is that your best effort? I would not have thought your imagination to be so lacking.'

A slight gasp escaped her lips before they pressed firmly together with annoyance.

Before she could retaliate he pressed a hand to hers. 'Do you always cross your fingers when you lie? Who told you that it saved you from the sin? Your nurse?'

Rosy stain flooded her face and the fingers encased beneath his straightened themselves. She shifted her feet uneasily. 'How did you know?'

'Mine said the same, much to my father's disgust!'

She smiled a small smile at that.

It seemed a shame to destroy the sudden rapport that had developed between them, but he could do nothing else if he meant to know just who was responsible for her hurts. A suspect loomed large in his mind, but he would not confront the man without first hearing Kathryn's side of the story. He lowered his head to hers. She was so close that his breath fanned a ripple across the curls framing her face, so close that the sweet scent of her filled his nostrils. One finger moved to tilt her chin, until her eyes were looking up into his. Ravensmede swallowed hard and resisted the urge to place his lips upon hers, to kiss her as thoroughly as he'd kissed her that night in the moonlit room. Temptation pulled him closer, beckoned him down a path he knew he had no right to tread. So close, so sweet. It seemed that her lips parted in invitation. He felt the stirrings of other interests and reined himself back with a self-denying hand. She was here for his protection, not the practised art of his seduction. But when he looked into Kathryn Marchant's face there was nothing practised about the erratic thud of his heart or the overwhelming urge to take her in his arms and never let her go.

He wondered as to his assertion to his grandmother. *I do not mean to ruin her*, he had said. But the woman standing so close that he could have plucked a sweet kiss from her lips stirred his blood like no one else. He wanted her. Had wanted her since that night at Lady Finlay's ball. A woman he could not allow himself to have; a woman who deserved better than the hand life had dealt her; a woman he had just made his grandmother's companion. Mentally he dowsed himself with cold water and focused on the matter in hand. And that was confirming Henry Marchant's guilt in the abuse of his niece. She was still looking up at him with such trust that it quite smote his jaded heart. With the gentlest of movements he touched his lips to the coolness of her forehead, before scanning her eyes once more.

'Will you not trust me with the truth?' he said softly.

For the beat of a heart he thought she would do just that. Her mouth opened to speak and then closed again. Her gaze dropped and the moment was gone. 'I cannot,' she whispered.

At least there were no more lies.

'What happened is in the past and will not happen again. I know that you only mean to help me…Nicholas…but…please, just let the matter go.'

His stomach somersaulted at the sound of his name upon her lips. What a glorious sound it was. 'I cannot do that, Kathryn.

You've been treated most cruelly and I cannot let any man get away with such injustice.' Beneath his fingers her hand trembled and she sighed a sigh of such fatigue and sadness and disappointment. 'Kathryn?' The word held an intimacy that he had no right to.

Slowly she shook her head and stepped back. 'No.' Her shoulders straightened and her face was filled with firm resolve.

He made no move to reclaim her. Just watched, and waited.

'No,' she said again with increasing determination.

There was nothing else for it. 'Then you leave me with no other option.' He waited for her response. Knew that it would come.

Her voice was small and tight. 'What do you mean to do?'

The slightest pause. 'I will speak with Henry Marchant until I know the whole of it. And then I'll decide what to do with him. Perhaps I should call him out.'

'No!' Her eyes widened in horror. 'You must not!'

'He does not deserve your sympathy, Kathryn.'

'No, please!' Her hands grasped at his arms, tightening, enforcing her will. 'You're wrong. It wasn't him…he's done nothing!'

Not Henry Marchant? His focus narrowed. 'Then who?'

Nothing, just the pressure of those slight fingers.

'Hell's teeth, Kathryn, tell me!' he growled with more force than he intended.

'Aunt Anna.' A faint whisper, barely more than the expiration of a breath. Cheeks so pale he thought she would swoon.

He moved to take her arms, unmindful that she still held his. A mirror of her stance, unnoticed in the incredulity that enveloped him. 'Are you telling me that Anna Marchant inflicted those bruises upon you?' His voice sounded cold and hard and distant even to his own ears.

'Yes.' Her body recoiled from his, and she stepped back until the chair was between them. 'You have what you wanted. Are you happy now?' The slight figure turned and fled, leaving Ravensmede staring at the library door that had just been slammed so adamantly in his face.

* * *

Kathryn stood still as a statue and stared down from the window of her bedchamber, although quite what made it hers she could not be sure since there was nothing of her own in it. A calm, light-filled room that was furnished with the finest furniture, or so it seemed to the woman who had made do for as many years as she could remember. It was as close to a sanctuary as she had come, even if it was owned by the man who had just caused her to reveal that which she had promised never to. But she could not have allowed him to meet Uncle Henry thinking what he did. The thought of exactly what Ravensmede had threatened to do twisted in her gut. Call him out. There was no doubt in her mind that he would have done just that…and more.

Her fingers kneaded at the tight spot developing behind her forehead, trying to forestall the headache she knew it would become. What would the Viscount do with the knowledge? *Oh, Lord, please do not let him speak of it, not to Uncle Henry, and certainly not to Aunt Anna herself. It would only make matters worse. Aunt Anna will deny all, cast me as a liar. I have no proof and they have provided me with a home all this time. And the scandal! Perhaps I should speak with Nicholas… Dear Lord, have I so quickly come to think upon him in such familiar terms?* The thought was really rather shocking. She pressed the cooling palms of her hands to her eyes. *Think, Kathryn, think!* She willed herself. *I have created this problem and therefore I can solve it.* So engrossed in her task was she that she did not hear the chamber door brush against the rug as it was pushed hesitantly open. Indeed, it was not until something tugged at her skirts that she jumped and gave a small exclamation of surprise.

'Why are you crying?' The pansy brown eyes were regarding her with concern.

One slender hand pressed to her breast before Kathryn bent and clutched the child to her. 'Maggie! You startled me. I didn't hear you come in.' She rearranged the locks of hair around the girl's forehead and kissed her. 'You were as quiet as a little mouse.'

Maggie smiled and touched small fingers softly to the shadowed areas beneath Kathryn's eyes. 'Why was you crying?' she repeated.

'I wasn't crying, moppet, just thinking.'

But the child persisted. 'But you was sad, wasn't you?'

'Just a little, but I'm not any more. Now, Miss Maggie, what are you doing out of bed?' Kathryn chided in a voice of mock severity.

Maggie was not fooled for one minute. 'Looking for you to tell me another story.'

Kathryn placed her hands on her hips and looked stern.

Maggie laughed.

'Oh, very well then, but only if you get back into bed. You must not get up until Dr Porter has checked your leg this afternoon.' Secretly Kathryn was pleased that the child felt well enough to wander. And, from the way she was jumping rather excitedly up and down, it appeared that the injury to her leg was perhaps not as bad as they had first thought. With one arm cupped protectively round Maggie's shoulders, Kathryn guided the small girl back along to the room from whence she had come.

The day passed quickly for Kathryn in her new role as Lady Maybury's companion, and she did have to admit that her first impression of that employment found it to be infinitely preferable to anything she had experienced in the house at Green Street. Ravensmede's grandmother was loud, opinionated and had evidently taken rather a shine to Kathryn. Beneath the old lady's harsh exterior was a heart of gold. She brooked no nonsense and did not suffer fools gladly, but when it came to her grandson it was quite clear to Kathryn that he held a special place in the lady's heart. It was just before three o'clock when the doorbell sounded. Miss Marchant was still seated at the lady's writing desk situated within Lady Maybury's rooms. With pen poised in hand and rather ink-stained fingers, she was waiting patiently for the dowager to dictate the next line of the letter. Her ladyship showed no sign of having heard the bell.

'Lady Harriet sounds to me to be indolent in the extreme. You must not hesitate to chastise her as such, my dear Frances, else you will never get her married off.' Lady Maybury was seated comfortably upon a pink chair. She paused to allow Kathryn to copy down her words, her head cocked to one side like a small lively robin.

Kathryn finished the sentence and glanced up. The clock on the mantel chimed three.

Lady Maybury ignored it. 'Lady Gardiner's daughter was quite the same, and look what became of her.'

The grey eyes drifted to the clock face.

'No, Frances, you must stand firm. It's the best advice I can offer.' Lady Maybury nodded her white curls forcefully. 'Do not pen the next words,' she instructed. 'They are for your ears alone. Harriet Kiddleby was an indolent child and she's now an indolent young woman. I blame Frances, of course. She always was too soft with the gel. If she doesn't act quickly, she'll be saddled with the wretched gel for the rest of her days. Frances never did have much sense.' A tap at the door interrupted Lady Maybury's tirade.

A footman entered and addressed himself to the dowager. 'Mr Marchant has arrived, my lady. He's in the drawing room with Lord Ravensmede.'

The snowy head graciously inclined. Only when the door had closed did she resume her conversation. 'Now, what was I saying? Ah, that's right, I remember now.'

'Should we not…?' Kathryn looked tentatively at the old lady.

'Make them wait!' came the abrupt reply. And so she did. It was some considerable time later and with a degree of mounting agitation that Kathryn came finally to pen the words, *remember me to Lady Augusta. Adieu—Yours ever, Eleanor Maybury.*

Ravensmede's grandmother offered no apologies for her tardiness. Rather, she cast a piercing eye in Henry Marchant's direction as if it were he who was making unfair demands upon her time. Kathryn sat at the old lady's side on the sofa and prayed fervently that the Viscount had not made any mention of her bruising. Her uncle looked distinctly uncomfortable, a sign that did not bode well. The tension in the room was thick and suffocating. No one spoke. She forced a smile to her face. 'Uncle Henry, how good of you to come. My aunt is not with you?'

'No.' He did not return the smile. 'Unfortunately she is otherwise engaged.'

Another awkward silence.

Her eyes sought Ravensmede's. His face was stern, forbidding even, but she thought she saw a softening in that shared moment. It was gone before she could be sure. His attention returned to the man sitting uneasily in the chair with his back to the door.

'Mr Marchant. As I explained in my letter, Miss Marchant has been kind enough to agree to become my grandmother's companion. You understand, of course, the honour that Lady Maybury is conferring upon your family with such an appointment?' Ravensmede had resumed the habitual arrogant drawl that had been missing for the past two days. A dark eyebrow winged as if daring Henry Marchant to disagree.

Henry cleared his throat and looked away. 'Quite. I have no objection to my niece accepting such a position *per se.*' The gruff throat cleared again and the large hands gripped the chair arms. 'However…' Henry looked at the marbled fireplace. 'My wife and I are concerned with the manner and speed with which the offer and acceptance have been made. Kathryn is like a daughter to us and naturally we can only be greatly concerned when she leaves our home for a drive around Hyde Park, and fails to return.'

'I understand your…*concern.*' The stress was on Ravensmede's last word. There was an iciness to his tone that Kathryn had never heard before. 'Indeed, it really is most commendable.'

Mr Marchant's gaze shifted uncomfortably.

Ravensmede's drawl intensified. 'The accident involving

the child that occurred during the drive has left my grandmother quite exhausted. At her age, I hardly expect her to
oversee the child's care amidst all of her other activities. Thus,
the immediate requirement for a companion to assist her arose.
Miss Marchant was the ideal candidate.'

Henry Marchant gave a little cough. 'And Lady Maybury
will be staying here with you?' The question dropped dangerously into the air.

Kathryn's stomach tensed. The unspoken inference was
obvious. And, if her uncle thought it, then so would everyone
else, despite all of Lord Ravensmede's persuasion. The
Viscount turned a glacial focus upon Mr Marchant.

Mr Marchant drew back against his chair.

'My grandmother has taken a house in Upper Grosvenor
Street for the Season,' said Lord Ravensmede.

Kathryn could not suppress a surprised glance in his lordship's direction. Hadn't Lord Ravensmede led her to believe
that they would be living here in Ravensmede House? His face
betrayed nothing.

'In that case, I can raise no objection. My niece is four and
twenty, and many years beyond the age at which she would
require my permission.' For the first time since entering the
room Henry Marchant looked at Kathryn. 'I hope that you'll
be happy in your new position.' His gaze skittered away. 'I'll
have your trunk sent round.'

'Thank you.' Kathryn had never been one to shirk her duty
and she did not do so now. 'I will call upon my aunt and Lottie
tomorrow to take my leave of them.' Belatedly she consulted
her new employer, 'If that is acceptable to you, my lady.'

A scowl flitted over Lord Ravensmede's face, and disappeared.

Before Lady Maybury could reply, Henry Marchant cleared
his throat and repeated the words that his wife had instructed,
'Regrettably, both your aunt and cousin will be out tomorrow.'

A small silence followed.

'Then the day after, perhaps?' Kathryn suggested.

'I believe them to be engaged on that day also,' he said awkwardly, and shifted in his chair.

Kathryn made to reply but Ravensmede was there first. 'How good of your family to be so understanding of the situation.'

Confusion clouded Mr Marchant's face.

The Viscount leaned forward towards the older man in a confiding manner. 'Some people are embarrassed by class differences, but clearly your lady wife is not one of them. Now that Miss Marchant is companion to my grandmother, she must exercise more discernment in her choice of those with whom she associates. It is well that Mrs Marchant understands that.'

Henry Marchant's cheeks stained a ruddy red at the insult, but he said nothing.

Seeking to alleviate the growing tension, Kathryn spoke to her uncle. 'Please send Aunt Anna and Cousin Lottie my regards and my thanks for all their kindness over the years.' From the corner of her eye she saw Lord Ravensmede's jaw twitch, and she almost smiled. Then Kathryn remembered Aunt Anna. If she had thought her aunt to be an enemy before, she had best have a care and watch her back from now on. Anna Marchant was not a woman to forgive or forget.

Henry Marchant nodded once. 'Of course.' He cleared his throat again and looked uneasy.

It was Ravensmede who finally brought an end to the charade. 'Then we bid you good day, Mr Marchant.' He stood over a head taller than Henry Marchant and looked down into the man's small eyes. 'Your niece will be safe with my grandmother, Mr Marchant. Have no doubt of that.' And beneath the polite reassurance was the veiled threat of something dark and dangerous. Henry Marchant felt it too and scuttled from the room with a speed surprising for a man of his girth.

Sunshine flooded the breakfast room the next morning as Ravensmede sipped his coffee. A plate containing the remains of kedgeree lay abandoned before him.

'It's quite impossible, Nicholas. I barely slept a wink last night, most probably as a result of that infernal Marchant rat. What kind of man stands by and allows his wife to beat his niece? He's despicable! Little wonder I was tossing and turning throughout the night!'

'Grandmama,' the Viscount admonished gently, 'you promised that you wouldn't speak of it. Kathryn did not want us to know of her aunt's guilt.'

'Fustian!' exclaimed his grandmother. 'The gel's still up with Maggie. She'll not hear me from there!' She winced. 'It's no good. I'm really not myself this morning. You and Kathryn will have to take the child home.'

Ravensmede's eyes narrowed. 'I'll send for Dr Porter.'

'No! There's nothing wrong with me that a few hours' sleep won't cure. Stop fussing, Nick. I'm not dead yet!' The old lady drew him a fierce stare. 'Just make sure you look after my companion.'

Ravensmede's mood lightened at the thought of Kathryn and a closed carriage. He quirked a smile. 'As you wish, Grandmama.' A small bow and he turned to leave.

'And Nick—' Her voice stopped him at the door. The faded green eyes glared a warning. 'Remember that Miss Marchant is under *my* protection.'

He raised an ironic brow and was gone.

Kathryn's arm tightened around the child sitting by her side. 'I promise I shall come and see you again very soon.' The carriage rumbled through the streets leading them to the rookeries in Whitecross Street and the little girl's home.

Maggie eyed her hopefully before looking over at Lord Ravensmede on the opposite seat. 'And will the pa come too?'

'I don't know about that.' She laughed. Somehow she could not imagine the Viscount of Ravensmede visiting a four-year-old girl in a street of overcrowded slums. But, come to that, she had not thought he would have paid for Maggie to have the best of medical treatments, cared for her within his own house and then personally delivered her to her parents.

Ravensmede leaned forward. 'Of course I will.'

'Good.' Maggie snuggled closer into Kathryn's side, feeling in the pockets of her new apron. The pretty white frills around its edge contrasted nicely with the matching pink-and-white high-waisted frock worn beneath it. An apple was produced and the carriage soon reverberated with the sound of Maggie's crunches.

'That's what I like to see, a good healthy appetite.' Kathryn stroked the little girl's clean, shiny hair, fixing the pink satin ribbons as she did.

She felt Ravensmede's gaze upon her and looked up to meet it. His mouth was not quite in a smile, and there was a solemnity about his eyes that made her feel peculiar.

The rest of the journey continued with Kathryn pointing out landmarks and shops to Maggie. Ravensmede made no effort to join in, just sat back and watched the woman and the child. Once they had arrived, Kathryn did not miss the purse that he pressed into Maggie's father's hand, or the kind words that he uttered to the child's poor work-worn mother. A kiss on Maggie's cheek and they were gone. Kathryn waved until the little girl and her family were just a speck in the distance, and wondered at what she could never hope to have. A child of her own. A family. She thrust the thought aside and looked at Lord Ravensmede. He had not spoken since their return to the carriage, just sat looking from the window as if his thoughts were elsewhere.

'You should not have said that you would visit her. She'll look for you and be disappointed when you don't come.' Kathryn spoke the words gently, not to chastise but merely to show him the error of his ways. What did a man like Ravensmede know of a child's fragile trust?

Then his eyes were on her, casting a spiral of excitement into her breast and down deeper into her stomach as they ever did. She ignored her body's response as best she could. 'What makes you think that I would lie to the child? Do you think so little of me?'

She felt the colour rise to her face at his continued scrutiny and the accusation in his voice. 'No, I just thought...'

'I know what you thought, Kathryn,' he said.

Anger flared. 'On the contrary, Lord Ravensmede, you know nothing of what I think! Don't presume to do so!'

He smiled at that. 'Ouch,' he said. 'The kitten has claws.'

He really was the most infuriating man alive. Deliberately she turned her face to watch the passing houses. And ignored him.

'You think me infuriating,' he said with unnerving accuracy.

'I didn't say so.'

'You didn't have to. And you think that I make promises I won't keep.'

'No.'

A cynical eyebrow raised.

'Very well, yes.'

His eyes did not leave her face and a sensual tone crept into his voice. 'I always keep my promises, Kathryn.'

Her blood tingled.

Anticipation grew in the punctuating silence.

'It seems that you have much to learn of me.'

Kathryn's heart thudded in her chest. Blood surged through her veins, visibly throbbing at the pulse-point in her neck. 'Lest you had forgotten, Lord Ravensmede, I'm companion to your grandmother. There is no need for us to know anything of each other.'

He did not appear in the least discomposed, just stayed leaning back against the seat with his legs stretched out before him. 'On the contrary, I care for my grandmother, and, as such, it's only natural that I take an interest in her health, in her life and...in any companion that she may have. Indeed, I would be failing in my duty if I did not undertake a thorough appraisal of your character, Miss Marchant.'

Her cheeks scorched scarlet. 'I do not think that is necessary, my lord.'

'Oh, but I assure you that it is. I am most determined to know you.' The words were low and mellow, scarcely audible over the rumble of the wheels and the passing shouts from the street.

She faced him defiantly. 'I do not care for the turn this conversation is taking, sir.'

He shrugged his shoulders as if to say that her consideration did not matter.

The balance of Kathryn's temper tipped. With one hand gripping the travelling strap, she reached up and banged twice upon the carriage roof. 'Stop!' she shouted loud enough for the coachman to hear. Her fingers tugged at the window. Her head whipped round in Ravensmede's direction. 'I'll walk the rest of the way.'

The carriage showed no sign of slowing.

'Perdition, Kathryn! Are you trying to kill yourself?' He grabbed at her hands, pulling them away from the glass. The carriage bounced over some bumps. She staggered, striving to keep her balance, and toppled over straight on to Ravensmede's knee.

'Dear Lord!' she gasped and tried to escape. But Ravensmede's arms had already closed around her. 'Unhand me at once!'

'And let you fall out of a moving carriage? I do not think so, Kathryn.'

'I was going to wait for it to stop,' she said with indignation.

'Really?' he said drolly.

'I refuse to stay in here a moment longer with you!'

No reply, just that nearly smile upon his face.

'Lord Ravensmede!' she gasped.

'Miss Marchant,' he replied.

He held her gently but firmly throughout her struggles until at last she realised their futility and relaxed against the hard muscle of his body. Still his arms wound around her, barring any route of possible escape. His clean scent of bergamot surrounded her and she was growing increasingly aware of the muscular thighs on which she was sitting and the tautness of his stomach and chest hugging the contours of her back. The pulse still leapt in her throat, throbbing with a speed that made her ragged breathing seem slow in comparison. It was no longer anger that drove her reactions, but something quite different, something that she most definitely should not feel.

He was a rake! He would take what he could, and cast her aside. To a man like Ravensmede she was easy prey, a nothing, a nobody. If his grandmother found out, then Kathryn knew that she would lose her new home and position...not to mention her reputation. And then where would she be? The thought gave her the strength she needed. Quite suddenly she pulled away from him and attempted to break free. At first she thought she would succeed. It seemed her stillness had lulled him into a false sense of security. But even as her body made to rise the large arms clamped her back down. The breath shuddered in her throat.

'Keep still, Kathryn. I would not have you hurt yourself.'

The words were so close as to tickle her ear. The sensation shuddered down through her core. Whatever she knew of Nicholas Maybury, it was not enough to still her traitorous body's response. She could have cried aloud. Instead, she forced herself to calmness, letting the seconds become minutes. When at last she had some semblance of control she spoke. 'Lord Ravensmede, you may release me now. I give you my word that I won't try to leave the carriage.'

Only the sound of his breath whispered past her ear.

'My lord?'

He did not speak. Slowly his arms relaxed and opened in a gesture of release.

Kathryn knew she should leap across to the opposite seat, but she stayed quite still, only swung her legs round to the side and moved her head so that she might look into his face. His gaze was trained on her, glittering with a force that made the breath catch in her throat. For in those eyes, those alluring green eyes, was a look of such tenderness as to shatter every belief Kathryn had of the man. A large hand moved to cup the back of her head, his fingers untied the ribbons of her bonnet and, casting it aside, threaded into the silkiness of her hair. She knew what he was going to do and still she did nothing to stop him.

With calm deliberation he manoeuvred her until their lips met. And in their caress was the escalation of passionate need. His mouth moved with slow sensuality, sliding and sucking, coaxing and nipping, until she found her lips lapping against his, giving as much as receiving. Just when she thought she was melting in the heat of his embrace she felt the tantalising tease of his tongue, sliding against her lips, invading her mouth, seeking her own. Tongue touched tongue in warm and moist intimacy.

A long low groan issued deep in his throat and his hands moved to stroke her back, sweeping down to cover the swell of her hip, pulling her closer against him. Breast against breast. Even through the layers of clothing that separated their two bodies Kathryn felt the strong steady beat of his heart. Her skin warmed and blossomed against his until there was an aching tightness in her breasts. Not knowing what she did, she rose against him, arching instinctively until their hardened peaks thrust against the firm muscle of his chest. His roughened jaw-line rasped at the scorch marks left by his lips.

'Kathryn!' The whisper was a shuddering caress, full of desire. His fingers wove their magic through the muslin of her dress, sliding round to move against the flatness of her stomach, and up, further, until they reached their goal. He groaned again, a low guttural sound. 'God, but you're beautiful.'

She touched her lips to his.

The coach ground to a halt. The thump of footsteps sounded and, not a moment after Kathryn found herself dumped unceremoniously on to the opposite seat, the door swung open. Ravensmede House loomed large in the background. A footman positioned the steps and stood back to await his lordship's descent.

The green eyes raised to hers. 'Kathryn…'

She didn't wait to hear the words. She didn't need to. Before Ravensmede could stop her she had clambered out of the carriage and was fleeing up the stone stairs to the front door.

Chapter Seven

If Lady Maybury noticed that her new companion's colour was rather high, or that the girl's lips were swollen from being thoroughly kissed, she kept such observations to herself. There was much work to be done with organising the packing and arrangement of her ladyship's luggage for the move to Upper Grosvenor Street. And the dowager seemed to be in a rather cantankerous mood with everyone except Kathryn. It was somewhat surprising that the lady's favourite grandson was also being included under this edict. The dowager's disposition had not improved by the time both she and Miss Marchant came to take their leave of the Viscount.

'Nicholas.' Lady Maybury presented a small withered hand to be kissed. 'You may call upon me next week and not before. I will be busy ensuring that all is in order and have no desire for a distraction. Do I make myself clear?' A rather chilly focus fixed itself upon her grandson.

Ravensmede was not indifferent to his grandmother's mood, but, not trusting exactly what that perceptive gaze of hers had fathomed, he did not enquire as to its cause. 'Perfectly clear, Grandmama. Never fear, I shall not disturb you before the appointed time.' He pressed a kiss to the papery hand and moved to face Miss Marchant, who to all intent and purpose was attempting to hide herself behind the tiny frame of his grand-mother. 'Miss Marchant,' he said politely, 'I trust that you have found your stay to be comfortable?'

'Yes, thank you, my lord.' There was nothing in her manner to suggest that all was not as it should be, apart from the slight tremor in her fingers when he pressed them briefly to his lips. Ravensmede felt it keenly, but could do nothing as she withdrew her hand and stepped away.

He suffered the baleful stare of a faded green eye and then the two women were walking down the steps to the heavily laden carriage and the journey that would remove them from the house in Berkeley Square. The door closed with a thump, leaving Ravensmede alone, save for the creeping sense of loss.

'Heard Lady Maybury has taken li'l Miss Marchant on as her companion. Rather convenient for you, I'd say.' If Lord Cadmount lounged any lower in the chair he would be in danger of slipping out of it. The brandy glass balanced delicately on one thigh as he gave his friend a knowing wink.

Ravensmede grunted and loosened the neckcloth that his valet had spent twenty minutes in tying. 'Then you'd be wrong.'

The pale eyebrows raised as high as they could. 'How so? Could it be that you've already bedded her and found her not to your taste?'

A dry laugh. 'Hell, Caddie! You know that I haven't.' The memory of her slender body pressed against his, the softness of those pink lips, the sweetness of her tentative response, intruded all too readily. He felt a stirring in his lower regions and clamped it down with frustrated determination. A gulp of brandy warmed his throat before he continued. 'As my grand-mother's companion, she should be safe from any such specu-lation.' He made no mention of the vile family from whom Kathryn was also now safe.

'Not quite,' argued his friend. 'There's always room for that wherever the woman is placed.'

'Not when my grandmother is involved,' replied Ravensmede.

'I agree that Lady Maybury would make a most formidable foe.' Cadmount sipped his drink and mulled his thoughts. 'Strange that Henry Marchant never looked to make a marriage for the girl. I know she's no schoolroom miss, but neither has she reached her dotage. Must have been keen to keep her in the bosom of his family. A charitable chap, wouldn't you say?'

Ravensmede's eyes darkened. 'Hardly that. Marchant lacks a backbone; he does little more than dance to his wife's tune. A less charitable couple I've yet to meet.' Something of the darkness lifted from his mood. 'Neither was their home a suitable place for a woman like Miss Marchant.'

Cadmount smiled. 'Ah,' he said softly. 'I think I begin to understand.'

The green eyes raised to his. One corner of his mouth flickered up. 'I doubt very much that you do, my dear Caddie.'

'And therein lies the rub.' A finger stroked thoughtfully at his chin. 'You still want her.' It was a statement rather than a question.

Ravensmede did not deny it. 'She's my grandmother's companion now, and even if she wasn't...'

'It would take a rake of the lowest order to seduce a woman who lost her mother and sister and found her father with half his head blown off.'

'Hell, I didn't realise that Kathryn saw her father after he shot himself.' Ravensmede's brows drew together.

'The chit found him all right. Couldn't have been a pretty sight. Had an interesting chat with Bertie Devon. He remembers the whole thing.'

'No woman should have to suffer that.'

Cadmount paused, then asked in a stolid tone, 'Do you mean to seduce her?'

Ravensmede blew a languid sigh. Seduce her? He had come damn near to doing so a week ago in his carriage. He gave Cadmount a cynical look. 'Do you think that I will?'

'I honestly don't know.'

A wry smile. 'My grandmother will take good care of her. She'll be safe there.' Safe from Anna Marchant, but was she truly safe from him?

Cadmount leaned over the chair and, catching his somewhat wrinkled coat up from the floor, set about rummaging in the pockets. 'Strikes me that the girl brings out the protective streak in you.'

Ravensmede crooked an eyebrow. 'Too much brandy, Caddie. Your imaginings run wild. Next you'll have me attending lectures by the Humane Society.'

'Now that would be something worth seeing.' Cadmount laughed. 'Are you telling me that you have no care for Miss Marchant?'

'I'm saying that the woman's suffered enough. She deserves to have some little happiness.'

The two men looked at one another.

'Undoubtedly we need another drink.' The Viscount walked without a hint of unsteadiness to retrieve the decanter.

'Won't help, old man.' Lord Cadmount shook his head sagely. 'Happens to us all sooner or later.'

Ravensmede rubbed at the darkening shadow of stubble on his chin as he refilled their glasses. 'Enlighten me.'

The finely painted miniature box nestled on Cadmount's palm as he regarded it with a knowing expression. 'Love.'

'You're most definitely foxed, Caddie.'

'Indeed I am,' said his friend, helping himself to a generous helping of snuff. 'But it doesn't mean I'm not right. Fancy a pinch?' The box was dangled enticingly towards Ravensmede.

'Why not?' He helped himself to some snuff and snapped the lid shut again.

Golden flames leapt high in the hearth, causing the logs to crackle and spit. The two men sat in comfortable silence, Cadmount knowing when he had pushed far enough, Ravensmede brooding on the growing fascination that he felt for Kathryn Marchant.

* * *

'Read me the last verse again,' Lady Maybury instructed.

Kathryn glanced up at the dowager's smiling countenance and then, lowering her eyes once more to the book, began to read.

> Whate'er the theme, the Maiden sang
> As if her song could have no ending;
> I saw her singing at her work,
> And o'er the sickle bending—
> I listened, motionless and still;
> And, as I mounted up the hill,
> The music in my heart I bore,
> Long after it was heard no more.

'No poet is quite as lyrical as Mr Wordsworth, and no lady reads poetry quite so well as you, my dear gel. You have a wonderful voice.'

Kathryn blushed at Lady Maybury's generous praise and lowered the book to her lap. 'Thank you, my lady. My father always liked to hear my sister and me reading, and we did so most nights in the parlour. Poems, essays, novels, anything would do, even the newspaper. Papa would listen as if he had never heard anything so interesting in all the day.' She paused and smiled, before adding quietly, 'They're happy memories.' She did not think of the bad ones.

'And did you read to your aunt and uncle when you came to London?' the old lady asked.

The rich brown curls swayed as she slowly shook her head. 'Oh, no, Uncle Henry reads the *Morning Post* and Aunt Anna does not much care for reading at all.'

'And the cousin? What did you say her name was—Lettie?' The ancient tone had sharpened imperceptibly.

'Lottie. I'm afraid my cousin finds reading rather irksome. She's of a more musical disposition, being very fond of singing and with a voice that's lovely to hear.' Kathryn carefully turned the page in the book nestled upon her lap. 'Indeed, my aunt is holding a musical evening very soon at which Lottie will be singing to Mr Dalton's piano accompaniment. Lottie has been practising for weeks.'

Lady Maybury showed not the slightest interest. 'I've just remembered our appointment with Madame Dupont. Come, we had best ready ourselves. She's rather high in the instep for a dressmaker, but I've never patronised anyone else in the last thirty years. Her designs are very much to my liking.'

Thus it was that, precisely two hours later, Kathryn and Lady Maybury came to be sitting within the tiny backroom of Madame Dupont's elegant establishment in highly fashionable Bond Street.

'But, my lady, it is such a colour as to bring out the fire in your eyes. A dark green silk will make the gown, damask is not at all right for this style.' The tall thin woman with the severe white chignon spoke passionately in an accent that still held the lilt of her Gallic origins. 'Most definitely *non!*' She shook her head defiantly.

For the first time since their meeting Kathryn saw Lady Maybury capitulate. 'Very well, Marie. I'll allow you to have your way in this one respect. A small turban in green and black should go very well, don't you think?'

'Indeed, my lady, very well indeed. And I shall add a few small ebony plumes as the finishing touch, yes?'

'Yes. Now that's enough for me at present, Marie. My companion Miss Marchant requires an evening dress for the same event. And we had better have a couple of afternoon dresses and another evening dress while we're at it.' Lady Maybury's small veined hand was pushing Kathryn forward in no uncertain terms.

Her companion, on the other hand, had very different ideas. 'My lady, it's really not necessary, I have a very serviceable evening gown and several other dresses too. I must insist that there is no need for anything more.' Kathryn thought of the few outmoded shabby dresses that had arrived in her old trunk from Green Street. She thought too of the six shillings hidden at the bottom of the trunk, next to the small battered bible that had belonged to her mother. The sum of her worldly savings would not suffice to pay for one of Madame Dupont's gowns, let alone four. 'Thank you for thinking of me,' she added hastily lest Lady Maybury think her rude.

The dressmaker's dark eyes swung back to the dowager.

'Kathryn,' Lady Maybury began, and Kathryn recognised it as her most autocratic tone. 'It is in the role of my companion that you require several new items of clothing. The choice is mine as is the reckoning of the account.' There was definitely more than a hint of the same imperious tone Kathryn had witnessed in the old lady's grandson.

Kathryn's cheeks flushed at the barely veiled implication. Lady Maybury did not care to be seen in the company of someone dressed so poorly. It was also evident that the dowager knew something of her companion's meagre means and thus felt compelled to pay for the clothing. Kathryn could not dispute that her dresses were probably of a state to cause her employer some degree of embarrassment, but she was also very aware of the pride that was lodged stubbornly in her throat. 'Thank you, my lady, but, kind as your offer is, you must know that I cannot possibly accept it. I will pay for the dresses myself.' The defiant little chin thrust up as she waited for Lady Maybury's reaction.

'Very well, my dear. It seems that you have your mind set over the matter.'

With a calm demeanour Kathryn nodded her gratitude and turned to face the dressmaker. She would worry over how to obtain the money later, when she knew the full sum owing.

If Lady Maybury felt any irritation towards her companion's insistence she hid it well and thus, at the end of the afternoon, they finally departed Madame Dupont's on very good terms with the promise of two completed evening gowns for the following week, and the rest to follow later.

* * *

The days passed with an easiness and speed that Kathryn had not experienced for many a year. Life with Lady Maybury was pleasant indeed. The old lady could be demanding in the extreme, but she was also kind, interesting and in possession of a rather wicked sense of humour, as her companion quickly discovered. Even Lord Ravensmede's visits to his grandparent failed to blight Kathryn's growing happiness. From the time of his arrival until his eventual departure she kept herself busily employed in tasks well away from the drawing room where Lady Maybury entertained. There was, after all, no point is jeopardising the harmonious existence into which she had fallen within the dowager's rented townhouse.

As Kathryn found contentment in her new life, her day-dreaming diminished. There were still times when, in her mind, she was the sole recipient of a certain nobleman's heart—a nobleman who did not want her as his mistress, but as his wife and the mother of his children. But this time, she kept the tall, handsome Viscount strictly confined to her dreams. Kathryn had learned her lesson well. Neither Lord Ravensmede, nor anyone else for that matter, would be allowed to ruin the chance she now had for happiness.

Warm golden sunlight spilled across the deep rosewood table in the parlour of the house in Green Street, highlighting a patch of dust that had escaped the maid's cloth and beeswax. Under ordinary circumstances such an omission would have been enough to earn the poor girl a clout round the ear and a thorough tongue lashing from the lady of the house. But, fortunately for the maid, matters within the Marchant household that afternoon were anything but ordinary. For Anna Marchant, sitting alone and bolt upright in the comfortable armchair beside the unlit fireplace, was reading the contents of a letter that had just been delivered by the letter carrier. A small gasp erupted into the emptiness of the room. The colour drained from her complexion. Her mouth gaped liked a landed fish. 'No!' she whispered aloud. 'It cannot be…' She smoothed the paper out upon her lap and then, grasping the sheet so tightly that her nails dug into her palms, made to read the small, neatly formed script once more.

26 May 1815
Amersham
Buckinghamshire

Dear Mrs Marchant

I beg that you will forgive the nature of the tidings that I write to impart, but I have just heard such news that renders me, in good conscience, unable to remain silent.

I was very pleased to make your acquaintance at Lady Finlay's recent ball, and I do not think that I was mistaken in finding that you are a lady of impeccable taste and judgement. However, word has just reached me here at my sister's residence that your niece, Miss Kathryn Marchant, has accepted the offer of a position as the dowager Lady Maybury's companion. As you will be well aware, Lady Maybury is the grandmother of the Viscount of Ravensmede, a nobleman of renowned repute. For reasons that I dare not put into writing, my dear Mrs Marchant, I am compelled to warn you against allowing your niece to take up Lady Maybury's offer. Suffice to say, I have evidence that, were it to become public knowledge, would most certainly jeopardise her reputation. I fear that Kathryn is not of the same genteel mould as you and your sweet daughter Lottie, but of that I will say no more lest this letter falls into the wrong hands and risks your family's embarrassment. It is unfortunate that I am forced to remain here in the country for a few days longer on account of my sister's confinement, but I assure you that I will return to London with haste and call upon you as soon as is possible.

With all good intentions
Your friend
Amanda White

By the time Mrs Marchant finished reading her mouth was
quite dry and her heart rate had kicked to a canter. What on
earth had that little bitch Kathryn been up to? Making a fool
of the family that had saved her from destitution on the streets,
if Amanda White's insinuations were to be believed. Mrs
Marchant folded the letter up and went to hide it in a safe place,
all the while musing on why she disliked Kathryn so very
much. The deed was done: Kathryn was already installed in the
dowager's house in Upper Grosvenor Street. Nothing in Mrs
White's letter could undo that, not without serving the entire
Marchant family up to the gossipmongers. And that was something that could not be risked. A sneer contorted her mouth,
and her eyes were filled with spite. Anna Marchant had no intention of meekly awaiting the return of the widow to discover
just what was going on with Kathryn, no intention at all.

Kathryn stared at her reflection in disbelief. She tried to
speak, her mouth even shaped to say the words, but none were
forthcoming. Her delicately shaped eyebrows rose and fell ex-
pressively and when still she could not speak she whirled
around and in three steps had gathered Lady Maybury into a
spontaneous embrace.

'I take it you're pleased with Madame Dupont's creation!'
chuckled the old lady.

Kathryn finally found her tongue. 'Indeed, my lady, it's
quite the most beautiful dress I've ever seen. When I look in
the mirror I see a stranger looking back at me. I'm nothing like
myself!' A slender hand patted the dowager's arm once more.
'Thank you for allowing me to repay your loan with such rea-
sonable terms.' As Lady Maybury's companion she was not
entitled to a wage as such, but her ladyship had insisted on

giving her a generous sum, all of which would now be consumed in paying for the outfit in which she was now attired.

'You are very welcome, child.' Lady Maybury smiled. 'I do believe Marie was right when she insisted upon this colour. It complements your eyes.' Her head perched to one side in contemplation. "Yes, Kathryn, you shall do very well.' One snowy eyebrow arched, mimicking the gesture so often used by her grandson. 'Very well indeed.'

For once in her life, Kathryn Marchant thought that perhaps that might just be true. The dress was of a sheer violet silk, high-waisted and cut so that the skirt draped enticingly to the floor with the merest suggestion of the curves hidden beneath. With a low décolletage it revealed rather more of Kathryn's other assets than she was used to, but her bruises were gone; when she suggested the addition of her fichu, Lady Maybury snorted and turned a more-than-querulous eye in her direction.

'There's no need for any such thing.'

Sprinkled liberally over the bodice were the tiniest cream pearls, which led the eye down to the broad cream satin ribbon that adorned Kathryn's waist as well as the edge of her short puffed sleeves. On her hands she wore an elegant new pair of cream gloves that reached up and over her arms to past her elbows. Her neck was bare save for the few chestnut tendrils that nestled about it. The mass of her curls had been gathered up high on the back of her head and fixed in place with pins and cream-and-violet coloured ribbons. A matching cream shawl and reticule completed the elegant ensemble. Little wonder that she scarcely recognised the woman looking back at her from the dressing mirror. Suddenly aware that she had been entirely absorbed in her own appearance, Kathryn turned to the dowager, who was resplendent in the forest green silk. 'You look lovely, my lady. Madame Dupont has truly worked her magic here tonight. We shall be quite the finest dressed ladies at Lady Cooper's ball.'

'I never doubted it for a moment,' said her ladyship in reply.

* * *

The ballroom was glowing with the light of a multitude of candles balanced in four enormous crystal chandeliers. Lady Cooper's affair was proving to be quite a success judging from the mass of people squashed within the confines of her ballroom. Kathryn and Lady Maybury had been fortuitous in finding seats close by the floor-length windows, which were opened in an attempt to remedy the stifling heat. Mrs Lee and Lady Hadstone soon arrived to monopolise the dowager's attention, leaving Kathryn to watch the proceedings upon the dance floor and around its periphery. She sipped her lemonade and enjoyed her contemplation. *The oppressive heat of the ballroom vanished, the air grew cool and sweet, scented with the freshness of grass and earth and blue sky. Instead of the press of sweat-drenched bodies were spacious marble chequered floor tiles and a flood of sunlight. Across the floor stood one large figure, immaculate in full evening dress, his green eyes light like tender young leaves, smiling his heart-rending smile...for her alone.*

'Kathryn!' The dowager's hand touched to her arm, and the spell was broken.

She looked at Lady Maybury, an expression of guilt blazoned across her face. 'I do beg your pardon, my lady. I'm afraid my thoughts had wandered a little.'

But the dowager's focus had shifted and was fixed quite firmly on someone else, someone that stood directly before Kathryn, someone of whom Kathryn was becoming rapidly aware.

'Miss Marchant,' he said. The deep melodic tone teased a shiver down her spine. 'A pleasure to see you again.' His bow was superbly executed.

'Lord Ravensmede.' She made her devoirs and tried to ignore the warmth that had suddenly pervaded her cheeks. *Distant and polite, stay distant and polite at all times*, she reminded herself. But it did not slow the thrumming of her heart or the acrobatic antics of the butterflies massing in her stomach.

He was dressed as if he had stepped straight out of her daydream: a finely tailored black coat worn with pale pantaloons that clung rather revealingly to his long muscular thighs. Well-shaped calves and ankles were encased in white stockings, leading down to a pair of highly polished black buckle slippers. A white satin waistcoat overlaid a snow-white shirt and neckcloth, beneath which it was clear that there had been no need for padding of any description. Nicholas Maybury was indeed a man of impressive physique. He turned to his grandmother and smiled. 'I trust this evening finds you in good health?'

'Never better, my boy. I have the constitution of an ox, as well you know.' Aside to her cronies she added, 'He's ever hopeful that I will shuffle off this mortal coil, but I do not intend to accommodate him for quite some time.'

Kathryn listened to the conversation continue for some little time, with Ravensmede politely exchanging small talk with all three elderly ladies. Notably he did not attempt the same with her. Indeed, his neglect was rather marked. Two strangers in a ballroom. Their kisses had never been. Respectable. The Viscount and his grandmother's companion—a class apart. It was what she wanted, after all, so why did it bring a heaviness to her heart? And then, at last, Lord Ravensmede's attention was upon her, and it was as if they were the only two people there.

His eyes met hers.

Her heart skipped a beat. It was her dream becoming a reality. She wetted her suddenly dry lips. Tried to shake off the enchantment in danger of overcoming her. Knew that she was staring at him in a highly inappropriate fashion. None of it made any difference. Kathryn glanced around, looking for a way to extricate herself from such temptation.

'Miss Marchant,' he said, and her name sounded like a caress upon his lips.

His lips... Her eyes were on them, tracing their outline. Firm, chiselled, with a hint of sensual fullness. Lips that had kissed her with such expertise. Her own mouth parted at the memory. Anticipation fluttered in her stomach. The breath trembled within her throat. She swallowed hard. Fought to regain some semblance of self-control. 'Lord Ravensmede.' How could she sound so calm, so unaffected, when she wanted so desperately to feel the press of his mouth against hers, the strength of his arms around her?

'The next dance is the waltz. I understand it to be a favourite of yours.' He did not appear to be in the grip of any such torrent of emotion. But there was something in his gaze that made the hairs on the back of her neck stand upright.

Kathryn's cheeks warmed. 'I…um…that is…' Her fingers slid to twist at the violet silk of her skirt. 'I do not think that…'

A corner of his mouth twitched. 'Grandmama, may I borrow Miss Marchant for the next dance? I promise to return her safely and I'm sure that these two beautiful ladies…' he turned the full force of his rakish good looks upon Lady Hadstone and Mrs Lee '…will engage you in such interesting and witty conversation that you shall not note her absence.'

Lady Hadstone and Mrs Lee giggled girlishly and fanned themselves with fervour.

Lady Maybury knew better. The tone of her voice was harsh, but the look in her eye was one of endearment. 'Why the blazes should I object?' And she turned her attention back to her friends.

Ravensmede smiled at that, then faced Kathryn again. 'Miss Marchant, would you do me the honour of partnering me for the waltz?' His eyes lingered at her lips before rising to meet her gaze.

Her throat was in danger of sticking together. The pulse at the side of her neck throbbed wildly. She prayed fervently that it would not show. 'Thank you, Lord Ravensmede,' she uttered weakly. From the corner of her eye she could see Mrs Lee and Lady Hadstone positively agog. For the sake of good manners she could not refuse him, and neither did she want to. 'I would be delighted.' And in her heart she knew it was the truth.

A large hand extended, closed around hers and tucked it securely into his arm. He did not speak until the music started and they were gliding effortlessly around the room. 'Are you happy with my grandmother?'

Her lashes swept up and she regarded him with surprise that he could ask such a question. 'Of course, my lord. Lady Maybury is very kind to me.' He smelled of soap and bergamot and something else that was uniquely him.

'It seems you have a short memory, Kathryn.'

She swallowed hard, aware that she remembered all too well a moonlit room and the dimmed interior of a coach. 'I don't know to what you are referring, sir.'

His eyes glinted with emerald lights. 'My lord? Sir? I think we know each other rather better than that would suggest.'

Her cheeks grew hotter. Did he know what he was doing to her? From the look on his face, most probably so. 'On the contrary, Lord Ravensmede, I'm companion to your grandmother. Any other mode of address would be quite inappropriate.' Despite the traitorous reaction of her body to his proximity, she was determined not to let her mask of polite indifference slip. Such a path was the rocky descent to ruin, nothing more.

'Do you deny then, *Miss Marchant*—' he stressed the use of her formal address '—that which has passed between us on two separate occasions?' His eyes held hers with an intimacy to which he had no right.

She bit uneasily at her lower lip, unsure of where his words were leading.

'Surely you do not forget that as well? Shall I remind you of the kisses that we've shared?' he teased.

She gasped and glanced self-consciously around. 'Ssh! Someone might hear you!'

'Then you do remember, after all.'

'Of course I remember,' she snapped. 'I'm unlikely ever to forget!'

'Why? Do my kisses affect you like no other's?' Ravens-mede laughed.

She could do nothing to prevent the intensifying rosy stain that scalded the fairness of her skin.

'Your face betrays you, Kathryn.' And for some reason he looked extraordinarily pleased about it.

'You are no gentleman to say such things!' she said, afraid of what she had revealed.

'I assure you, Kathryn, I'm no gentleman at all.' A wicked twinkle set in the green eyes. 'But that is something of which you are, no doubt, already aware.'

'Lord Ravens—'

A dark eyebrow arched. 'Tut tut, Kathryn, what must I do to make you use my given name?' His gaze dropped pointedly to her lips.

'Nicholas!' the whisper ejected with alacrity.

He smiled. 'Much better. So now that we've sorted one small problem, let us deal with another. Why have you been avoiding me?'

Her denial was too quick. 'You're mistaken.' The chestnut tendrils cascading around her neck shook. She was not wanton. No matter the strength of his left hand surrounding hers, or the undeniable heat that emanated from the touch of his right against her waist. No matter that she quivered with the hope that he would kiss her, as he had before. She must strive to show him that he erred in his opinion.

'I've visited my grandmother on five occasions and not once have you been present. Do you mean to tell me that she sent you away when she knew I had arrived?'

'No. I was simply engaged with other chores.'

'I've told you before, Kathryn Marchant, you make a poor liar.'

Her eyes met his at the shared memory of the last time he had uttered those words.

His hand tightened upon her waist.

She trembled beneath it.

'I owe you an apology, Kathryn. That day in the carriage, I should not have taken advantage of you. Forgive me.' The edge of his thumb delicately caressed her fingers.

Right at this moment in time she would have forgiven him anything. 'I was not entirely blameless in the situation,' she admitted. 'I should not have…' She glanced away. 'I ought not to have…' Was there any polite way of saying what had to be said? Silver eyes met smouldering green once more. 'You know very well what I'm trying to say, Nicholas.'

A knowing smile was her only answer.

She cleared her throat nervously. 'No such thing must happen again. I'm Lady Maybury's companion, and even if that were not the case…' Anxiety widened her eyes. 'I would not have you think me anything other than respectable.' There, she had said it.

The music filled the silence between them.

'I do not think anything else,' he said, and a strange expression came over his face. 'And as you rightly said, you're my grandmother's companion. Do you think that I would do anything to dishonour her?'

'No.' It was the truth. There seemed to be a genuine bond of affection between the Viscount and his grandparent.

He was still looking at her in that peculiar way. 'Are you truly so averse to my company, Kathryn?'

She sighed. The lie refused to form upon her lips. 'I'm averse to any impropriety that might blight my reputation. My good name is all that I have left.'

'I do not seek to damage it,' he said softly.

She should treat him with the cool distance that propriety demanded, but she could not. 'If we are agreed that no such thing should happen again between us, then there is no reason that we cannot be friends.'

'Friends?' He rolled the word around his tongue in careful consideration. It would certainly be a novelty. 'Friends do not avoid one another, Kathryn.'

'No, they do not,' she said quietly.

'Well, in that case…' the side of his mouth quirked '…we shall be friends.'

The last bars of 'Ach! Du lieber Augustine' sounded in the ballroom.

Kathryn had no opportunity to speak further with Lord Ravensmede that evening. It seemed that his taking her on to the floor had acted as a signal as to her availability as a dancing partner, for no sooner had she taken her seat once more than she was approached by first one young man and then another. She tried to decline as politely as possible, knowing that she was present only in the capacity of a companion, but Lady Maybury was having none of it and, at her insistence, Kathryn was forced to accept each and every one of the flood of dance invitations. While partnering Captain Brent for the quadrille she became aware of Lord Ravensmede's scrutiny and during the Scottish reel with Mr Parket she saw that he had stood up with an elegant young blonde lady. After that he disappeared and Kathryn focused her attentions on remembering her dance steps.

Chapter Eight

Ravensmede carelessly dropped the neckcloth on to the chair and massaged the knot of tension at the back of his neck that had been growing all night since witnessing Kathryn in the arms of another man, or several other men to be precise. He sighed and loosened his shirt, glad that he had instructed his valet not to wait up. The night was still young, certainly for someone of the Viscount's lifestyle, but he had no inclination to attend his club, and still less to visit Millicent Miller. He wondered whether he had been a trifle hasty in paying his latest mistress off. He paced around the bedchamber, restless, discontented. Each time he closed his eyes an image appeared—Kathryn smiling at someone, and that someone wasn't him. Little wonder he'd been forced to leave early. He poured himself another large and aromatic brandy and lay back still clothed upon the bed.

Perhaps Millicent was exactly what he needed. A pretty face and willing body to ease his frustration. But the thought went no further. The need that gnawed at him was specific, and he was quite sure that only one woman could remedy it. He had no notion for any of the women that had served as his mistresses. Indeed, he had no notion for anyone or anything other than his grandmother's companion; a woman whom life had treated harshly, who, until he had quite literally stumbled upon her at Lady Finlay's ball with that dreadful blonde cousin, had battled alone through life's trials. The thought of what she had witnessed after her father's suicide, and, worse still, at the hands of the woman who called herself her aunt, nipped at Ravensmede. Yet Kathryn had endured and refused to be either cowed or embittered by her experiences.

Perdition, but she was beautiful. He had known it from the first, when she was hidden behind that monstrosity of a grey garment that passed for a dress. His grandmother's influence had unmasked Kathryn's real beauty for all to see. She was not pretty in the mundane sense of the *ton*. Rather her eyes had a silver sparkle, and that smile… He had scarcely been able to draw his eyes away from the sight of Kathryn, encased in the violet evening dress that emphasised the gentle curves of her figure.

And when he'd first approached her, only to find her with that faraway look in her eyes, he wanted nothing other than to pull her into his arms and kiss that delectable mouth that moved so readily to laughter. It had nigh on been his undoing, causing as it did certain physical reactions that were hardly appropriate at a society ball, least of all in front of his own grandmother. He'd been forced to concentrate his attentions on his grandam's cronies in the hope of preventing what could have been an embarrassing situation for them all.

His fingers raked the dark ruffle of his hair. What was this obsession he felt for Kathryn? A desire to bed her, and yet he recoiled from treating her in such a despicable way. He was growing soft. Never once in all the years of playing the rake had he suffered such a revelation of conscience. And all because he'd developed a fancy for his grandmother's companion. Truth to be told, much more than a fancy.

It was time he took himself in hand. She was just a woman, like any other. The brandy trickled down his throat, soothing the edge from his emptiness. A smile crooked across his face. Yes, Kathryn Marchant was definitely all woman, but she was nothing like any of the others. Maybe, just maybe, Kathryn had already offered him the solution to his problem. It was almost as if he heard again the soft whisper of her words within his bedchamber, *there is no reason that we cannot be friends.*

Slowly and carefully he placed the empty glass upon the bedside table, stripped off the remainder of his clothes and crawled beneath the covers. For the first time in ten years Ravensmede was sound asleep before the clock struck midnight.

The sunshine flooded the breakfast room, basking both Kathryn and Lady Maybury in its golden light. Her ladyship was devouring a plate of chops, her appetite being disproportionately large for so small and frail a person. Her companion was satisfied with a mere egg on toast. Behind Kathryn's plate was propped *The Times*, from which she was reading aloud the announcements, between mouthfuls of breakfast.

'Lord Barclay has the common sense of a flea. Engaged to Wilhelmina Turbet? Mark my words, the girl will bore him rigid in less than a month. Just like her mother—nothing between the ears, I'm afraid.' Lady Maybury helped herself to yet another slice of toast.

Kathryn poked an errant curl behind her ear and smiled mischievously. 'But I thought that's precisely what a gentleman demanded of his wife. Did not Lady Hadstone say there's nothing less attractive than a clever woman?'

'Ho!' screeched her ladyship at the top of her voice. 'Amelia's three daughters couldn't hold a single thought in their heads between them. She's not likely to say anything else! Fortunately for her, their dowries were large. Had them off her hands in no time, even though they each had the brain of a small carp, and the face to match.'

The two ladies were laughing at Lady Maybury's scathing observation when the footman entered to announce the Viscount of Ravensmede, followed closely by the man himself.

'Grandmama, Miss Marchant.' He gave a nonchalant bow.

'Forgive the early hour of my call. I wished to catch you before you made arrangements for the day.'

'Nick,' murmured the dowager with pleasure. 'Come and join us for a spot of breakfast.' She indicated the empty seat to her right-hand side and rammed another mouthful of pork into her mouth. 'I'm sure Miss Marchant will not object.'

Kathryn smiled at both grandmother and grandson. 'Of course not.'

Lord Ravensmede helped himself to a little toast and some coffee.

'What's wrong with you, boy?' The dowager's brow wrinkled. 'Picking at your food like a sparrow. Are you sickening for something?'

Ravensmede took his grandparent's jibes with good nature. 'I've already broken my fast. I'm merely accommodating your hospitality, ma'am.'

Lady Maybury grunted, but the faded green eyes remained unconvinced.

'Have you made plans for today?' Ravensmede sipped his coffee, but abandoned the half-eaten toast.

'Apart from attending the Opera House tonight, we are as yet undecided.'

'Then perhaps you'll allow me to accompany you on a visit to the exhibition of the Society of Painters in Oil and Watercolours. From there we could travel to the British Museum.' His gaze flitted from his grandmother to her companion.

The old lady smiled, a fiery light appearing in her eyes. 'What do you say, Kathryn? Shall we attend?'

Kathryn could barely conceal her surprise in being asked. 'My lady, I'm happy to abide by whatever you should decide,' she said with the utmost diplomacy.

'Don't flannel me, gel! Do you want to go or don't you? It's a simple enough question.'

The heat rose in Kathryn's face, creating two small spots of colour. 'I would very much like to see the paintings.' With calm deliberation she folded the newspaper over and laid it on the table.

'Good,' announced the dowager, and then said to her grandson, 'Come back in an hour, we shall be ready then. Haven't had time to finish m'breakfast,' she grumbled. 'Blasted interruptions aren't good for the digestion. Off with you, then!' And the formidable little lady held her cheek up for Lord Ravensmede's kiss before shooing him from the room.

It was very different from the last journey she had made in this same carriage. Kathryn drew her mind carefully away from that avenue of thought. Seated beside Lady Maybury with a well-behaved Lord Ravensmede opposite, things could not have been more dissimilar. Despite the warmth of the fine summer day and the firmly closed windows, Lady Maybury insisted on being covered with the vast expanse of her favourite travelling rug. Its woollen folds overlapped on to Kathryn's legs, making her feel hot and sticky before they'd even arrived at Spring Gardens. She still wore the shabby blue muslin gown as her new afternoon dresses were yet to be delivered; a fact for which she was grateful, given the coolness of the simple material. Fortunately Lady Maybury had not demanded that her companion wear a spencer, although the mud-brown bonnet was an absolute necessity. They arrived at the exhibition while it was still relatively quiet and so were able to enjoy an unimpeded appreciation of the fine collection of water-colour and oil paintings.

'I simply must sit and have a closer look at these paintings,' said her ladyship, seating herself on one of the green-and-pink painted benches within the gallery.

Kathryn touched a hand to the dowager's arm. 'Are you quite well?'

A snort of disgust greeted her concern. 'You're getting as bad as m'grandson, miss. Can't I enjoy the merits of Mr Fielding's work without those around me becoming fixated on m'health?'

'I beg your pardon, my lady, I didn't mean to—'

'No one ever does, it is—' said the dowager with mounting exasperation.

Ravensmede's voice interrupted smoothly. 'Grandmama, allow me to suggest that I accompany Miss Marchant around the room, while you view Mr Fielding's paintings in more detail.'

Kathryn looked rather uneasily towards Lord Ravensmede. 'I—'

The old lady did not shift her gaze from the paintings on the wall before her. 'Very well, Nick.' And then, as if remembering Kathryn, she turned her head and mumbled, 'Go ahead, gel.'

Without further ado Kathryn felt her hand being tucked into the Viscount's arm, and then she was quite literally whisked to the other side of the expansive airy room.

His voice was deep and mellow, laced with a hint of amusement. 'Please do forgive my grandmother, Miss Marchant. I'm sure she didn't mean to be so…forthright in her opinion.' Given that they were in such a very public place, he released her arm and stood back to consider the painting before them.

'Your grandmother is honest and always speaks her mind. It's a trait that I much admire,' she said in stout defence of her employer, and stepped likewise to view the same work. With her head perched to one side she studied Mr Robson's watercolour showing a rather sombre scene of a castle on a rock. 'Mmm, it's a very atmospheric scene,' she said. 'Do you like it, my lord?'

'It's well executed and undoubtedly of excellent technical expertise, but as to actually liking it…'

'Can you not feel the sheer rugged rock on which Stirling Castle is built, the bleakness of the vast view, and the humidity of the grey cloud-layered sky?'

A nearly smile hovered at his mouth. 'Enough to make me feel an inkling of gratitude that I'm here instead of there,' he said drolly.

Kathryn's eyes lit with passionate enthusiasm. 'But *there* is freedom unbounded, wildness untamed—see the mountains in the background. And *here* is something altogether different.' Her eyes met his and she smiled. 'Mr Robson has succeeded very well in showing us that. He truly is a great artist.'

'You sound as if you have a real interest in art.'

Her lips curved up in readiness. 'I know very little of the subject, but when I was younger I enjoyed painting very much.'

'And now?'

A shrug of the shoulders. 'And now I have other things to occupy my time. What of you, my lord? Do you paint or sketch?'

Ravensmede laughed. 'Not at all. Let's just say my talents lie elsewhere. But I appreciate good art, especially that depicting the sea.'

'Really?' The genuine surprise was evident in her voice. 'Seascapes are my favourite too. I remember once, many years ago, my father took us to Cornwall to visit his old friend. All those rugged sea views, it was bliss!'

They looked at Mr Robson's painting in companionable silence, each caught in their own thoughts, unaware of the other bodies that drifted by. And by the time Kathryn had been returned to Lady Maybury's side she felt quite sure that beneath the rakish exterior of Nicholas Maybury lurked another man altogether: a man who was infinitely likeable.

'I'm sorry that you didn't get to see more of the museum, Miss Marchant.' Lord Ravensmede's voice dropped in volume. 'My grandmother's constitution is not what it was.' He glanced ahead to where Lady Maybury was tottering down the pathway of Montagu House. 'Perhaps we could return another day.'

'That would be most agreeable, my lord.' Kathryn caught up with the dowager just in time to hear her cursing.

'Where the hell is the blasted carriage?'

'Edwards will be walking the horses. He shall arrive presently,' Lord Ravensmede reassured his grandmother.

'Lady Maybury, Lord Ravensmede,' said a coldly polite

voice. And then added, 'And, of course, Kathryn.' Anna
Marchant and her daughter stopped before the Viscount and his
grandmother.

'Aunt Anna, Lottie.' Kathryn inclined her head in greeting.
It had been some weeks since she'd left Green Street and in
all that time she had never once set eyes again on any one of
her relatives. She was surprised at just how easily their
memory had been erased from her life. Now it was as if that
miserable time had never been. Both Marchant women were
immaculately dressed, their golden-blonde curls peeping from
beneath their splendid bonnets. But the perfection of their appearance did little to hide the coolness of their eyes. 'How nice
to see you both again.' It was gratifying to find that her time
with Lady Maybury had not blunted Kathryn's ability to play
a part well.

Unfortunately Anna Marchant was not gifted with such
thespian skills. Her narrow lips pursed to a fine line across her
face, and the fair eyebrows could not quite prevent their involuntary scowl. 'Indeed, dear Kathryn.'

Young Lottie's gaze was having trouble detaching from
Lord Ravensmede's visage. When eventually she managed to
prise it away, it flitted back and forth between the Viscount and
her pauper cousin. 'We're on our way to the dressmaker. Mama
has promised me a new gown for my musical evening and Mrs
Thomas wants one final fitting before it will be complete.'

Mrs Marchant looked pointedly at the familiar old gown in
which her niece was garbed.

A movement from the Viscount drew her attention, as he
stepped forward, partially obscuring her view of Kathryn. 'How
very interesting,' he uttered in a voice that would have curdled
the freshest of milk.

'Dear Kathryn.' Mrs Marchant ignored him and managed to
force a smile to her mouth; it did not extend anywhere near as
far as her eyes. 'What good fortune that we've chanced to meet
like this.'

Lottie's jaw dropped and she stared with puzzlement at her mama.

'We've missed you so, haven't we, Lottie?'

Lottie looked at her mother as if she had run mad.

'Haven't we, Lottie?' said her mother again and pressed a forceful hand to Lottie's arm.

'Yes, of course,' said Lottie.

Kathryn looked from the false geniality on her aunt's face to the perplexity on that of her cousin.

'We wanted to be sure of your attendance at Lottie's musical evening,' said Mrs Marchant.

Lottie positively scowled at her mama.

'Things just wouldn't be the same without you, dear Kathryn. And your uncle would so like to see you again.'

Her uncle had revealed no such inclination at their last meeting, thought Kathryn grimly. Nor did she relish the thought of spending an evening in the house in Green Street. But there seemed to be no way to decline the invitation graciously. 'Thank you, Aunt, I shall enquire of Lady Maybury if it is permissible.' She prayed that her ladyship would judge otherwise.

Mrs Marchant glanced at the dowager. 'I promise we shall take very good care of your companion,' she said with forced jollity.

Lady Maybury's eyes brightened. 'A musical evening, did you say? They are quite my favourite form of entertainment. We shall be happy to come.'

Kathryn's heart sank.

'How delightful,' said Mrs Marchant weakly, and the smile on her face appeared to be suffering under the strain. 'It shall, of course, be the smallest and most modest of affairs.'

Lady Maybury appeared undeterred.

'Then I shall send you a card with all of the details,' Mrs Marchant said. 'And now we really must rush. We cannot keep Mrs Thomas waiting. Please do excuse us.' With one rapid inclination of the head she placed a hand behind Lottie's back and pushed. 'Goodbye, Lady Maybury, Lord

Ravensmede, Kathryn.' And without another word she steered her daughter towards their carriage as fast as she could manage.

Lord Ravensmede raised a cynical eyebrow at his grandparent. 'An interest in musical evenings? I seem to recall that you were afflicted by no such tendency last Season.'

'Fiddlesticks!' declared the old lady. 'Your memory's going, boy. Never missed an invitation to a musical event in m'life.'

'I had not thought you would have included Mrs Marchant in your circle.' His lordship's voice never normally betrayed emotion. But on this occasion Kathryn thought she could detect the subtle undertone of disapproval.

One faded eye glittered rather threateningly in Ravensmede's direction. 'Would you have Kathryn go without me? I have a notion to hear the chit sing, nothing more.' Then fatigue showed in her face. 'Take us home, Nick. I must have my nap in preparation for tonight's outing and time is getting on.'

Anna Marchant was up to something, Ravensmede was certain. Why should the woman suddenly be so eager for Kathryn's attendance…and seemingly on her own? The invitation had been issued to Kathryn alone. His grandmother had taken the liberty of inviting herself. Mrs Marchant's lack of enthusiasm for Lady Maybury's presence had not escaped his attention. For the rest of the day Ravensmede found himself to be pondering the question. It was the foremost matter in his mind as he dispatched the note to Cadmount. He had still not resolved the issue when a footman announced Lord Cadmount's carriage. Five minutes later the two men were *en route* to Haymarket.

It did not take long for Cadmount to become aware that his friend's attention was otherwise engaged. Conversation was scant for the duration of the journey. Cadmount had his suspicions as to the cause of Ravensmede's somewhat brooding mood, but knew better than to test them at that precise moment. It was only when they had seated themselves within the auditorium that Lord Cadmount understood Ravensmede's sudden urge to attend the opera this evening.

'Isn't that your grandmother with li'l Miss Marchant over there?' The fair brows indicated the direction of the sky-blue box not so very far from Cadmount's own.

'It appears you may be right,' drawled Ravensmede. 'Shall we…?' He did not wait for the answer, but was up and threading his way through the crowds with leisurely determination.

'Lord Ravensmede.' Kathryn could not prevent the sudden gallop of her heart.

'So you decided to join us,' said Lady Maybury quite matter of factly. 'Lord Cadmount.' The snowy white head dipped, sending the deep red plumes balanced thereon into a frenzy.

'Your servant, ma'am,' said Lord Cadmount and bowed. 'You look as exquisite as ever, dear lady.'

'Flatterer!' shrieked her ladyship, but she smiled and fanned herself all the same.

Kathryn tried hard to keep a straight face. It appeared that Lady Maybury had rather a soft spot for her grandson's friend. Her eyes flitted once more to Lord Ravensmede, who was looking devilishly handsome. 'You made no mention, sir, that you planned to attend tonight.'

'No, I did not.' His gaze held hers for a moment longer, raising in Kathryn the peculiar tension she had felt before when he had held her in his arms or pressed his lips to hers. She looked away, unwilling to allow such feelings to resurface.

For the rest of the evening nothing in Lord Ravensmede's manner or speech was anything but formally polite, but she could not dispel the odd sensation that he was, by his very presence, lending her his protection, and not at all in the scandalous way he had once suggested. And when, at the end of the evening, Ravensmede and Cadmount assisted Lady Maybury and herself to her ladyship's carriage, Kathryn was surprised to find that she did not wish to say goodbye.

* * *

The next day Kathryn entered the breakfast room to find a parcel and a small box sitting on the breakfast table.

Her ladyship barely raised her eyes from *The Times*. 'Could they print this confounded news any smaller? I can't see a damn thing!' she complained.

'Would you like me to read to you?' Kathryn knew how her ladyship hated to admit just how much her eyesight had deteriorated. It was their usual routine, Kathryn reading aloud, the dowager interrupting with comments, both learning the news of the day, both discussing their subsequent views and opinions. 'I'm sorry I'm late, my lady. I overslept a little. I hope I haven't kept you waiting long.'

For morning time Lady Maybury appeared to be in an unusually good mood. 'It's of little consequence. My stomach can't be kept waiting for breakfast and I knew you would arrive shortly.' She helped herself to another chop and a couple of devilled kidneys. 'Couldn't sleep then, gel?'

Kathryn lifted the coffee pot. 'No. I slept like a top,' she lied. 'I can't think why I didn't waken. It must have been all the excitement of yesterday.' She most certainly was not about to admit that she had lain awake half the night thinking about the lady's grandson.

'What excitement?' asked Lady Maybury between mouthfuls of kidney.

'Why, our visits to the painting exhibition and the museum, and, of course, the opera.'

Lady Maybury smiled. After a few minutes in which Kathryn sipped her coffee and ate some eggs, the elderly voice asked, 'Aren't you going to open them?'

'Open them?' Kathryn asked, rather unsure of herself, and her eyes drifted to the packages sitting across the table.

'It is your birthday, is it not?'

Kathryn let out an exclamation of surprise. 'Yes, but how did you know?'

'We Mayburys have our ways.' The old lady smiled, and pushed the small dark box towards Kathryn. 'A small token of my affection, gel.'

Kathryn stared at the box, her hand touched to her lips.

'Open it.'

The box was shallow and rectangular in shape, with an external covering of blue chinoiserie painted silk. Inside, on a lining of plain white silk, lay a strand of ivory pearls and two matching single-pearl drop earrings. Kathryn gasped. 'They're beautiful!'

Lady Maybury's smile broadened. 'Happy birthday, Kathryn.'

'I…' The words faltered and then she was up out of her seat and throwing her arms around the dowager. 'Thank you,' she whispered in a voice thick with emotion, 'it is a long time since anyone remembered my birthday, and never with such a truly lovely gift.'

Lady Maybury patted Kathryn's hand. 'I'm glad that you like them. Now, open your other present.'

Still standing, Kathryn looked at the large parcel on the table.

'Hurry up, then. My curiosity's getting the better of me.' Lady Maybury resumed her attack on her breakfast. 'When one gets to my age one's family take steps to curtail all excitement. It has the effect of making some ladies, not to put too fine a point on it, overly inquisitive.' One ancient hand removed itself from the cutlery for long enough to push the parcel further in Kathryn's direction.

The brown paper crinkled beneath her fingers as she picked at the knots in the string.

'For heaven's sake, gel,' huffed her ladyship, and, extracting a small, finely crafted pair of scissors from a pocket in her dress, she reached across and snipped the string. 'You'll be there all day with those knots. No point in wasting time.' Lady Maybury attacked her chop once more, but her eyes were trained firmly on the parcel.

Kathryn peeled back the wrapping to reveal a wooden box

filled with the brightest range of water-colour pans. Inserted in cunningly designed compartments within the set were small pots for holding water and a narrow drawer containing the finest sable brushes. 'It's wonderful!' Her fingers traced the contours of each and every part, touching with a care that suggested reverence.

'What's that beneath it?' A silver fork stabbed towards the paintbox.

With the box positioned carefully on the tablecloth, Kathryn saw that the parcel also contained a pad of cut paper sheets and a box of sketching pencils. 'Who on earth could have sent me…?' The letter was folded in half and lay at the bottom of the pile. Even before she read the words her heart leapt, for there at the top of the paper was the Viscount of Ravensmede's crest. Fingers fluttered to her cheek as her eyes skimmed the boldly penned script.

Her ladyship laid down her cutlery upon the emptied plate, dabbed a napkin to her lips, and emitted a small burp. 'Do you like m'grandson's gift?'

Kathryn's emotions were in quite a flurry. Abruptly she found her chair, and stared at the pile of art materials before her. 'It's…exquisite! But…' She plucked distractedly at the apron of her dress before running her fingers across the beech paintbox. The clear grey eyes raised to the dowager's. 'I can't accept it.'

'Why ever not?'

'It's not that I'm not grateful, because, of course, I am. It's just…well… not quite appropriate that I receive a gift from a…' She couldn't very well describe Ravensmede as a rake to his own grandmother, so she searched frantically for a suitable word, and found one: '…man.'

'Man!' Lady Maybury's tone cast the word in derision. A cackle rent the air as she seemed to find Kathryn's statement of extreme comic value. When she had stopped laughing long enough to speak, her ladyship helped herself to more coffee and said, 'I thought the fact he's reputed to be one of London's most notorious rake-hells might have influenced you more.'

Kathryn balked at the lady's words and flushed with embarrassment. It seemed that nothing similar affected Lady Maybury's sensibilities.

'It's all a load of stuff and nonsense, of course. Rebelling against his father's hand and the like. Wanted to fight for his country. Tried to buy himself a commission. Charles, m'son, soon put paid to that. The two of them have been at loggerheads ever since. Nick's not cut out to be a rake and a wastrel. He's just bored; there's nothing and no one to tax his mind. Never had a real challenge in his life, errant puppy that he is. Things have fallen too easily into his lap all along.' The distant look in her eyes faded. 'For all of his reputation, Kathryn, I'm certain that, in this at least, Nick is well intentioned. It is a birthday gift, nothing more. I see no impropriety. My advice to you, gel, is to accept the art materials with grace. Besides, I enjoy watching others paint. It soothes m'nerves.'

In all the time Kathryn had known the dowager she had seen no evidence to suggest that the old lady was afflicted with anything that could be remotely described as a nervous condition. The paintbox was very beautiful. She cast a longing look at it.

'So you'll paint for me this afternoon,' coaxed Lady Maybury.

Using the water-colours and brushes and paper that Lord Ravensmede had bought for her? His letter wishing her birthday greetings was still clutched between her fingers. She folded it and placed it on the table. 'Yes, my lady, of course I will.'

A week later Lord Ravensmede was standing in the library of his grandmother's rented townhouse, browsing through the water-colour studies that lay upon the table. The assortment mainly consisted of still-life studies, carefully contrived arrangements of flowers and fruits. All were of a good artistic standard, but what really caught his eye was the single sheet at the very bottom of the pile. Kathryn Marchant had captured every aspect of his grandmother's personality in those few brush strokes. The intelligence and perception within that gaze, the kindness and loyalty beneath that harsh façade, and, most tenderly of all, the hint of vulnerability in the grand demeanour. It was something that Ravensmede guessed few others besides himself had ever glimpsed. It was not a posed portrait of rigid formality, but a natural moment frozen in time. His grandmother looked as if she were watching Kathryn, but without the consciousness so usual in those sitting for a portrait. Ravensmede found it hard to draw his eyes away. A noise at his back signalled Lady Maybury's entry.

'Quite the little artist, isn't she, Nick?' Then, without waiting for an answer, she continued, 'I didn't know my face was so revealing. Seems that our Kathryn has a very real talent when it comes to portraits. Unlike most, she can look beneath the veneer we present to the world.'

Our Kathryn… The expression hit Ravensmede like a bolt from the blue. *Our Kathryn…* It seemed so right that she was one of them, a part of their family. Aware of his grandmother's scrutiny, he shook the thought from his head and looked directly at her. 'Grandmama…you do know what you're about with Anna Marchant tonight, don't you?'

'Of course,' she said. 'Thought I would send her into that viper's nest on her own, did you?'

'No, I thought that you might find an excuse that Kathryn need not endure such a farce,' he said wryly.

The old lady chuckled. 'Doubting your old grandam's wisdom, Nick?' She caught his large hand and held it sandwiched between her own. 'Kathryn's attendance this evening will put paid to any suggestion that all is not well between her and her relatives. We do not want any gossip arising over either that or the haste of her move to Upper Grosvenor Street.'

'Indeed not,' said Ravensmede. 'But Anna Marchant seemed too eager that Kathryn attend Lottie's musical. Given the fact that the woman can barely conceal her dislike for her niece, I wonder why that might be.'

'As I said, it would be commented upon if Kathryn were not present. And the Marchant woman is determined to curry favour with the *ton*.'

'Maybe,' said her grandson, 'but I have the feeling there is more to Mrs Marchant's invitation than meets the eye.' His lips curved in a mocking smile. 'I fancy that I too have a notion to hear the chit sing.'

A voice floated in from the hall.

'That will be Kathryn.' The dowager drew him a strange little look. 'The aim is to stamp out gossip, not start it. Is your presence really necessary?'

'Absolutely,' answered her grandson.

The two moved towards the door.

Kathryn's sense of dread that had fast been escalating over the past week had reached a pinnacle. No matter how many times she told herself that she was being foolish, no matter how much she insisted that Aunt Anna would never behave with anything other than congeniality before the dowager, Kathryn could not rid herself of the fear. She did not want to set one foot back in the house in Green Street. Even just thinking about the place brought a cold nausea to her stomach. The memory of the three long years that she had lived there would not be easily erased. It was one thing meeting Aunt Anna out in the street, quite another venturing back into her aunt's own domain—where all the power was, and always had been, in Mrs Marchant's hands. Nothing bad could happen, not in Lady Maybury's presence, or so Kathryn reassured herself. But despite all of her efforts, she could not quell her mounting apprehension. It was therefore with a considerable amount of relief that Kathryn descended the staircase of the dowager's house to discover that Lord Ravensmede had every intention of accompanying his grandmother and her companion to Miss Lottie Marchant's musical evening.

* * *

'Kathryn...and Lady Maybury,' gushed Anna Marchant with a sickly smile plastered across her face. 'So pleased that you could both make it to our little gathering.' The ladies were in the middle of their devoirs when Mrs Marchant spotted the tall dark presence by the doorway. 'Lord Ravensmede!' It was all she could do to prevent the smile slipping from her face. 'What a pleasant surprise.'

'Mrs Marchant,' he said lazily, and watched her through narrowed eyes while she led them across the room to where Lady Finlay was chatting with Lottie.

'Lottie dearest, look, some more guests have arrived to hear you sing. Cousin Kathryn, Lady Maybury, and...and Lord Ravensmede.' Anna Marchant looked up to see his lordship smile. It was something that bore a startling resemblance to one of the great black wild cats in the royal menagerie, being unaccountably menacing. The Viscount's eyes held the suggestion of a threat.

Lady Finlay stared short-sightedly at Kathryn. 'I can't say that I remember meeting you before, Miss Marchant.' She peered long and hard. 'Have we been introduced?'

Kathryn raised her chin a notch and endured the scrutiny. 'No, indeed, my lady, I don't believe I've had the pleasure.'

'My cousin was present at your recent ball as my companion, but that was before she was persuaded into Lady Maybury's establishment.' The words were innocent enough, but no one present was in any doubt as to the intention behind them. Charlotte Marchant intended to set her cousin firmly back in her place.

'Indeed,' drawled Lord Ravensmede from Kathryn's side. He looked at Lottie with an air of utter boredom. 'My grandmother insisted that Miss Marchant is such delightful company that she simply would not hear of anyone else as her companion.'

Kathryn felt her hand being tucked into Lady Maybury's arm. 'Such a lovely gel,' said the dowager.

With such overt championing, who would dare to stand against it? Certainly not Lady Finlay. Especially when Lady

Maybury leaned forward and hissed in her loudest stage whisper, 'Her mother was one of the Overton Thornleys.' The snowy white curls nodded knowingly.

Anna Marchant looked as if she would have liked to throttle the dear old dowager there and then. 'Ah, here is Mr Dalton. Now we can all take our seats for tonight's entertainment. I'm sure that no one will be disappointed with my darling girl's performance.'

'I'm sure that young Lettie will not let you down,' said Lady Maybury.

Lottie's baby-blue eyes squinted in displeasure and she looked demandingly at her mama.

'Lottie,' said Mrs Marchant with emphasis.

The dowager's smile contained all the warmth of a hooded cobra. 'Yes, indeed, dear little Lettie. Let us hope she's as talented as her cousin.'

'Her name is Charlotte, which the family shorten to *Lottie*.' Anna Marchant positively snapped the sharp retort.

Aristocratic cheeks were sucked in all round and a knowing look passed between the ladies of the group as they ambled to take their seats in Mrs Marchant's drawing room.

Kathryn found herself seated between Lord Ravensmede and Lady Maybury in the row of chairs furthest back in the room. His lordship sat closest to the door, as if he hoped to make a quick escape should Lottie's musical ability prove not to his taste. Kathryn hoped fervently that he would not leave. Just his presence made her feel safer, allaying the worst of her fears regarding her aunt and the house in Green Street.

She sneaked a look up at him through downcast lashes. He was relaxed in the chair, as if he had not a care in the world, long legs stretched out before him, dark hair worn fashionably short, and an expression of bored indifference upon his face. His attire was immaculate as usual. A deep blue tail-coat, above which showed a white high-pointed collar and a snow-white

neckcloth tied in a simple but stylish knot. Her eyes slid lower
to where one hand rested on his thigh. A light sprinkling of dark
hair showed on the back of the hand. His nails were short and
clean, his skin a light honey coloration. It looked to be a strong
squarish hand; a hand used to taking what it wanted, and one
that Kathryn knew was capable of the most tender caress. Her
abdomen gave a little flutter and she swiftly moved her eyes
on from his hand to the thigh beneath it. That did not help
matters. Not when the thigh, encased in tight buff-coloured
buckskin, was so long and muscular, and the front of his coat
was so very short. Her cheeks grew warm and she quickly
raised her gaze to find herself staring directly into his eyes.
Something warm quivered deep inside her. He smiled, and the
quiver became a somersault.

'Are you comfortable enough, Miss Marchant?' There was
something in his look that made her think that he had more than
an inkling of her thoughts.

'Yes, thank you, my lord, quite comfortable.' She nodded
and glanced away, unwilling to let him see just how much he
affected her.

Fortuitously Mr Dalton sounded the first notes upon the
piano and then Lottie began to sing, and Kathryn was saved
from any further embarrassment.

Chapter Nine

Lottie had just finished her third rendition to rapturous applause when Anna Marchant threaded her way quietly to the back of the drawing room, to stand beside the Viscount of Ravensmede's chair. She ignored Ravensmede, smiled sweetly at his grandmother and leaned towards Kathryn. 'Dearest niece,' she whispered, 'may I have a minute of your time?'

Kathryn's heart began to thud within her chest and a certain uneasiness started to squirm within. A sense of foreboding rippled down her spine. For one awful moment she was seized by the sudden overwhelming desire to just run through the door and keep on running—far away from Aunt Anna and this house. Her eyes flickered towards the door longingly. And then common sense prevailed. Kathryn knew very well that there was no way out. She could not refuse to speak to her aunt. So she took a deep breath, looked at the dowager, and said quietly, 'Please excuse me, my lady.' Then she nodded and rose to follow Mrs Marchant.

Ravensmede stood to let her leave. As she squeezed past she heard the silk of her skirt slide against his legs, and smelled the clean citrus scent of him. She looked up to read the unspoken question of concern in his eyes, and tried to hide the fear in her own. Then she had passed him and was following Aunt Anna across the floor and out of the drawing room.

Anna Marchant waited until Kathryn was seated in the small room before closing the door behind her. The click of the latch echoed in the silence.

Kathryn recognised it as her aunt and uncle's own personal parlour. It was much smaller than the drawing room and nowhere near as ornate. The décor was a cool combination of duck-egg blue and pale grey, with no hint of warmth or welcome. A small pile of tinder, sticks and coal dross had been set up within the hearth in readiness for a fire. The temperature of the evening outside meant it had not been lit; the chill in the parlour suggested that it should have. Kathryn suppressed a shiver. Nothing of the summer warmth pervaded the little room. The light of the candles in the wall sconces flickered within the gloom. She noticed that the heavy blue curtains had been pulled to shut out the daylight. Everything about the place felt dim and dank and claustrophobic. Her fingers smoothed nervously over the silk of her skirt. 'You wished to speak to me, Aunt?'

'Yes.' Mrs Marchant took the chair between Kathryn and the door. Now that they were alone all pretence of amiability had disappeared. Her eyes were a cold hard blue; her lips pursed to a thin, narrow line. 'I wish to know exactly how matters are between you and Lady Maybury.'

Distrust tutored Kathryn's words. 'Why, they are very well indeed. Lady Maybury is both kind and thoughtful. I could not ask for more.' She waited to see what this game was about.

'And how fares the child?'

'The child?' Kathryn stared at her aunt.

'The child that necessitated such a sudden and immediate move to Ravensmede House.'

Kathryn's fingers pleated the violet silk of her skirt between them. 'Lady Maybury's house is in Upper Grosvenor Street,' she said carefully. 'Maggie, the little girl who was involved in the carriage accident, is recovered and back living with her family.'

'How fortuitous.'

Kathryn said nothing. A horrible suspicion was forming.

'Does Lord Ravensmede spend much time visiting Upper Grosvenor Street?'

'No.' The violet silk twisted tighter in her hands.

'But I've heard he's inordinately fond of his grandmother.'

Kathryn could guess where this was leading. Perspiration beaded cold upon her skin. 'We're missing Lottie's singing.'

'So we are.' Anna Marchant smiled a vicious little smile. 'Then I had best come straight to the point, hadn't I?' The faint strains of music and a high pitched melodic voice drifted through the barrier of the door. 'Certain rumours have come to my ears, Kathryn, rumours involving you and some very improper behaviour.'

The blood rushed in Kathryn's ears. She felt the tripping of her heart. Her eyes widened in shock.

'If you are intent on destroying your reputation then I have a right to know exactly what you are up to.'

Kathryn rose from her chair, her cheeks scalded with embarrassment and anger. 'How could you say such a thing? Any rumours to which you may have listened are false.'

'Don't give me that, you little bitch,' snapped her aunt. 'I know that you're lying; it's written all over your face.'

'I think I should return to Lady Maybury now,' said Kathryn with a great deal more control than she felt.

'Oh, no, I haven't finished with you yet, miss.'

Kathryn hid her growing fear and made to move towards the door, only to find her way blocked by her aunt.

'You're going nowhere until you tell me exactly what's been going on.'

'Aunt Anna—'

'Don't "Aunt Anna" me! You leave here with Ravensmede and his grandmother on the premise of going for a drive in Hyde Park, and the next minute you're installed in the old woman's house as her companion, without so much as a by your leave. The first that your uncle knows of it is a letter from Ravensmede!' Mrs Marchant advanced towards her niece.

Kathryn instinctively backed away.

'Do you think I know nothing of his reputation?' The older woman's mouth twisted to a snarl.

'The child's leg was injured in her fall, and Lady Maybury was in need of immediate assistance,' said Kathryn with force.

'And what of Ravensmede?'

'He could not be expected to look after a four-year-old girl.'

'But he could look after you, miss, very well indeed.'

Kathryn stiffened at the insult. 'You malign both his lordship and me!' She thrust aside the memory of just exactly what she and the Viscount had shared.

Mrs Marchant stepped closer. 'He's the only man to have shown an interest in you, though God knows why he should have taken notice of so plain a creature. And why else would her ladyship have taken you up? It stands to reason, if you're indulging Ravensmede's interest.'

'Lady Maybury would never stoop to such a scandal. Her reputation is beyond reproach.' The eyes that were normally a clear pale grey became dark and stormy.

'Lucky for us all,' said Anna Marchant, 'else your reputation would be in tatters, miss.' She took another step towards her niece.

Kathryn felt the press of the wall against her back. 'My reputation is unblemished.' A sliver of guilt stuck in her throat.

Mrs Marchant stepped closer still. 'That's not what I've heard, and I mean to have the truth from you, you selfish little trollop. You have no thought in your head for anyone other than yourself.'

Kathryn scanned the room for an escape route, but the only way out was the same way through which she had entered.

'If you cast your reputation to the gutter then what of Lottie? Innocent of all blame, yet she'll suffer just the same.'

'Aunt, you're mistaken—'

Anna Marchant's hands closed hard around the tops of Kathryn's arms. 'Tell me what you've been up to, girl, or, so help me, I'll have the truth from you one way or another!'

'Leave me be!' Kathryn struggled to free herself, but her aunt was much larger and stronger.

'Tell me!' Anna Marchant said again and tightened her grip.

Kathryn's ordeal went no further: the door of the parlour swung open.

Anna Marchant spun to face the intruder, her hands dropping to her sides.

'Mrs Marchant,' said the man's voice, but for all its drawl there was in it an unmistakable flint-like quality.

Anna Marchant flushed to the roots of her golden hair. 'Lord Ravensmede,' she said, unsure of quite how much the Viscount had seen or indeed heard.

His expression was one of cold contempt and every line of his face held the promise of retribution. Mrs Marchant surreptitiously backed away towards the corner of the room.

His gaze slid to Kathryn who still stood, as if pinioned, against the wall. Her face had drained to a powder white. 'Miss Marchant, my grandmother has need of you.' The words were innocent enough, but the tone was loaded with danger. 'You appear to be somewhat distressed. Has someone upset you?' His focus drifted questioningly towards Anna Marchant, and the colour of the woman's cheeks darkened to a deep puce.

Kathryn's hands kneaded at the violet silk. 'No!' she almost shouted, then more calmly, as if regaining control of her emotions, 'No, I am quite well, thank you, my lord. I was just about to return to the drawing room.'

'As I'm sure is Mrs Marchant,' he said smoothly, and waited for the golden-haired woman to cross the floor before them. Anna Marchant did not look back. Only then did he place a supportive hand on the small of Kathryn's back and guide her in her aunt's wake. Lottie was still singing as they quietly settled back into their seats. No one commented on the ladies' short absence.

Kathryn never knew how she made it through the rest of that evening. Certainly the knowledge that Lord Ravensmede was never far from her side gave her strength. She could hazard a very good guess at what would have happened within that horrible little room had he not interrupted. A nausea was rising in her stomach and she longed for nothing more than to flee from the house in Green Street. One look at Lady Maybury's face told her that was not possible. The dowager seemed to be in her element, relaying stories of Kathryn's artistic abilities, introducing her new companion to all and sundry, ensuring that everyone knew just who Kathryn Marchant's mother had been. Through it all Kathryn endured with a smile, a murmur of the right response, and an interested expression as the most trivial of stories were told; and all the while she was conscious of the Viscount standing so very close by, guarding her with his presence.

Strangely enough, at the end of the evening it was not Lottie's musical achievements that were talked of by all the best people. Rather, the sudden emergence of the quietly refined Miss Kathryn Marchant, with her water-colour talents, held that coveted spot, thanks to Lady Maybury.

Anna Marchant had some inkling of the matter and it did not please her. 'It was a mistake to invite your cousin,' she conceded to her daughter in the few quiet minutes they had alone. 'I learned nothing, and, because of that battleaxe dowager, Kathryn has managed to steal your thunder.' She flicked a gaze at her daughter. 'For heaven's sake, don't you dare start crying. Do you want them talking of your hideous red blotchy face instead of tonight's performance?'

Lottie's pouted lips trembled, but she swallowed back the tears that threatened to fall. 'I saw you take her out of the drawing room. And then Lord Ravensmede went and fetched you both back.'

'Interfering villain! I fancy that I must be right in my supposition.'

'Mama?' Lottie's still-watery eyes opened wide and round in bewilderment. 'I don't understand.'

'No, you never do.'

Lottie's lips began to quiver again. 'But that mean cat has ruined my evening.'

'She could ruin a whole lot more than that,' said her mother ominously.

Fortunately the comment was lost upon Lottie, who continued unabated with her complaining. 'Only see how Mr Dalton is looking at her, I'm sure he means to offer for her instead of me. Oh, I shall never forgive her if he does. How I wish she was living back here, then you could box her ears and none of this would ever have happened.' Lottie's voice whined close to hysteria.

'Calm yourself.' Her mother moved a blonde ringlet from across Lottie's cheek. 'Unlike you, my darling, your cousin is a nobody.'

'But Lady Maybury said Kathryn's mother was one of the Overton Thornleys, and everyone was much impressed,' she snuffled.

'Elizabeth Thornley was a strumpet and her family disowned her. The Overton Thornleys wanted nothing more to do with her or her children. Why else do you think we were forced to take Kathryn into our home? Just because Lady Maybury has her in favour does not alter that fact. It was not so long ago that Kathryn was scrubbing floors and washing your linen. Hold that memory close. She may have tried to steal this evening from you, but I don't mean to just stand by and watch that little bitch get away with it, or anything else for that matter, my dear. No. Cousin Kathryn may find she has a little surprise coming to her.' Mrs Marchant's hand turned to stroke her daughter's bright golden locks. 'Just you trust your mama, Lottie. I shall see that Kathryn gets her due, be very assured of that.'

'Such a delightful evening, thank you, Nick. You may call on us tomorrow,' said the dowager when Ravensmede's town-coach halted outside her house in Upper Grosvenor Street.

'I'd rather call on you now.' Lord Ravensmede's eyes flickered towards Kathryn before returning his grandmother's gaze.

'As you will,' she said.

Only once they were all seated within the dowager's drawing room did she speak again. 'Kathryn, my dear, could you go and fetch me a suitably interesting book from the library? I've a mind to hear you read a little before I go to bed—that is, if you're not too tired.'

'Certainly, my lady.'

Lady Maybury waited until the door closed behind Kathryn before turning to her grandson. 'Well, out with it. I take it you want to tell me what went on between Kathryn and her aunt.'

Ravensmede didn't even comment upon his grandparent's bluntness. 'Anna Marchant had her pinned against a wall and was threatening her when I found them.'

'Good gad! Little wonder the gel looked powder white when you brought her back through.'

Ravensmede looked directly at his grandmother. 'I need to talk to her…alone.'

A white eyebrow arched high.

'I would know exactly what Mrs Marchant was up to this evening.'

The faded green eyes held his. 'You know that I should not allow it,' she said quietly.

'And you know I would not ask were it not so important.'

They looked at each other for a moment longer.

'Very well,' Lady Maybury uttered at last. 'I need not say the rest.'

Ravensmede nodded, and dropped a kiss to the lined velvet cheek. 'Thank you.'

When Kathryn returned to the drawing room, complete with book in hand, it was to find Lord Ravensmede standing by the unlit fireplace. Of Lady Maybury there was no sign.

She hesitated halfway across the rug, as if a little unsure of herself. 'My lord…where is Lady Maybury?'

Ravensmede saw the pallor of her cheeks and the signs of fatigue around her eyes. 'Sit down, Kathryn.'

'I think she'll like this one.' She gestured to the small leather-bound book gripped within her hand. 'It's a collection of works by Lord Byron.'

He said nothing, just waited for her to sit down upon the sofa.

'Perhaps I should check if she needs my assistance.'

'Kathryn...' and the word sounded like a sigh on his lips '...my grandmother has retired for the night. I want to speak with you before I leave.'

Her eyes widened. 'I do not think that's a good idea, my lord.'

He shrugged. 'I disagree.'

She was still wearing the violet-and-cream evening dress. He noted how well the colour became her, how enticingly it fitted around her small bosom. The neckline was plain, the violet silk a fine contrast to the exposed smooth white curves of the tops of her breasts that rose and fell at such regular intervals. Suddenly conscious that he was staring, he dropped his gaze lower to where her fingers plucked at her skirt. He knew then the level of her unease. 'You need not be afraid, Kathryn. I only wish to speak to you.'

'What do you wish to discuss?' A note of caution sounded in her voice.

'That which happened this evening at your aunt's.'

Her fingers tightened around the violet material. She swallowed. 'There is nothing to say about that, sir.'

'Oh, but I think there is, Kathryn.' He watched a hint of panic flit across her face.

Silence stretched between them.

'Kathryn.' The word acted as a prompt, as he knew it would.

'We...we had a disagreement, that's all.' Her focus shifted away to study the pattern on the rug.'

'Then it must have been a very heated disagreement; she had you against the wall when I walked in.'

'She was merely making her point, rather forcibly.'

'She was threatening you,' he said succinctly.

'No…she was just—'

'Damnation, Kathryn, why are you trying to protect her?'

She glanced up at him then and he caught a glimpse of guilt and embarrassment in her eyes, before her gaze skittered away again. 'I-I'm not.'

'Then you're hiding something from me.'

'No!' The denial did not ring true, and he knew it.

The violet silk was suffering a thorough pulverisation beneath her fingers.

He leaned back against the mantel, rested his booted foot upon the fender, and watched her. 'Your lying does not improve with practice.'

She rose swiftly from the sofa. 'It's late, Lord Ravensmede, and I have much to do tomorrow. Please excuse me, sir.'

He pushed off from the fender and moved swiftly to stand before her. 'No.'

Indignation stared from the silver eyes. 'I beg your pardon,' she said stiffly. 'It's not seemly that we're here, alone, at this time of night.'

Exasperation rose in Ravensmede's throat. 'It's not seemly that you're lying to me,' he growled.

'Lord Ravensmede,' she said primly.

'Miss Marchant,' he countered.

She made to turn towards the door.

'I did not excuse you.' He saw the slight body stiffen. Felt a scoundrel for what he was doing. Knew he must do it for Kathryn's own sake.

'I can stand here all night, my lord, and there will still be nothing more to say.'

One step, and the distance between them disappeared. 'Tell me,' he said roughly. His hand closed around her arm. He felt her start beneath him, try to pull away. She looked up at him, fear blazoning in her eyes. Shock kicked in his gut at the realisation of just what she thought. 'I'm not going to hurt you!' One by one he uncurled his fingers so that she was free. 'God help me, I could *never* hurt you.' They were standing so close that the hem of her skirt brushed the gleaming toes of his long black riding boots; so close that he could hear the whisper of her breath and smell her sweet scent. 'Don't you know that by now?'

Her eyelids fluttered shut.

Next to him she was so small, so slender. It pained him that she believed he could have struck her. 'Forgive me if I frightened you, Kathryn.'

There was a catch of breath in her throat and then those beautiful eyes raised to his once more. 'I'm sorry,' she said, and her, words were so quiet as to scarcely catch his ears. 'I didn't mean to…'

'Hush.' With great tenderness he cupped one hand against her cheek and stroked a delicate caress across the silken skin. It seemed that there was a great stillness within him and a peculiar ache across his chest. It was a novel sensation for Ravensmede. Beneath his fingers her skin was warm and smooth. And her eyes clung to his like a woman drowning. She made him feel both powerless and omnipotent at the same time. 'You need not tell me if you really do not wish to. I sought only to save you from the worst of your aunt.' For all that he wanted to help her, he could not bear her pain.

Her eyes shuttered. 'Oh, Nicholas,' she sighed. 'You, of all people, cannot.'

He touched his lips against her forehead, not kissing, just resting them there, trying desperately to give her some small comfort.

'Aunt Anna said…'

He pulled back, rested his hands loosely, lightly, against her shoulders, and watched the hint of a blush stain those pale cheeks. Kathryn would not meet his gaze. 'What did she say?' he asked as gently as he could.

A deep breath. A tremor of tension beneath his palms. 'She said that there were rumours.'

There was a sudden coldness in the pit of his stomach.

'She implied that I…that we…' Her hand moved to worry at her skirt. But his moved faster, catching her fingers back up and threading them through his own. 'That we?'

'That we have behaved improperly.'

Only the ticking of the clock on the mantel punctuated the silence in the room.

'She wanted to question me on the matter.'

'I see,' said Ravensmede. His fingers pressed a gentle reassurance against hers. He controlled the anger rising within him, didn't want to distress Kathryn any more than she was already.

'And she's right, isn't she?' said Kathryn quietly. 'We haven't behaved as we should.'

'Perhaps I haven't behaved entirely as I should, but you've done nothing wrong.'

Her chin came up and she squared her shoulders. 'I'm every bit as guilty as you, Nicholas. I wasn't unwilling.' Colour flared in her cheeks.

His blood quickened at her bold admission, and his heart gladdened that she was not indifferent to him. 'Your aunt can know nothing for certain; she's fishing for trouble.' But even as he said the words, Ravensmede thought of someone who most definitely knew enough to destroy Kathryn's reputation. The fact that he had parted with a hefty sum to buy the woman's silence did not make him feel any easier. Amanda White's discretion could not to be entirely trusted. He could only be thankful that she had been persuaded to leave London for a while.

Kathryn sighed. 'I only hope that you're right.'

How could he reassure her? He traced his thumb against the inside of her wrist, slowly, intimately. 'We shared a few kisses, Kathryn, nothing more. There's nothing so very wrong in that.' A few kisses…it sounded so innocent, but Ravensmede knew better. Kathryn Marchant's kisses were fit to overwhelm a man's mind. One taste of her lips was enough to snare a fellow for life. And even had that not been the case, even if her mouth had been hard and dry and unyielding so that he never touched her again, he had already done enough to sully her name if the truth were to come out. He thrust the thought aside. 'You said yourself it will not happen again...and now we are just friends.' It was what she wanted, what she *needed,* to hear; or so he told himself.

Hurt flashed in her eyes, and then was gone so quickly that he thought he must have been mistaken. She stared down at her feet.

He squeezed her hands in what he hoped was an encouraging manner; struggled to ignore the smell of her perfume drifting up from her hair, and the tantalising touch of her fingers still entwined within his own. Ruthlessly he quelled the desire to wrap his arms around her and crush her to him. Loosening his hand, he took her chin between his fingers and gently raised her face so that he could look into her eyes. 'I look after my friends, Kathryn,' he said slowly. 'I won't allow Mrs Marchant to hurt you again.'

She nodded. 'Thank you,' she said softly.

He could resist no more. Sliding his arms round her back, he pulled her into his embrace, and then just held her, with the softness of her curves pressed against him, and the smell of her filling his nose. She made no protest, just clung to him as he clung to her, her breath warm and moist against his chest. He dropped his lips to rest against the top of her head. And they stood there, as if they would merge together as one for all eternity.

In the days that followed Miss Lottie Marchant's musical evening Kathryn heard nothing more from her aunt. It seemed that Ravensmede had been right in his assertion that Mrs Marchant had been untruthful about the existence of injurious rumours, for, from the very next day following the event, it became clear that Kathryn had been taken into the bosom of the *ton.* Invitations to balls and routs and parties arrived at the house in Upper Grosvenor Street by the score, and all were extended to both Lady Maybury and her companion.

For the first time in her life people looked *at* Kathryn instead

of *through* her. There was definitely no danger of her being
ignored. People who had previously not deigned to notice her
were suddenly keen to be seen chatting with Lady Maybury's
protégé. She lost count of the number of requests she received
from people asking her to paint their portraits. And a number
of gentlemen took to calling in the hope of fixing Miss Marchant's attention. It was akin to the past fantasies played out in
her head, unreal in every aspect except that when she opened
her eyes it did not vanish. Kathryn should have been happy, and,
indeed, she was content of sorts. But something was missing,
and that something left an emptiness within.

Since that night when he had held her so tenderly in Lady
Maybury's drawing room, Lord Ravensmede had been careful
to avoid being alone in her company. He was a model of polite
consideration. Indeed, Kathryn would have gone as far as to
describe him as the very epitome of gentlemanly behaviour. But
there was a new distance between them, as if he had withdrawn from her. It was the right thing to do, the proper thing
to do. Especially for a viscount to his grandmother's companion. So why did she feel a constant ache in her heart?

We shared a few kisses, he had said, *nothing more*. Was that
all it had been to him? Didn't he too feel that the world had
turned upside down? Clearly not. But then he was a rake.
Everyone said it. A man who was used to taking what he wanted
from women and moving on. Just the thought of that was
enough to turn her blood cold. She should be glad that he was
behaving with the utmost respectability. And then she remembered the dark smoulder in his eyes when he kissed her, the
gentle insistence of his lips upon her, and the tenderness of his
touch…and she knew that against all rhyme and reason, what
she really wanted from Nicholas Maybury was not in the least
respectable.

'Oh, it has been an age since I was in Brighthelmstone. Such
a good idea of m'grandson. To escape from the infernal smells

of the town will be a blessed relief. I only hope the sea air is not too cold. At my time of life one cannot be too careful about catching a chill.' Lady Maybury drew her shawl around her as if she already felt the gusting of the bracing sea air, instead of the stifling heat of London. 'Are you finished, my dear?'

Kathryn was engaged in yet another portrait of the dowager, this time a sketch in charcoal and chalk. She bobbed her head to the side, considered the work carefully, and, after a stroke here and a smudge there pronounced that she was.

The briefest of knocks sounded upon the library door behind Kathryn and then footsteps sounded upon the wooden floor.

'Nick!' Lady Maybury's face illuminated as her grandson came forward to sweep a kiss to her hand.

'Grandmama,' and, turning to the slight figure half-hidden behind the large wooden drawing board, 'Kathryn.' He made to politely lift her hand, but she pulled it back before he could reach it.

A smile lit her face as she set the board down on the floor and wiped her palms on the dark stained apron covering her dress. 'I'm afraid that I'm quite covered in charcoal.' As if to prove her point, she extended one hand and several slender fingers dangled temptingly in front of his face. It was clear to see that Kathryn was telling the truth, for her hands were indeed ingrained with a thick black dust.

'I've seen cleaner hands on a climbing boy,' he laughed and, before she could protest, plucked the dirty little hand into his and kissed it. 'Let it not be said that Lord Ravensmede could be deterred from his manners by a few grains of charcoal.'

'Your manners are quite impeccable, sir. I don't think you need worry that such an accusation could be levelled at you.'

Her grin was less than ladylike, but it smote Ravensmede's heart just the same. Several wild curls had escaped her chignon and were draping artlessly around her throat, the grey eyes were clear and bright, and her skin, beneath the daubs and smudges of black dust, was of a creamy luminescence. There had been too many days of polite formality, too much self-restraint. Before her appeal the Viscount's will-power began to crumble. In a moment of weakness he touched one thumb tenderly to her cheek, and then, suddenly conscious of exactly what he was doing and his grandmother's perceptive gaze, said lazily, 'More charcoal.' A large snow-white handkerchief was produced and he quickly wiped at the offending mark. 'That's better.'

Lady Maybury's mouth shaped as if to catch flies, before she snapped it shut. Kathryn said nothing, but could not prevent the flood of colour that warmed her face. The skin that he had touched with such betraying intimacy burned as if branded.

Ravensmede replaced his handkerchief, unwittingly transferring a small quantity of charcoal dust on to the pocket of his coat in the process, which he then proceeded to inadvertently share between his chin, and his cheek. He wandered away from the faded green scrutiny and feigned an interest in a shelf of books. At the other side of the room he could hear the scrape of Kathryn's chair and the movement of the drawing board upon a table.

'If you would be so kind as to excuse me, my lady, I'll attempt to remove the worst of this mess. A good shake of my apron outside and a hand scrub should suffice. And then I'll wipe the floor in here just in case—'

Lord Ravensmede glanced up from the book he had just extracted from the shelf. 'My grandmother employs servants to do that, Kathryn; you are not one of them. Is that not so, Grandmama?'

Lady Maybury looked from her grandson to her companion. 'Yes, of course.' Then, waving her hand in a dismissive gesture, 'Mary won't mind a little extra dust to sweep in the morning. Don't bother the gel just now.'

'Very well. I'll go and clean myself up. I'll come back later when you have need of me.' Kathryn started towards the door.

'Kathryn.' The single word stopped her progress immediately. 'We plan to discuss our forthcoming trip to Brighthelmstone. I would have you here.'

Kathryn had frozen halfway across the library floor. When she turned around, Ravensmede could see the deepening colour of her cheeks.

'Fustian, Nick! Must you always be so high-handed? I don't know where you get it from. Let the gel tidy herself. We can wait for her return before we start upon the plans for Brighthelmstone.' Lady Maybury peered down the length of her short little nose at her grandson. 'Besides, I can't think of a thing until I've had some Madeira and cake. Be so kind as to ring the bell.' She turned to Kathryn, who was still standing rather awkwardly in the middle of the room, unsure of what to do. 'Well, what are you waiting for, gel? Off you go.'

The door closed quietly behind the slight figure and the dowager and her grandson were left alone. Neither spoke. The slow steady tick of the grandfather clock marked the passing of the seconds.

And then the faded green gaze fixed its focus upon Ravensmede. 'Are you going to tell me what's going on?'

'Nothing's going on.'

'You seem uncommonly concerned with m'companion.'

A dark eyebrow arched. 'I'm merely being polite.'

'Polite, my foot!' sniffed the old lady. 'You fancy the gel!'

Ravensmede laughed. 'You've been reading too many romantic novels, Grandmama.'

'Don't try to flannel me, boy, I'm not so old that I can't see when a young man's ardour is up, even if he is m'own grandson.'

'Whatever I feel about her is irrelevant—she's your companion, nothing more.' The broad shoulders shrugged.

'I'm trusting you to remember that, Nick,' she said and fixed a belligerent eye on her grandson. 'I've put in a lot of effort to establish Kathryn in the eyes of the *ton*. Got plenty of respectable young gentlemen interested in her. Won't be long before one of them makes her an offer.' She sniffed. 'But one whiff of scandal and that will soon change. I don't want you ruining things for Kathryn, or for myself.'

'I've no intention of ruining anything,' Ravensmede drawled. 'As I said before, my interest in Kathryn is purely philanthropic.'

'Then you should take care to remember that until I can find her a husband,' said the dowager.

The thought of Kathryn marrying one of Lady Maybury's young gentlemen did not please the Viscount. His grandmother clearly had the bit between her teeth and was progressing her plan at an all-out gallop. It was time that Ravensmede slowed things down a little. 'Have a care you don't tire both Kathryn and yourself out, Grandmama. I've never seen you attend so many balls and routs as in these last weeks. When was the last time you spent the evening in?'

'Stuff and nonsense!' declared the old lady with a considerable degree of venom. 'I'm not in m'coffin yet. Why should I want to be sitting in here all evening when I can be out enjoying m'self. And as for Kathryn, the gel's as strong as a horse. We'll go out every night if we damn well choose!'

'You already do. But just think, if you make yourself ill what will happen to your plans for Kathryn then? She cannot go out alone.' That made Lady Maybury think; he could tell by the closed look that settled upon her face.

'It won't be for much longer,' she said. 'I'm very close to success. Indeed, if it were not for our holiday to Brighthelmstone I would be expectant of her receiving a proposal in the next few weeks.'

Ravensmede secretly blessed the forthcoming trip.

'Mr Roodley and Mr Williams have both been attentive and I have been warned that Lord Stanfield and Lord Raith have expressed more than a passing interest in my gel. She'll make a good marriage before this Season is out, or I'll eat my hat.'

'Roodley and Williams would bore Kathryn silly within a week of their company. As for Stanfield…the man's one of the biggest lechers in the country. And Raith's old enough to be her father. Are any of them really a suitable match?' Ravensmede flashed a lazy smile. 'I don't think so, and when you think about it, neither will you.'

Her ladyship cast him a determined look. 'I fully intend to catch her a husband, Nick.'

Ravensmede examined his nails, as if the matter was of such little importance to him. 'I fail to see the rush. Couldn't you just take her home to the dower house at Landon Park with you, and bring her back again next year?'

'The gel's four and twenty! Another year shan't be in her favour. I have Kathryn's best interest at heart when I say that I mean to secure her an offer as soon as possible.'

A wave of disgruntlement swept over the Viscount. The thought of Kathryn Marchant married to another man goaded him to irritation. For all that he'd sworn he would not touch her, for all his good intention for friendship and nothing more, he knew them both for the lies they were. Nothing and everything had changed from that moment at Lady Finlay's ball. He wanted her as much as ever—no, if he was honest, even more so. Then, her standing had been little better than a servant, and now, thanks to his grandmother, she was an eligible young lady on the marriage mart. Eligible to everyone other than himself. He gave a dry little smile and continued to sip his Madeira.

Chapter Ten

With a tap at the door, Kathryn walked into the room. She had changed into one of her new afternoon dresses and tidied the wayward curls of her hair. Her hands were still pink from being scrubbed with soap, but all signs of the black dust had disappeared. As soon as she entered she had the feeling that she had just interrupted an awkward silence. 'I hope the Madeira has refreshed you, my lady.'

'Never more so,' replied her ladyship. 'I was tempted by a second slice, but managed to resist.' She passed Kathryn a slice of sponge cake on a delicate painted plate. 'Help yourself to Madeira, my dear.'

Kathryn did as she was bid and then settled herself down in the empty chair next to the table. It was positioned beside the dowager and directly opposite the Viscount, so that she could not help but obtain an excellent view of his face. He certainly looked to be pondering something. She wondered what his grandmother had said to make him so. Perhaps more strikingly, though, he had a faint thumbprint of charcoal dust upon his chin and a smaller but similar mark upon his cheek. Her eyes flitted towards Lady Maybury who seemed to have observed nothing out of the ordinary with her grandson's appearance. Kathryn's fingers twisted at the skirt of her dress. What to do?

She couldn't let Nicholas leave the house like that—he'd be a laughing stock within five minutes. But to point it out when his grandmother had failed to do so was to risk embarrassing both the dowager and her grandson. Perhaps Lady Maybury would notice before that time came. True to form, the old lady was suffering none of her grandson's silence.

'Well?' A haughty brow rose. 'We are waiting for your discussions on Brighthelmstone.'

Ravensmede seemed to shake the contemplative mood from him, and started to recount the arrangements he had made. 'My servants shall travel down tomorrow to ensure that all is ready for us upon our arrival. We will leave on Thursday, take a leisurely journey with one overnight stop on the way down, thus arriving on Friday. No point in making the journey uncomfortable for you.'

His grandmother made what sounded to be a snort of disgust at this point, but he ignored it and continued undeterred.

'Once in Brighthelmstone I've rented us a house for the month. I'm told it has a good position with unimpeded views of the sea. It's on The Steyne and not far from the Prince's Pavilion.'

'Sea views?' Kathryn could not keep the excitement from her voice.

Ravensmede's mouth curved into a smile, the first since she had returned to the room. 'They're reported to be most scenic.'

Her face lit with delight. 'I can scarcely wait.'

'You will be taking your sketching and painting materials?' He was looking at her with an unfathomable expression.

She smiled. 'Of course! Nothing could stop me. You know how I treasure them.'

His voice was a low husky murmur. 'Yes.'

Their eyes met across the table and held.

'Kathryn, my dear,' Lady Maybury interrupted. 'Do you think I have enough shawls? I should so hate to catch a chill. They do say that the sea air is rather invigorating.'

'Perhaps we could check this afternoon, and if you're not

happy we could go shopping for some more.' Kathryn ignored the flush that had leapt to her cheeks and turned her attentions to the dowager. 'Are you warm enough just now? If not, I could fetch you a thicker shawl.'

'I'm pleasantly warm and cosy,' said the old lady.

A subtle knock at the door and a footman appeared. 'Lady Kiddleby to see you, my lady. I've taken the liberty of showing her to the drawing room.'

The dowager's brow wrinkled. 'Frances here? I wasn't expecting her.' She turned to Kathryn. 'This is not like her at all. I had best go to her at once. Come along, gel.'

The footman gave one delicate cough. 'Lady Kiddleby asked that she see you alone, my lady.' He coughed again. 'Her ladyship appears somewhat distressed.'

'Dear, oh, dear,' muttered Lady Maybury. 'No doubt Harriet has been upsetting her mama again. This shouldn't take long.' She drew her grandson a warning stare. 'I trust Nick shall not make a cake of himself in my absence.' She stared at him a moment longer before rising from her chair and leaving.

A silence.

The moss green eyes were on Kathryn.

'Would you like another glass of Madeira? Some more cake, perhaps?' She lifted the bottle.

'No, thank you.'

Another silence.

'I wondered if I might speak bluntly to you, Kathryn.'

The butterflies flocked within her stomach. She netted them down. 'Certainly, Nicholas.' She saw the tug of his mouth at her use of his name.

He touched a finger to his lips in a gesture that she had not seen him use before. 'I'm concerned about my grandmother's health. You see how much she hates to admit the slightest weakness and would never tell either of us if she were unwell. All these late nights are taking their toll on her. For all her protestations, she's in her eighty-first year with a weak heart, and I fear her hectic lifestyle of late is in danger of making her ill.'

The hand of guilt laid heavy on Kathryn's heart. 'I'm afraid you may be right. I know Lady Maybury enjoys going out but…I cannot help but wonder that she has my interest too much at heart.' She nibbled again at her lip and wondered if she should be confessing such things to her employer's grandson. 'At many events she's insistent that I accept every invitation to dance. Indeed, it's now quite common that I spend the evening upon the dance floor and not in Lady Maybury's company at all.' The grey eyes raised to Lord Ravensmede's with mounting anxiety. 'I have tried to refuse, but she won't have it. I feel that her fatigue is, in part, my fault.'

'My grandmother is forthright in her opinions, and once set upon a course is not easy to dissuade. You must not blame yourself, Kathryn, and, indeed, I did not mean that you should do so.' He reached across the table and gently took one of her hands.

'Is there anything I can do to remedy the situation?' She thought she saw something akin to guilt flicker within his gaze and then it was gone.

'The only way my grandmother would be persuaded to stay in on an evening is if you, yourself, Kathryn, were to feel unwell.' It was there again, an uneasiness in his eyes.

She understood very well what he was asking her to do. 'Yes. The odd headache…' Her words trailed off and she stared at the charcoal dust smears upon his face. She touched a finger to those imprinted places, but upon her own face instead of his. She couldn't let him leave like that, and the dowager's poor eyesight was unlikely to notice. Her finger tapped very deliberately against her chin. 'You have a little…' The finger tapped harder.

Ravensmede's focus sharpened like that of a starving man shown food.

'And here.' The finger had moved to poke a spot on her own cheek.

'Kathryn?'

'A little charcoal, just here.'

The dark head shook its denial. 'No, your face is quite clean,' he said slowly, and licked his lips. The green eyes had darkened considerably and were watching the movement of her fingers intently.

'But yours is not,' she replied with a wry smile. 'Somehow you must have touched the charcoal dust. And it's now on your face.'

A large hand rubbed ineffectually at a clean patch of skin on his cheek.

'No, it's over some more.'

'Here?' The fingers slid too far to the left.

'No, back a bit.'

Again he missed the mark.

'Move forward a little.' Before she could contemplate and dismiss the impulse she half-rose from her seat, reached across the table and moved her hand to touch his face. Then slowly and with what amounted to a caress she rubbed her thumb against the square edge of his chin until no trace of the charcoal remained. From there her fingers slid to his cheek. She could feel the roughness of the first hint of stubble on his skin, was so close she could smell the bergamot of his scent. With calm deliberation she kept her gaze fixed on the charcoal-shadowed skin. A sharp intake of breath that was not her own made her forget her purpose. His eyes were a deep, dark green, and in them was a hunger that made her forget where she was and just what she was doing.

'Kathryn,' he whispered. And contained in that single word was both pain and longing.

She could not speak, could not move, just stared into those dark mesmerising eyes.

His face crept towards hers until she could feel the warm stir of his breath tickle her cheek.

Chest compressed. Heart expanded. A sudden rush of blood to her head.

The smouldering gaze dropped to her lips.

Yes, she wanted to shout, but no words came. His skin brushed hers. Cheek touched cheek.

'Kathryn,' he said, and it was almost a growl. The need in his voice mirrored that in her soul.

Yes! Please. Did she have to plead? Their noses nestled. Lips so close to imagine their feeling. Touching…almost. Nothing existed outside that single moment. Locked in time, alone. 'Nick!' her voice was hoarse, barely recognisable as her own. She wanted *him*, nothing more.

His mouth claimed hers in sweeping possession.

A sigh and her lips opened in sweet surrender. Wanting all he would give, giving all he would take. Urgent. Demanding. The table jabbed at the front of her thighs as he pulled her into his arms. She felt the press of his hands upon her back, warm, caressing.

Footsteps sounded outside the door. A knock.

Before she could even register what was happening, Kathryn found herself quite suddenly pushed back into her chair.

By the time the footman entered the library it was to find a rather startled-looking Miss Marchant sitting bolt upright in her chair, and Lord Ravensmede lounging rather too comfortably back in his. 'Beggin' your pardon, my lord, but her ladyship has asked if Miss Marchant would be so kind as to come through to the drawing room.'

Kathryn's legs were shaking so badly that, had she not already been seated, she was positive she would have fallen. Her heart pounded in her chest. 'Yes, certainly. I'll come right away.'

Lord Ravensmede gave a nod of his head, and the footman retreated. 'Kathryn.'

A blush coloured her cheeks and her fingers plucked at the material of her skirt. She did not raise her eyes. 'I…I must go.'

Ravensmede stood. 'Until Thursday then,' he said politely and bowed.

Only when she reached the door did Kathryn look back to meet his eyes and see that they held a most determined promise.

* * *

Mrs Marchant was busy at her needlework within the drawing room of the house in Green Street when the visitor arrived. No sooner had the maid whispered the lady's name in Mrs Marchant's ear than the lady herself appeared in the doorway.

'My dear Mrs Marchant!' gushed the female voice. 'Anna. I came as quickly as I could. I'm only just returned to town as of last night.'

Anna Marchant's eyes widened momentarily and then she regained her composure. 'Amanda.' She smiled. 'Please do come in and take a seat.'

'Thank you. You're too kind,' said the widow and arranged herself on a stylish gold-covered armchair.

'How was your visit to the country?' enquired Mrs Marchant with politeness. 'I trust your sister is well again.'

'I cannot stand the country,' confided Mrs White. 'The roads are in a terrible state—it takes an age to travel anywhere; there is a dearth of anything remotely interesting; and the assemblies are positively backward in terms of their fashion and the clodhoppers who patronise them. All in all a thoroughly boring experience.' She did not mention that her ennui more specifically arose from the absence of rich young men to fawn over her beauty. The country squires and parsons in the vicinity were all elderly or grossly overweight or both. Amanda White had found much time to brood upon matters in Amersham…and subsequently the insult Ravensmede had dealt her in that little room at Lady Finlay's ball had become honed and magnified in her memory.

'And your sister?' prompted Mrs Marchant again.

'Delivered of a bawling son,' came the curt reply. 'But that is not of what I came to speak. My letter—'

'Came as a great shock to me. I must confess I'd no notion of that which you suggested. My niece has always behaved with the utmost decorum,' Anna lied.

'My dear Mrs Marchant, it pained me to have to be the bearer of such bad tidings; I felt I had little choice but to warn you of the danger.' The afternoon dress was cut to display Amanda White's curvaceous figure to perfection, its deep ruby-red coloration complementing the lush darkness of the widow's elegantly coiffured hair, and the smooth sheen of her pale skin. 'Not long after I'd sent the letter I learned that Lady Maybury has indeed taken the girl up as her companion.'

The accusation hung in the air between them.

'Your letter arrived too late,' said Mrs Marchant crisply. 'Kathryn had already accepted the position, and, whatever you might suggest, Lady Maybury has a lineage without blemish. The Mayburys are not without influence.'

The widow pouted her pretty lips while a sly expression slid across her eyes. 'Indeed, but it makes no difference to what Miss Marchant is about.'

Much as Anna Marchant disliked her niece, she realised full well the consequences of any slur on Kathryn's name. The Marchant family would not escape unscathed. And so it was with this in mind that Mrs Marchant prepared to defend her niece's reputation. 'Kathryn is a young lady of impeccable values. I must insist that your fears as to any improper behaviour are quite mistaken, Mrs White.'

'I saw her with my own eyes, Mrs Marchant, behaving little better than a common whore.'

A sharp inhalation of breath. 'Mrs White! I must protest!' Both women rose to their feet.

'I thought to tell you only because I know you hold a fine and respectable standing within society; I did not think that you would want your own reputation jeopardised by your niece's scandalous behaviour.' She shrugged her beautiful shoulders. 'But if you are not interested in your niece's dealings…' Mrs White made to leave.

'There is no need for such haste,' said Anna Marchant with feigned sweetness, as she moved swiftly to block her visitor's exit path. 'Your concern for my family is admirable.' It was a lie, of course. The pretty young widow had no concern for anyone other than herself. Anna knew quite clearly that Amanda White's world revolved singularly around herself and her pretty looks. Not that it made one blind bit of difference to Mrs Marchant. But it did make her wonder as to exactly what game Amanda White was playing with her letter and her visit. A smile moved across Mrs Marchant's lips. 'Sit down again, Amanda,' she said. 'I would hear what you have to say.' Before the afternoon was out Anna Marchant intended to have the answer to all of her questions in full.

Mrs White swished her skirts and sat back down before the words were even out of her hostess's mouth. It was clear that she had had no intention of going anywhere. Mrs Marchant's smile stretched wider. 'If you can bring yourself to tell me all, my dear,' she added.

'Dearest Anna,' simpered Amanda White. 'I shall strive to do what is right.' And proceeded to describe the scene she had interrupted between Lord Ravensmede and Kathryn Marchant at Lady Finlay's ball. Every possible embellishment was added, so that not only was Ravensmede kissing Miss Marchant with a passion (which of course was true) but he was kneading upon her breast and clutching her against him in the most carnal of manners. Mrs White gave no mention as to her own assignation with the Viscount and said she had wandered into the room quite mistakenly.

'Why did you not tell me at the ball?' asked Mrs Marchant, barely able to hide the rise in her temper.

'Lord Cadmount whisked me away just as I was about to. And then Ravensmede practically bullied me into going to the country. I was fearful to do anything other than he bid.'

Anna Marchant had trouble in believing that. The young widow was a woman more used to controlling men than being controlled by them.

'You must have enough influence over the girl to bring her to her senses before it is too late. Surely you can make her give up this ridiculous affair and move back here with you? You're her aunt; she'll listen to you. Forbid the girl any further contact with Ravensmede. It's not too late to salvage some semblance of her reputation. The fact that she's his mistress has not yet become common knowledge. There's still time, if you act now.'

So that was what Amanda White wanted: Ravensmede…for herself. Mrs Marchant said somewhat coldly, 'Kathryn has always been disobedient and stubborn. There is, and always has been, little love lost between us.'

'Oh, dear,' said Amanda without the slightest emotion. 'It would be such a shame if anyone else was to learn of your niece's indiscretion. Especially now that she's Lady Maybury's companion, it wouldn't take much for the whole town to deduce that she's Ravensmede's mistress. Poor Lottie, I suppose she shall not remain unaffected by Kathryn's shame.' Mrs White looked slyly at the older woman. 'And you had such hopes of a good match for your daughter.'

Anna Marchant's teeth clamped tightly shut. Her top lip curled with unconcealed contempt. She knew very well exactly what Mrs White was about: blackmail. Get Kathryn back to Green Street, or the widow would spread her gossip. And the thought that Kathryn had allowed her to be put into such a position fuelled the hatred already burning in Mrs Marchant's breast. 'Very well, Amanda. Since you place me in an untenable position, I will do as you ask, but I must warn you it may take some little time.'

'The longer you take, dear Anna, the more chance there is that I may inadvertently let something slip. I can be such a forgetful puss at times.'

'Then the sooner I start, the better,' said Mrs Marchant.

Mrs White took the hint and soon only Anna Marchant sat alone in the drawing room, cursing the widow, trying to think how she could lure Kathryn back from Lady Maybury, planning just what she would do to her when she did.

The journey to Brighthelmstone was pleasantly uneventful. Although the road appeared to be dreadfully busy with carriages and carts, Ravensmede assured both Kathryn and his grandmother that the level of traffic was quite normal. The journey, having been designed not to tire Lady Maybury, was conducted at a leisurely pace. Ravensmede's large closed carriage was well sprung and he had ensured not only a mountain of travelling rugs for his grandmother's warmth but also a basket of provisions including the most refreshing lemonade Kathryn had ever tasted. Lady Maybury alternated between watching the passing countryside, chatting and napping, the latter activity occupying the greater part of her time, thus leaving her companion to fill her own time as best she could. As far as Kathryn was concerned, it was fortuitous indeed that Lord Ravensmede had chosen to ride alongside the carriage rather than travel within its small interior.

Following what had flared between them in the library, being alone in the Viscount's presence was not something with which Kathryn trusted herself. And she had only herself to blame. It was true that he had kissed her, but she was well aware that her own actions had precipitated such a response. Touching her fingers to his face…whatever would he think of her? Kathryn gritted her teeth at the all-too-obvious answer to that question. How could she repay the dowager's kindness by encouraging her grandson, for there was no doubt that that was what her behaviour amounted to? It was behaviour in keeping with Aunt Anna and Cousin Lottie's taunts. Tired fingers kneaded against her forehead, and she sighed. The passing hedges and fields became nothing more than a distant green blur.

'Kathryn? What's wrong? Are you sickening for something?' Lady Maybury's voice interrupted her reverie.

She glanced up in surprise, thinking the dowager to have still been sleeping. 'No, my lady. I have the slightest of headaches, nothing more.'

'Then we must make a stop at the next inn and allow you to wander and stretch your legs. Perhaps it's being cooped up in here that has brought it on.'

'Oh, no, please do not.' The thought of having to face Lord Ravensmede again so soon was not something with which she felt comfortable.

The faded green eyes narrowed in their focus and lingered upon Kathryn's anxiety-ridden countenance.

Blood scalded her cheeks under the scrutiny. 'I mean… please don't stop for me. I would rather press on with our journey.' She plucked at the material of her skirts. 'I'm so looking forward to arriving in Brighthelmstone,' she said with false brightness.

Lady Maybury remained singularly unconvinced. 'Indeed,' she said drily. 'We've first to spend the night at Horley Common.' Not once had that relentless green gaze faltered.

'Yes.' Kathryn did not know what else to say. The old lady was looking at her as if she could see her innermost thoughts. If that were indeed true, Miss Kathryn Marchant would find herself turned off without so much as a reference, and then what would she do? Half of London's bachelors would not be dangling after her then!

Neither woman spoke and the dowager had not shifted her attention.

'Has Nick done something to upset you?' The question fired out of the silence.

Kathryn's heart missed a beat. She forced herself to stay calm. 'No. Lord Ravensmede has been nothing but polite at all times.' She chewed at her lip. 'What makes you think so?'

'An idle thought, nothing more.' The dowager tucked the blanket higher, so that it almost reached her chin. 'Still, if you say there's nothing in it…' One white brow raised in enquiry.

'Nothing at all, my lady,' Kathryn speedily replied. 'I…I'm very happy as your companion, Lady Maybury. Indeed, I've never been happier, and hope that nothing will jeopardise my position.'

The snow white curls nodded once. 'And I'm very happy to have you as my friend.' Lady Maybury relaxed back against the seat and snuggled beneath her blankets. Within a matter of minutes her eyelids had shuttered and the gentle wheeze of her snoring filled the carriage.

That night in the King's Arms coaching inn and for the entirety of the journey Ravensmede behaved with the utmost propriety. Nothing in his speech or manner betrayed in the slightest that he felt anything other than the appropriate civil concern for his grandmother's companion. Neither did he suggest at any time that he should share the carriage, even when he was subjected to a rather heavy rain shower. So by the time the small party arrived in Brighthelmstone to take up residence within their rented accommodation, Kathryn had managed to rein her wayward emotions under sensible control once more.

The episode in Lady Maybury's library was banished far from her thoughts, and she was able to relax, firm in the belief that she would not tempt fate by allowing herself to spend any time alone in the company of Lord Ravensmede. The trip to the seaside resort was the chance of a lifetime and she did not mean to spoil the opportunity with silly worrying. She would not shatter Lady Maybury's trust in her. And as for her own trust in herself, she knew that now, where Nicholas was concerned, that was something on which she could not completely depend. If she did not want to ruin her new life as the dowager's companion, then Kathryn had better have a care…especially here in Brighthelmstone.

'I trust you find the house to your liking?' Ravensmede sipped at his coffee the next morning and watched the ladies across the breakfast table.

Lady Maybury's ferocity of attack on a pile of carved ham mellowed slightly. 'I'm never anything but completely uncomfortable when anywhere but Landon Park, but…' she sniffed '…I suppose I will suffer to endure it.'

'Kathryn?' the Viscount asked politely.

'It's beautiful both inside and out, and our every comfort has been thought of. You spoke truthfully when you promised splendid views of the sea. I haven't seen the like for many a year.' She paused and looked at Lady Maybury. 'It was very kind of you to arrange that my bedchamber was seaward facing. It's a dream come true to wake up each morning and look out at the shoreline.'

'If you would be so good as to pass me that dish of eggs, Nick.' The dowager pointed to the silver heated dish on the serving table and waited expectantly. 'Had nothing to do with me, dear gel. It was Nicholas that took care of all the arrangements. Gave us the scenic chambers, took the one at the back for himself.' She helped herself to four large poached eggs and several slices of toast.

'Grandmama...' Ravensmede laughed '...I swear your appetite is expanding for a lady of such sylph-like proportions.' He did not want to discuss the sleeping arrangements, or the fact that there was a scant four feet of landing separating his chamber from Kathryn Marchant's. Such thoughts were dangerous and that was a direction in which he could not afford to wander if he did not want to disgrace them all. And anyway, hadn't his grandmother determined that Kathryn would be spoken for before the Season was out?

The old lady laughed. 'You'll not get round me with such flattery. Quite how these young females survive on fresh air and lemonade I shall never know. It's not natural. In my day we ate all we could and our stays did the rest. Wretchedly uncomfortable to wear, but a dashed necessity. Didn't pick at our food like sparrows then, I can tell you.'

'I fear you're embarrassing Kathryn.'

'Stuff and nonsense,' replied his grandparent. 'Kathryn's not some milk-and-water miss just out of the school room. Likes a good serving of food herself. No silly nonsense with this gel, is there, Kathryn?'

'I hope not, my lady.' Kathryn smiled at the dowager.

Ravensmede remembered Kathryn Marchant's collarbone outlined starkly against her bruised skin, and her gaunt cheeks when they had first brought her back to Ravensmede House. She had no need to starve herself; Anna Marchant had only been too willing to undertake that task, and her cruel treatment had had nothing to do with slender figures, of that he was quite sure. He brushed such disconcerting thoughts aside and forced his mind to more pleasant avenues. 'I've already paid my respects to the Master of Ceremonies and we are therefore welcome to attend all balls at both sets of assembly rooms. Those in the Castle Inn are on Mondays, and on Wednesdays the balls are in the Old Ship. Card parties are on Wednesdays and Fridays, and on Sundays there is a promenade and a public tea. There's also the theatre in North Street, and of course Brighthelmstone races. If you let me know which you prefer, I will make the necessary arrangements.'

His grandmother nodded. 'Yes, indeed. I think a shopping trip is first in order so that we may familiarise ourselves with the town. A walk along the pier, and a closer inspection of that monstrosity that the Prince Regent calls his Marine Pavilion would also be of benefit. I've a notion to view the new stables and riding house built in the Indian style. Thereafter, we'll see which cards arrive.'

'And the theatre?' her grandson prompted.

'I shall think about it,' the old lady pronounced.

And so their holiday by the sea began very well.

The Castle Inn suite of rooms were superbly adorned in the classical decorative style of Robert Adam. It seemed that the fine weather had brought out all of the town's polite society, for the rooms were filled despite the departure of many local families to London for the Season. It was a cosier affair than the grand London balls with less of those who called the tune that the rest of the *ton* were happy to dance to, nevertheless

Kathryn hovered close to Lady Maybury. Despite arriving as a stranger, Lady Maybury soon discovered some old friends, through which numerous introductions were made. Thus, as had become usual, Kathryn's dance card was soon filled.

Nicholas chatted politely to the rather awestruck young men who flocked to meet the notorious Viscount of Ravensmede. He danced with the flustered giggling débutantes and made great efforts to ensure that his grandmother's friends' granddaughters were not ignored. And through it all he watched every move that Kathryn made, knew every man with whom she danced. It was a self-inflicted torture to which he readily ascribed. Indeed, he had taken great pains to ensure that they were not too much in each other's company that evening. He had brought her here to enjoy herself, to let her paint the sea scenes so dear to her heart. Damn it, but the girl deserved some little joy in her life. The last thing he intended doing was allowing some uncontrollable instinct spoil the whole set-up they had worked so hard to achieve. He'd damn well not risk both her and his grandmother's happiness, not to satisfy some selfish whim of his own. But he had to admit that his growing obsession with his grandparent's companion had never felt less like a whim.

'Your servant, Miss Linton.' Ravensmede delivered the simpering girl back to her mother, bowed and beat a hasty retreat. The chit's mama's eyes were positively ogling with speculation. 'Grandmama, you seem to be in high spirits.' Lady Maybury was fanning herself with an exuberance he'd rarely seen.

'Of course I am,' she crowed loudly. 'I haven't seen Jane Ballantyne for an age. All her granddaughters are married and she has twelve great-grandchildren to boot. I have only a paltry four to compete. What is that compared to twelve? And you show no signs of obliging me.'

'You begin to sound like my father, ma'am,' the Viscount replied. 'It is a favourite topic of his and has been for the last few years.'

The volume of her voice dropped somewhat. 'You cannot blame him, Nick, he does not wish all that he has worked for over the years to pass to the dreadful Herbert.'

Ravensmede thought of the selfish connivance of his cousin Herbert and was forced to agree. 'Neither do I. But I'll marry when I'm good and ready, and not because m'father wills it.'

The dowager raised one cynical white eyebrow. Any reply she might have made was forgotten when Lady Farrow, who was seated some six feet away, gestured at Lady Maybury and shouted, 'Is not the next dance the waltz?'

'I do believe you're correct, Hetty,' came the reply.

Just the mention of the dance was enough to have Ravensmede glancing around for Kathryn. He soon spotted her across the room partnering some fair-faced youth for a country dance. The final bars sounded and soon the couple were making their way back towards Lady Maybury. No sooner had Kathryn been deposited beside the dowager than a most insistent Mr Silverton appeared to spirit her away.

Her eyes turned to Ravensmede in question. The action was not lost on Lady Maybury, who seemed to positively encourage the young gentleman's interest in her companion. 'Off you go, Kathryn,' she said before turning to her grandson. 'He seems a delightful young man.'

Ravensmede could do nothing while the woman who had come to haunt his dreams was led out on to the floor and allowed herself to be held quite properly and at the allotted distance by Mr Silverton. She had never danced the waltz with anyone other than himself. And now she was in Silverton's arms. It was for the best, her best, or so he told himself.

'Nicholas,' Lady Maybury said, 'I have a need to seek the retiring room. Be so kind as to watch over Kathryn until I return. Do *not* let the gel come after me, and make sure that she dances with the next gentleman whose name is upon her card.' Lady Maybury drew him a fierce look and then disappeared across the room, leaving only the lingering scent of her lavender perfume.

Ravensmede was forced to watch Kathryn and Mr Silverton dance the whole of the waltz, before that young man returned her to him.

She smiled and a spasm of desire shot through him. 'Is all well with Lady Maybury? She is not here.'

'A visit to the retiring room. She'll rejoin us shortly.'

'Then I should assist her.' Without waiting for an answer she made to move towards the door.

His hand caught her arm. 'No, Kathryn. She has asked that you stay here. You know how she hates a fuss.' With a gentle tug he pulled her back towards him.

'Yes, you're right. I should wait for her to return.'

Sliding his fingers down to meet her hand, Ravensmede delivered a gentle squeeze. 'Did you enjoy your waltz?' The cream silk of her glove was smooth beneath his fingers. His hand encompassed hers possessively.

She glanced up at him, the hint of a blush just beginning on her cheeks, then peered around to check that no one was close enough to see what was happening between them.

'Nicholas,' she whispered, 'I—'

Whatever she intended to say was cut short by the return of Mr Silverton, followed closely by the dowager.

'Sir…' Lady Maybury tapped her fan in fake reproof against the young man's sleeve. 'I do believe you've already stood up with my companion not so very long ago.'

Mr Silverton smiled a charming smile. 'That is indeed the case, but with a lady as beautiful as Miss Marchant all others pale to insignificance. I would be honoured if she would stand up with me again.'

Lady Maybury smiled in her most agreeable manner. 'Well, as it's you,' she said indulgently.

'You have my undying gratitude, my lady,' replied Mr Silverton and moved to face Kathryn. 'I do believe you've granted me the honour of agreeing to partner me for the quadrille.'

'I…I…' Mr Silverton's name was indeed written upon her

card against the quadrille. Kathryn shot a glance at Ravensmede. The expression on his face was unreadable.

'Don't dally, Kathryn,' urged the dowager.

She had little option but to place her hand in Mr Silverton's
and allow him to lead her out on to the dance floor...again.
'Thank you, sir.' Kathryn's impression of Harry Silverton from
their waltz was confirmed during the quadrille. He seemed a
pleasant enough young man, even if he was prone to a rather
overly dramatic turn of speech. It was all Kathryn could do to
keep a straight face when he waxed lyrical on the extent of her
beauty. She was sure that he lavished the gush of compliments
upon every woman with whom he danced. She endured a
eulogy on her fine eyes, but when he started to compare her hair
to a cascade of rich autumn leaves she laughed and begged him
to tell her something of the town of Brighthelmstone instead.
When at last the dance was over Mr Silverton returned her,
breathless and smiling, to Lady Maybury.

Mr Silverton bowed low to both the dowager and Kathryn.
'May I have your permission to call upon your companion, my
lady?'

'*I* have no objection to your calling, sir,' said Lady Maybury,
'but you have yet to ask Miss Marchant her opinion on the matter.'

Three faces turned to Kathryn, who was looking both surprised and a little awkward.

'I...I think perhaps...'

'Thank you, my dear Miss Marchant, I shall count the
minutes until we meet again,' said Mr Silverton.

It was then that Kathryn noticed the dangerous darkening
of Lord Ravensmede's eyes and the glacial stare that he drew
Mr Silverton. Harry Silverton saw it too. With a speedily
executed bow the young gentleman was gone, leaving Kathryn
to face Lord Ravensmede.

Chapter Eleven

The journey home was rather stilted. Lady Maybury seemed drained of energy, and lay back against the seat with her eyes closed. Lord Ravensmede's ill humour did not recede. His manner was distant and he seemed loath to converse. Only Kathryn, balanced precariously next to the dowager, was desperate for a chance to clear the air. She looked hopefully at Lady Maybury, but the old lady's eyes remained shut. And the Viscount had not yet glanced in her direction. Silence reined supreme. She cleared her throat in an attempt to draw his attention.

The dark profile did not turn from the window.

'Nicholas,' she said softly.

He looked at her then, but she could scarcely see his face through the darkness.

Where to begin? 'I…' It was clear that Mr Silverton's presumption had annoyed him. She was being paid as Lady Maybury's companion, not to court a suitor while the dowager sat alone and fatigued. She tried again. 'I did not encourage Mr Silverton's attentions.'

'Didn't you?' He sounded quite unlike his usual self. There was a distance in his voice, so different from anything that she had heard previously. And exactly what did he seem to be implying?

A gentle snoring sounded from the dowager.

'Of course not! We came to Brighthelmstone for the sake of Lady Maybury's health.'

Ravensmede did not correct her misconception.

'I'm her companion. It isn't right that gentlemen should call upon me here.'

'Then why did you not refuse your permission?'

She faltered. Why indeed? Shock, disbelief. She had fully intended to do so, but Mr Silverton had been too quick in his assumption. 'I didn't grant him my permission,' she insisted with a degree of stubbornness.

'I don't think that Mr Silverton understood that to be the case.'

He was taunting her! How could he change from the caring, passionate man she knew to the arrogant goading creature that sat before her now? Kathryn felt her temper rising. Not only had she to somehow contrive to get rid of Mr Silverton, but she now also had to explain herself to the Viscount. 'Then he's a fool,' she snapped.

'Kathryn, you must have given him some sign to encourage his attentions. Believe me, I know when a gentleman is intent upon securing a lady's interest. And you appeared to be enjoying his company immensely,' he said meaningfully.

'Indeed I did, sir, but with the exception of being civil, I assure you that I have given that gentleman no indication that his attentions would be welcomed.'

Silence.

She could just imagine the arrogant arch of his eyebrow at her reply, and it irked her, as did his ridiculous assumptions. 'How could you even think that I would encourage him?'

'How indeed?' Irony laid heavy on his words.

An exasperated sigh escaped her. 'You're being unfair, my lord.'

'And you're being completely fair, are you, Kathryn?'

A blush rose in her cheeks. 'I know my place,' she said quietly. 'Be assured that I have no intention of receiving Mr Silverton as a visitor.'

'Really? I think that my grandmother may have other ideas on that matter.'

'Then think what you will, Lord Ravensmede,' she said, 'your mind is clearly made up, far be it for me to try to change it.'

'Kathryn Marchant, you are the most infuriating of women.'

'Of that I'm most heartily glad!' she retorted.

The volume of Ravensmede's voice increased. 'God help me, you drive me to—'

'Nicholas?' Lady Maybury's croaked through the darkness.

'Grandmama,' the Viscount replied with forced serenity. It sounded as if his teeth had ground together.

'Why are you shouting at my companion?'

'I beg your pardon, ma'am.'

Kathryn felt the old lady raise herself up on the seat. 'It isn't my pardon you should be begging,' she said quietly. 'I haven't a mind to find myself a new companion quite yet.'

A slowing of the carriage. The crunch of footsteps outside the door.

'Forgive me, Miss Marchant.' Following his stiff words, the Viscount opened the door and jumped down from the carriage before the steps were in place. He waited until they were fitted before helping first Lady Maybury, and then her companion, out into the gloomily lit darkness. The glow of the street lanterns was not sufficient to safely light their path up the stone stairs to the front door of the house so Ravensmede took both ladies' arms in his to act as guide.

Kathryn felt the tension in the muscles beneath her fingers, though her touch was light as a dragonfly and knew the man beside her was angry beyond belief. What she did not yet fully understand was why. Assuredly she should not have answered him back, but his accusations were silly in the extreme. As if she would encourage any man's attentions! Her mind flitted back to the passions she had shared with Nicholas. Oh, heavens! She began to have an appreciation of his point. If she could respond so readily to him, then he had every reason to believe her a woman of loose moral fibre. Oh Lord, what a web she had spun herself into!

Mr Silverton waited only as long as the following afternoon to call upon Miss Marchant, and had the audacity to bring with him quite the most ridiculously outsized arrangement of flowers that had been seen for a long time.

'Ah, Mr Silverton.' Lady Maybury sounded encouraging.

'Lady Maybury, a pleasure to see you again, ma'am. Is Miss Marchant—'

The dowager smiled a smile of sweetness and light. 'She is almost ready. A young lady's *toilette* must never be rushed, sir. The result would be too disastrous to imagine.'

'Indeed, my lady. I didn't mean to hurry Miss Marchant. I'm happy to wait upon her leisure.'

'I'm sure you are.' The smile deepened.

Mr Silverton smoothed his neckcloth. 'Is Lord Ravensmede at home?'

'Why, did you wish for a word?' her ladyship asked.

'No, no,' Mr Silverton said with undue haste. 'I was merely being polite. No need to disturb his lordship.'

'Quite,' agreed Lady Maybury, and then confided, 'It is for the best. He can be prone to a cantankerous disposition when disturbed by unannounced visitors, although I'm sure that would not be the case with you.'

Mr Silverton appeared to have developed an irritation in his throat. He coughed loudly and shifted from one foot to the other.

The awkwardness of the moment was alleviated by the appearance of a maid who quietly informed her ladyship that Miss Marchant was feeling unwell and would not be able to receive Mr Silverton.

The dowager's brows knitted. 'What nonsense is this?' She peered at the unfortunate maid. 'She was as fit as a fiddle not half an hour ago. Tell Kathryn to come down this instant or I shall be forced to fetch her myself.'

Five minutes later Kathryn entered the drawing room to have the huge mass of flowers suddenly thrust upon her.

'How kind, Mr Silverton. Perhaps if I were to just put them down here until—'

The dowager interrupted. 'Of course, my dear. The maid shall see to them. What's all this about feeling unwell? Perhaps it would be better to postpone the drive until another day.'

A look of hope entered Kathryn's eyes.

'I shall ring for tea and cakes and leave you young things together.' She smiled again at Harry Silverton. 'And ensure that Lord Ravensmede knows not to disturb you.'

The young man coughed and glanced around nervously as if he thought Lord Ravensmede was about to appear..

With Nicholas's accusations still clear in Kathryn's mind, Lady Maybury's suggestion seemed unbearable. 'Thank you, my lady, but there's no need. I feel quite recovered.'

'Well, if you're sure,' said the dowager somewhat doubtfully.

'Absolutely positive,' said Kathryn.

'In that case, be sure to have a lovely time on your drive.'

Kathryn eyed Lady Maybury anxiously. 'I shall not be long, my lady.'

'Take as long as you like, dear gel.' The old lady's hand waved imperiously. 'No need to hurry back.'

Mr Silverton's nerves vanished in an instant. He beamed his gratitude at the dowager.

'Off you go, then,' said Lady Maybury from the other side of the drawing room.

The couple walked across the brightly decorated rug.

Just as Mr Silverton's hand touched to the door handle the elderly voice boomed, 'You will bring m'gel back safely, won't you, sir? I fear that I have a tendency to overprotectiveness when it comes to m'companion.'

The young man flushed an unbecoming shade of puce, and announced dramatically, 'Indeed, my lady. I shall guard Miss Marchant with my very life.'

Lord Ravensmede did not enter the drawing room until he had heard the bang of the front door. He strolled nonchalantly to the window and watched while Harry Silverton drove Kathryn away in a hideously over-decorated green-and-black painted phaeton.

'I fancy Mr Silverton is quite taken with her. If I'm not mistaken, an offer will be forthcoming before we leave for London,' said his grandmother from behind his shoulder.

'Unfortunately it appears that you may be right,' he said.

One white brow lifted. 'He's heir to a small fortune, I'll have you know.'

'True, though it's earned through trade.' Ravensmede's eyes were still trained upon the diminishing dot in the distance.

'What's wrong with that? He may not be an aristocrat, but he's wealthy enough to provide her with a life of comfort.'

'Harry Silverton's father owns a string of coffee houses across the country, as well as a sugar plantation in the West Indies. The family are from Bristol and are here only for a short break.' Despite the bright sunshine in the room a sombre aura clung to Lord Ravensmede. 'I've a notion that Kathryn wouldn't approve of the Silverton family's interest in slavery.'

His grandmother frowned. 'Good gad!'

'It's also rumoured that they have significant investments in the overseas slave trade, although if Lansdowne's bill goes through that won't last for much longer.'

'Blast! That means Silverton won't do at all. Can't have her marrying into a family like that.' She eyed him sharply. 'I suppose I should be thankful that you've been thorough in your enquiries, m'boy.' The old lady wandered across the room and sat herself neatly upon the sofa. 'Is there any gentleman either here or in London that you would recommend as a husband for Kathryn?'

'No.' The Viscount's reply was definite.

Lady Maybury's eyes were focused upon her grandson's face. 'But if you were to give the matter some thought, perhaps you would be able to come up with a suitable candidate.'

'I do not think so, ma'am.' Ravensmede's lips compressed into a hard line.

'It's unlike you to admit defeat with such ease,' his grandmother goaded.

An ache was growing in the Viscount's chest. 'I'm not normally asked to play matchmaker.'

She sighed. 'Does not Kathryn deserve this little happiness? A husband, children of her own?'

'She's happy as she is. There's no need for her to marry.'

'You wish her to stay a companion to me for ever? And what when I'm dead, what will happen to her then? Servant to another old woman? Or, worse still, mistress to some man? Believe me, Nick, when I tell you that it's no life for a girl like Kathryn. I know this is not easy for you, boy, but it's for the best. So, please, just give the matter a little thought.'

He sighed, running his fingers through his hair. 'Very well. I promise I'll give serious consideration to what you've asked.'

The faded green eyes held his with a sudden intensity. 'I sincerely hope so, Nick. I've come to care very much for Kathryn, and as an unmarried lady she's vulnerable…in all sorts of ways. I cannot rest easy until I know the gel is settled in marriage.'

'Grandmama, you've saved Kathryn from a life of misery, and offered her a home with you. What harm can come to her? She's safer now than she's ever been.'

'Is she?' she asked in a strange tone of voice. The old hand moved to clasp his, and she sighed. 'Life is never that simple.'

At last Kathryn saw the blessed emergence of the familiar front door. If the phaeton had not stood so high upon the ground, she would have leapt down herself without having to suffer the indignity of Harry Silverton's hands around her waist.

'Mr Silverton!' she chided when he seemed reluctant to relinquish his hold upon her person.

The gentleman's corn-gold hair glistened in the sunlight. His deep blue eyes held admiration. 'You're such a vision of loveliness as to make a gentleman forget himself.' But he released her nevertheless. 'Will you be attending Lady Richardson's ball tonight?'

'I don't know what Lady Maybury has planned. As her companion it's my duty to accompany her in whatever her wishes might be.' She struggled to remove her fingers from Mr Silverton's clasp and attempted to hurry up the stone stairs to the front door.

Mr Silverton matched her every step. 'May I be so bold as to suggest that I call again tomorrow? We could perhaps drive further out into the country.'

'No. I don't think so, sir.' Kathryn wished to spare Mr Silverton's pride; had seen the effects of her cousin's cruel words too many times not to feel some sympathy for the young man standing so hopefully beside her. 'I believe Lady Maybury has already made arrangements for tomorrow.'

'Then I shall call the following day.' They were standing beside the heavy wooden door.

Kathryn made to press the bell, but not before his fingers plucked her hand to his lips. 'No.' She surreptitiously tried to pull away, while taking care not to create a scene. 'I thank you for your kind invitation, and indeed I've enjoyed our pleasant drive today, but I cannot accompany you again any day this week.' Mr Silverton's grip was surprisingly strong.

'Why ever not, Miss Marchant?' The blue eyes held hers with rather too much intimacy than that with which she was comfortable. 'Without you I shall fade as a flower deprived of sunlight.' He pulled her closer.

'Because she'll be accompanying me,' a deep voice drawled as the door swung open.

Kathryn had never been so relieved to see Nicholas. 'Lord

Ravensmede,' she uttered faintly, unsure of how much of the conversation he had overheard.

In one swift movement he had plucked Kathryn to stand behind him in the hall, leaving the golden-haired young man upon the step. 'I bid you good day, Mr Silverton.'

Harry Silverton lingered only a moment longer, then, with a low and elaborate flourish of a bow, he was gone.

The door slammed in his wake.

'Oh, Nicholas, thank you!' Relief swamped Kathryn. She wrapped her arms around the Viscount's body in a bear hug and pressed her cheek to the broad expanse of his chest. 'I thought he would never go. He was so very insistent and I didn't wish to be unkind.' Freshly laundered linen, and soap, and bergamot tickled her nose. She relaxed against him. 'I can only pray that he doesn't mean to make me an offer!'

His hands touched to her back in a gentle gesture.

Her eyes were still closed, her body nestled into his.

Ravensmede stood very still. It seemed that even his breath had halted.

There was the sudden rattle of china and a footman carrying a heavily loaded tea tray appeared at the top of the staircase leading up from the kitchen.

Kathryn's eyes sprung open, her body tensed for flight.

The footman did not look in the entwined couple's direction once. He merely trotted across the hallway, tapped politely on the library door, and waited until a loud female voice bid him enter.

'Thank you, Toby,' said Lady Maybury. 'I thought I heard a carriage outside. If Miss Marchant has returned, have her come through for tea.'

By the time the footman had reappeared to impart this message Kathryn was standing innocently by Lord Ravensmede's side. Meekly she turned towards the library door.

'Ah, Nick as well,' said the dowager and raised an eyebrow. 'You had best come in before the tea grows cold.' Only once three cups of steaming tea had been delivered in the finest of saucers did Lady Maybury continue between sips, 'Why, my dear gel, has Mr Silverton overtaxed you?' The faded green eyes peered sharply at her companion's face. 'I do declare that your colour appears unnaturally high and you seem to be a little out of breath.' The dowager appealed to her grandson. 'Am I not right, Nick? Pray do examine Kathryn's visage.'

It was true that Kathryn had indeed appeared a trifle flushed upon entering the library, her embarrassment due to the realisation that she had just thrown her arms around Lord Ravensmede and her wholly inappropriate action had been witnessed by a footman, who was now guaranteed to delight in informing the whole of Ravensmede's staff of what he had seen. Beneath the dowager's blatant scrutiny the faint rose bloom intensified to a scarlet flame of colour. Had the dowager heard her words to Nicholas? Did she have any inclination of exactly what her companion had just done? Kathryn forced herself to meet the faded green gaze. There was nothing of shock or anger there, only a little sadness.

'Grandmama, I'm sure Kathryn's cheeks are flushed only from the fresh air.'

'Perhaps,' said Lady Maybury. 'I'm all-agog to hear the news regarding her drive with Mr Silverton. Pray tell all, my dear.'

Kathryn took a fortifying gulp of tea. 'We travelled along the coastal road in order to enjoy the views. They are indeed quite spectacular.'

'How far along the coastal road?' said the Viscount.

'To a place named Rottingdean, whereupon we turned around and came back by the same route.'

Lady Maybury frowned. 'I had thought Mr Silverton's drive to be limited to the park.'

Kathryn did not want to cause trouble for the young man, but neither was she prepared to risk giving the impression that she liked him. 'He thought that I would prefer the scenery along the coast.'

'And did you agree to this change of plan?' asked the dowager.

A pause. 'No.'

'Shall Mr Silverton be calling again?' A white eyebrow raised in enquiry.

Ravensmede's gaze slid to Kathryn's.

'No,' she said, 'I hope that he will not.'

The old lady sighed. 'It is just as well.'

Kathryn's eyes widened. 'I thought—'

Lady Maybury leaned towards Kathryn. 'I had high hopes for you and him. He seemed such a personable young man too. But that was before I learned where his family's money comes from.' She sniffed disapprovingly. 'Slavery,' she said succinctly.

Kathryn's cup clanked back down against her saucer, and said quietly, 'Then it is for the best that he will not be coming back.'

A silence followed.

'You said the views along the coastal road are impressive,' said Ravensmede.

'Yes, they're wonderfully scenic.'

'In that case, why don't we travel the route ourselves? We could spend the day on the beach, Cook can pack us a basket of food…and you can take your paintbox. Would tomorrow suit?'

Kathryn's eyes lit up, and she smiled before waiting politely for Lady Maybury to deliver her verdict.

'It's certainly a splendid suggestion, but Kathryn and I will go alone. We've been monopolising you, Nicholas, and we should allow you to pursue your own interests for the day. You will grow bored with constantly escorting an old lady and her companion.' She faced her grandson. 'Is that not a better idea?'

Ravensmede returned his grandmother's look in full. Something unspoken flashed between them, something slightly dangerous that conflicted with the smiles upon their faces.

Sensing the underlying current, Kathryn felt unease prickle between her shoulder blades.

'A veritable genius,' replied Lord Ravensmede. 'Your concern for my welfare is admirable, Grandmama, but I am of a mind to enjoy the beach tomorrow too. You would not forbid my interest?'

Faded green eyes locked with bright green, in a battle of wills, and then the dowager inclined her head. 'Not this time,' she said.

Anna Marchant left the maid to close the gaping front door and hurried towards the parlour at the back of the house, pulling off her gloves and straw bonnet as she went. Just as she expected, she found her husband sitting comfortably spread out upon the sofa reading a newspaper. He glanced up briefly as she shut the door firmly behind her, then resumed his examination of the article in which he appeared engrossed.

'You're back sooner than I expected,' said Mr Marchant without taking his eyes from the paper. 'Did the visit not go well?'

'The place is empty. A serving girl told me that Lady Maybury and her companion have gone to Brighthelmstone.'

'So?' Mr Marchant could barely keep the boredom from his voice.

'With Lord Ravensmede.'

'So?' he said again.

'Oh, for heaven's sake!' snapped Mrs Marchant. 'Must I spell it out for you?'

Henry Marchant slowly lowered the newspaper from before his face and looked at his wife with an irritated expression. 'Madam, I'm sure that is what you intend, so hurry up and be done with it.'

'Lord Ravensmede has hired a house for them all in Brighthelmstone. He is living in the same premises as Kathryn!'

'And his grandmother,' pointed out Mr Marchant.

'It's all of a sham, I tell you. He's taken Kathryn as his mistress under the guise of her being Lady Maybury's companion.'

'Nonsense! Eleanor Maybury wouldn't risk her reputation with such a thing. And I doubt that even Ravensmede would drag his own grandmother into such a scheme. Besides, if Ravensmede wanted Kathryn as his mistress, he would have taken her by now, and as blatantly as he did all of the others.'

'Whatever you say, the rumours are already starting, Henry!'

she snapped. 'Think what they'll do to Lottie. Where will her chances of a good match be then, when her cousin is publicly denounced as a slut?'

'I'm sure you're mistaken, Anna.'

'There's very much more danger than you realise.' She thought fleetingly of Amanda White's threat. 'I'm sure that a trip to Brighthelmstone is in order.'

Mr Marchant's eyes rolled up into his head. 'I think you're overreacting, my dear.'

'You'll see who is overreacting when your niece is the talk of the town and your own daughter's chance of marriage is ruined because of it. Hasn't Kathryn lived as part of this family for the past three years? Do you think I've learned nothing of the girl's nature? I've said all along that she is a sly and wanton miss, and now I'm proved right. Will you let her destroy Lottie's chance? Are you content to let your brother's daughter ruin everything for your own flesh and blood? Mark my words, if one hint of this comes out before Lottie has made a match, then she'll be on the shelf for ever!' Mrs Marchant pressed a small lace handkerchief to her eye and gave a sniff.

With the weary resignation of a man who knew full well that his wife would give him no peace, Henry Marchant closed the newspaper, folded it in two and sat it upon his lap. 'What do you wish to do?'

'Fetch Kathryn back from Brighthelmstone. Have her live here with us.'

'You dislike the girl immensely, Anna. Why do you want her back here?'

'If she's under our control, then we can limit any danger she might do. She's safer where we can keep an eye on her.' She made no mention of Mrs White and what the widow had insinuated. 'For the sake of my daughter's future I'm prepared to suffer Kathryn's presence.'

Mr Marchant digested his wife's words. 'Kathryn is now

four and twenty. We cannot force her to come back with us. The last time I saw her she seemed determined in her role as Lady Maybury's companion. And I don't suppose she can have too fond a remembrance of this house.'

'Why should she should think of us with anything less than gratitude? Had it not been for this family Kathryn would have ended up in the gutter. However, I concede that she always was a selfish, addle-brained miss, and perhaps that has biased her memory,' said Mrs Marchant. 'That's why I have a plan.' For the first time since entering the parlour she smiled. 'You need not worry, Henry. A little family trip to partake of the sea air and Kathryn will return with us to Green Street.' Her smile broadened. 'And then she'll be sorry, very sorry indeed, for all the trouble that she's caused.'

The day was fine and warm with a pleasant sea breeze. They had encamped on the beach at a secluded spot not far removed from the town of Worthing, and enjoyed a tasty lunch from the depths of the hamper. Lady Maybury, having battled valiantly against the combined effects of fatigue, heat and a full stomach, lost the struggle and finally succumbed to sleep beneath the shade of her parasol.

Kathryn sat on a small stool placed upon the sand. The wooden drawing board was balanced on her thighs, and she stared completely entranced by the vast expanse of sea that stretched before her.

'Do you mind if I watch while you paint?' Ravensmede sat down beside the slight figure that seemed dwarfed beneath the drawing board. He could not see her face beneath that hideous monstrosity of a bonnet. Momentarily he wondered why she was still insistently wearing the mud-brown hat; he knew full well that his grandmother had been doggedly trying to add to her companion's wardrobe piece by piece.

She turned then and looked up. 'I don't mind, but I warn you that it shall not take long before you grow deeply and thoroughly bored.' The small pink mouth curved in a tantalising smile. An errant curl fluttered across her cheek.

She was teasing him! One dark eyebrow arched wryly. 'Perhaps. I've never watched an artist at work. This will be a new experience for me.'

'Then I hope it will be an enjoyable one.' She fixed her paper into place and, after checking the sharpness of her pencil, began to sketch.

'I thought you meant to paint the scene.'

'Yes. But I'll draw it out first in pencil so that I may rectify any mistakes I make. Only when I'm happy that I have the proportions correct will I begin to paint.' All the while her hand moved swiftly, lightly against the paper, her gaze flickering constantly between the sea and the white patch of paper.

Ravensmede's gaze flitted from the view to the paper to the fine bones of the woman's face. She was clearly intent on her task, her gaze never wandering once. There was an openness about her expression, as if she had let fall the careful guard of politeness. This was the Kathryn that he'd witnessed humming behind the tree in St James's Park, who had gazed unseeing at a blackened fireplace in her aunt's house, and smiled when he touched his fingers to her cheek. It was the first time she'd knowingly let him witness her escape, to wherever it was she went when she looked so faraway. He could see the same look in her eye, as if she were present in body only and her mind somewhere else altogether. 'You must have had a very good drawing master!' The faint marks on the paper were beginning to take shape.

A laugh that caught on the wind was carried out to sea. 'I taught myself! Anyone can sketch if they practise enough, and believe me I practised!' Still her gaze moved methodically between the lapping water and the white page. Her eyes were narrowed and her face crinkled against the sun. 'Have you tried your hand at it?'

'As a child, never since. My mother said it was quite the most ugly picture she had ever seen. My talents lie elsewhere, or so I am told.'

Only then did she pause, and look up into his face. 'I'm sure your mother was wrong.' Her voice was quietly serious and her eyes filled with compassion. Then she smiled and the moment was gone, as quickly as it had arrived. She resumed her scrutiny of the view. 'I can teach you if you like.' It was uttered lightly, as if it were of no importance. The pencil scraped against the page, making a vertical line here, a horizontal line there.

A blossoming of warmth erupted in Ravensmede's chest. He longed to lay his arm across her shoulders, to hold her to him. 'I would like that very much, Kathryn.' Since his dismissal of Harry Silverton he had felt extraordinarily happy. Knowing that she held the golden-haired youth in no regard and had sought his own protection gladdened his heart. It was better than winning a fortune night after night at the gaming tables. Better than an evening spent drinking with Caddie and the boys. And infinitely better than any time he had spent in any other woman's company. He watched while she covered the entirety of the page, excepting the odd patch here and there, in pale blue paint.

As if in answer to his unasked question she offered an explanation. 'It's a wash to unify the background. It should also stop the glare from the sun bouncing up from the page and dazzling my eyes. Conditions today are perfect and it should dry in no time. Would you like some paper and a pencil?'

'For now I'm content to watch you. But I'll hold you to your promise of sketching lessons.' The sun beat down with a relentless strength. 'Kathryn, would you mind if I removed my coat?'

She did not look up from mixing her paints. 'Of course not. You must be melting beneath all that wool.'

He peeled off the offending item and laid it down by his side. The cooling breeze fluttered through the fine lawn sleeves of his shirt, and he toyed with the idea of removing his waistcoat and neckcloth, but thought better of it. Daubs of paint were stroked on to the paper by her delicate hand. Just watching fascinated Ravensmede. The slow repetitive action, sometimes tentative, sometimes bold, held his attention so that he could not look away. A sheet of calm sparkling water, clear and deep, of quite the brightest turquoise coloration he had seen. Small waves lapping against the shoreline in the distance. Cloudless blue sky stretching out far to the horizon. She captured it all. And the air of peace that surrounded them. Nothing sounded except the soft rush of the sea on the sand and the cry of the gulls circling high overhead. It was enough just to sit by her, to be in her presence. No need for words. Soft sugary sand warm to the touch, all yellow and fawn, golden and white. On and on she painted, as if driven by the magic of the place to set down a record of what had existed for this one afternoon. And all the while Ravensmede sat by her side.

One last brush stroke and she cocked her head to the side. 'Mmm.' It was a gentle sigh of consideration. With deliberate care she set the board aside and clambered to her feet. 'Pins and needles in my legs.' She wiggled and stamped her feet to ease the numbness and, unmindful of her bonnet ribbons that were flapping around her chin, pressed the weighty drawing board into the Viscount's hands. 'Please can you hold this, just so that I may check that I haven't missed anything. I always find looking at it from a distance helps.' Without waiting for an answer she moved several paces away and turned to inspect the painting.

Ravensmede looked down at the drawing board. 'You've captured the view splendidly.'

'And you, sir, are looking at it upside down!' came the cheeky reply.

His mouth curved to a grin. 'I beg your pardon, but I can imagine how it will appear the right way round.'

'Here, let me hold it while you look.' Just as the board was halfway between them, a gust of wind lifted Kathryn's bonnet clear off her head. She loosed her grip on the board in order to catch it back, just as Ravensmede engaged in the same idea. The drawing board dropped to the sand, bouncing on its side before fortuitously landing on its back. The ties that had secured the painting dislodged in the fall, and, before either Kathryn or Nicholas could move, the sheets of paper were sent flapping and tumbling along the sand. 'Oh, no! That's all the paper I have left!' The bonnet forgotten, Kathryn scrabbled along the shore, and successfully captured the newly finished coastal painting along with four blank sheets. Another five blew ever further away.

Nicholas caught her elbow. 'You have the painting. Let the others go. We can buy some more.'

'No, paper is costly and all my money is accounted for. Please!'

With that look in her eyes and the long wind-blown hair tumbling in a cascade of curls reaching far past her shoulders, Ravensmede would have granted her anything. In a gallant gesture he chased the sheets until at last he had caught each and every one. His exertions had taken him quite some distance along the beach, but when he looked round the slight figure was running towards him. Her hair glinted a reddish golden brown in the sunlight and was billowing wantonly in every direction. A pair of finely shaped ankles and calves were visible each time the wind gusted around her skirts; moreover, the material was blown to cling revealingly against the shape of her thighs and hips. As he collected the papers into a tidy pile, one caught his eye. It was not blank, but contained a pencil drawing executed in great detail. The breath caught in Ravensmede's throat. His eyes raked the picture a moment longer before he bent low to the ground as if catching the papers up to him, and slipped the folded sheet into the secret inner pocket of his waistcoat.

'Nicholas!'

He glanced up and, with a smile upon his face, closed the empty distance between them.

She was breathless and pink-cheeked, wild and wind blown, and, judging from the look on her face, enormously glad to see him. Lord, but he could have taken her in his arms and tumbled her upon the sand there and then.

'Did you catch them?'

'Every last one!' He passed the sheets into her hands, and, unable to help himself, caught her to him and pressed a kiss to the top of her head.

She did not chastise him. Rather one small hand reached up and squeezed his arm. 'Thank you,' she said simply.

'Come on, we had best get you back to Grandmama. She won't be pleased when she wakens.'

The silver-grey eyes were lit with pearly hues. 'Perhaps she's still sleeping and has not seen this débâcle.'

The Viscount laughed and gently swept his thumb across the bridge of her nose. 'I was thinking more about your freckles. Although, personally, I find them quite delightful.' He cast her a wicked grin, held her hand in his and walked back towards his grandmother.

It was fortunate that the Viscount spotted Kathryn's hairpins in the sand close by her abandoned drawing board, and more fortunate still that the young lady had managed to secure her hair in some vestige of a respectable style before the dowager awakened. Alas, the mud-brown bonnet had been swept far out to sea, a mishap that caused his lordship much rejoicing. Indeed, Lord Ravensmede could not remember a more enjoyable day.

Chapter Twelve

It was one quiet afternoon close to the end of the second week of their holiday when Lady Maybury announced her intention to host a ball at her grandson's townhouse.

Lady Maybury continued, 'I haven't told him of m'idea yet, and I don't want you letting the cat out of the bag, young lady. It wouldn't do to pester him with all the details when we can sort those out ourselves.'

'But shouldn't we check that he's happy to host such an event first, before making any arrangements?'

'He shall not be hosting the ball. That's my job,' said the dowager. 'I assure you, Kathryn, he'll be most pleased with my efforts.'

'But…'

Lady Maybury raised an eyebrow. 'Are you questioning that I know what's best for m'own grandson?'

Kathryn saw all the warning signs and sought to pacify her employer. 'No, not at all, my lady. If you've made up your mind then—'

'My mind is made up,' came the adamant reply. 'Fetch paper, pen and ink and let us begin the list of guests. There's no time like the present. And remember that it's to remain, for the minute, a secret from Nicholas.'

'Of course.' Kathryn did as she was bid and waited.

Soon the dowager was reeling off names. 'Lord and Lady Radford, Lord and Lady Finlay, Lady Hadstone, Mrs Lee, Lady Farrow, oh, and Mr and Mrs Barchester and the Misses Barchester, but most certainly not Mr and Mrs Palmer—they're too vulgar for words.' She sighed and waited for Kathryn's neat script to stop. And then the pause stretched a little longer. 'Naturally, when Nicholas is married, his wife will take over such duties. This is likely to be the last time I'm able to play hostess for him.'

Something cold wrapped itself around Kathryn's chest and squeezed. She was quite unable to move. 'I didn't realise that the Viscount was betrothed.'

'Oh, he isn't…well, not officially.' Lady Maybury leaned forward and lowered her voice. 'If I'm not mistaken, that is something that will be remedied before the Season is at a close.' She gave a sage nod of the head. 'M'son Charles—that is, Nick's father, Earl Maybury—thinks it's more than time that the boy settled down and all that, what with him having sown more than his fair share of wild oats.' She sniffed.

A tinge of colour touched Kathryn's cheeks.

'Still, the least said about that side of things the better. Afraid us Mayburys are not a patient lot, as you may already have guessed, m'dear. But even Nick can't hold out much longer against his father. Charles's practically got it all arranged. Gel is from a decent family, good breeding and money too. Can't think why Nick's being so confoundedly stubborn. Wretched boy's got to marry at some time or other.'

Kathryn reeled as if she had suffered a hard blow to the stomach. 'May I…' she steeled herself to ask the question, knowing full well that she should not, that it was none of her business '…enquire as to the name of the lady that the Earl has in mind?'

The old lady's eyes washed bright with compassion. 'Her name is Miss Francesca Paton, my dear, and m'son is very de-

termined that Nick weds her.' She stretched out one small hand
and touched it consolingly to Kathryn's.

The slow terrible thud of Kathryn's heart intensified, and
deep within the pit of her stomach she tasted the sourness of
nausea. It seemed that there was a ligature tightening around
her throat.

'There may very well be two weddings. Your future should
be assured.' The dowager smiled a small smile. 'I'm very determined to catch *you* a good match.'

'No, my lady, that really isn't necessary,' Kathryn gasped.
'I'm here as your companion, not to find myself a husband.' In
her distress she gripped the pen as if she would snap it clean in
two, her fingers inadvertently touching too close to the nib and
bleeding a large stain of ink across her skin.

'Tush! Don't you want a husband and children of your own?'

'I...' She struggled to keep the emotion from her voice.
'I'm happy here with you.'

'As I'm happy to have you here. But you deserve a life of
your own, gel, and I mean to see that you get it.'

The flow of black letters upon the page began to swim. A
strange dizziness was rolling up towards her head. She forced
herself to inhale deeply, slowly, willed herself not to yield to it.
Determination clamped her teeth hard together, and made her lips
stiff and immobile. Surely she wasn't about to faint? She *never*
fainted. Not Kathryn Marchant. But the dizzy sensation was expanding and black spots danced in the periphery of her vision.
Sweat prickled down the length of her spine, and her chest felt
so tight that she feared she could not draw the air into her lungs.
She shut her eyelids tightly, struggling to regain control, doggedly
telling herself that she would not faint, not here, not now, not
when the dowager might guess the terrible truth.

'Kathryn.' The old lady's voice was soft. 'It is for the best.'

One breath, and then another. In. And out. She forced herself
to breathe deeply, fingers clinging for dear life to the arms of
the chair. Slowly the darkness receded, but the terrible weight

upon her chest lay there still. It took great strength to hide the utter bleakness that swept over her. The constriction in her chest had spread to her throat, wherein the lump was making it difficult to swallow. But for that terrible tightness all else had grown numb, a creeping lack of sensation that rendered her trapped upon the Sheraton-style mahogany armchair. She could no longer see the words that she had penned so carefully on the neatly cut sheet, could scarcely see the paper itself. 'Please excuse me, Lady Maybury. I fear I'm feeling a little unwell,' she managed to say through lips that could barely move.

'Unwell?' A concerned old hand touched to Kathryn's arm. 'You have gone very pale of a sudden. And you feel so hot! Mary shall take you straight to bed. You'll feel better after a little rest.'

'I'll finish the guest list in the morning,' murmured Kathryn and laid the paper and pen down carefully beside the inkstand on the desk.

'Stop worrying over that. There's time enough yet.' The old lady tried to look severe and for the first time failed miserably. 'I'll brook no disobedience, gel, so off to bed with you.'

'Yes, thank you, my lady.' Kathryn kept her eyes averted, frightened of losing her last vestige of control, and quietly hurried from the room.

Not one last drop of blood lingered in Kathryn's face as she climbed the central staircase towards her bedchamber. Slowly, methodically her fingers worked at the material of her skirt, pleating and smoothing and pleating again, in a rhythmic repetitive motion. And all the while, with each and every step that she took, she wondered why it had taken such a revelation for her to realise the truth. Not that Lord Ravensmede was to marry. As Earl Maybury's heir that had always been a foregone conclusion. Perhaps she hadn't expected it to happen quite so soon, but that in itself was not the issue. No, the truth was much worse than that. In her time as Lady Maybury's companion, she, plain, penniless Kathryn Marchant, had fallen head over heels in love with Nicholas Maybury; a man who was not only an aristocrat and enormously wealthy, but also a rake. And the reward for such a foolish action could only be a broken heart.

At the same time as Kathryn was treading silently up the central staircase by the maid's side, Lord Ravensmede was sitting at the small reading table by the window of his bedchamber in the house in Brighthelmstone. Before him, spread out upon the fine polished cherry-wood, was a drawing. The piece had been executed with a fine attention to detail, capturing every nuance of the sitter, conveying, by the skilled use of line and shade, that person's precise character. Ravensmede studied every last pencil mark upon the paper until at last he sat back in the chair and smiled. It was clear that the artist viewed the model in a positive light. Indeed, he would go as far as to say that there was a distinct tenderness in the rendition. And that thought was a most appealing one to the Viscount, given that the artist was none other than Kathryn, and the model—himself.

Quite when she had secretly sketched his likeness he did not know. These last weeks in Brighthelmstone had only confirmed what he knew of her: that she was kind and compassionate and imbued with a freedom of imagination that allowed her to escape the mundane, the tiresome, and the downright painful. Whether it be through the pictures set down on paper or those that she wove in her head, Kathryn was an artist, and a passionate one at that.

Beneath that meek and mild exterior was hidden an ardour. But Ravensmede had seen beneath the mask, had known the essence of her from the very first night of their meeting, when he'd mistaken her for Amanda White—as if there could ever be any comparison. Mrs White was little better than a courtesan who sold herself to the highest bidder. Kathryn was quite simply the most amazing woman he had ever met. Lust or desire did not go near to explaining the compulsion he felt for her. Just to be near her, to make her laugh, to ensure her safety, to hear her voice, and hold her within his arms… It was far and beyond anything he had ever known.

A door opened across the corridor. Female voices. One that sounded to be the maid, the other so quiet as to almost hide its owner. But he didn't need to hear Kathryn's voice to know that she was near. Awareness coursed through him. And he knew that he could no longer ignore his need to see her, to watch her smile, to touch his lips to hers. Sandwiching the portrait between two blank sheets of paper, he hid it carefully under some papers within a drawer. Then, waiting until he heard the maid make her way along to the servants' stairwell, he quietly opened his door and stepped across the corridor to Kathryn's bedchamber.

Kathryn heard the light knock at her door and scrambled up from the top of the bed. 'I'm just coming,' she said in a small controlled voice. Before she had taken one step further Lord Ravensmede entered, closing the door noiselessly behind him. Her hand clasped at the bedside table. She could not speak.

'Kathryn!' Shock widened his eyes. Whatever he had been expecting to see, it wasn't the state of distress that he now witnessed. He reached her in two strides and without the slightest hesitation pulled her into his arms. Scanning her face, he took in the unnaturally white cheeks, and the haunted look in her eyes. 'What in Hades has happened?' His clasp was gentle, his hands firm and reassuring against her back.

'Nothing at all. You need not concern yourself with me, sir.' She struggled to release herself from his embrace, but he was having none of it. 'Lord Ravensmede, I must insist that you unhand me. It isn't fitting that you should be here in my bedchamber or that you have your arms around me.' The pale lips pressed tight together as she spoke the words quietly and with as much dignity as she could muster.

'What is this nonsense, Kathryn? I had thought us to have reached an understanding. Are we not friends?'

She lowered her face that he might not see her pain. 'Indeed we are, sir.'

'Then I would know what this about.'

'I made a mistake,' she said, choosing her words carefully. 'We cannot go on as before…even if we are friends. I'm your grandmother's companion…and I'm happy with that.'

'Have you had word from your aunt?' he asked suspiciously.

'No, of course not. She doesn't even know that I'm here.'

'Is it my grandmother?'

'No.' The word was determined and defiant.

'Then why are you so upset?'

'I'm not.'

A single dark eyebrow arched. With slow deliberation he traced a thumb down her cheek.

'No!' She twisted her face away. Then with more control, 'Please do not.'

His hand stilled in mid-air, then dropped back down to her arm. 'Tell me what's wrong, Kathryn.'

'I cannot.'

Silence hummed.

'Kathryn,' he said.

Slowly, unable to help herself, she looked round at him.

His eyes were dark as the depths of a forest where the light does not reach.

Beneath his gaze Kathryn felt her resolve waver. For there she could see concern and kindness…and something else, something for which hope flared…then died when rational thought intruded. It seemed that she had to drag the breath into her lungs, force it back out again. Pain burst anew into a thousand piercing shards at just how much she had come to love this man.

She could not tell him. Had to preserve some scrap of pride. He desired her…as she desired him, to touch, to kiss, to hold. He liked her, of that she was sure. But he did not love her; could not love her as she loved him. Before the summer was out he would be betrothed to another woman…married even. And

Kathryn would be alone once more. She chided herself for the fool that she was. Even as he looked at her as if he could see into her very soul, she lowered her eyes.

She wanted to scream and cry and beat her hands upon the breadth of his chest. She wanted to condemn him for each kiss, for every caress of his hand, the very smile on his face, the tender light in his eyes. How dare he tempt her to love him knowing full well nothing decent could ever come of it! The pain seared across her chest, tightening her throat. Through all the storm of emotions she held herself erect, clinging to her dignity, never once yielding to the sensations that battered her. 'Please leave now.' Those three small words so quietly, so politely spoken were more devastating than if she had roared at the top of her voice.

'No, not until you tell me what's going on.' One hand slid up the length of her arm to grip upon her shoulder.

She trembled beneath his touch. 'Please don't touch me.'

The green eyes widened, but her heart was so wounded she did not see his hurt.

His grip loosened until his fingers were nothing more than a featherlight touch. They lingered for a matter of seconds longer and then slowly, as if by an act of immense will-power, they were gone. And now, even though there was nothing holding her to him, she felt the warmth of his proximity, felt the urge to wrap her arms around him, bury her face against his chest. Her breath was uneven and shallow, coming in fits and starts, gasps and shudders. She forced herself to step back, to reject temptation before it caught her completely. One tiny step backwards, and then another.

He made to follow.

'Lord Ravensmede,' she said as coldly as she could.

Frustration boiled. 'Damnation, Kathryn, just tell me!'

For one tiny sliver of a moment she nearly did, and then common sense came to the fore once more and she shook her head.

She composed her face, unwilling to have him witness the

full extent of her humiliation. 'I fear I have the headache, sir. If you would be so kind as to leave me to my rest.'

Nicholas's gaze did not falter. He made no move.

She swallowed hard. Her heart shuddered. 'Please, Nicholas,' she whispered. 'Don't make this any harder than it already is. Just go.'

He looked at her for a moment longer, then turned and walked towards the door.

Ravensmede only suffered Kathryn's new cold formal treatment for two days before a visit from Harry Silverton forced a change in matters. The Viscount was staring moodily out of the library window, sipping his brandy when the footman arrived.

'Beggin' your pardon, m'lord, but her ladyship sent me. Mr Silverton has arrived and is refusing to leave until he's seen Miss Marchant.'

The ejection of Mr Silverton was to prove rather more problematic than Lord Ravensmede anticipated.

'Ravensmede, you dashed scoundrel!' Harry Silverton bellowed upon Ravensmede's entry to the drawing room.

'Mr Silverton, I must urge you to refrain from shouting when my grandmother is present.' Ravensmede looked meaningfully at the dowager perched uneasily on the edge of the sofa.

The younger man swayed a little unsteadily on his feet. 'Where have you hidden her?'

'If by *her* you're referring to Miss Marchant, then I regret to inform you that she is at present not in to any visitors, nor is she likely to be so in the near future.'

'You confounded cur!' The young gentleman's words had a distinctive slur to them. 'You mean to keep her for yourself. To have her as your mistress when a decent man like me would ask for nothing but her hand in marriage!' The stench of alcohol pervading the room intensified as Mr Silverton staggered closer.

Ravensmede's eyes narrowed at the insult, but he had no intention of bandying insults with a young man who was quite clearly well and truly foxed. 'I will ask you to leave, Mr Silverton, before you make even more of a fool of yourself than you have already.'

'Damn you, Ravensmede, but I love her, and I ain't leaving until I've seen her to tell her so.' He scrabbled about in his pocket and produced a sheet of folded paper. 'I've written a poem to her beauty. I mean for her to have it.' He tried to focus on the sheet for several minutes, but to no avail.

'I shall not ask you again, sir.' The Viscount's voice cut sharply through the room.

'I've heard all about you. Who hasn't? The infamous Viscount of Ravensmede and his affairs with the ladies, and the gaming tables.' The youngster sneered. 'A rake, a libertine and more! I've seen the way you look at Miss Marchant and I don't like it.' The dramatic effect of this little speech was somewhat ruined by the enormous belch that succeeded it. 'I do beg your pardon,' said Mr Silverton.

'You've said quite enough for one night, sir. And if you won't leave of your own accord, then I will throw you out, you insolent dog!' Lord Ravensmede moved to effect his threat.

'Stay where you are!' Silverton produced a pistol and waved it in the Viscount's direction. The poem fluttered unnoticed to the floor.

Lady Maybury, who had hitherto been silent throughout the two men's exchange, leapt to her feet. 'How dare you threaten m'grandson, you odious toad! Put that infernal thing away this instant!'

Mr Silverton looked momentarily at the barrel of his pistol as if he were surprised to find the object in his hand. 'I do beg your pardon, my lady. I was just trying to explain to Lord Ravensmede that I…' he hiccuped and waved the pistol as he spoke '… am here to prevent him ruining Miss Marchant. I mean to have her as my wife, you see.'

'Yes, I see only too well, sir, that you are going about courting m'companion in quite the wrong manner. Not only are you rather the worse for drink, but I'm offended by your presence.' Lady Maybury sniffed and cast him the haughtiest of looks.

'I didn't mean to insult *you*, my lady. *You* are not a rake of the worst degree.' He gestured the muzzle in the dowager's direction as he stressed the word *you*. '*You* do not mean to keep her from me.' The pistol pointed directly at Lady Maybury, the young man's finger lingering unwittingly around the trigger.

Ravensmede had seen enough. He knew exactly how dangerous a weapon could be, particularly in the hands of a man who had clearly spent the best part of the day in the consumption of brandy if the reek was anything to go by. His grandmother was at risk and that was not something he was prepared to tolerate. Moving with a speed and agility that surprised them all, Ravensmede launched himself at the golden-haired visitor, placing his own body between the pistol and the old lady at whom it was levelled. The momentum of his flight carried both men to the floor, but not before an almighty roar reverberated around the drawing room. The stench of gunpowder arose, along with a plume of blue smoke.

Lady Maybury screamed.

Ravensmede clambered up from the prostrate body.

Harry Silverton's bright blue eyes stared up, round, unblinking.

The dowager scrabbled towards her grandson. 'Thank God you're safe!'

The door swung open. Pounding steps as the butler and two footmen clattered in.

'Escort this gentleman from the house. A carriage shall be required to send him on his way.' Ravensmede bent to retrieve the pistol from where it lay discarded upon the floor. 'He no longer has need of this.'

A soft gasp came from the doorway.

She was by his side, hands on his sleeve, eyes wide with fear. 'Nicholas?' No polite and distant 'Lord Ravensmede' this time.

He smiled a lazy smile, and pulled her against the right-hand side of his body. 'Mr Silverton was just leaving.'

Kathryn grabbed both of his arms and stared up into his face, all thoughts of propriety forgotten in her concern. 'What happened?'

An unmistakable wince, and an involuntary withdrawal.

'Nicholas?' With an escalating dread Kathryn let her gaze travel slowly to where her right hand clutched.

The material of his coat was warm and wet beneath her fingers. She drew them back, swallowed hard and looked down at the glistening red stain. The grey eyes swivelled to meet his. 'You're bleeding.'

'The smallest scratch, nothing more.'

Lady Maybury stepped closer, her bony fingers clutching to her throat. 'You're shot,' she whispered in disbelief.

Her words seemed to rouse Harry Silverton from his faint. The gentleman raised himself cautiously to his elbows, terror dawning upon his countenance. 'Was an accident.' And with that he groaned and gingerly replaced his head upon the polished wooden floorboards.

Time ceased. The moment stretched unending, until at last the dowager gave a frightened little mew. 'So much blood.'

'Grandmama.' Ravensmede stepped forward to reassure the elderly lady who was tottering rather unsteadily on her feet.

As if awakening from a stupor Kathryn sprang to life. She moved to gently, but firmly, place Lady Maybury in the closest armchair. 'My lady, please do not alarm yourself. It's as Nicholas says, a flesh wound that bleeds prolifically.' Even as she uttered the reassurance her own fears, her own darkest dread, were being thrust deep down, hidden far out of sight. But from across the years came an image of another man she had loved, of the faint lingering smell of gunpowder, and the raw stench of blood...and her father's lifeless fingers resting upon his desk, still wrapped around the handle of the pistol. Her eyes shuttered. Dear God, not Nicholas, never Nicholas. He could not die…she would not let him. Determination rose. She gritted her teeth hard, shock still kicking in her gut. Pushed away all memories, all thoughts of fear and panic. Allowed instinct to take over. Kathryn would do whatever she had to…for Nicholas's sake. So, having dealt with the dowager for the minute, she instructed the butler to send for a physician, the first footman to fetch boiled water and clean linen strips, and the remaining footman to collect four warm blankets from the press upstairs. Only then did she turn her attentions to Nicholas.

For all of the bemused expression that he presented to her, she could see the pallor in his face. It seemed that something grabbed hold of her heart and squeezed until it was tight and painful. She breathed deeply, squared her shoulders, and moved towards him. 'Nicholas, we must remove your coat.' Her voice was surprisingly calm and controlled. 'Here, let me assist you.'

'I assure you, Kathryn, there's no—' The deep voice got no further.

'Assure me only of your compliance, sir,' she said quietly.

A dark eyebrow arched, but before he could utter his protest she was peeling the fitted coat from his body.

She removed first the sleeve from his uninjured arm and then, without pausing, she caught him unawares and pushed him back on to the sofa.

'I think I might manage on my own,' he said wryly.

But her small bloodstained fingers were already on his arm, easing the cloth away from his wound. The coat was delivered close to the dowager's feet in a heap. His neckcloth and waistcoat received similar treatment and soon lay on top of the crumpled coat. Kathryn worked with a calm quiet efficiency that belied the frenzied beat of her heart.

She cleared her throat. 'Now for your shirt.'

'I beg your pardon?'

'Please remove your shirt, Nicholas.' Arms akimbo, smoky grey eyes that glistened with determination…and something else that she could not quite hide, Kathryn was unaware that she presented a most formidable sight, enough to make a man's pulse race, especially a man whom she'd been avoiding for the past two days.

The sensual mouth grinned wickedly. 'You're putting my grandmother to the blush, Kathryn.'

'I'm sure that Lady Maybury will forgive me this once,' she said with a great deal more confidence than she felt. 'Please, sir, for I don't mean to ask you again.'

His smile deepened and he deliberately lay back upon the cushions, and waited.

'Very well, my lord.' She swallowed hard, gathered her courage together in both hands, and, stepping forward, effected her action in one fell move. The tear of linen sounded loudly in the room. Shock showed upon his face. And she knew that, whatever Nicholas had been expecting, it was not to have her quite literally rip the shirt from his body. Having disposed of the front and one arm of the garment, she lingered over the injured limb, gently easing the material away from the wounded area. The sight of the bloody mess of flesh was almost her undoing. *The smallest scratch* he had said, but Kathryn's heart turned over at what she saw once the last vestige of shirt had been removed. A few inches over and the ball would have lodged itself in his chest. A wave of dizziness swept through her at the thought.

'Kathryn!' Lady Maybury gave a weak protest.

Kathryn took a deep breath and pulled herself together. Such weakness would not help him. 'Don't worry, my lady. I know what I'm doing. All shall soon be ready for the physician's arrival.' Kathryn flung the words of reassurance over her shoulder, but there was no such assurance or confidence within. She forced herself not to think, just to act. 'Once we have this cleaned up, he shall be able to see the damage clearly.'

When the first footman eventually returned with two basins of boiled water that were still steaming and a small pile of linen strips, it was to a scene in which his master was lying semi-clothed upon the sofa with his grandmother's companion clasping his arm. It was the same footman that had witnessed Miss Marchant and the Viscount embracing by the front door not so very long ago. The man was wise enough to keep his thoughts to himself and made no sign as to having observed anything remotely untoward.

'Very good, Toby. Place the basins down here by me and the rags close by. Thank you.' She gave the footman a little nod and moved the bowls to exactly where she needed them. 'And Toby, send Mr Silverton home in the carriage as Lord Ravensmede instructed.' A nod of her head indicated the young gentleman's prone body.

'Yes, miss.'

Then the second footman returned with the blankets and, having sat them upon the table, made to help carry the inebriated man from the room.

Kathryn washed her own red stained hands thoroughly in one basin before wetting the linen rag. For the first time since removing his clothes she sought Nicholas's gaze. Kathryn was unable to help herself; her hand fluttered to lightly cup his face. 'Although I'll be as gentle as I can, Nicholas, my cleansing of the wound is bound to cause you pain.' Her thumb stroked a gentle encouragement. 'I'll contrive to act as quickly as is possible.'

His eyes held hers. 'This isn't work for your hands, Kathryn.'

'Perhaps you're right,' she admitted softly. 'But I'll finish what I've started all the same.' She looked at him a moment longer, wanting to kiss the worry from his face. One last stroke of her thumb, a little smile, and then her hand left his face, and her gaze dropped once more to his injured arm.

'Dear Lord, but I'm too late!' a mumbled utterance escaped Mr Silverton's lips as the footmen manoeuvred him through the doorway. One pink-lined eye fixed itself on the woman bending low over the naked torso of Ravensmede. 'Miss Marchant!'

Kathryn did not divert her attention. Nothing else mattered save for Nicholas and his wound.

By the time Nicholas's arm had been cleansed and the deep furrow ploughed by the trajectory of the lead ball exposed, the Viscount lay back upon the sofa white-faced and with a grim line to his mouth. Perspiration beaded his forehead and upper lip, but he made no sound. There was a nausea in Kathryn's stomach at the pain her cleansing and probing had caused him. But the task was done now. The wound was tightly bound. And Kathryn could only be relieved. Taking his hand in hers, she guided it to lie across the top of the sofa back, allowing her fingers to linger when they should not have, desperate to give him some small comfort. There was nothing of embarrassment, no sense of impropriety at what she had done. Her thoughts were with Nicholas, and Nicholas alone.

His hand closed around hers. There was no strength in the light touch of his fingers, only the gentleness of a caress.

Green eyes met grey, and the smile they shared was both intimate and loving. It lasted only a moment, but it was enough. Kathryn tucked two warm blankets snugly around him, placed a cushion placed behind his head, and moved away. She had done what little she could; now there was Lady Maybury to attend to.

As she bent to hand the hot sweet tea to his grandmother, he could see that some of her hair had escaped her chignon, and was curling around her neck and shoulders. The long sleeves of her dress had been rolled back down into place, but the skirt and bodice were still marked with a liberal application of his blood. He knew that she had not been unaffected by what had just happened, had felt the slight tremble in her fingers, and admired her all the more for her courage. Her voice, quiet and clear, soothed, as did the slender scrubbed fingers carefully adjusting the mountain of blankets surrounding the old woman. He wondered that someone who had received so little care through-

out her own life had so much to give. His grandmother looked
pale and infinitely older than usual. A frown crinkled his brow.

'Kathryn,' he said.

She hurried across.

His gaze twitched to the dowager and back to the woman
standing above him.

As if reading his mind, she bent her face lower to his.

'My grandmother should not have witnessed this. Her
heart… She needs to rest. Help her up to her bedchamber.'

The grey eyes were filled with compassion. 'Nicholas, Lady
Maybury has suffered a great shock. What she needs now is to
know that her grandson is safe, that you've taken no great hurt
and will recover,' she said quietly.

'I told you, it's nothing more than a scratch.'

'Maybe so. But you bled like a stuck pig. You must reassure
her yourself by behaving as normal. It would be better if we
did not retire until the physician arrives.' And with that she
hurried back to attend to his grandmother.

He gave a slight nod in acquiescence, and smiled. Kathryn
Marchant had courage and honour…and his love.

Kathryn stood alone by the window in her bedchamber and
stared out at the expansive shimmering sea views. The water had
a turquoise-green hue reminiscent of that captured in the many
paintings of Mediterranean subjects that she'd seen over the
years. The rhythmic sweep of the waves lulled and pacified her.
White spray frothed where the waves broke upon the shoreline.
Cool sea air flooded in through the open window, filling the room
with its own peculiar scent: salt and seaweed and freshness.
Curtains billowed in the stiff breeze and several strands of hair
fluttered unnoticed across the pale skin of the woman's cheeks.
Still, silent, outwardly serene, the image she presented was far
removed from the turbulent emotions twisting within.

No matter that the physician had declared the Viscount to
have been extremely lucky or that the damage to Lord Ravens-

mede's arm was minimal. Rest, clean dressings, and it would soon be healed, or so the doctor had said. The memory of Nicholas's blood smeared upon her palms would not leave her. So much blood that she could have cried her fears aloud on the spot. She had wanted to clutch him to her, to take his pain upon herself, anything but face the awful terror of that moment, when her mind was filled with the worst of imaginings.

Death. It had a starkness about it that pared everything else to insignificance. So she had done what she had to, in order to remedy the situation, with no consideration for propriety, without the slightest notion of how her actions might be construed. He was alive and well. Now she could think of nothing else except how close she'd come to losing him. And that cast quite a different light on all of her best-made resolutions. Her façade of coolness and politeness and distance had crumbled to dust. Nicholas might well marry Miss Paton, but that didn't change the fact that Kathryn loved him with a love so strong that it frightened her. She knew now that she couldn't just turn her back on him, and walk away as if their friendship had never been. Not for all of Lady Maybury's warnings, not even for the sake of her own good name. Kathryn Marchant was changed for ever.

Chapter Thirteen

Kathryn's hand trembled before she clenched it into a fist and knocked lightly against the mahogany wooden panels of the door. Her heart was thudding fast and loud, and she swallowed to alleviate the dryness in her throat.

'Come in.' His voice alone caused a fluttering within her stomach.

She smoothed her skirt down with nervous hands and, before her courage could desert her, opened the door and stepped into Lord Ravensmede's bedchamber.

His eyes widened momentarily at the sight of her standing there so awkwardly by the doorframe. 'Kathryn?' And then, as if catching himself, 'Please…come in.'

Her fingers betrayed her, plucking at the pale green of her afternoon dress, in small furtive movements. For a moment it seemed that she had not heard him, for she stood stock-still and cautious as a deer scenting the wind. Then, just when he would have spoken again, she did as he bade, shutting the door silently behind her.

'Nicholas.' There was a silver light in her eyes and the first hint of a rose blush in the apple of her cheeks. The rich russet brown of her curls had been arranged up behind her head tidily as if she had only just combed and pinned them. Already two curls had contrived to free themselves to dance enticingly against the creamy white skin of her neck. She stopped short of the bottom of the bed, her eyes flitting between him and the floor.

He could see her unease and the tension that ran through her slender body by the repetitive touch of her fingers to her skirt. Yet there was something in her gaze when it rose to meet his, something new, something that was both soft and generous yet, paradoxically, with the same determination he had witnessed the previous day in the drawing room when she had tended his wound with such calm competence. His senses tingled. She should not be here, in his bedchamber, while he sat beneath the bedcovers clad only in a nightshirt. He held his breath and waited for what she had come to say.

As if reading his mind she started, 'I know that I shouldn't be here, but I wanted to check that you…that your arm has not worsened.'

'It's the smallest scratch, nothing more. I'm only in bed today to satisfy my grandmother, and of course my own slothful nature.' He stretched out his injured arm, clenching and unclenching his fist as if to demonstrate the proof of his words. 'But thank you for your concern.'

The colour bloomed in her face. 'I should go.'

'No.'

The word hung between them.

'Kathryn,' he said a little more gently, 'come and sit here beside me. I would speak with you before you leave.'

She showed no sign of complying.

'I want to thank you for what you did yesterday. The physician said that your quick action saved me much blood loss from the wound.'

'Anyone would have done the same.'

'Even to the point of forcibly unclothing me? I do not think so,' he said with a roguish smile.

Kathryn's cheeks were now blazing a fiery hot red. 'Yes, well…' she muttered and stared down at her feet. 'That couldn't be helped. The wound needed my attention and you weren't proving to be of much assistance. I'm sorry if I embarrassed you.'

It was the same expression that she had used at Lady Finlay's ball, for the slip in her dance steps…and their shared kisses in the moonlit room. Ravensmede felt a warmth expand within his chest as the memories flowed. 'You could never embarrass me, Kathryn.'

The clear gaze slid up to meet his, and he felt a flood of desire and need and tenderness. A shy smile spread across her mouth.

'The other day when you sent me away, what had happened to upset you so much?' It was a question that had worried at him since walking in to find her in that state within her bedchamber. For all that she had endured he had never seen her so affected, not until that day. The sight of her pain and the sound of the formality in her voice had made him want to snatch her into his arms, to kiss her long and hard and passionately until she told him what was wrong. And that whispered plea, *Please, Nicholas, don't make this any harder than it already is*, had torn at his heart. For Ravensmede, a man used to taking what he wanted, when he wanted it, such impotence was frustrating. His grandmother knew what the matter was about, with her little looks of feigned innocence, and contrivance to keep him away from her companion. But the old lady had stubbornly refused to be forthcoming and doggedly changed the subject each time he had mentioned Kathryn's name.

He watched her fingers catch at the material again, grip it hard. 'It's of no consequence,' she said.

'Kathryn…' He raised one eyebrow and peered at her as if he would fathom the truth in that way.

But her head just shook a quick denial. 'It doesn't matter, not now.'

He heard the slight breathless catch in her voice, watched her take a single step closer. His right hand stretched towards her, reaching out for her, a gesture of conciliation and more.

It seemed that she hesitated, her gaze unmoving upon his

hand, her face impassive. Then her eyes flickered up to his and he could see their colour had darkened to a soft smoky grey. The moment stretched. Time stilled. Awareness narrowed until there was only the two of them in existence. Thud of heart, flutter of pulse. Her small hand slid into his, his fingers closed around hers. From there he did not know quite how she came to be in his arms or his lips pressed against hers, possessing and yielding all at once.

She was warm and soft, an alluring mix of innocence and passion. His hands swept the length of her back, down to the curve of her hips, pulling her closer. Her mouth opened beneath his, inviting further exploration. The tip of his tongue slipped within, teasing, tantalising. Tongue touched tongue, lapped together, twisting, licking, sucking. All rational thought fled. She was his, to pleasure, to worship, to love. Even as he clutched her closer he heard the little mew sound in her throat, felt the nuzzle of her breasts against his chest. All of Lord Ravensmede's good intentions were lost.

His lips traced a pattern along the delicate line of her jaw to find the tender skin beneath her ear. She gave herself up to the sensations rippling through her. From the strange ache down deep and low in her pelvis to the pulsating heat in her thighs, Kathryn embraced what was happening to her. This was far beyond any dream. It was urgent and wicked and wild, but Kathryn wanted it never to stop. She needed to feel Nicholas's arms around her, wanted his mouth on hers. Her fingers caressed against his cheek, stroking down over the rough stubble of his chin. All the love that she felt welled up and flowed out to him, spilling over in every touch, in every kiss. And in her mind the silent words whispered again and again, *I love you, I love you,* until she knew not whether she gasped them aloud.

He plucked the pins from her hair, one by one, until the glorious mass of curls hung free. His fingers tangled within the heavy chestnut tresses, revelling in their glossy softness. Her hair smelled fresh and clean as if she'd rinsed it in a wash of lavender water. His hands followed her hair down to where it brushed against her breasts, cupped the two small mounds, massaging them through the material of her dress with gentle passion.

The soft white skin grew more sensitive with each caress, every stroke, until she thought that his heat would scorch her. And then when his fingers eventually found passage beneath the pale green bodice, to burrow under every layer of separating material to capture the bare skin of her breasts, she could not contain the sudden sharp inhalation of breath. Instinctively her back arched, thrusting her taut nipples hard against him, seeking more of something that she did not understand. Each and every touch sent sparks of pleasure writhing deep into her stomach. Rational thought had long since fled.

The groan growled low in his throat and his arms locked around her as he twisted and pushed her down so that she lay on the bed beside him. 'Kathryn,' he gasped her name as if it was air and he was a man suffocating for want of it. 'Kathryn,' he whispered again as he rolled his length on top of her.

'Oh, Nicholas,' she sighed and wrapped her arms around him.

A voice sounded from the direction of the stairs on the landing beyond the door of Ravensmede's bedchamber. 'What do you mean I can't go in there! I don't need you to announce me to m'own grandson,' bellowed Lady Maybury. 'If I want to see Lord Ravensmede I'll damn well see him!'

Kathryn and Nicholas froze as the full realisation of their situation hit them.

The dowager's small feet thumped noisily down the corridor, growing ever louder as she made her way to her grandson's bedchamber.

Kathryn's eyes widened in horror. She tried to scramble up, to repair the loosened bodice, the long curls that flowed wantonly over her shoulders. But Nicholas's hand stayed her frantic panic. He shook his head, touched a finger to her lips, and imprisoned her wrist with his other hand.

A sharp knock sounded at the door. 'Nicholas, are you decent?' Lady Maybury's words came clear through the mahogany.

''Fraid not, Grandmama,' said Ravensmede with a lazy drawl. 'I wouldn't want to shock your delicate constitution by the sight I present at this minute.' His eyes glowed wickedly as he looked down at Kathryn lying beneath him.

'Don't be absurd,' came the withering reply. 'I've seen it all before. Had you naked on m'knee before you were in breeches.'

Despite the predicament they found themselves in, Ravensmede smiled at his grandmother's words. 'Grant me ten minutes,' he said laughingly.

A surly-sounding grunt. 'I'll be back in five,' the dowager said, and the footsteps receded back along the landing.

Only then did a very white-faced Kathryn release the breath she had been holding. Realisation of her predicament screamed loud. And now that her ardour had disappeared without a trace, she was suddenly shamefully aware that she was on Lord Ravensmede's bed, with the man himself lying atop her. Nicholas had not the least look of embarrassment; indeed, he was smiling down at her in what could only be described as a positively dangerous manner. Her eyes widened with growing horror. 'N-Nicholas…' her tongue stumbled over his name, as she tried to free herself from her position.

The wickedness of Nicholas's smile intensified and slowly his face moved towards hers…to drop the smallest, innocent kiss on to the tip of her nose. 'Kathryn Marchant, you are quite the most beautiful, beguiling woman I've ever met.' Without another word he rolled off her and, leaning down, helped her up to her feet. In one fluid action he had reached around to the back of her dress and fastened the buttons he had undone not so very long ago. Everything about him was smooth, lazily efficient and supremely confident.

The same could not be said for Kathryn. Not only was she in a state of abject shock at the extent to which passion had pushed her, but her hands were shaking so much she could barely fashion her hair into some semblance of order.

'Here, let me,' he instructed, and simply turned her around, coiled her hair into a neat chignon and pinned it into place with much less fuss than any abigail would have caused.

'How do you—'

'Don't ask.' He spun her round, delivered a final kiss to her mouth, took her by the hand and guided her towards the door. 'And now you had better go before my grandmother decides to return.'

'Nicholas…' Kathryn bit at her bottom lip.

'We'll talk about this later, Kathryn.' Opening the door by the smallest crack, he scanned beyond, then, giving Kathryn's fingers one last reassuring squeeze, pushed her towards the door directly across the landing; the door that led into her own bedchamber.

It was exactly five minutes later that Lady Maybury made a reappearance, and an hour after that when she finally left him to his rest. And all the while Lord Ravensmede was forced to pretend that he had not just reached a decision of monumental proportions. Not until his grandmother left the room did he allow himself to think back on the woman who had come to him out of concern and whom he, in return, had practically seduced. Had not his grandmother come knocking at the door of his bedchamber he wondered if he would have had either the strength or the sense to stop what he was about.

Kathryn absorbed him, totally, completely. Just touching her, kissing her, made him forget all else. What chance had he then when she lay beneath him on his bed? It was enough to drive any man mad. For all these years Nicholas Maybury had called the tune when it came to women. And heaven knew he had practised it often enough, on rich women, powerful women; all of them widowed or well experienced at their profession, some of them even other men's wives.

Now one woman had changed all that. One woman alone

could have called any tune she wanted, and he would have danced to it a thousand times over. One woman alone had the power to gladden his heart, to make him feel dizzy with desire, or to cast him into a doldrum of depression. She was neither wealthy nor titled, neither fashionable nor flirtatious. As Cadmount had so accurately observed, she was not even his type. None of it made any difference. Nicholas loved her. And he meant to marry her. The woman's name was Kathryn Marchant.

It was only later that same evening when he made enquiry of his butler as to the whereabouts of his grandmother and her companion that he discovered them to have departed for a dance in the local assembly rooms. First instinct told him to seek them out, check that Kathryn understood that his intentions were honourable—hadn't he given her every reason to think otherwise? Second thoughts suggested he wait where he was. Care must be taken to ensure that no contrary gossip linked Kathryn's name with his. As his wife she would be safe, but until then... Reputations were a fragile thing in the hands of the *ton*. He was sure that his grandmother already had her suspicions about his relationship with her companion, and was warning him off. Why else was she doing her damnedest to keep them apart? It was for the best that Kathryn be seen in Brighthelmstone without him. Soon they would be together. Ravensmede would have to content himself with that. But had he known what was unfolding in the assembly rooms, the Viscount would have decided very differently.

The air was unpleasantly stuffy and hot within the assembly rooms, and the fact that her dance card was full did not help matters. Lady Maybury was chatting with lively animation to a group of elderly ladies, and looking very pleased with the fact that Kathryn had not yet been off the dance floor. Parson John Andrew, who had a keen interest in lepidopterology, was describing to Kathryn in some detail the differences between the

Red Admiral as compared to the Blue Butterfly, a feat to be much congratulated as they were engaged in dancing a robust Scottish reel at the time. The tempo of the music increased, urging the dancers to skip faster, twirl their partners with more force. Reverend Andrew's face grew redder, and his breathing more laboured. Sweat dribbled down his cheeks and chin. By the end of the dance both Kathryn and Reverend Andrew were much relieved. The gentleman mopped at his brow with a large white handkerchief before setting off to fetch two glasses of lemonade for the delightful Miss Marchant and himself.

'Kathryn?' The woman's voice inflected with surprise. 'Is that really you? What a surprise to find you here, my dear.'

The skin on the back of Kathryn's neck prickled. It was a voice she knew well, and one she had not thought to hear in this part of the country. She looked up to meet the cold blue eyes of Anna Marchant. 'Aunt Anna, the surprise is mutual.' Then, as Lottie stepped from behind her mother, 'And Cousin Lottie too. I had not thought to meet you both here in Brighthelmstone.'

The harshness in Mrs Marchant's eyes faded and she looked almost contrite. 'Our visit is not one of pleasure,' she said in a hushed tone. 'It is Mr Marchant...'

It seemed to Kathryn that her aunt was smaller than she remembered. 'What of Uncle Henry?'

Mrs Marchant swallowed, and compressed her lips as if trying to control some strong emotion assailing her. 'He...'

Guilt and concern pricked at Kathryn's conscience. She noticed the pallor of her aunt's face as she waited for what was to come.

'He has taken an inflammation of the lungs.' Mrs Marchant clasped her perfectly manicured hands together and held them to her mouth. There was a suspicious sheen about her eyes. 'The doctor is not optimistic. He said...' Her eyes squeezed momentarily closed, and, when they opened again, there was in them a vulnerability Kathryn had never seen before. 'He said that clean sea air was our best hope. Hence I brought Mr Marchant here with all haste.'

Lottie clasped at her mother's hand and let out a little sob. 'Poor Papa.'

'It came on so suddenly,' said Mrs Marchant. 'One minute he was fine and well, and the next…' She glanced anxiously at Kathryn.

'I'm so sorry. I didn't know.'

'He insisted that I bring Lottie here tonight. Was so adamant that I dared not refuse him for fear of bringing on another coughing fit. We will not stay long and then we will get straight back to him.'

'Please send my uncle my best wishes that he recovers his good health as soon as possible.'

'Of course,' nodded Mrs Marchant, then paused before she added, 'Mr Marchant would benefit from your visit, Kathryn, that is, if you can find the time to see him. I believe it would make a difference to him.'

'I—I'm not sure—'

But before she could say what she would have, Anna Marchant interrupted, 'I haven't always treated you fairly, Kathryn, and for that I beg your forgiveness. Only now do I see things in a different light.'

The two women looked at one another, before Kathryn nodded and gave a small smile. 'If you tell me where you are staying, then I will visit my uncle.' So shocked was she by the news of her uncle's illness and the drastic change in her aunt that Kathryn failed to notice the gentleman until he stood directly by her side…rather closer than was seemly.

'Sorry to interrupt, Miss Marchant…' and he bowed '…but it's imperative that I speak with you on a matter of privacy.'

'Mr Silverton!' She could not keep the shock from her voice. The last time she had seen Harry Silverton he was being carried in a drunken stupor out of the drawing room of the rented house on The Steyne and into Lord Ravensmede's carriage. An image of a blood-soaked Nicholas flashed into her mind, and fear flickered. Both Aunt Anna and Lottie were looking at Mr Silverton with expressions of curiosity. Kathryn deliberately edged herself away from the young man's proximity, while making the necessary introductions. 'Aunt Anna, Lottie, this is Mr Silverton, whose family are enjoying the summer in Brighthelmstone. Mr Silverton, this is my aunt, Mrs Marchant, and my cousin, Miss Lottie Marchant.'

Mrs Marchant's devoirs went unnoticed as Lottie stepped forward into Harry Silverton's line of vision. 'Miss Lottie,' he said with awe, and stared at Lottie as if she was an apparition. 'Is this an angel I see before me?' And before the stunned Lottie could reply, he plucked her hand into his and placed upon it a reverential kiss.

Kathryn looked from Harry Silverton's stunned visage to her cousin's flushed excited one. Lottie was ogling right back at Mr Silverton.

Mrs Marchant cleared her throat. 'We must be going, Lottie, come along.'

'But I've only just arrived,' protested Mr Silverton, 'and not yet had the pleasure of dancing with the beautiful Miss Lottie.'

Lottie's lips moved to a pout. 'Mama, we are scarcely here.'

Kathryn had no wish to speak to Silverton, especially knowing all that he had done to Nicholas, but she was wise enough to realise that the young man could be dangerous. It would be better to hear what he proposed to say over the matter. 'You wished to speak to me, Mr Silverton?'

Harry Silverton blinked like a man struggling to free himself from a drugged daze. 'Did I? It's of no matter, now.' He bestowed his most charming smile upon Lottie, and held out his hand for her dance card. 'May I hope to secure a dance with you, Miss Lottie?'

Kathryn could see quite clearly the way that things were progressing, especially after her aunt learned of the Silverton family's wealth. She was, therefore, considerably relieved when the Reverend Mr Andrews, carrying two glasses of lemonade, finally found his way back to her. And even more relieved when that same gentleman informed her that Lady Maybury had developed a headache and wanted to leave the assembly rooms.

During the journey home in the carriage Kathryn thought about her uncle's ill health, and the change in her aunt's manner. She thought about the sudden and rather overt attraction between Mr Silverton and Cousin Lottie. But most of all she thought about Nicholas Maybury, and of what had happened between them on his bed that very afternoon.

In the days following Nicholas and Kathryn's illicit tryst not one opportunity presented itself for them to speak together privately. Lady Maybury guarded her companion with all the tenacity of a terrier. Naps were forgotten. The independent old lady vanished. Her temper did not. She developed a need to have Kathryn with her at all times, from breakfast time to dinner. The very night of their return from the assembly rooms, she developed a nocturnal fear that necessitated Kathryn moving into Lady Maybury's bedchamber to keep her company. Matters grew even worse the next morning when Kathryn asked for leave to visit her uncle. The dowager embarked on what amounted to an inquisition over Uncle Henry's illness and Aunt Anna's invitation—and then claimed that she could not spare her companion even for half an hour. Every evening there were dances and trips to the theatre—all very public affairs—all with Ravensmede very much consigned to the background if her ladyship consented to his company at all.

In a way Kathryn was thankful to the old woman. She both desired and dreaded the time when she would be alone with Nicholas. She loved him, knew now that she could deny neither him nor herself. It was just a matter of time. Lady Maybury's tactics were only deferring the inevitable. Kathryn had her suspicions as to how much the dowager knew, loved the old lady all the more for trying to protect her poor companion.

Nausea rose at the thought of what becoming Nicholas's mistress would mean: a slap in the face to Lady Maybury for all that she had done to help Kathryn, and the loss of her own good name. No matter how hard they tried to keep the affair hidden, it would come out—such secrets always did. And what about when he tired of her, when he found some other woman to fill her place? The thought churned cold in her stomach. She was a fool a hundred times over, a fool caught between the devil and a high place...with little idea of how to solve her quandary.

Within the drawing room of the rented townhouse in Brighthelmstone Mrs Marchant was pacing with a great deal of excitement. 'You're certain, Henry, that Mr Silverton means to ask her?'

'Yes, he asked my permission to pay suit to Lottie. The boy is clearly besotted with her and wants to marry her.'

'Very good. Lottie will be married before either of us thought,' purred his wife. Her blue eyes narrowed and her slash of a smile broadened. 'I like Mr Silverton immensely. He has such very interesting tales to tell...particularly concerning our niece and Lord Ravensmede.'

Mr Marchant worried at his chins. 'There is an indecent haste about the affair. Mr Silverton is talking as if he means to marry Lottie tomorrow. They have only known each other a matter of days!'

His wife delivered him a withering look. 'What's to know? Harry Silverton is an only son; he has two sisters, and his parents are elderly. He stands to inherit his father's chain of coffee houses and sugar plantation in the West Indies. Not only that, but he's currently worth fifteen thousand a year, and will receive a large and fashionable new townhouse in Bristol as part of his wedding gift from the old man.'

'But he's trade, and I thought you wanted better for Lottie; a baronet at least, you said.'

'Bah, half the aristocracy have pockets to let. Fifteen thousand. And think what he stands to inherit.'

Mr Marchant nodded in agreement. 'I concede it to be a fortune.'

'Although I should prefer Lottie's wedding to be a grand affair, I would not want to stand in the way of true love.'

Her husband rolled his eyes.

'And there would be other advantages to them marrying sooner rather than later.'

'I see none,' said Mr Marchant somewhat sourly, 'other than the cost to my pocket.'

'There is the little matter of Kathryn. Have you forgotten about her?'

'The chance would be a fine thing,' he muttered beneath his breath, then spoke out loud, 'What difference can Lottie's marriage make to Kathryn?'

Mrs Marchant cheeks grew rather red from excitement. 'Why, if Lottie has already caught herself a husband, and we distance ourselves from Kathryn, then any damage that attaches itself to her reputation will not affect us.'

'She is still our niece.'

'We will publicly disown her. And with Lottie safely wed and sent to Bristol, then what harm can Kathryn do us?'

'Then I can cease this pathetic charade of illness in an attempt to lure the girl here?'

'Yes.' Anna Marchant beamed. 'We no longer need coax the little trollop back to London with us.' That had only been to please Amanda White and that woman had just been rendered powerless. She laughed aloud at the good fortune Harry Silverton had brought them.

'Hallelujah,' said Mr Marchant with sarcasm.

'You must concentrate on persuading Mr Silverton to London. He needs to visit Doctors' Commons as soon as possible—and come to Green Street with a special licence in his pocket. If we play our cards right, we should have Lottie married by next week. And then I can turn my attentions to Kathryn. I'll send her a note today telling of your unexpected recovery and that we have to leave Brighthelmstone. Do you know that I actually had to apologise to the little bitch the other day? How I'm longing to make her suffer for that. She's made her bed, and now I mean to make sure that she damn well lies in it. By the time I've finished, Kathryn Marchant will wish that she'd never been born.'

Less than a fortnight later and Lady Maybury was proving to be as demanding as ever. The two women sat at the breakfast table, the dowager consuming a second helping of ham and eggs, Kathryn sipping her coffee and reading aloud from the notices in *The Times*. Of Ravensmede there was no sign. Kathryn was trying hard to keep her thoughts from his possible whereabouts when one particular marriage announcement caught her attention. Her words faltered. The coffee cup stilled its motion halfway to her mouth.

Lady Maybury glanced up from her plate. 'Pray continue with the next one. I want to see if Mrs Pearsall's granddaughter's marriage to young Fox is in there.'

With exaggerated care Kathryn set the coffee cup down upon the table. There was the tiniest of pauses, and then she started to read again. 'On Friday June 25, at her father's house in Green Street, by the Reverend J. Blundell, Charlotte, only daughter of Mr and Mrs Henry Marchant of London, to Mr Harold Silverton, only son of Mr and Mrs James Silverton of Bristol.' Lottie had married Harry Silverton!

'Good gad!' exclaimed Lady Maybury. 'I thought they only met at that wretched dance the other week.'

'They did, but it was immediately apparent that their interests were captured.'

'Well, never you mind, Kathryn. He's a nincompoop. Showed his true colours when he came round here, brandishing that pistol in m'face. You'll catch better than him. Mark my words.'

'I don't understand.' Kathryn's brow rumpled in perplexity. 'Aunt Anna was different the last time we spoke. She seemed changed: softer, kinder somehow. She wanted to put the past behind us, to start anew. And then when she sent that letter telling of my uncle's sudden recovery and their intended return to London, she made no mention of Mr Silverton. I thought...' She shook her head. 'It doesn't make sense.'

'You thought what? That your aunt would at least inform you of your cousin's wedding?'

'I should know her better than that,' said Kathryn.

'So you should. A leopard doesn't change its spots,' replied the dowager, giving Kathryn a strange little look. 'What a surprise that your aunt was up to organising a wedding so soon after Mr Marchant's recent illness. But then the speed of your poor dear uncle's recovery was truly miraculous. Such a shame I couldn't spare you to visit him...' She raised her eyebrows with just the faintest suggestion of cynicism, before turning her attention once more to her breakfast plate. 'Now read the rest of the announcements before m'eggs grow cold.'

The first leg of the journey back to London was, as Kathryn expected, both slow and tedious. There was little conversation between the ladies as Lady Maybury managed to sleep almost continuously with no regard for the jolting of the carriage. Despite his recent injury Lord Ravensmede accompanied the carriage on horseback, the thud of his horse's hooves never far away.

He watched her pale face at the carriage window.

She studied the dark figure that rode so close by.

Green eyes met grey, again and again, binding the man and his woman together, promising what was to come.

She worried as to his arm, and that he should be riding.

He worried as to why she should look so anxious when he meant to claim her for his own.

Mile after mile. So close as to almost touch, so near as to almost whisper. Yet they could do nothing. By the time the coach entered into the yard of the King's Arms at Horley

Common, the tension between them was unbearable. The party was shown to their bedchambers, given some little time to refresh their travel-stained selves, then the landlord showed them to a private parlour and dinner was served.

At the first opportunity Ravensmede addressed himself to Kathryn, 'How did you find the first part of your journey?'

'Comfortable, thank you, my lord.'

'Don't lie,' interrupted the dowager between mouthfuls of salmon and boiled potatoes. 'It was damnably uncomfortable. It was all I could do to manage the briefest of naps. You really must have that carriage seen to, Nick.'

'I will do so upon our arrival in town,' he replied.

A silence descended upon the little group.

Kathryn poked at the small mound of potatoes on her plate, and tried not to look at Nicholas. She could feel the burn of his gaze upon her, could feel her face colour beneath his scrutiny. Surely the dowager would notice if he continued to stare so? She sought to distract her employer. 'My lady, how do you find the fish? Is it to your taste?'

Lady Maybury shovelled a large portion of the salmon steak into her mouth before replying. 'I'm afraid to say that it's barely edible. When one's appetite is as fragile as mine, it's important that only the best quality of food be consumed.' A large swig of wine passed her lips. 'The potatoes are hard, the pie is lacking in flavour and the soup is too poor to comment upon. I'm forced to nibble upon a meagre portion to sustain my strength.' The shrewd pale eyes swept over Kathryn's barely touched food. 'You would be wise to do the same, my dear, for our journey tomorrow will be as long as today and you heard what the landlord said of the weather.'

'It's going to rain,' supplied her companion quietly, and ate a little more of the pie.

Ravensmede drew a mocking smile at his grandmother. 'Perhaps then you will agree to let me travel awhile inside the carriage, instead of banishing me to the road.'

'The fresh air is good for you, boy,' she said. 'Besides, I thought you enjoyed riding.'

He raised an eyebrow and glanced across at Kathryn, before refilling all three glasses with claret.

Kathryn concentrated on watching the pale red liquid slosh against the glass. Within her chest her heart had kicked up to a canter. She ignored it, along with the peculiar battle of wills that seemed to be going on between Ravensmede and his grandmother. 'May I suggest an early night, my lady. You must be very tired and tomorrow will be more fatiguing than today.'

For once the dowager appeared to be in agreement. With a shrewd expression she patted Kathryn's hand. 'Go on ahead, gel. I shall not be long. Just want to finish m' wine, then I'll be up.'

Kathryn nodded and began to rise, but Nicholas was there before her. 'I'll escort Miss Marchant to her room.'

The blush in Kathryn's cheeks intensified. The flurry of her heart hastened. One glance up into those green eyes that glowed so bright beneath the flickering flame of the candles and she froze, for there was everything of intimacy and possession in Nicholas's gaze. It was as if a hand reached in and squeezed Kathryn's heart. 'Really, there is no need, my lord.' She felt his fingers brush her arm, felt too the instinctive sway of her body towards his. 'I—'

The dowager interrupted. 'Kathryn is right, Nick. Besides, I want a word with you.' She fixed a belligerent eye upon her grandson.

Kathryn's eyes shuttered for the briefest moment. Every nerve in her body was vibrating and taut. What she had feared was about to pass. For Kathryn could not shake the unassailable conviction that Lady Maybury knew. As surely as they were sitting here within the little parlour, as surely as the attraction that flowed between Nicholas and herself, the dowager knew. Why else was the tension wound so tight between the three of them? Dread weighed heavy on her chest. She rose swiftly to her feet, unwilling for either Lady Maybury or Lord

Ravensmede to witness her fear. 'Thank you, my lady.' With every last scrap of dignity that Kathryn possessed she turned and, without a backward glance, walked quietly from the room.

'Well?' said the dowager.

'Well?' said her grandson.

'Enough is enough, Nicholas. Don't think to fob me off this time with some tale of "there's nothing going on". I'm not in m'dotage yet, and I'd have to be deaf, blind and stupid not to see what's right in front of m'very nose.'

'I have not compromised her, nor do I intend to,' said Ravensmede.

'You came damn near to doing so. If it ever gets out that she visited you alone in your bedchamber, then I can assure you that she'll be well and truly ruined...and even I won't be able to save her.'

Ravensmede was genuinely shocked. 'You knew?'

'Of course I knew. What do you take me for, some kind of gibbering idiot? You've been looking at her like you're going to eat her. Why else do you think I've had to resort to guarding the gel night and day? Shouldn't have to do it from m'own grandson.'

His fingers raked through his hair. 'It's not what you think.'

'It's everything that I think and more. Hell's teeth, Nick, I thought you had some semblance of care for her. Couldn't you have just kept your breeches on for once?'

'They've never been off,' he protested, and then he remembered that he had been wearing his nightshirt the day that Kathryn had come to his bedchamber.

A snowy white eyebrow raised and a faded green eye stared hard.

'You're much mistaken, Grandmama.'

'Faugh! I know a seduction when I see one.'

'Grandmama,' He pushed the glass away.

'You might not have a care for the gel, Nick, but I'll be

damned if I just sit back and let you ruin her in a public inn of all places, and make a fool of me in the process.' The faded eyes flashed their angry determination.

He lounged back in his chair. 'Contrary to what you think, I care very much for Kathryn,' he said quietly. 'Do you honestly think I would seek to ruin the lady whom I mean to make my wife?'

Lady Maybury's jaw gaped. 'Did you say *wife*?'

'Most certainly so.'

'I had no idea.'

'Evidently not.'

'But…' The dowager shook her head in disbelief, unable to finish what she had started. A silence grew between them, and then, at last, Lady Maybury asked, 'Does Kathryn know of your intentions?'

Ravensmede's mouth crooked. 'For some strange reason I have been unable to find Miss Marchant alone these past weeks to ask her.'

'Well, I wasn't to know. I thought you were planning on bedding her!' said his grandmother indignantly.

'So you won't be insisting on my riding tomorrow?'

'Only if you behave yourself,' said the dowager. 'You aren't home and dry yet. Better have a care until the ring's on her finger.'

'You're taking the news remarkably well.'

'I find myself resolved to the situation. She might be m'companion and without a penny to her name, but she's got breeding; anyone with an eye in their head can see that. Besides, I like the gel. She's good for you.'

Ravensmede set his napkin down on the table. 'I'm glad we agree.'

'However, there is Miss Paton to consider.'

'Any possibility of an alliance between Miss Paton and me existed only in m'father's head.'

'Your father won't agree.'

'So much the better.' He paused. 'My father might protest, but he'll be relieved that I've chosen to marry at all.'

'If you say so, Nick. But the sooner you tell him about Kathryn the better.'

Ravensmede smiled, but gave no reply.

'You know, of course, there's bound to be gossip. It's not every day one's grandson marries one's companion.'

'There's always gossip.'

'Not about my family there isn't!' The dowager peered haughtily at him.

Ravensmede laughed. 'The tabbies wouldn't dare discuss my misdemeanours in your presence, Grandmama. They're really rather afraid of you.'

'I don't know why!' she snorted, but the glimmer of a smile touched to her lips. Then the smile faded. 'If you marry her, you'll find yourself related to Henry and Anna Marchant. You cannot alter the fact that they are her uncle and aunt.'

'The Marchants have no part in Kathryn's life now, nor will they do so in the future. I mean to see to that.'

'Then, your mind's made up.'

'Yes, Grandmama, my mind's made up.'

They looked at one another in silence for a moment.

'To Kathryn, the future Viscountess of Ravensmede.'

Clink of glasses in a toast, and then the wine was drained, and the small private parlour stood empty.

Chapter Fourteen

The next morning, when it came time to depart, Ravensmede was in the process of escorting Kathryn and his grandmother out to the waiting carriage when they came face to face with a lady and gentleman known to them from London.

'Mr and Mrs Parker.' Ravensmede bowed politely.

Ernest Parker's chubby cheeks took on a ruddy hue. 'Lord Ravensmede, Lady Maybury. Arrived last night from town, travelling down for a brief sojourn in Brighthelmstone. Emily has a notion to try one of those bathing contraptions.' His wife's head nodded in the most peculiar manner and she seemed to be having difficulty in meeting the Viscount's gaze.

'We too have been enjoying the delights of Brighthelmstone.' The dowager smiled. 'May I introduce my companion, Miss Marchant.' An elderly hand of surprising strength thrust Kathryn forward.

Emily Parker's expression froze into one of horror. For one awkward minute there was silence. Then, without even so much as a glance in Kathryn's direction, Mrs Parker grabbed her husband's arm in a lock that would have crushed a smaller man, and announced, 'Dear Lady Maybury, I'm afraid we really must leave. Please do excuse us.' And with that she practically ran across the courtyard, dragging her husband in her wake.

Ernest Parker cast a silent appeal at Lord Ravensmede. 'Your servant, sir,' came the gruff utterance as he disappeared into the carriage.

'Well, of all the most ninny-headed females, Emily Parker must take the biscuit!' said Lady Maybury with a scowl. 'Such an appalling lack of manners, I'm not surprised she's not invited anywhere of consequence.'

Ravensmede cast a curious look at the Parkers' carriage, but the door had been shut and the curtain closed across the window.

The dowager's breast puffed dangerously towards high dudgeon. 'How dare she slight m'companion. Kathryn's got more breeding in her little toe than that creature shall ever have!'

'My lady,' cajoled Kathryn from the lady's side, 'I'm not in the least offended. No doubt it is still too early in the morning for Mrs Parker.'

Lady Maybury seemed marginally calmed by Kathryn's words and allowed herself to be steered across the yard to the waiting carriage.

The landlord's predictions concerning the weather proved to be true. The day was quite the foulest that the summer had seen. Blustery cold winds and one heavy rain shower after the other slowed their journey considerably. The roads were muddied and filled with expanding puddles, the sky grey and forbidding with rain.

In contrast to her behaviour of the past fortnight, Lady Maybury showed not the slightest objection to her grandson sitting within the carriage beside her and her companion. Indeed, she positively encouraged Lord Ravensmede's presence, something of which Kathryn could only be glad on seeing the deterioration in the weather conditions. And rather than keeping a close scrutiny upon his person as she had taken to doing of late, the dowager was not five minutes into the journey when she fell asleep beneath her mound of travelling rugs. The snuffle of her snore competed with the rumble of the wheels and the pounding of the horses' hooves.

Kathryn looked at Nicholas.

Nicholas looked at Kathryn sitting at Lady Maybury's side.

He seeming to fill the whole of the carriage with his presence just by sitting on the seat opposite.

'At last,' he said.

Kathryn's gaze flickered towards the dowager.

'My grandmother is an extremely heavy sleeper.'

A tremor of panic fluttered through her.

Something of her feelings must have shown on her face, for Lord Ravensmede moved back to lounge against the squabs. 'I only wish to speak to you.' The smouldering intensity in his green eyes sent a shiver of anticipation from the top of her head down to the very tips of her toes. He did not look like he wanted to talk to her. Everything about his long lean body seemed poised to pull her into his arms and ravage her mouth with his. A lazy lop-sided smile spread across his face and he stretched out his legs so that his booted shins brushed against her skirt.

She waited.

'When you came to my bedchamber in Brighthelmstone—'

'Nicholas…' Her throat was dry and his name little more than a whisper. Her eyes flicked nervously towards the sleeping form of the dowager. 'We do not need to discuss this.'

'I think that we do,' he said.

She gave a little shake of her head, and a curl escaped down to drizzle against her cheek. 'Things need not change.'

'They already have.'

'We could be friends just as we were before,' she said, grasping at straws.

He sat upright and leaned forward, oblivious to the shake and heave of the carriage. 'We both know that there is much more than friendship between us, Kathryn.'

The breaths came small and fast and shallow in her chest. Her gaze dropped to the floor. 'There should not be.'

'*Should* does not enter into it. There is, and it's clear that you cannot remain as my grandmother's companion for much longer.'

She raised startled eyes to his. 'I would not hurt Lady May-bury.'

'Neither would I.'

'Then why…'

'You know why,' he said and, reaching across, laid his hand over hers.

His touch was light yet possessive. He was right. Kathryn knew very well the answer to her question. He could not take his grandmother's companion as his mistress.

The noise of hooves and wheels and rain and snores filled the minutes.

'There is something that I want to ask you.'

Her heart lurched. She withdrew her hand from his, her fingers stumbling to the skirt of her travelling dress and gripping for dear life at the material. She knew what he was going to ask, had known it for quite some time. Now that the moment had come she feared that her courage had deserted her. It was one thing to be drawn into it while in the throes of passion; it was quite another to agree to it in the cold light of day. An arrangement. To suit them both. He desired her. She loved him. And for the sake of that love she would bear the shame that being his mistress would bring. But this wasn't how it was supposed to be. For all that had passed between them, for all that she had tried to convince herself, she knew that if he asked her here, sitting in his travelling coach, with his grand-mother asleep by her side, she would refuse him.

'No,' she whispered. 'Do not say it.'

A curious expression flitted across his face. 'But you don't yet know yet what I mean to ask.'

She swallowed hard. 'Even so, I would not have you ask it here, in front of Lady Maybury. That…that would not be right.'

A dark eyebrow arched in the familiar gesture that she had come to know and love, and he subjected her to a long knowing scrutiny. When at last he spoke there was a gentleness to his words. 'I'll warrant my question is not the one you expect it to be, Kathryn. But…' he captured her hand again in his and stroked his thumb against her skin '…if you would prefer I took a more conventional route with my proposal then so be it. I will wait until we reach London.'

She blushed and stared down at where their hands joined. 'Thank you.'

The coach rumbled on. The rain continued to pour. The dowager's snoring grew louder. Nicholas watched Kathryn. Kathryn watched the passing countryside…until they reached London.

The next morning was fine and warm, with no sign of the unseasonable weather of the previous day. Kathryn sat alone in the carriage, content with what she had found during her visit to young Maggie. The visit had distracted her thoughts from Nicholas and had been most enjoyable. The little girl's pleasure at the doll made the selling of the last of Kathryn's papa's books worthwhile, and the tasty biscuits and cakes from the dowager had doubled both the child and her brothers' pleasure. Beneath the warm golden sunlight Kathryn recalled the small hands pressed to hers and the laughter in those large pansy eyes. Maggie was a joyful delight for all her squeals and clambering.

A slender hand pressed to her cheek as she remembered how the child's mother had thanked her for the food parcels that had seemingly arrived with conscientious punctuality every week since Maggie's return home, and for the job in which her husband was now employed. Nicholas. There could be no one else responsible, after all. The knowledge made her smile. Beneath that devil-may-care attitude was a man who cared about a poor child's welfare, a man who doted upon his elderly grandmother…and a man who was going to ask her to become his mistress… just as he had before. Only this time she would give him a very different answer.

A barouche passed close by, travelling only marginally faster than that belonging to Lady Maybury. Miss Dawson's face looked out.

Kathryn raised her hand in salutation through the open window and smiled.

Miss Dawson's cheeks reddened and she turned her head away with a startling abruptness.

She must not have seen me, thought Kathryn, and returned to her musings without the slightest hint of rancour.

It was only later that same day that she had cause to remember the incident and place quite a different interpretation upon it.

It was late that evening when Ravensmede made himself comfortable in the wing chair within the library of his own house in Berkeley Square and accepted the brandy glass from his friend.

Cadmount's white fingers drummed upon the chair arm. 'How is the delightful dowager?'

'In fine mettle.'

'And li'l Miss Marchant?' asked Cadmount a trifle too innocently.

'She's well. I'm meeting them both at the King's later this evening, if you want to come.'

Cadmount coughed discreetly. 'You encountered no problems in Brighthelmstone?'

'No. Should I have?'

The fair-haired man cleared his throat and avoided Ravensmede's eye. 'You did bed her.'

Ravensmede carefully set the brandy glass down upon the table. 'Question or statement? Before you start down that line, Caddie, there's something you should know: I mean to marry Kathryn.'

Cadmount sighed, reached for the decanter and refilled Ravensmede's glass. 'In that case, best drink it down, old man,' he instructed. 'There have been some developments while you were away, and you ain't going to like them, not one little bit.'

The atmosphere within the King's Theatre was stuffy and oppressive, too many bodies crammed into too small a space, and all for Mr Kelly's benefit night. Those in the gallery were in jovial form and were already shouting and laughing even before the play had begun. When the curtain finally rose on the comedy *Road to Ruin* their crude comments grew louder, thus creating a raucous atmosphere in which the actors struggled in vain to portray their parts with some level of decorum. The dowager's face showed all too well exactly what she thought of such a coarse display.

'No sign of Nicholas yet?' Lady Maybury fanned herself with vigour.

'No, my lady.'

'Not like him to be late, but then he does have other things on his mind at the minute,' she said, resting her faded green gaze knowingly upon her companion.

Kathryn glanced uneasily at her employer. Surely the dowager did not know what her grandson was planning? 'Does he?' she asked, trying not to sound guilty.

'Most certainly,' said Lady Maybury with a twinkle in her eye.

A smile, then Kathryn decided to steer the conversation to safer ground. 'Are you enjoying the performance, my lady?'

'Blasted nonsense with those louts crowing in the background. Damnable waste of time,' she pronounced with venom. 'And it's so uncomfortably hot in this wretched place.'

'Would you like me to fetch you a lemonade before the curtain goes up again?'

'Would you, dear gel?'

'Of course.' And so saying Kathryn exited the box, brushing against the scarlet curtains as she did so. She had barely walked more than a few paces when she became aware of the libidinous stares of several gentlemen who were loitering close by the marble pillars. With an averted gaze and a determined thrust of the chin she headed to the stairwell, only to be intercepted by Lord Stanfield.

'Miss Marchant,' he said. 'Enchanted to see you again. I hope that you enjoyed your stay in Brighthelmstone.'

'Indeed, sir. It was most enjoyable.' Something in the man's manner made her uncomfortable, not that his words could be faulted. He was politeness itself, but beneath the polished veneer... It hardly seemed possible that this was the same man she had danced with so many times in the weeks preceding Brighthelmstone. There was a subtle change, something that she could not quite define.

He lingered a trifle too long over her hand, pressed his lips that bit too ardently to her fingers.

She retrieved her hand and saw his focus drop to her bosom where it remained in undisguised and leisurely pleasure. 'Please excuse me, Lord Stanfield,' she said coldly and moved swiftly past. The thump in her chest and heat in her cheeks persuaded her she had not misinterpreted his behaviour. Thrusting the thought from her mind, she made her way down the stairs and started to traverse the crowded hallway to the queue at the refreshments table. A hush descended, marred only by whisperings and snide laughter. On either side men and women slowly, deliberately, turned their backs to her. There could be no mistaking that clear signal, a cut to her face.

With a hammering heart and trembling legs Kathryn held her head up and walked with quiet dignity towards the table. The crowd parted before her, contempt upon the faces of the fine ladies before they turned them away, and something worse upon the gentlemen's. And then straight ahead, barely a few feet away, she saw Mr and Mrs Marchant. Her eyes met those of her aunt, and for a moment she thought that the woman meant to help her, to rescue her from the nightmare in which she suddenly found herself. Anna Marchant smiled, and her eyes were cold, hard chips of ice. There was nothing of kindness and everything of malice contained in her look. Vulnerability had long fled, as had any vestige of all other pretence. With slow deliberation Mrs Marchant turned to present her back. Uncle Henry followed suit. Voices buzzed in the background. Kathryn swallowed down the aridity in her throat and refused to be beaten. She walked on through the cleared route hedged by a line of smartly presented backs. With her eyes fixed ahead she purchased two lemonades and turned to retrace her steps, running the gauntlet once more. Quite how she did so with such cool reserve she would never know, not when the very ground seemed to loom up towards her.

Halfway up the stairwell she encountered Mr Roodley on his way down. Although he did not address her, his knowing brown eyes swept brazenly over her body as he passed.

The safety of the box was in sight when she felt the firm touch of a hand upon her bottom. Lecherous sniggers sounded from a small group of gentlemen lounging against a wall. Kathryn stopped, and drawing herself up to her full height, turned with icy fury. She would never know the image she presented at that moment, with her ashen skin and stormy grey eyes, her small nose flared and full lips parted in readiness for battle, the steady rise and fall of her breasts and the rigid stance of her body. Indignation personified. Deathly silence. The pulse thrummed in her throat, as one by one she fixed her chill gaze upon them, until their leers and smiles vanished and they looked away. Then she turned and walked to the box, white knuckles gripping the glasses for dear life.

'Oh there you are, my dear. Thank you.' Lady Maybury gratefully sipped at the lemonade. 'So refreshing.' The faded green eyes raked her companion's countenance. 'Kathryn?'

She could not speak, sat frozen in a state of shock, the lemonade untouched before her.

The dowager's hand gripped to hers. 'What is it? What has happened? You look as if you've seen a ghost…and you're shaking.'

'I'm feeling a little unwell. I'm sure it will shortly pass,' she whispered. 'Please do not concern yourself, my lady.'

Lady Maybury frowned, 'But I am concerned, gel, and do not give me that old flannel of feeling unwell. You left here fine enough ten minutes ago and return looking like death warmed up. Am I not entitled to some explanation?'

Her hand pressed to her brow. Where to begin? What to say? Blasted, pulverised, unable to think straight. Kathryn squeezed her eyes shut and swallowed hard at the memory of what had just occurred. But what *had* just happened? And why? Her fingers trembled as they pulled at the silk of her skirt. Why? The question sounded again and again in her mind. The reason did not matter, not once Lady Maybury witnessed the sorry state of affairs upon their exit. It was perhaps fortuitous that they had arrived at the theatre early to beat the crowds, thus stalling the inevitability of what was to come.

'Kathryn—' the elderly voice sounded close to her ear '—come, we'd better get you home, my dear.'

'But Lord Ravensmede—'

'Will know where to find us,' finished Lady Maybury. 'There's nothing to worry about.'

At the sound of such genuine concern Kathryn could bear her shame no longer. 'I'm sorry, my lady, so very sorry. You've been so kind, like my own grandmother instead of an employer. I would do anything to save you from... Please forgive me.' Her voice ruptured into hoarseness and she spoke no more, just touched the frail old hand to her cheek in a gesture of affection.

'Come on,' came the imperious command.

'The play is not yet finished.'

'A bigger load of tripe I've yet to see. I'll not waste any more of my time on it. Hurry along now.' Lady Maybury rose from her seat.

'My lady, there's something you should know before you...before you leave this box.' Kathryn's fingers plucked nervously at one another.

A white eyebrow raised in a gesture similar to that so favoured by the lady's grandson.

The smoky grey gaze dropped to the floor. 'It seems that I have…incurred the condemnation of…that is to say, I have invoked the displeasure of…'

'You may explain it to me in detail once we're home. I've no mind to stay here any longer.' Lady Maybury swept from the box with regal elegance, seemingly oblivious to the whisperings and raising of viewing glasses all around.

They passed few people of any significance on their way from the theatre to the carriage, but the manner of those in their path soon enlightened Lady Maybury as to the cause of her companion's distress.

'Of all the most idiotic, petty and malicious behaviours!' The dowager was working herself into a lofty dudgeon. 'How dare they cut m'companion!'

'Their treatment of me is inconsequential, but I'm dismayed to see that Lady Collins was so frosty to you, my lady. I'm sorry that you should be so affected. I will, of course, leave at once to save you further embarrassment.'

'Don't be ridiculous,' the lady snapped fiercely. 'You were quite the toast of the town when we left only a few weeks ago. And while in Brighthelmstone you barely strayed from the view of my beady eye.'

Kathryn thought of the hungry kisses from Nicholas's mouth. She remembered the warmth of his body lying on top of hers and the press of his bed against her back. The memories brought a guilty heat to her cheeks. Mercifully the carriage interior was dim.

'This abominable treatment is without the slightest merit.'

Kathryn said nothing.

The remainder of the journey continued in silence with the dowager brooding and Kathryn in a state of numb disbelief.

The ladies did not have to wait long before Ravensmede arrived at Upper Grosvenor Street.

'Grandmama, Kathryn.' The green gaze saw in an instant the

tension etched upon the girl's face. 'I went to the theatre first. My apologies for being late.'

'Well, you're here now, thank goodness. Kathryn and I have encountered something of a problem.' The dowager threw off her cashmere shawl in a flurry, ordered that the brandy decanter be brought to the library and ushered both her companion and her grandson into that small cosy room.

'If I may be so bold as to comment, ma'am, you appear a trifle put out,' said Ravensmede, trying to gauge just how far the gossip had spread. 'Was the play not to your satisfaction?'

She waved the butler away, shut the door with a decisive thud and poured three glasses of brandy. Kathryn was then pushed unceremoniously down into a chair and a glass pressed firmly in her hand. 'Drink!' commanded the dowager.

It seemed the gossip-mongers had been busy. Ravensmede could see the tremor in the girl's fingers.

A minute's pause and the glass raised to those lips that were so unnaturally pale. She sipped on the spirit, made a face at the strength of its taste, and swallowed it down.

His grandmother wasted no time in emptying the contents of her glass and soon had it refilled.

'Grandmama.' Ravensmede made to take his grandparent's arm. 'Perhaps you should sit down and tell me what has happened.'

'Polite society,' said Lady Maybury acidly, 'has decided that m'companion is no longer acceptable. Kathryn has received the cut direct.'

'I see,' replied Ravensmede without the least surprise.

'And we have no notion as to the cause of this sudden outlandish behaviour,' said the old lady.

His eyes skimmed to Kathryn once more, but she had not moved one inch, just sat with the brandy glass gripped within her fingers, the amber liquid almost untouched. 'Ah,' he said softly, 'I think I may be able to help you with that.'

Two pairs of eyes swivelled to his.

There was no easy way to say what must be said. A dagger twisted in his gut at the very thought, but he rose nevertheless, without a shadow of the anger and pain that troubled him. He leaned back against the small wooden desk and stretched out his legs before him.

Time slowed within the library. No one spoke. No one moved. They sat as statues and waited.

He could defer no longer. 'It seems that there's a malicious rumour circulating regarding Kathryn's relationship with a certain gentleman. The couple are believed to have behaved without propriety.'

The fire crackled in the grate. The soft wheeze of Lady Maybury's breathing.

He looked up at Kathryn's white face, her eyes huge and dark, overwhelmed by the blackness of her pupils.

'With whom am I purported to have established such a…relationship?' The words forced from her bloodless lips.

Ravensmede calmed the leap of his pulse. The merest twitch of the muscle in his jaw.

She was watching him still, a mask of calmness across her face.

'With myself,' came the dry reply.

Silence echoed.

'They think you're keeping m'companion as your mistress?' Lady Maybury questioned with alarming candour.

A sharp intake of air from the slender figure opposite, and the stormy grey eyes with all their hurt, all their fury, all their incredulity, dropped to the floor.

'It would appear so, ma'am,' Ravensmede conceded.

She turned to face her grandson. 'Then you had better speak to Kathryn,' said the dowager, and walked out of the room.

The latch clicked into place. The grandfather clock ticked its slow steady rhythm.

'Tell me the whole of it,' Kathryn said in a small, tightly controlled voice.

'It's better that I don't.'

Her shoulders squared back, her chin thrust out in defiance. 'I need to know.'

He gave a curt nod. 'Harry Silverton has been busy informing anyone who will listen that I was responsible for the ruination of a young lady acting in the capacity of my grandmother's companion. He's adamant that he witnessed you within my arms while I was in state of some undress upon the sofa in the drawing room of our rented accommodation.'

Kathryn's temper flared, 'What nonsense! He's misinterpreting the whole thing. Where is the mention of his drunken state, or the fact that he shot his pistol at you?' Her eyes flashed and colour burned in her previously pale cheeks. 'Can we not discredit his lies?'

'Even if we could, I'm afraid that Silverton's tale is not all.'

'There's more?' An incredulous frown wrinkled her brow.

He reached for her.

Adamant, she shook her head. 'No. Just tell me.' If he touched her, the last of her brittle control would shatter.

In a calm mellow voice the Viscount proceeded to apprise Kathryn of the worst of their problem.

'And you have seen this printed leaflet yourself?'

'Yes,' he said grimly. 'Cadmount kept one copy and destroyed all the others he could find. Unfortunately, it seems that the damage was already done.'

She held out her hand. 'May I see it, please?'

'I'm afraid it is a crude and vulgar piece, not fit for the eyes of any lady.'

'Not even the subject of its story? Have I not a right to know?'

His eyes did not leave her face. 'It is where it belongs, Kathryn, burned to a cinder.'

She swallowed hard, determination and anger and devastation glinting in her eyes. 'What exactly did it say?'

An uncompromising expression slipped across Ravensmede's face.

'Tell me.'

His jaw set firm.

'Would you have me alone ignorant of what all of London is saying?' She saw the flicker in his focus, knew he was weakening. 'Please, Nicholas.'

He sighed. 'It is a tale in which the Viscount of R. and the widowed Mrs W. arrange an illicit liaison in a back room at Lady Finlay's ball. The widow arrives, only to interrupt a scene of impropriety between Lord R. and a certain Miss M., whom he later installed as his mistress under the guise of his grandmother's companion.' He did not tell her that every tawdry detail of the encounter had been obscenely exaggerated.

Kathryn's face paled. 'Only Mrs White knew,' she whispered.

'Mrs White is hardly portrayed in a flattering light within the article. Had Amanda White been responsible, I'd warrant it would have read a tad more in her favour.'

'Who would do such a thing? Pay from their own pocket to print and distribute such a spiteful piece of work? No one else knew.'

The bright green eyes narrowed of a sudden. He indicated Kathryn's barely touched glass of brandy. 'It might be a good idea to take another sip…a big one.'

Kathryn gripped her hands together tightly to stop them from shaking. 'You know, don't you?'

His gaze faltered. 'It is not pleasant,' he said.

'None of it is.' A terrible coldness was spreading through her body, tensing each and every muscle. And the dread of foreboding writhed in her gut. She waited, watching his anger vie with compassion, his rage with tenderness.

There was nothing but the moment and the waiting.

'I've spoken to the printer and the boy who delivered the article and instruction to him.'

'Already?'

His shoulders shrugged. 'I was still late for the theatre, and I would not have had you face that alone for all the world, Kathryn.' Their eyes locked. 'The boy took me to the house from where the letter was sent…'

She wetted the dryness of her lips. Suddenly knew the name that would pass his lips. The blood roared in her ears, so loud she feared she would not hear him.

'It was in Green Street. The woman who paid for the article was your aunt.'

Even as he confirmed what she feared she sat still as a statue in the chair, unmoving, lifeless, her expression frozen, her eyes wide and unblinking. And then her eyelids shuttered.

She did not hear him move, was not aware that anything had changed around her until she felt him kneel before her and pull her into his arms. His warmth thawed her, his strength anchored her. All around her a storm was breaking, and he was her only haven. She felt the wetness upon her cheeks, tasted the salt upon her lips, and did not know that she was weeping. A sobbing escaped her throat before she could catch it back. She laid her face against his chest, felt his hands upon her back, reassuring, protective. They did not speak; they did not have to.

A dam had broken, and all the misery, all the suffering, everything that Kathryn had so carefully stoppered through the past years rushed out. Fear and frustration and fury. Hurt and betrayal and grief. In three long years she had not wept, not once. Now that the tears had started it seemed that they would never cease. She wept until there were no more tears to weep. When finally she stopped there was nothing. Just an emptiness, and the throb of her head and the gritty nip of her eyes.

She noticed then the damp wool of Nicholas's coat lapels against her cheek, the warmth of his arms wrapped around her. Noticed too that she was standing, her body pressed into his, although quite how or when she rose from the chair she could not say. Neither of them moved. Both seemed content just to be, unmoving in the calm hush of peace. Steady thud of heartbeats, gentle rise and fall of breath. It was a place in which she could rest for ever. Seconds stretched to minutes,

minutes dragged to hours, until at last his fingers found her chin, tilted her face up towards his, and Kathryn knew she could hide no longer.

'I never meant for this to happen,' he said.

'I know.'

A little pause.

'You know too that you'll have to marry me.'

A rapid inhalation of air. She should have known it was coming. He was too honourable a man to do anything else, despite all that society thought him. A proposal of marriage from Nicholas Maybury, the man that she loved, the man of whom she had dreamed. She should have been ecstatic with happiness. But she wasn't. He was a viscount, heir to an earldom, wealthier than she could imagine. She was untitled, poor, with neither dowry nor connections. Moreover, he was expected to marry Miss Francesca Paton, if the scandal had not already jeopardised that arrangement. Kathryn could not hope to wed...not as a fallen woman. She was alone, and would stay alone.

There was also the small matter of love. She felt it. He did not. Her eyes closed. She thought of Nicholas's father and the Earl's expectations. She thought of Lady Maybury and of all that the dowager had done for her. She thought of Miss Paton waiting patiently for Nicholas's offer of marriage. But most of all she thought of Nicholas and how much she loved him. Her pulse steadied. When her eyes opened Kathryn knew what she must do. 'No,' she said quietly. 'I know no such thing.'

Nicholas gave a crooked smile. 'You do now.'

'No, Nicholas.' She captured his fingers within her hand. 'I thank you for your kind offer, but I'm afraid I cannot be your wife.'

'Kathryn, you're ruined. You've no other choice but to marry me.'

Slowly she shook her head. 'It's my reputation that's ruined, not myself.'

'You'll exist as a pariah, not received in any decent house.

If you think your treatment harsh so far, it will only get worse.'
His gaze razed her. 'Men will think you an easy target for their
attentions. You'll be subjected to the worst of their lechery.'

Still she did not speak.

'You must know that you cannot possibly continue as my
grandmother's companion.'

Her head bowed. She swallowed hard. 'I understand.'

The green eyes narrowed as if he understood for the first
time the absolute certainty of her resolve. 'Don't be ridiculous,
Kathryn. You've no other option.'

'I can think of one,' she said, and her cheeks burned pink at
the audacity of what she was about to suggest.

A tiny frown creased between his eyebrows. 'Pray enlighten
me,' he said in a quietly dangerous voice.

Her fingers still touched lightly against his. She could not
look him in the eye. Drawing all of her courage together, she
forced the words out quickly before she could catch them back.
'Once before, in St James's Park, you made me…a different
offer. Yesterday, in the coach on the way back from Brighthelmstone, you would have asked me the same thing. If the
offer is still open…I accept.' She felt his fingers stiffen beneath
hers. Saw the incredulity in his eyes.

He gave a spurt of ironic laughter. 'Let me check that I understand you correctly, Kathryn. You'll consent to become my
mistress, but not my wife?'

It sounded so brazen that she felt the heat spread from her
cheeks to burn the very tips of her ears. 'Yes,' a hoarse whisper
of agreement.

'May I ask why?'

She loosed his hand. Stepped back. Met his gaze. 'I would
not force you to a *mésalliance*.'

He said nothing, just waited expectantly.

The explanation came tripping out of her mouth unbidden.
'I am not titled or wealthy. Indeed, I cannot bring you either a
dowry or connections.'

No reply.

'And this is not the first scandal to attach itself to my family name.'

Still he did not speak.

She found herself rambling on. 'It would not be fair to either Lady Maybury or your father.' Her eyes darted away. 'And then there is Miss Paton.'

'What of Miss Paton?' he asked, and his face was leaner and harder than ever she had seen it.

'You have long been promised to marry her.'

'Have I?' His focus pulled her back, never wavering for a moment. 'And what if I say that it is not true? That I have no need of more money. That each and every one of the reasons you list is nothing more than an excuse. And that the proposal I would have made you yesterday was one of marriage.'

She shook her head, knowing that his honour forced him to deny the truth.

'Yet you still offer yourself as my mistress?'

The breath felt trapped within her lungs. Her fingers gripped against her skirt. She could feel his tension as clearly as if it were her own.

'Why would you do that, Kathryn?' he said silkily, and moved closer.

She could not tell him. Would not speak of love. That small last vestige of pride held strong. She stepped back, striving to maintain a distance between them.

'You think that is what you want, do you?' Without any further warning he pulled her to him, crushing her in a brutal embrace. His lips raked hers, punishing, hard, taking what they would. This time there was no tenderness, no teasing affection. It was a kiss to brand her, a kiss of possession.

She was powerless to resist such an assault.

At last he raised his face from hers and the determination in his eyes took her breath away. 'I disagree. Besides, the offer I made you in the park no longer stands, Kathryn.' He released her and stepped away, watching while she stumbled back into the chair. And then he was gone, leaving Kathryn more confused than she had ever thought possible.

Chapter Fifteen

It was early the next morning when a commotion sounded in the hallway of Ravensmede House.

'I don't give a damn what he's doing. I want to see him, and I want to see him now!' A man's face contorted with fury as he strode uninvited into the drawing room. The volume of his voice carried throughout the house.

Within the breakfast room Ravensmede set down his coffee cup. He waved away the footman and without further dalliance moved swiftly and sleekly along the corridor to meet his father.

They faced each other across the drawing room.

The Earl was almost as tall as his son; his silver locks glistened in the sunlight that streamed into the room through the four large-paned windows. 'So it has come to this,' he said, 'as ever I knew it would.' His hand slipped into the pocket of his immaculately tailored coat and withdrew a folded piece of paper. With a deft flick of his wrist he unfolded the paper and, turning it round so that his son might see the printed side, dangled it between the tips of two fingers as if he thought to contaminate himself from its touch.

One glance at the sheet told Ravensmede all he needed to know. It was Anna Marchant's leaflet.

'You've gone too far this time, boy. What the hell do you think you're playing at, dragging your family into your schemes? I didn't think that even you would stoop so low as to attach such scandal to your own grandmother's name.'

Not one glimmer of emotion showed upon Ravensmede's face. Only the slight tension around his jaw betrayed the mask for what it was. 'For that I beg her forgiveness. It was never my intention.'

'God knows I've tried my best to warn you, but you always were intent on going your own way.'

'So it would seem, sir,' said Ravensmede coolly.

'And what of this Miss Marchant?'

'Surely your sources will have told you of her? It seems they have not omitted aught else,' came the gritted reply.

The Earl's eyes narrowed. 'I've heard something of Mr and Mrs Henry Marchant. If that family's character is any estimation of their niece, you are well caught by your own folly.'

'Kathryn has the misfortune to share her name with those people, nothing more.'

A silver brow arched in an arrogant gesture Ravensmede himself so frequently used. 'It matters little,' he said. 'It's one thing to waste your time and your money with widows and harlots, it's quite another to seduce unmarried young *ladies*, especially those that must make their own way in the world.'

Their gazes met and locked. 'For once we are in agreement, sir. Nevertheless, I would have you know that the leaflet is nothing but a piece of malicious spite. Miss Marchant is a lady of unimpeachable virtue.' In his mind he heard again the whisper of her soft voice. *Once before, in St James's Park, you made me a...different offer. If the offer is still open...I accept.* The thought of what it must have cost her to say those words wrenched at his heart. She was an innocent...in every aspect of the word. He would not have his father think otherwise. There could only be one real reason why Kathryn had declined marriage in favour of a more illicit relationship. And Nicholas had a very shrewd idea just what that might be. 'You may say what you will, sir, but I mean to marry Miss Marchant all the same.'

Lord Maybury sauntered to the brandy decanter and poured two large glasses. He lifted one himself and left the other for his son to retrieve. 'I'm relieved to hear that for once you're prepared to do the honourable thing. Whether you laid a finger on the girl or not is irrelevant. To all intents and purposes she's well and truly ruined.'

Ravensmede did not move from his stance next to the blackened grate. 'I assure you that the leaflet does not figure the slightest in my plans, sir. I have intended making Kathryn my wife for some time.' The expression on Nicholas's face was one that the Earl had never before seen.

Maybury grunted. 'And what of Miss Paton?' A swig of brandy disappeared down his throat.

A dry laugh erupted into the silence. 'There was never the remotest possibility that Francesca and I would marry. We would not suit, no matter how much you and her father will it otherwise.'

Silence hissed around them, and from both faces the same green eyes looked out.

The glass banged against the mahogany of the table as Maybury set it down hard. 'I think that I should meet Miss Marchant.'

'We may see her in half an hour's time at Grandmama's house.'

'It's a trifle early to call upon ladies,' the Earl protested.

'The visit has already been arranged: there is someone else whom I want Kathryn to meet.'

Kathryn lay awake all the night through, worrying over what to do. Sunlight was infiltrating the blinds and the birds chirping a lively racket by the time she finally reached a decision. Only then did she succumb to the oblivion of sleep. It seemed only minutes later when there was a knock at the door to her bedchamber, the pad of feet, and the rustle of skirt material. The aroma of freshly brewed coffee and bread still warm from the oven drifted to her nose. Kathryn groaned, pulled the bedcover over her head and rolled on to her stomach.

'Beggin' you pardon, miss, but her ladyship said as how I was to bring you a little breakfast.' The maid set the tray down on the bedside table and moved across to the other side of the room.

'Thank you, Betsy. How very kind.' One bleary eye peeped out from beneath the covers, just as Betsy raised the blind, and bright white sunlight flooded across the room. Another groan escaped Kathryn.

Betsy cast a curious look in the direction of the bed. Lying late in bed was out of character for Miss Marchant, who was normally up and about with the larks. But then again, if the gossip below stairs was anything to go by, the situation that the dowager's companion now found herself in was far removed from normal. The maid wondered if the rumours were true. Lord Ravensmede was a fine-looking gent, and as the old saying went, there was no smoke without fire. Certainly Toby knew more than he was letting on; no doubt his lordship had greased the footman's palm to keep him quiet. 'Are you ill, miss? Shall I fetch Lady Maybury?'

Kathryn pushed herself upright, and sat back against her pillows. 'No, I'm quite well, thank you, just tired. The coffee shall revive me admirably.'

Not by the look of the dark shadows beneath Miss Marchant's eyes it wouldn't, thought Betsy, and then remembered the other message that she had been instructed to impart. 'Oh, I nearly forgot miss, her ladyship would like to see you in the drawing room at ten o'clock.'

Kathryn glanced at the clock on the mantel. 'It's half past nine now!'

'Yes, miss.'

'Heavens! How on earth could I have slept so late?' Kathryn swung her legs out of the bed.

'I'll fetch you some warm water, miss.' And Betsy disappeared.

Kathryn drank the coffee down and ate two bread rolls smeared with honey. There would be no room for weakness in today's dealings. She was under no illusion as to what the dowager wanted to say. The old lady could hardly be expected to keep on a companion whose name had been linked so scandalously with the lady's own grandson. Even Nicholas had said as much.

Nicholas. The mere thought of him made her feel uncomfortably warm. The uncomfortable feeling expanded at the memory of what had passed between them yesterday. Kathryn's cheeks flamed. It was bad enough to offer herself like a common trollop. His rejection was a thousand times worse. She blew out air from between her lips, feeling the sting of shame yet again. He had offered her marriage. Marriage, for goodness' sake! Better than all of her dreams put together. To spend the rest of her life as his wife... How very easy it would have been to say that one tiny word, yes. Yes.

Yes! She should have shouted it from the boughs of the trees. But she had thought better, and now the offer was gone. As was his desire. He had said she was ruined, and so she was. With little money and nowhere to go, Kathryn knew her options were limited. She could only pray that the gossip would not reach Hampshire. Her mother's relatives were her last hope. With a heavy heart she moved to fetch the old trunk she had brought with her from Green Street.

It was only a little after ten when Kathryn was washed, dressed and ready. She had turned a deaf ear to Betsy's protestations and worn her old blue muslin dress. The trunk sitting ominously by the door was as empty as when it had arrived. Madame Dupont's skilfully fashioned dresses, for which Kathryn had not yet fully reimbursed Lady Maybury, were left hanging in the clothes-press. The pearl necklace and earrings gifted by her ladyship sat neatly in the jewellery box on the dressing table. Kathryn was unadorned. Her fingers carefully skimmed her hair just to check that none of her neatly pinned curls had escaped. A deep breath, a squaring of her shoulders, one final smoothing of her skirt, and then she opened the door and walked towards the drawing room...and Lady Maybury's dismissal.

The scene within the drawing room was not what Kathryn expected. She stood for a moment, unnoticed, staring, drinking in the sight before her. The dowager sat in her usual chair by the unlit fireplace, chatting ten to the dozen. Her expression was warm and lively, her manner familiar as if she knew the young woman who was seated demurely upon the nearby sofa very well indeed. In a glance Kathryn could see that the girl was tall and willowy, with silky dark brown hair worn in an elaborate coiffure. Two tiny white pearls dangled from her ears. Her white-and-pastel-blue dress was well cut and fashionably stylish. Everything about her bespoke money and breeding, and she wore it all with an air of effortless relaxation. Kathryn's fingers strayed self-consciously to her own shabby gown. By the window stood two men, both tall, both with the same green eyes, both wearing the same defiant arrogance, one with hair as dark as night, the other whose head had silvered with age. Kathryn's heart skipped a beat as it did whenever she saw Nicholas. It was not hard to guess the identity of the older man standing by his side.

The little group looked comfortable, at ease, like they belonged together. There was only one outsider. For a minute she felt the urge to turn and run, and then the moment was gone. Before she could think any further as to what was going on, she heard Nicholas's voice.

'Miss Marchant,' he said, and made his way to her side. 'Come in.'

She ignored the hammering of her heart and held her head high. 'Lord Ravensmede,' she replied politely, and gave a small curtsy. And then turning to his grandmother, 'Lady Maybury.'

Although she was careful to keep her gaze averted from his, she could feel his scrutiny. Just his voice was enough to set her insides aquiver. She set her face determinedly and prayed that her cheeks did not appear as scalded as the rest of her felt.

He wasted no time in the introductions. 'This is my father, Earl Maybury.'

The man by his side bowed. 'I'm pleased to welcome you to our family, Miss Marchant.' Pleased did not describe the expression on his face. Appraising came closer.

Kathryn froze at the implication of his words. It was clear that Lord Maybury misunderstood the situation. She glanced at Nicholas, waiting for his reaction.

Ravensmede made no notice of having heard anything untoward. He met her gaze with a strange look, as if he was poised, as if he was waiting. There was a pause that was slightly too long for comfort, and then he said, 'Kathryn, this is Miss Francesca Paton.'

Kathryn stifled the gasp, blinked back the black dots swimming before her eyes and breathed deeply. The dizziness diminished. A warm hand pressed against the small of her back. Without looking she knew it to belong to Nicholas. She forced herself to step towards Miss Paton, away from the support that Nicholas offered. 'Miss Paton,' she said, and was relieved to hear that her voice sounded a deal calmer than she felt.

Miss Paton made her reply.

An awkwardness followed.

Then the dowager rose to her feet, and smiled. 'There's something to which I must attend. Please do excuse me.' And she tottered out of the door.

Nicholas stepped closer. 'My father and I must also take our leave of you…for now.' Then they too were gone.

A pair of fine hazel eyes turned upon her. 'Miss Marchant, please do come and sit beside me.' She patted a hand to the cushion to her left. 'Nicholas has told me all about you.'

Not *all*, Kathryn sincerely prayed. 'Thank you, Miss Paton,' she said with as much dignity as she could muster, and seated herself on the sofa.

Miss Paton leaned forward and smiled. 'Please call me Francesca.' Her expression was open and honest and sincere. 'You must be wondering as to the reason for my visit at such an early hour.' Without waiting for an answer she continued. 'Firstly, I came to wish you happy.'

Every muscle in Kathryn's body stiffened. She wetted her lips, unsure of what to say.

'And, secondly, I wished to meet for myself the lady that has finely succeeded in capturing Nicholas's heart.' Her smile broadened and there was a definite twinkle in her eyes.

Kathryn tried to smile, but her mouth seemed unwilling to respond. Something akin to a grimace stretched across her face. 'I fear that you may have misunderstood the—'

Miss Paton let her get no further. Her hand touched to Kathryn's in a gesture of friendship. 'Miss Marchant,' she started, and then said as an aside, 'Or may I call you Kathryn?'

'Of course,' murmured Kathryn.

'Kathryn, let me tell you how heartily relieved I am that Nicholas has at last decided to marry. You know my father and Lord Maybury are great friends, and have for years been trying to force a match between Nicholas and myself.' She laughed. 'Have you ever heard anything more ridiculous?'

It did not sound in the least ridiculous to Kathryn. Miss Paton was heiress to a considerable fortune. Lord Ravensmede was heir to an earldom. There was no disputing that the two were well matched. Kathryn held her tongue.

'Why, my dear Kathryn, Nicholas and I would not suit at all. He's a dear man, and a very great friend of the family, but that is all.'

'I thought…' Kathryn found her voice at last. 'I thought that there was an informal betrothal between you both, an understanding that you would marry.'

'Oh, no, not at all!' Miss Paton exclaimed. 'Besides, my interest lies elsewhere.'

Kathryn watched as two pink patches suddenly appeared on Miss Paton's cheeks. 'You have a *tendre* for someone else?'

Miss Paton's cheeks dimpled, and her face lit up. 'There is a certain curate. He's kind and diligent and of quite the most admirable character. But he's a little shy of approaching my father. Little wonder, for although Papa is the best of fathers, he can appear a tiny bit intimidating in his manner to those with whom he is unfamiliar.' Worry washed across Miss Paton's face. 'I beg you will not speak of it, Kathryn. We have told no one, though now that you've taken care of Nicholas for me, the way is clear for Thomas to speak to my papa.'

A weight lifted from Kathryn's shoulders. 'Your secret is safe with me. And I sincerely hope that you and Thomas find happiness.'

'Thank you,' said Miss Paton.

'No, thank *you*, Francesca,' Kathryn said, and meant it.

They moved to talk of the weather, and then discussed the Duke of Wellington's recent victory against Napoleon. Miss Paton told Kathryn all about the magnificent firework display at Vauxhall Gardens to celebrate the event. From there talk led on to the latest fashions, and then the birth of Lady Harrington's twins. Never once did she make the slightest mention of the most scandalous rumours sweeping every drawing room in London, especially those concerning Lord Ravensmede and his grandmother's companion.

Indeed, when Nicholas returned, alone, it was to find the two women chatting as if they were the best of friends.

Within a few minutes of the Viscount entering the drawing room, Miss Paton took her leave.

Nicholas leaned against the mantel above the fireplace.

Kathryn stayed where she was upon the sofa.

He was careful to keep his face expressionless. 'Did you and Miss Paton find anything interesting to discuss?'

Her face raised to his and he could see that much of the earlier tension had vanished. The silver eyes held a glimmer of mischief. 'Perhaps.'

He moved from the fireplace to take up the seat that Miss Paton had so recently vacated. Kathryn edged closer to the opposite arm of the sofa. He arched an eyebrow. 'Scared?'

'No. Should I be?'

A nearly smile pulled at his mouth. 'Most definitely so. I've just neatly disposed of two of your objections to marrying me. Two more to go and then you're mine, Kathryn Marchant.'

Shock rippled across her face. 'You still wish to wed me?' There was a definite breathy catch to her voice. 'Even after…'

'*Especially* after your proposition.' His eyebrow twitched.

Colour flooded her cheeks. 'It was not a proposition,' she said stubbornly.

He gave her a knowing look. 'If you say so.'

Her gaze fluttered away, and her fingers picked at the skirt of her dress.

He couldn't afford to let himself touch her…not yet. He produced a letter from his pocket and threw it on to the sofa between them. It was addressed to Miss Kathryn Marchant. No other direction had been added.

She peered at it suspiciously.

'Open it.'

A moment's hesitation, and then she did. The wafer broke beneath her fingers and the paper unfolded to reveal the lines of black flowing script. Disbelief creased her forehead. Slowly, concentrating on each word, she read the letter's contents again. 'It's from my uncle. He has enclosed a banker's draft for five hundred pounds…as a dowry.' The paper fluttered to her lap. She stared at him. 'I don't understand.'

'You're his brother's daughter. It is only to be expected that he would supply you with a dowry.'

'But…the scandal…my uncle and aunt have disowned me.'

'It would appear that they have changed their minds.'

Her eyelids shuttered momentarily. She pressed her fingers to her lips, as if to stopper any flow of emotion.

'So it seems, Kathryn, that you now have a dowry…if you should choose to use it as such.'

'I…' He could see her confusion.

His voice gentled. 'Which leaves only your last excuse… your family.'

'You cannot change that, nor would I wish you to,' she said softly.

'Why would I want to, when you have such good connections?' A wry smile curved. 'I have it upon the best of authorities that your mother was a Thornley of Overton.'

She wiped the emotion from her face, fixed her expression to one of blandness. Several heartbeats passed. 'Before you say any more, Nicholas, there is something I should tell you.' Not one movement. Not one betraying flicker of her eyes. 'This is not the first scandal to be attached to my family name. My father…' An image of her papa lying slumped upon his desk, a spent pistol in his hand. She stopped. Cleared her throat. The blink of her eyes lasted just fractionally too long. 'My father…' Again it seemed she could not bring herself to say the words.

'I know, Kathryn,' he said, wishing to spare her the worst of it.

Her gaze clung to his. 'How did you find out?'

'Does it matter?'

She shook her head, inadvertently dislodging a few curls. 'No. I suppose not. It's just that I've never spoken of it. Never. But not one day has passed without its memory. So much blood…and the pistol still in his hand…and his face…' She caught at her lower lip with her teeth.

He moved then. Closed the space between them, until their legs touched together on the sofa. Took her hands in his. Gripped them firm. 'I did not mean to remind you.'

'I cannot forget,' she said. 'But with time it grows easier, and there are other things that help me not to think of it.' Such as daydreaming and the man who sat so closely by her side, but she would never say so.

Her fingers were small and cool beneath his. His thumb stroked at the back of her hand. 'Your father's death was a tragedy, but the blame is not yours. It has no bearing on our marriage.' He leaned back against the sofa, keeping her within his gaze, watching the emotion cloud the brilliance of her eyes. 'So,' he said, 'Kathryn Marchant, will you do me the honour of becoming my wife?' Blood pulsed through the pulse point at the side of his neck. Thud. Thud. Thud. His hand still covered hers. Everything was still. Motionless. Breath caught and held, waiting to exhale.

She looked at him, really looked at him, as if seeing him for the first time.

His grip unwittingly tightened.

'Yes,' she said, in a whisper. And a small sigh escaped her.

Whether it was a sigh of sadness or resignation or relief, Nicholas did not know. He pulled her into his arms and dropped a kiss to the top of her hair.

It was Kathryn who pulled back. Kathryn, whose free hand touched to his cheek, her thumb brushing against his lips, tracing down to his chin. He saw her eyes drop to his lips, sensed her need. And then her mouth touched to his, her lips moving in sweet tentative enquiry.

The green eyes sparked. His lips answered her call, sliding and teasing, caressing and tickling.

Her mouth opened in sensual invitation.

The hot moisture of his tongue penetrated. She met his probing with her own. Tongue lapped against tongue.

He groaned and pulled her fully into his arms. 'Kathryn!' The rawness of emotion rendered his voice hoarse. His hands moved upon her back weaving patterns of age-old magic that she could not ignore.

Her fingers threaded through the burnt umber of his hair. Deep within her was an ache of longing. The hardness of his chest grazed her breasts, and she thrust against him and felt the thrum of his heart beneath that warm solid wall of muscle.

His hand moved to claim first one breast and then the other. Much more of this and he would be lost. The last vestige of reason pulled him back from temptation. Gently he eased himself away, looking her full in eyes that smouldered with passion and emotion. 'Sweetheart,' he said, 'it's a good thing I already have the special licence. I don't think my restraint will last much longer.'

With only two days to go before the wedding Lady Maybury decided a mammoth shopping expedition was in order. 'It's such a shame that there's not time to have a new gown made for you. We'll have to make do with a new bonnet and gloves. Oh, and a bandeau perhaps, and stockings…and a matching reticule.' The dowager was warming to her theme. 'And most definitely a new and rather exciting nightdress.' She slid a mischievous look at the young woman by her side.

Kathryn ignored the heat rising in her cheeks. 'It's very kind of you to offer such luxuries, but I already have more than enough.'

'Nonsense,' replied Lady Maybury. 'I can't have my granddaughter dressing in rags. We shall start with Miss Walters, move to Madame Devy, and Mills, then work our way along to Mrs Shabner, not forgetting Millards.'

A sigh was stifled as Kathryn allowed herself to be led into first one shop, then many more.

The day was warm in the extreme. Lady Maybury did not appear to notice. She was busily immersed in yards of ribbons and lace, and had just dispatched their footman to empty his arms of the multitude of parcels into the carriage.

'How dashed inconvenient!' Lady Maybury's nose wrinkled with irritation.

The woman serving behind the counter looked up, shock displayed across her face.

'James has taken the turquoise turban and I need it in order to select the best matching feathers.'

'I'm sure we can make a very good guess at which colours will suit,' Kathryn said.

The dowager raised an imperious white brow. 'Indeed we will not. When he returns, I'll send him back for it.'

Kathryn thought of the rising heat of the day. She thought of the footman's warm woollen coat, and the long walk he would have to reach their carriage. 'He's only just left and cannot have gone far. Perhaps I could stop him in time.'

'My dear gel—'

But the slender figure was already disappearing through the doorway.

The shop assistant sniffed, but said nothing.

Kathryn scanned the street and there in the distance was the retreating footman struggling under his load. Without a further thought she hurried towards him. Her breath became laboured and she felt the sweat bead upon her brow. 'James!' she said in a loud voice.

The footman disappeared around the corner.

Kathryn walked faster still. From out of nowhere an arm snaked around her waist, pulled her into an alleyway and slammed her hard against a wall. Her scream was rendered useless by the hand clamped across her mouth.

'Out walking alone, Kathryn, without even the accompaniment of a maid? What will people say? But then I'm forgetting that your reputation is already in tatters.'

She stared up into the face of Anna Marchant. Kathryn ceased her struggles, the blood draining from her cheeks until, beneath the heat of the day, a cold tremor pricked upon her skin.

The kid-clad hand dropped from her lips, but the grip remained around her wrist.

'Aunt Anna!' she exclaimed, unable to believe who it was that stood before her.

The older woman's lips smirked. 'Why so pale, niece? Did you think to play me for the fool quite so easily?'

'I don't know what you mean,' she whispered, feeling the stirrings of fear.

'Oh, but I think that you do, Kathryn. Sending Ravensmede to blackmail your uncle into paying a dowry.'

'Blackmail? I thought…' The words trailed off.

'You thought what?' sneered her aunt. 'That your uncle paid the money out of some sense of obligation? Affection, even? So sorry to disappoint you, my dear, but only Ravensmede's threats forced Mr Marchant's pen to paper. You could rot in hell for all we care.'

Realisation hit Kathryn between the eyes. 'He used the leaflet.'

'Very good. Did you like it? Really most effective, even if I do say so myself. Because of it, Amanda White dare not show her face. Did you know that she's left the country? Ran away to Italy, so they say. And you and Ravensmede are the scandal of London. All according to plan. Such a shame that he discovered my part in the affair.'

'Nicholas threatened to reveal the truth if Uncle Henry did not supply a dowry?'

'Of course. What choice did we have?'

It made sense. Kathryn looked directly into her aunt's eyes and saw the depths of the other woman's hatred. 'Why did you do it, Aunt Anna? Why should you want to destroy me so much as to publish such a thing?'

A smile stretched across Anna Marchant's face. 'Why do you think? I loathe you. I've always loathed you since the minute you crossed the threshold into my house. Trying to make claims upon your uncle's affection, thinking you were due our hospitality. I saw what you intended from the start. Trying to cast my own daughter into the shade, thinking yourself superior, and always with that look upon your face as if nothing we did could ever touch you.'

Kathryn stared as if she could not believe the words tumbling from her aunt's mouth. 'You are mistaken, Aunt, much more than you could ever know.'

The thing that passed for a smile upon Anna Marchant's face faded. 'No, Kathryn. I know full well what you are.' The ribbons of her bonnet danced in the breeze. 'I never wanted to take you into my home. You may thank Henry and his sense of duty for that. But why should my family and I suffer? It was not our fault that your slut of a mother died, or that your pathetic sot of a father killed himself.'

Instinct took over. Kathryn drew her hand back, and an almighty crack reverberated through the alley.

The imprint of Kathryn's hand, stark and red, appeared upon her aunt's cheek.

For a moment the two women just stared at each other, and then Anna Marchant's voice dropped to a snarl. 'You're going to regret that,' she said, and tightened her grip around her niece's wrist. 'You think to thwart me, but I won't let it happen. Ruined before all of London, and somehow you end up forcing Ravensmede into marriage in an effort to outdo your cousin. Lottie catches herself a decent gentleman for a husband, but you have to go one better with a viscount, and a rich one at that. Do you think after all that has happened that I shall just sit back and let you marry Ravensmede, and worm you way back into society's favour?'

'Take your hand off me.' Inside Kathryn was shaking, but her voice was clear and calm.

'Gladly,' said her aunt, and released her grip on her niece's wrist. She stepped back.

Kathryn made to leave.

'Not so fast.' Anna Marchant drew the small pistol from her reticule and aimed it at Kathryn's forehead. 'I'll see you dead first.'

Kathryn's heart hammered hard enough to escape her chest and her legs wobbled. 'You'll never get away with it. Lady Maybury is in the shop just a few yards along the street. I was merely trying to catch her footman. If I don't return soon, she'll come looking for me.'

'I know exactly where the old woman is. Did you think that I just chanced to be here? I was following you, awaiting my opportunity… which you have very obligingly just handed me.' A low hollow laugh sounded. 'I'll be long gone by the time the footman returns and the dowager realises that you're not with him.'

The pistol poked closer. Kathryn determined not to flinch.

'Just think, dear niece, a lead ball in the head, the same as your papa.' Scrape of metal, and the pistol was cocked.

A thousand thoughts flashed through Kathryn's head in that single moment. Images of her father, her mother, her sister, scenes from throughout the years of her life. But one picture dominated all others: Nicholas Maybury. And her one regret was that she would die without telling him of her love. Her eyes closed of their own volition. Her heart was beating in a frenzy, blood pumping so hard that it sounded like the rush of wind in her ears. Yet somewhere in the middle of the storm of emotion was an unexpected calmness, a silent place, a peaceful place.

'Kathryn!' The deep masculine voice echoed, and all at once she knew she was safe.

Somehow, by some sliver of chance, he was here. 'Nicholas!' she gasped.

'Ravensmede?' Anna Marchant swung to face the tall athletic figure. She paled, gulped and stumbled back in the opposite direction.

Kathryn had never seen such a look upon Nicholas's face. The green eyes glowered dark and menacing, the deep brown of his eyebrows drawn low and angled warned of a mood as black as the devil's. His hair rippled around a face that was the antithesis of colour. Even his lips, pressed firmly together, glowed with an unearthly pallor. Everything about him was still, tense, controlled. Dressed entirely in the deepest darkest black, he loomed a huge stark silhouette against the skyline. A chill stole through the air, the sky dimmed as a cloud obliterated the sun. 'Mrs Marchant,' he said in a voice filled with menace.

Kathryn shivered.

Anna Marchant's eyes widened and with fumbling fingers she swung the pistol towards Ravensmede.

'No!' Kathryn grabbed for her aunt's arm, deflecting the pistol's aim.

A loud bang. Smell of gunpowder. The drift of wispy plumes of blue smoke.

And when the smoke cleared Anna Marchant was lying on her back amidst the filth of the alley, bonnet askew, eyes bulging in terror. The dark figure stood above her, a large pistol trained on her sweating forehead. He crouched lower to look directly into the woman's eyes and when he spoke it was with that same terrible quiet control. 'Death can be mercifully quick, Mrs Marchant.' He touched the pistol muzzle between her eyes. 'And then again, there are ways to make it slow and painful.' The muzzle slid down to rest against her collarbone.

'Please,' came the high pitched whimper. 'Please.'

'Please what?' he asked. 'Do it quickly? I don't believe that the choice is yours to make.'

'No, don't kill me. Please don't kill me.' A sob sounded.

Ravensmede pressed the pistol a little harder. 'Crying for yourself, Mrs Marchant? Do you think that your tears of self-pity will stay my hand? After everything that you have done to make Kathryn's life miserable, to hurt her, even trying to kill her, there is nothing that can do that...'

Anna Marchant began to weep in earnest.

'Save to spare Kathryn the distress of witnessing such an act. She's suffered enough because of you. For her sake, and her sake alone, I'm prepared to offer you an alternative. England would fare better for your absence, madam. Therefore, you should remove yourself, your husband, your daughter, and the slanderous Mr Silverton to a place overseas with immediate effect. I'm sure that Silverton can make arrangements with his contacts in the West Indies. So, what is it to be?'

Mrs Marchant whimpered.

'Speak up, Mrs Marchant. Let us hear your decision.'

'We'll leave the country.'

'Never to return,' pressed Ravensmede.

'Never to return,' repeated a shaken Anna Marchant.

'I'm glad that we both understand the situation. Make no mistake, if you renege on this agreement I'll see you hanged for your attempt on Kathryn's life,' said Ravensmede, and removed the pistol to his pocket. He rose and walked slowly over to Kathryn.

His eyes scanned her face. 'Are you all right?'

Words would not come. Her head nodded, never for a minute breaking their gaze.

And then his arms were around her, strong, and safe. He pulled her to him and held her like he would never let her go.

The sun shone from a glorious cloudless sky as Kathryn made her way down the sweeping staircase of the house in Upper Grosvenor Street on Earl Maybury's arm. She was dressed in a simple gown of cream silk that, with its fashionable high-waist, flattered her petite stature. The décolletage swept low, revealing the gentle swell of her breasts. Tiny shimmering beads adorned the bodice and the edge of the short puff sleeves. Her hair was worn high with the soft curls allowed to drape teasingly down to her neck. Threaded throughout the chestnut locks piled upon her crown were narrow bead-studded ribbons of the palest cream, highlighting the rich red undertone of her hair.

'It's not too late to change your mind. Are you sure you can wed such a scoundrel, even if he is my son?' teased Lord Maybury.

She inclined her head as if deep in thought. 'To wed Nicholas,' she said softly, 'is something of which I thought only to dream.' Then the strange intensity of the moment was lost. She laughed and her curls danced. 'Does he know that you're inciting me to such rebellion?'

His shoulders shrugged. 'Most probably—he would expect nothing less.' The sunlight burnished the silver of his hair. 'I may be Nicholas's father, but for today I also take the role that your own dear papa should have had.' He tucked her hand into the crook of his arm.

'Yes.' A sad little smile stole across her face.

'I'm sure that he would have approved of your marriage.' He patted her small hand. 'That is, once he got to know Nick, of course.'

They laughed and stepped from the staircase on to the cool marble floor of the hallway.

Kathryn stopped and glanced at the door ahead of them, the last barrier that remained between her and Nicholas Maybury. Once she stepped beyond it there would be no going back.

'You plan to keep him on his toes, then?' The green eyes twinkled mischievously. 'Even though you are but fashionably late, he should have started to worry by now. I never thought to see him so tamed.'

Taking a deep breath, she stepped forward and allowed Lord Maybury to open the door.

He was standing facing the priest, with Cadmount by his side. A tall, imposing figure at the best of times, Kathryn thought she had never seen him look so magnificent as he did today. The ebony coat looked to have been sculpted upon his body and highlighted the snow-white sheen of his neckcloth, shirt and waistcoat. Long muscular legs were wrapped in white breeches. Even his deep dark brown locks had been shaped to perfection. Her heart turned over and she felt strangely shy.

Lord Maybury deposited her by Nicholas's side and moved back to sit beside the dowager and Miss Paton.

The palms of Kathryn's hands grew suddenly clammy and her throat dry.

Then the tall figure by her side smiled down at her, and there was such warmth and tenderness in his eyes that she quite forgot her nervousness and relaxed in his protective gaze. And when the priest asked her what she knew he would, she was able to answer in a clear voice without the slightest hint of a tremor. The ring slid smoothly on to her finger as if it had always been destined to fit there.

It seemed that the ceremony had barely started when she heard the priest pronounce them man and wife.

Nicholas's hands moved to take her arms.

She raised her face to receive the chaste kiss that would seal their union.

His lips slid intimately over hers with a prolonged passion that raised the colour to her cheeks.

'Nicholas!' she whispered in scandalised tones and made to pull away.

He held her tight. 'It's quite all right, sweetheart, we're married now.' He smiled a wicked smile and shot her a smouldering glance. And throughout the day when he looked at her she could see the promise in his eyes.

When he entered her bedchamber she was standing by the window as if mesmerised by the luminous glow of the full moon. Curls of chestnut hair cascaded over her shoulders, leading his eye down to the sheer cream gossamer of her nightdress and the barely concealed skin beneath. Small bare feet peeped out from under the hem of the nightdress and the slender hands were held loosely by her side. Although he had not spoken, she must have heard him and glanced round over her shoulder. A shy smile flashed at him, 'Nicholas.' But she did not change her stance, turning her face once more towards the moon.

Ravensmede felt his loins harden at the very sight of her. He had longed for this night for so long and now it was here, finally, at last. Kathryn was his, his wife, to have and to hold, to love and to cherish, for ever. With determined effort he schooled his passion and moved slowly towards her, until he stood so close behind her that the cream gossamer brushed the black satin of his dressing gown.

She shivered.

'Are you cold?' He touched his hands to her shoulders, sliding them down to capture her fingers.

'Just a little. It's this nightdress, it's just so…' She blushed and looked back at the moon.

'So very becoming,' he supplied, and slipped his arms around her so that her back was pressed full against him. The clean scent of her hair drifted up. Unlike most of the women that he had known, she wore no perfume, but her own sweet smell was intoxicating enough. He lowered his face to the red-brown curls and inhaled. By their own accord his hands crept up to cup her breasts. The soft thunder of her heart raced beneath the small firm mounds and he thought he detected a slight tremble in her body. 'Don't be afraid, sweetheart, there's nothing to fear.' A kiss dropped to the top of her head.

'I know,' she said and, twisting round in his arms, buried her head against his chest. 'It's just that there's something I need to tell you, something I should have told you a long time ago, had it not been for fear and for pride.' She laid her palms flat against his chest, and gave her bottom lip a little nibble. 'But when I stood in that alley with Aunt Anna's pistol in my face, I realised that I had been a coward not to tell you the truth: I love you, Nicholas.'

'I know,' he said. 'I've known since you turned down my offer of marriage in favour of a more scandalous proposition.'

'Oh.' Embarrassment warmed her cheeks. Her eyes held level with his chest. 'From all that you've done for me, I know that you must feel some measure of affection, and…and desire…and I want to tell you that it is enough. It doesn't matter that you don't love me in return.'

His thumb and forefinger captured her chin and tilted her face up to his. 'Some measure of affection and desire,' he said and moved his lips to hover above hers, 'goes nowhere near it, Kathryn.'

It seemed that her heart shuddered to a stop.

'I want you…' his head lowered to hers '…I need you…' until their lips almost touched '…I love you…' and they shared the same breath. 'Why else did you think that I went to so much trouble to make you my wife?'

She caught her breath.

'I love you, sweetheart,' he said again in a voice that was low and seductive. 'Completely. Utterly.'

The clear grey eyes darkened to a deep smoky charcoal. A gasp escaped her and his mouth closed over hers.

It was a kiss of longing and of love. A kiss to prove the words he had spoken. A kiss of passion and of need.

The last barrier crumbled. Nicholas loved her. Loved her, just as she loved him. He was her husband, and she was his wife. Kathryn gave herself up to the sweetness of the moment.

Nicholas teased. He tantalised. His hot breath seared the path his mouth had taken, slowly, enticingly, determined to prolong her pleasure.

Beneath the slick caress of his tongue, her lips parted in invitation, offering herself to his touch, his taste. Her palms flattened and crept up and across the broad strength of his back, her fingers sliding on the cool satin of his robe.

His hands skimmed down to her buttocks, the sensual massage a prelude to the grip that pressed her to the hard core of his arousal.

A soft moan escaped her lips.

With shaking fingers he untied the ribbons of her thin filmy gown so that it fell from her shoulders, exposing the pearl lustre of her skin.

Her eyes flickered open and she watched his gaze travel over every inch of her bare body.

'My love,' he said and fluttered soft kisses to her eyelids, her cheeks, across her passion-swollen lips down to the pale column of her neck and further. She arched against him as his mouth moved over the softness of her breast, his tongue washing its rosy peak with erotic precision.

Slender fingers threaded through his dark locks, pulling him to her, guiding him to her other breast. Shallow reedy breaths. Her hardened nipples ached with desire. Something fluttered and contracted deep within her. 'Nicholas.' She whispered his name, not fully understanding the escalating need. A liquid warmth melted between her thighs as he suckled her taut peaks. Then his mouth was gone.

A tiny sound of frustration, and her hands attempted to guide his head back to where it had lain. But Nicholas had other plans. Slowly, deliberately, he traced a line of tiny butterfly kisses beneath each breast then dipped lower, getting down on to his knees to follow the central line of her stomach, down across the soft plain of her abdomen.

'Nicholas!' Her eyes opened wide and round.

The green gaze found hers, and lingered with ardent intensity while his lips slid lower over the smooth silk of her skin towards that most secret of places.

Her legs trembled as his tongue tasted her sweetness and his hands, which had been steering her hips so expertly, gently lifted her and lowered her on to the bed.

He raised his head to hers, their eyes never leaving each other's for a moment, even when their lips met in honeyed reunion. His long, toned body covered hers, the tight muscles rippling beneath the sheen of sweat that drenched his skin.

Naked and hot, their bodies entwined beneath the silver glow of the moonlight. There was no need for covers, the heat of their passion scorched all that it touched. His low murmurs of encouragement caused her breath to come in short pants. She rose against him, unwittingly rubbing the tip of his heated desire. His fingers caressed her hidden moistness, sliding in sensual circles while his kisses played upon the soft whiteness of her inner thighs. Beneath the laboured breaths he felt the urgency of her need.

'Nicholas.' Her arms pulled him closer, until their skin slid together with the moisture of passion. Her lips trembled beneath his, heavy lids shuttered over eyes in which the pupils were huge and dilated.

He moved to take her then, thrusting once into the heat of her molten core.

A sharp intake of air. The grey eyes opened, stared up into his, searching.

He held still. And then his mouth found hers and indulged in slow deep sensual passion. Between those sweet swollen lips his tongue lingered, then lunged in a steady rhythm until he felt her tension loosen. He felt the first tentative wriggle of her hips, and a deep sensuous smile curved to his mouth. When those slender fingers wove a pattern of delight upon the firm muscle of his buttocks he could wait no longer. His muscles tensed to spiral them both into an ecstasy of oblivion for the first of many times that night.

Sunlight flooded the breakfast room. The Viscountess of Ravensmede smiled up at the tall handsome man by her side.

'You should not have risen so early,' he chided. 'I would not have you tired for tonight.' His eyes darkened with simmering desire, as he stared down into the face that he loved so well.

She laughed and, for Nicholas, it lit up the room brighter than any sunshine ever could. 'I promise that I shall not be tired, but what of you, dear heart? I would not want to wear you out,' and her voice held a husky teasing edge. The blush rose in her cheeks at the boldness of her words.

'Minx!' he chuckled. 'At this rate it won't be long before we're able to fulfil young Maggie's expectation of us becoming the *ma* and the *pa!*'

'A child of our own,' she said wondrously.

'Children,' he corrected. 'I don't mean to let you off that easily.' Drawing her to him, he placed a tender kiss upon her lips. His dark glossy hair mixed with the rich red-brown ringlets dancing temptingly at the sides of her beautiful face. He moved back to stare into her eyes, eyes that were of a serene silver coloration. 'I love you, Kathryn Marchant!' he declared with passion and kissed her again, mindful not to spoil the arrangement of her new and highly fashionable lemon silk dress. What was once a dream was now reality.

* * * * *

Silhouette® Desire®

**Introducing an exciting appearance
by legendary
New York Times bestselling author**

DIANA PALMER
HEARTBREAKER

He's the ultimate bachelor...
but he may have just met
the one woman to change his ways!

Join the drama in the story of a confirmed
bachelor, an amnesiac beauty and their
unexpected passionate romance.

"Diana Palmer is a mesmerizing storyteller
who captures the essence of what
a romance should be."—*Affaire de Coeur*

Heartbreaker *is available from Silhouette Desire
in September 2006.*

THE PART-TIME WIFE

by *USA TODAY* bestselling author

Maureen Child

Abby Talbot was the belle of Eastwick society;
the perfect hostess and wife. If only her
husband were more attentive. But when
she sets out to teach him a lesson and files
for divorce, Abby quickly learns her husband's
true identity...and exposes them to scandals
and drama galore!

On sale October 2006 from Silhouette Desire!

*Available wherever books are sold,
including most bookstores, supermarkets,
discount stores and drug stores.*

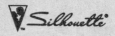

nocturne™

Save $1.⁰⁰ off

your purchase of any Silhouette® Nocturne™ novel.

Receive $1.00 off
any Silhouette® Nocturne™ novel.

Available wherever books are sold, including most bookstores, supermarkets, drugstores and discount stores.

Coupon expires December 1, 2006. Redeemable at participating retail outlets in Canada only. Limit one coupon per customer.

52607136

SNCOUPCDN

nocturne™

Save $1.⁰⁰ off

your purchase of any Silhouette® Nocturne™ novel.

Receive $1.00 off
any Silhouette® Nocturne™ novel.

Available wherever books are sold, including most bookstores, supermarkets, drugstores and discount stores.

Coupon expires December 1, 2006. Redeemable at participating retail outlets in the U.S. only. Limit one coupon per customer.

5 65373 00076 2   (8100) 0 11265

SNCOUPUS